COLLABORATORS

DEBORAH J. ROSS

Praise for Collaborators

First-rate world-building from a writer gifted with soaring imagination and good old-fashioned Sense of Wonder.

—C.J. Cherryh

A compelling tale of political intrigue, and well-meaning intentions creating disastrous tragedies. ... and a romantic and intellectually sexy gender discussion wrapped up in a compelling novel.

—J. M. Frey, Lambda Literary Award reviews

The alien biology and first-contact dynamics are handled unusually deftly; the narrative polyphony weaves complex melodies and harmonies. [The] world is effortlessly immersive and teems with fully realized characters.

—Starship Reckless

Keeps the reader's interest with solid prose and... adventure.

—Publisher's Weekly

Collaborators takes the familiar plot of "first contact" and makes something new of it. Its evocation of an alien species and culture is both fascinating and enlightening, and [Ross] uses that culture to draw parallels and contrasts to our own human behavior which are sobering and yet also hopeful. Do yourself a favor and read it!

—Kate Elliot

Collaborators tells a story that resonates deeply with our own history, yet at the same time evokes a culture and people unlike any on Earth. [It] is not only a rousing good story, it is also the kind of thoughtful fiction that offers new insights with each reading.

—Catherine Asaro

COLLABORATORS

by Deborah J. Ross

Thirsty Redwoods Press

COLLABORATORS

Published by Thirsty Redwoods Press
P.O. Box 1412
Boulder Creek CA 95006
Cover design: Maya Kaathryn Bohnhoff
Cover image: Dreamstime
Copy editor: Linda Nagata
Interior design: Steven Popkes
ISBN: 978-1-952589-00-3

Acknowledgments

I offer my heartfelt thanks to the people of Lyons, France, who extended such warm hospitality to me during my sojourn there, everyone from the women of *Rhône Accueil* to the professors at the University to the farmers at the *marché*, our neighbors and the parents of the children my own daughters attended school with. Thanks to all those who made that experience possible.

I also want to express my appreciation for the people who believed in this story during its long gestation: to my agent, Russ Galen, to Debbie Notkin, C. J. Cherryh, Jane Fancher, Mary Rosenblum, Catherine Asaro, and Kate Elliott; to Phyllis Nelson for many conversations about engineering and laser spectroscopy; and to the friends I met at Gaylaxicon 2004 who kept asking when the book was coming out.

This revised version owes much to Linda Nagata, for her thoughtful insights and suggestions. Any remaining shortcomings are my sole responsibility.

Table of Contents

For Elizabeth

Maps

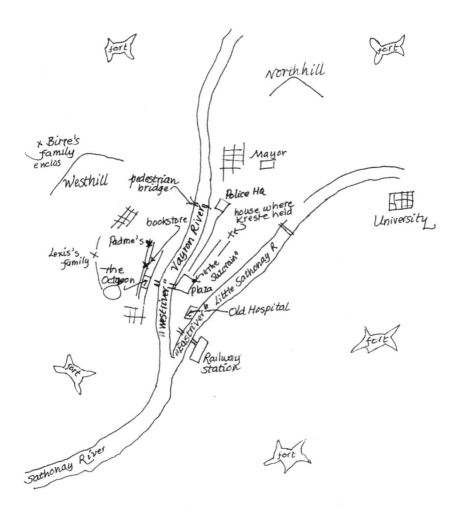

fort

fort

Northhill

x Birre's
family
enclos

Westhill

Mayor

pedestrian
bridge

Police HQ

bookstore

house where
Kreste held

"Vayron River"

University

Padme's

Lexis's
family

the
Octagon

"the
Suzerain"

Plaza

"Westriver"

Little Sathonay R

"Eastriver"

Old Hospital

fort

fort

Railway
station

Sathonay River

fort

Miraz

Prolog

Miraz: SPACE SHIPS SIGHTED OVER CHACARRE, Report by Talense. Throughout northern Chacarre, hundreds have reported sighting unknown airborne objects believed to be alien space ships. Kreste's representative declined comment until the official science report is completed, but clan sources indicate a flurry of communications between the Helm offices and their counterparts in Erlonn. We have received one report, quickly denied as rumor, that troops have been secretly stationed near the Erlind border.

Hoax or sensation? Conspiracy or political gambit? No one is willing to say. Meanwhile, the people of Chacarre are watching and waiting for answers.

Hayke and his two children had carried blankets out to the hills beyond their farm near the Erlind border. They ate leftover potato rolls while the light faded from the sky. Early summer heat hung in the air, sweet with the smell of the ripening hay. The world softened into shadow, tone upon tone of layered gray except for the ghostly white of Hayke's fur. Night-hoppers chittered; the grass rustled with the passage of a snake.

Torrey, the older child, had been out in the fields all day. Sun had bleached the downy fur on his face to platinum, probably his last season of that pure, shimmering color. He was growing fast. Little Felde played his pipe to any living thing that would sit still and listen.

Slowly the first pale stars emerged: the Archer, the Water-Dove, and the Serpent, which Wayfolk called the Grommet. Felde loved hearing the story of the little grommet who sang such wonderful music to the stars that when he died, they could not bear to lose him. Torrey insisted he was too old for such tales. Tonight he was hunting other quarry in the skies.

Hayke, lying back on the blanket and gazing up at the stars, felt an absurd sense of tenderness. He loved both his children, but Felde, the one he had not carried... Felde was special. Perhaps because Felde was the last child he and Rosen would ever have, perhaps because it was Rosen who had borne him. Loss, still poignant after five years, pulsed through Hayke.

"There it is!" Torrey pointed to the northeast at the unwinking mote of light.

"Sharp eyes," Hayke said.

Felde snuggled close, curling his arms around Hayke's chest. "Are they really people from another star?"

"That's what they say, little one."

"Adso says it's all an Erlind plot," Torrey said. Adso was fourteen and Torrey's closest friend.

"I'm not saying Adso's wrong-minded," said Hayke, "but imagine if you'd never set foot off this farm, never seen anything but hens and woolies, and then one day someone told you about the great city of Miraz. Thousands of people, all eight clans living together in one place. Towers and bridges and museums. Trams and temples. You'd think he was making it up."

"I'd think his brains were corked!"

"But he'd be telling the truth, wouldn't he?" said Hayke.

"Dim-Dim, what's *corked*?" Felde piped up.

Torry choked on his own laughter. Hayke hushed him.

Felde lifted his head. "I'd like to meet the star people."

"You, grub?" Torrey said. "What would you do if you did meet one? Run away howling?"

After a moment, when the night had fallen quiet again and the stars seemed even closer, Felde said in his child's voice, "Do you know what I'd do if I met the star people, Dimmie?"

"No, little one. What would you do?"

"I'd play my music for them."

Hayke tightened his arms around Felde, felt the child's bones like a delicate sculpture. The heartbeat, soft and light against his own. His crest fluttered with a tenderness he could not speak. He had no words for how very precious this child was to him. Rosen... Rosen would have loved him very much.

He wished with all his heart that Rosen might have lived to see this night, this unwavering star of hope.

PART I

Chapter 1

A smoky haze filled the corridor leading to Medical section of the interstellar ship *Prometheus*. The air was supposedly safe to breathe, but if Sarah Davies let her thoughts drift, she imagined a tell-tale numbness in her lips and fingers, and fine tremors in her eyelids, the first signs of acricyanate poisoning. She raked a fringe of black hair back from her forehead, felt the mixture of skin oil, dried sweat, and dust, and promised herself a water shower once environmental systems stabilized. *When*, she thought. *Not if.*

The corridor was barely wide enough to pass an emergency stretcher. A dozen of Sarah's shipmates sat or leaned against the wall, holding on to the railing. She knew them—junior scientists like herself, computer wizards, support personnel. A pair of women in soot-grimed command uniforms moved among them. One carried a first-aid tray, the other a touchpad.

Sarah clasped the extended hand of an engineering tech. The bandage over one eye was new but already stained yellow. His other eye looked glassy, bewildered. Like her, he'd worked repair while the more seriously injured were cared for.

Her attention diverted, Sarah lost her balance and went half-tumbling in the partial gravity. Her back muscles throbbed in protest. One shoulder slammed into a wall and luckily not the hydroponics technician with the bandaged knee. The repair tools tied to her belt thwapped against the last set of bruises. She grabbed the rail and righted herself, swearing under her breath, and wondered for the hundredth time how she'd gotten herself into this mess.

Astrophysicist's chance of a lifetime. Right.

Witness the birth of stars! Plumb the secrets of gas clouds! Discover the genesis of supraferric elements, analyze the electromagnetic and nuclear interactions in presupernovae! Right.

Study with the legendary Vera Eisenstein... For an instant, an echo of feverish joy pulsed through her.

"Right," Sarah whispered under her breath.

The man at the door wore a strip of white cloth around one sleeve. Sarah recognized him as one of the applied math people who had emergency medical training. He nodded and waved her through without a smile, exhausted rather than unfriendly.

Sarah paused at an open door, one hand on the frame. An airpad, suspended from its armature, dominated the room beyond. It covered the patient like a quilted glove, monitoring vital functions, immobilizing injuries, and controlling shock. A woman rested there, only her face and arms exposed. Her eyes were closed, her hair a tangle of iron-gray curls. A ventilator mask covered her mouth and nose. One hand rested beside a touchpad; a computer monitor was clamped to the side of the airpad frame by a clamp. Complex mathematical notations filled the screen, ending in the middle of an equation. It took Sarah a few moments to realize this was a preliminary analysis of the space-time distortions near the "dark" hole

I should have known that a spine fractured in six places wouldn't slow her down. "Dr. Vera?"

The woman on the bed stirred. Eyes bright as polished onyx snapped open.

Sarah felt her body less solid for a moment, as if the ship had wobbled in its spin. "I'm on double-shift, so I can't stay more than a few minutes. I haven't been able to find out anything more about the spectrometers. The primary array section was the worst hit. We haven't been able to get in there yet. It's flooded with acricyanate."

One eyebrow arched upward. "I wonder how *that* happened." The components were stored in non-reactive form.

"Chemistry's best guess is a weird compressed-gas effect while we were caught in the gravity loop." *Prometheus* had been built to withstand the stresses of a six-year voyage in deep space; a hidden "dark" hole was another matter.

"Damn," said Dr. Vera.

Sarah closed her eyes, thinking of the delicate crystal diffractometers and gossamer metallic screen antennas, the instruments that had drawn her into a world beyond imagining, the electromagnetic spectrum from visible light to X-ray and radio frequencies. Maybe the remote probes for the particle energy instruments had survived.

What was the point? Since they were orbiting a planet around a G-type star very like their own sun, they clearly were not anywhere remotely near where they were supposed to be. Their mission was to study a region of new stars and pre-supernoval gas clouds, a "stellar nursery" where unique, fleeting events, unknown in their own area of the galaxy, could be observed and recorded.

Beneath Sarah's feet, the ship creaked and shuddered. She tried to smile for Dr. Vera. Her face hurt with the effort. It wasn't possible, she thought, for anyone to be this tired.

"So you're back with us, Dr. Vee," came a voice from the doorway.

Sarah watched Chris Lao enter, still awed by his energy. Together their team had cut away the fused and curdled wreckage of the primary navigational control unit and set up the jury-rig that had got them this far. Even when she and Mae Brown from the Nuclear Physics Department had been forced to stop, hands and faces burned in a dozen places, eyes like sandpaper, cracked ribs protesting with every breath, Chris had kept on. By that time, though, he'd given up swearing in English and switched to Mandarin.

Chris touched Sarah's shoulder. She glanced at him, questioning. He wouldn't meet her gaze. He said something inconsequential to Dr. Vera, who muttered a few words about military baboons.

A wave of heat shot up Sarah's spine as she realized that Hammadi had chosen Chris for the first-contact team, not her. She felt a slash of jealousy, a chill of relief, a pulse of bone-deep weariness and then fear—for him, for them all.

"Good luck down there," she managed to say.

The muscles at his temple rippled. "That's what I came to tell you. I was sure Hammadi would pick you, with your minor in sociology, or else stick with his own people."

Chris was a logical choice, given his facility with languages. Most of the scientific staff could read at least one language besides English, but Chris had grown up bilingual in English and Chinese and spoke several others—French, Hungarian, and Russian—as recreation.

"Who else?" Her voice came out husky.

"Sergei Bartov from Engineering, and Celestin Bellini."

Sarah frowned. Why not another physicist, or someone with secondary training in biology or planetology? Les Bellini, however, was Hammadi's golden boy.

Dr. Vera's eyes gleamed. "What's the latest on the planet?"

"Our orbit will hold for now," he said. "Downside, the civilization is remarkably like our own, mid-twentieth century."

"Parallel evolution?" Sarah asked.

Dr. Vera came alert. Life was common in the galaxy, as were planetary systems, but it rarely progressed beyond microscopic forms. Current theory held that the higher the evolutionary level, the narrower the range of possibilities. Intelligent life might well be limited to vertebrate, mammalian, primate. And, by the same thinking, humans would tend to alter their physical environments in similar ways. So went Trowbridge's Principle.

"We've located two major industrial centers and a handful of secondaries," Chris went on. "Sergei says, based on the air pollution analysis and radio transmissions, they should have an adequate manufacturing capability—metal components for the star drive, plus copper and manganese wire of pure enough grade. Max Elliott says we can salvage enough of the lanthanide dopants for the focusing lasers. We'll have to shuttle it up and do the electrophotonic processing here."

Dr. Vera nodded. Sarah remembered the huge fight she'd had with United Terran brass over the design of the focusing lasers used in the navigation unit. Bob Kwambe, Dr. Vera's counterpart and opponent in the navigation-system debates, had been on board the *Celeste*, the second expedition ship.

They should have ended up about where we did, Sarah thought. *If they were caught in the same gravity loop. If they made it out alive. If…*

She shivered. "I've got to get back to work."

Dr. Vera turned to the monitor, her hand already skimming the touchpad, rearranging factors. "On your next visit, bring me the data keys for the AU *List of Gravitational Lens Anomalies* with the mathematical appendices nd the latest edition of Misner, Thorn, and Wheeler. And find me a real monitor. I can't fit the equations on this one."

The physician on duty, a tall black woman with abrasions livid across one cheek, paused as she rushed by. "Thanks for the break. Every moment she's not sleeping, she's trying to get up or demanding access to equipment buried somewhere."

"Take my advice and get out of her way," Sarah said. "You'd have more luck standing in front of a whirlwind."

"Tsunami," said Chris.

Sarah remembered the honors lecture she'd attended as an undergraduate, the first time she'd heard Dr. Vera speak, the very moment she had decided to become a physicist.

"Science is not about measuring things."

Sarah repeated the words to herself. *"It's about asking questions, about asking what the answers mean, about getting inside the very heart and nature of the universe. About being alive and human."* Those words had set a fire in her mind, a hunger that drove her through graduate school, through the mission selection process. And here, in orbit above a planet she never expected to see.

Had she come here to ask questions or to discover answers? Or to die?

Chapter 2

High above the rolling farmland of Chacarre, light sheeted off the billowed clouds. The airship floated above the clouds, vast and silver-skinned. Slowly it proceeded toward Erlind, passing over the southernmost tip of Joosten. The sound of the immense propellers was muffled inside the heated, pressurized viewing deck. By now, most of the passengers had returned to their seats or to the restaurant level for a late breakfast.

Ferro-az-Kerith stood at the curved glass, gazing down at the sunken fields that gave Joosten its folk name, the Drowned Lands. Oblique sun burnished his face and hands to amber beneath his sparse lanugo fur. Thicker, longer hair draped like a mane to his shoulders. A clan pendant depicting Maas, the Sixth Aspect of the god, hung between his small breasts. Beneath his simply-cut tunic, his hips were narrow, belly flat, a singleton body never transformed by polarization and pregnancy.

As the other passengers moved about, exchanging comments and gestures, Ferro registered the nuances of tone, the scraps of conversation, the latest jokes, even the subtle shifts in posture. Traders, traveling beyond the security of their own clans, often sensed the first shifts in political tides.

Far below, geometric fields gave way to pastures, and then to the broken hills that marked the boundary with Erlind. The land rose steeply. Outcroppings of stone appeared and pastures dwindled to veins of green. Here the light dimmed, or maybe it was the dark color of the rock itself, the naked, twisted earth, that gave rise to that illusion.

Ferro felt the starkness of the border as a shivering through his bones. He told himself it was all imagination, this drop in temperature. He'd made the trip to Erlind before, first as a student, then as personal agent for the Helm of Chacarre. Up here he felt the transition from Chacarre to neutral Joosten and then to Erlind as a change in the very soul and texture of the land.

It is the days and the times that give rise to moments of such unease, he told himself. *Nothing more.*

He ran the tips of his fingers over the enameled face of his medallion, silently chanting the resonant musical tone *ma* to evoke the divine attribute of charisma. Or, he added glumly, protection against its demonic inversion, apathy. But apathy had never been one of his shortcomings.

As an antidote to the lingering mood, Ferro replayed in his mind the meeting he'd had with Kreste before he left Miraz. In Kreste's presence, he never felt the subtle outclan tension but a deep, abiding warmth. He told himself this feeling carried no personal significance, it was because Kreste was Helm to all Chacarre.

More than a century ago, the first Helm united the Eight Clans of Chacarre to stand against Erlind in the Last Great War. Since then, the office had passed from parent to the most worthy child like a sacred trust. What Chacarre would have been without its Helm—fractured by feud and rivalry, easy prey for a united enemy—Ferro shuddered to think. What Chacarre might yet become—that was his dream as well as Kreste's.

"In the guise of a minor embassy functionary, you'll have a chance to meet these 'space aliens'," Kreste had said. "If they seem genuine, find out why they came to Erlind first, what they seek to gain there, and what understandings they have come to. And make sure they're made aware of... political realities."

"Such as the state of relations between Chacarre and Erlind."

Kreste had signaled agreement, then with a fluid twist, turned the gesture into one of caution. "The Erls have only a short time to wrest whatever advantage they can from the situation. That will make them eager, perhaps desperate, to hold on to their prize."

"I serve Chacarre," Ferro had replied.

Now Ferro pushed himself away from the airship railing, thinking that a cup of heated wine might dispel the chill that coiled around his spine. As he turned away, he caught movement at the periphery of his vision, a sun-bright mote.

He blinked. Everything at this height, the clouds, the airship, the passage of the landscape below, moved with an unhurried, almost languorous pace. Time itself seemed suspended. The blur of light, more energy than shape, plummeted like a stricken bird, then leveled out and raced eastward.

Ferro held his breath, captured by the eerie, unbelievable speed. His crest leapt to its full height and the hair along his neck quivered. He grabbed the railing, pressing against the glass, straining to follow the rapidly disappearing object.

"Seventh Name!" someone behind Ferro cried out. "What *was* that thing?"

Passengers, Chacarran and Erl alike, rushed to the window. They crowded together, jostling each other and gesturing. The view deck rang with their voices. Their bodies reeked with a sudden, sulfur-edged tang.

Ferro felt the primal instinct to lose himself in the group excitement. His neck ruff quivered, and his breath hissed between his bared teeth. He forced himself to stand still.

Two servers dashed out from behind the wine table, calling for order.

The nearest grabbed a passenger and pulled him away from the others. With fewer people jammed together, the group panic reflex faded.

"An alien space ship!" someone said in Erlindish. "That must be it!"

"Nothing natural could move that fast," someone else said in Chacarran. "It must have been—"

"What, a beacon kite, all the way up here? Did you see how it whipped across the sky?"

"Where did it come from?" one of the new-pairs murmured in the Drowned Lands dialect.

Ferro stared out the window again. Something had changed in that moment. He expected the heavens themselves to crack open, altered by what had happened there. As far as he could see, the expanse of blue stretched on, as unbroken and serene as ever.

It was he who would never be the same.

Ferro and the other travelers shuffled across the windswept landing field. The terminal building looked like an oversized barn, low and squat. Age-darkened timbers framed its walls. The stones were irregular, with a faint sheen.

The airship loomed behind the terminal building, its metallic curves blocking half the sky as it strained against its tethers. Technicians threw up flexible scaffolding and swarmed up its sides, checking gas gauges and tension cables. Hovercraft filled the air with their racket and the stench of oil smoke, while a high-pitched loudspeaker blared out announcements in Erlindish and Chacarran. Behind Ferro, a child whimpered in his parent's arms.

Everyone filed through terminal doors to the border control area. As he passed the armed Erlind guards, Ferro kept his crest lowered, his features bland and composed. He must appear dull, unworthy of any special attention.

The arrival lounge teemed with passengers and the people meeting them. Ferro hated how they crowded together, bumping each other, hated the raucous sound of their language, and most especially the odor of boiled callet that always seemed to cling to them.

Reporters pushed among the passengers, shouting questions. The airship must have casted ahead the news of the sighting. A press reporter grabbed Ferro's arm, pinning him against the solid bulk of another passenger. "You, what did you see?"

Ferro felt a prickling along his spine. The skin around the roots of his crest burned. He smoothed his crest with his free hand. "I saw only what everyone else saw. Let me go."

"Give me a statement from the Chacarran point of view."

Ferro twisted away, trying to maneuver through the crowd. His satchel caught between two jostling sightseers and he tripped. A hand hooked under his elbow brought him upright again. He found himself breast-to-breast with a buxom young person, Chacarran by the cut of his clothing, wearing an orange clan token.

"It's all right. I'm from the embassy." The Chacarran took Ferro's baggage and deftly threaded his way through the crowd. "We heard about the sighting and thought you might have a little trouble here."

Outside the terminal, the sky seemed too clear, as if a protective veil had been ripped away. Ferro followed the aide to a car parked in the restricted zone. Settling himself in the second seat, he gazed out the windows. His heartbeat slowed and the creeping fire along his crest receded. Normally, he thought, the ambassador would not send someone to meet a subordinate. He prayed that all Seven Aspects of the god would bless Dorlin for making an exception this time.

The street buzzed with people, trams, and pedal-cyclists. Push carts were doing a brisk business selling boiled callet wrapped in leaves, skewered chunks of spiced apple, and cheese buns. Above them fluttered bright pennons and cheap foil kites. They passed a public arbor, its trellises thick with flowering rosellias.

"What are they saying out there?" Ferro asked.

"You know these people," the young Chacarran said. "They'll believe anything their leaders tell them."

The traffic dwindled to a handful of private cars and an occasional tram. Striped shadows cut across the avenues as they passed a row of ancient columns representing the unbroken dynasty of the ruling House Ar. A troop of children scampered after hoops of red-striped gold, a pair of teachers at their heels.

"What about you?" Ferro persisted.

The aide's crest raised a fraction. "Frankly speaking?"

"Youngster, this is a casual conversation, not an interrogation."

"Then yes. Yes, I do believe it. If someone's hoaxing us, it isn't the Erls. They're as taken in by this thing as we are."

We must not be taken in. That's why I'm here.

At the embassy, Ferro was escorted to Dorlin's office, small yet elegantly appointed in Chacarran fashion. He sat in a chair of carved rufino wood and glanced around at the tapestries. Greenish shadows from the planters mottled the subdued colors.

After a few minutes, Ambassador Dorlin entered. Like the young aide, he was Keshite, under the aegis of the Second Aspect of the god. Ferro had met him once before, years ago at an official function in Miraz. He was the only one in the embassy aware that Ferro's authorization came directly from Kreste.

Dorlin offered Ferro shallan, the honey-smooth liqueur that was one of the few pleasures to be found in Erlonn. "You were on that flight."

"It was no airship," Ferro said. "Nothing we or the Erls can build could move that fast." He added, choosing his words carefully, "There's speculation that the entire matter of the space aliens is a hoax, one created for a specific effect." Meaning, as Dorlin would understand, a cover-up of Erlind military activity, which was why Kreste had reinforced the most vulnerable stretches of the border.

Dorlin set his glass down. "That was our first reaction here, too. The Erls are very good at pretending nothing ever happens that they haven't engineered themselves. This time, it won't work."

Ferro swirled his drink, watching the patterns of golden light. "If there are... beings... from space who can build a ship like that, what do they want here? With us? With the Erls?"

"The Erls say," Dorlin remarked, "that the aliens want to establish friendly contact."

The Erls say... Ferro repeated to himself. "Are they like us, then, these aliens?" *In all the ways that count?*

Dorlin made a noncommittal gesture. "They offer no reason why they have set down *here*." In Erlonn, he meant, instead of Chacarre or anywhere else. "At least, none that the Erls are willing to divulge."

"Speeches delivered at public events are notoriously superficial. Perhaps a more intimate setting, free from outside influences, would yield a deeper understanding."

Dorlin gestured in agreement, a circular cupping movement. "I will see that such an opportunity is arranged. Meanwhile, your name is on the list of embassy personnel for the formal reception at the Old Erlking's Palace tomorrow night."

Erlonn: "TERRANS" REVEALED TO PUBLIC! Report by Lansky, special correspondent from Miraz (cleared by the Erlind Board of Censorship): Hundreds of reporters, scientists, and Erlind officials, as well as the general public, filled Erlonn's Auditorium of Central Magnificence this morning to hear the first official announcements on the newly-authenticated space aliens. A hush filled the enormous hall as the Director of the Erlind

Academy of Science and Medicine reported the results of their analysis of the artifacts and persons which have caused such an uproar in recent days. In answer to widespread skepticism, he reiterated the academy's position, which is that the aircraft in which they landed could not be fabricated by any established technology.

The Sub-Director for Medicine stated that the three "Terrans" appear to be a completely different, independently evolved species. In his opinion, the superficial similarities in body structure and features represent a remarkable example of parallel development.

The high point of the conference came when the "Terrans" greeted the assembled crowd, addressing us in Erlindish by means of vocal decoder instruments. The three, named Celestinbellini, Laochristopher, and Sergeibartov, are remarkably humanoid in appearance, despite their patches of baldness and supernumerary digits. (See accompanying artist's sketches.)

When asked their purpose in coming here, they replied that they brought greetings of peace and friendship from the people of Terra to the people of Bandar, their name for our world. A partial transcript of the interview follows.

Question from the audience: What are your first impressions of the world?

Answer: Your planet is very beautiful and remarkably similar to our own. We hope to discover areas of commonality and mutual benefit.

Question: How can we be sure of your peaceful intentions?

Answer: We are vegetarians.

Question: How did you travel here?

Answer: We cannot respond in any terms that would make sense to you.

Question: Please excuse the intimacy of this question, but are all three of you polarized?

Answer: Our funding agency is the United Terran Peacekeeping Force.

Question: Isn't it true that you are in fact not aliens from another star, but cleverly disguised and coached Shardian actors?

Answer: Yes, our people also enjoy drama and music very much. We look forward to attending your performances.

Question: Why have you come here?

Answer: We have established contact with your people to exchange scientific, industrial, and cultural resources. Specifically, we offer to trade technological knowledge for certain items to be manufactured to our specifications.

Question: What items? What are their nature and function?

Director of Erlind Academy of Science and Medicine: This concludes the evening's interview. No further questions will be permitted.

Chapter 3

Ferro halted just inside the portal of the Old Erlking's Palace. Beyond the gates, with their age-worn carvings of heroes and monsters, columns of pinkish stone curved inward, joining to form a ribbed ceiling. He felt as if he were about to be swallowed by an enormous beast.

The crowd swirled with color, the reds and oranges of the ruling House, the browns and greens of the Chacarran Embassy staff, the furs of the Valads. Two dignitaries from Shardi swept past, their gauzy robes billowing around them. The mingled scents of spice incense and citron lingered in their wake.

A minor Erlind official came to stand beside Ferro. Ferro expected the Erls to watch him, although perhaps not this obviously. He moved off, making his way through the crowd to the refreshment table, and accepted a glass of wine. As he was about to take a sip, the odor of rancid auroch grease stung his nostrils. He composed his features, smoothed his crest hair, and turned around. Sure enough, the Valad standing there wore the ceremonial vest of his clan, embellished with loops of braided hair and embroidery.

"My friend," the Valad dignitary said in Chacarran, "what pleasure it brings me to see you again!"

"Na-chee-nal!" Ferro switched to Valad and continued, "I didn't expect to see you here." He peered at the newest insignia on the vest. "Ambassador to Erlind? My congratulations on the promotion. May it bring you honor."

"The glory is to my clan. But what of you? Are you here in an official capacity?"

"As you can see, I am the wine taster."

"Then I wish you joy." The Valad ambassador lifted his glass, with a comment about the excellence of Chacarran wine. Most of Valada might be too far north for the best-producing wine trees and the Valads themselves uncomfortably close to their roots as nomadic raiders, but they appreciated sensual pleasures. As a youth, Ferro had spent a summer in Ah-rhee-koh-nah-tee, ostensibly perfecting his pronunciation of Valad but also enjoying enthusiastic mutual pleasuring. It was then he'd first met Na-chee-nal. Now Ferro sighed, wondering when he might enjoy such a holiday again.

Before either could say more, metallic clashing resounded through the room. Ferro winced, for the hallowed cymbals of Erl were painful to anyone not already deaf. It would be an unthinkable breach of courtesy to cover his ears as the sound swelled and reverberated. After it died down, his ears kept ringing. The only consolation was that every other non-Erl in the room was in the same condition.

The Erlind minister descended the stairs, wearing formal garb, a floor-sweeping cloak of crimson wool, twin swords, and helmet topped with sprays of gilded feathers.

Three figures stood at the top of the stairs. The crowd hushed, all eyes lifting. No cosmetics, no disguise, no trick of theatrical technique could create the broad shoulders and narrow hips, which could mean only one thing: polarization.

Ferro pushed forward, anxious for a closer look at the aliens. They must be strange indeed, he decided. Who in his right mind would send breeding couples on any kind of mission? How could any real work be accomplished? And what kind of creature would expose unborn young to such risks?

Be careful, Ferro told himself. *These creatures are not human. It's dangerous to judge them by civilized standards.*

Accompanied by an Erlind guide, each alien descended the stairs and began a circuit of the room, greeting each guest in turn. The process was slow, for the translation devices had to be re-set for each language. Yet, Ferro mused, everyone in the room spoke several languages in common, Erlindish and Chacarran at a minimum. The aliens must be unaware of even the simplest customs.

One of the Terrans approached Ferro and raised a hairless hand in greeting. Ferro could only stare in wonder. Every hair root on his body tingled. His eyes darted from the hands with their five stubby fingers to the naked, light brown skin, the glossy hair and curiously-shaped eyes, oval instead of round. He caught a whiff of a faintly tangy odor, strange but not offensive.

Words issued from the thin metal box the alien wore around his neck, badly inflected but understandable, conveying wishes for friendship.

Bemusement struck Ferro as he framed a formal reply. How could intentions of these people be anything except peaceful? Breeding couples rarely had time or energy for anything else. Yet a race that could build such a space-faring vessel must not be lightly dismissed.

The alien, having finished his prepared greeting, paused before turning away.

"When you've finished with this ceremony," Ferro gestured to the room, "I hope you will have the chance to visit my own country. I would share the wonders of my city with you." What was the alien's name? Ferro searched his memory of the press conference and came up with the unlikely sounding name, "Laochristopher."

The alien glanced down at his translator box. "You are from another continental district. Chacarran?"

"Yes. My people have our own traditions of hospitality... and other things." Ferro wished he could read some trace of emotion in Laochristopher's black eyes or in the mantle of glossy hair that lay unmoving against his scalp. "Perhaps we could continue this conversation at the Chacarran Embassy?"

After the briefest pause, the alien made a peculiar bobbing movement with his head. Inflectionless words of agreement issued from the translator. Then a trio of Erls in the regalia of House Ar drew the alien into their midst.

When finally the aliens had been escorted from the grand hall, Ferro found that the Valad ambassador had also disappeared. Which was just as well, he reflected as he returned alone to the Chacarran Embassy. After the day's extraordinary events, he needed to sleep tonight.

Ferro, acting as Dorlin's aide, arranged a reception for the Terrans later that week. Such an event would usually have included a banquet of Chacarran specialties such as chilled flower-petal soup, ice-cured miniature vegetables, or terrine of nuts and wild mushrooms. The Erlind scientists insisted they had not completed the tests to make sure the Terrans could eat human food, so other arrangements had been made.

On the appointed evening, Ferro took his post inside the ornamental steel gates of the embassy. Chacarran military officers, armed and taut-eyed, stood facing the crowd outside. Most of the guests, those Chacarran notables who happened to be in Erlonn on business, had already arrived.

The night breeze had not yet sprung up, and the air felt as if a glass dome had descended on the city. Even the excited voices of the crowd were muffled. The last rays of the sun gleamed on the Erls' rifles. Watching them, Ferro's crest quivered, then lay still.

A Chacarran guard screened the guests at the entrance to the embassy building. A sudden flurry of activity, hands waving, voices raised, caught Ferro's attention. "I regret," he heard the guard say, politely but firmly, "but this invitation is not valid."

"What do you mean, *not valid?*" The accent was Chacarran and the robe of Shardian satin had been woven with a clan emblem, yellow for Sotir, first Aspect of the god. "Don't you realize who I *am?*"

"This," the guard handed the card back, "is a forgery."

"There must have been some mistake! I paid good money for that invitation!"

"If there is a mistake, I'm sure it can be remedied," the guard said smoothly.

Collaborators

Ferro, in his guise as minor official, hurried over. "How may I serve?"

"You see, there's been this dreadful error," the Chacarran guest turned to Ferro. "First my invitation was issued in the wrong name and now this Keshite *person* refuses to honor the replacement, which I was fully assured would be valid, only I didn't want to bother *dear* Ambassador Dorlin with such a trivial detail and—"

"Please allow me to resolve this problem," Ferro said. "In what name was the original invitation issued?" He took the name and went inside to check it against the official roster. As he expected, it was not there. When he returned to the gate, the wealthy Chacarran was gone and the Terrans had arrived with their honor guard.

Dorlin came forward, his senior secretary a pace behind, and gestured with both hands in greeting. One of the Terrans moved his five-fingered hands in response.

Ferro watched as the guards secured the gates, then followed the others into the embassy. The central chamber was far less grand than the Old Erlking's Palace, yet to Ferro's eyes it excelled in grace. Pennons and hangings in the colors of the eight traditional Chacarran clans enhanced rather than disguised the room's elegant proportions. Flower planters flanked the refreshment tables along the walls. In the open space, a half-circle of chairs, each with its footrest, faced a long straight bench. The style, called shield-and-crescent, was uniquely Chacarran. The Helm's Bench, or Shield, created a focus for the room without giving priority to any one clan. Ferro had suggested it as a deliberate contrast to the triangular configuration with the Erl-King at the head.

Dorlin and his senior aide sat on the bench with two of the Terrans. Ferro took his place on the far side of the Terran, Laochristopher. The half-circle filled, the clans arranged in traditional order. Many wore ribbons on their sleeves or circlets of fresh flowers in clan colors. Some carried musical instruments ornamented with rosettes.

Rising, Dorlin gave a formal speech of welcome. Ferro couldn't help glancing at the Terrans, at their muscular shoulders, the bony angles of jaw and collarbone, the way their broad chests tapered to narrow hips. Something nameless and uncomfortable stirred within him. He was near enough to touch Laochristopher's sleeve, to inhale the faintly salty odor, to feel the warmth from the Terran's bare skin. He himself had never paired; he'd always assumed the reason was because his work had come first. It was impossible—*unthinkable*—that he could respond to an alien, polarized or not.

After Dorlin concluded his opening remarks, the second Terran, the one named Celestinbellini, rose in turn. The words from the translator box sounded flat and stale, rendering the speech more equivocation than information. Everyone in the audience circle listened raptly.

The evening was to be a traditional Chacarran feste, in which representatives of each clan offered performances, speeches, or impromptu music or drama. The clans performed in traditional order: Sotirites, of the First Aspect of the god, whose color was yellow, and attribute, loyalty, came first. A mated pair, elderly and dignified, chanted a part-song around the mystical tone *ur*. The melody was very old, perhaps even from the days of the Prophet. Ferro watched the Terrans, trying to understand their response. He thought he saw their peculiar, bare-skin faces twitch from time to time. Their manes, flat and unmoving against their skulls, looked incapable of any emotional expression.

The young Keshite aide who'd greeted Ferro upon his arrival appeared in the doorway. Ferro immediately noticed the jagged state of his crest and his nervous gestures for attention. In keeping with his disguise as a minor official, Ferro hurried over. He hoped the trouble wasn't the wealthy Sotirite with the forged invitation again.

"Reporters," the aide said as the doors closed behind them. "Our own."

Ferro touched the aide's sleeve in reassurance and told him to go back to his post. Ferro noticed the guard at the entrance of the reception hall, standing with legs braced apart, blocking two people in the drab-colored belted coats favored by Chacarran reporters.

"I don't care who you are," the guard said. "This is a restricted event, by invitation only. I have no orders to admit press."

"How much did the Erls pay you to censor us?"

The guard's crest ruffled, and Ferro could see he was keeping his temper only with an effort.

The second reporter's fur was grizzled with age, but the residual traces of polarization still showed through his coat. Something in the movement of his eyes, the controlled demeanor, struck Ferro as familiar. Memory supplied a name.

Talense, from the Interclan Agency in Miraz, had a reputation for nonpartisan coverage. The smaller, single-clan news services rarely ventured beyond their home territory.

"I thought I recognized you," Ferro said to the second press. "I've followed your work for years. But I can't help you. This is truly a private function."

Talense made a gesture of impatience. "Chacarre deserves more than Erlind propaganda! Lansky here wrote the report on the first conference with the space aliens. If you read it, you know the Erls cut the questioning off suddenly. We want to know what they were hiding."

If the decision were his, Ferro would have let them in. With his years of experience at sensing nuances and implications, analyzing evasive answers, Talense would make a natural ally. But he could not, in his present role, go openly against Dorlin's orders.

"It's no use," Lansky said, making a gesture of disgust.

"If we act like the rest of your guests," Talense said in a quiet, intense voice, "no one need know who we are."

Ferro hesitated. It was as if the press had read his thoughts, offering him the opening he wanted. He sent a tiny quiver of indecision along his crest.

Talense spotted the ripple. "In your place, I'd try to set up a relationship with these aliens, counteract whatever lies the Erls have fed them. I'd also want to find out as much as possible about them and for that, I'd use every reliable source at hand."

Ferro waited a pulse beat, then another. "Is that an offer?"

Talense raised one hand in the gesture that sealed a formal agreement. "If you don't tell us what to write, it's a promise."

Ferro turned to the guard, pitching his voice to convey authority. "I'll handle this now." He led the two reporters around to the side entrance.

He turned to them, watching eagerness and suspicion clash in their eyes. "You look like everyone else, behave like everyone else. Your questions sound like everyone else's. No gear, no notebooks, no special attention."

Lansky's fur quivered with excitement. Talense, calmer, was already slipping off his coat. Underneath, he wore a simple beige tunic of the sort favored by travelers, which never looked really good or really bad.

With Ferro as escort, none of the guards within the embassy challenged them. They slipped through the doors to the central chamber and stood along the planters. In Ferro's brief absence, the feste had proceeded. The Terran Laochristopher was standing, reciting. The translator box had been turned off. His voice made strange sounds, rising and falling in pitch. Singing, almost. The effect wasn't unpleasant, just eerie.

Ferro slipped into his own place. When Dorlin glanced his way, he gestured, palm downward, *Everything under control.*

Everyone stood up, servers removed the furniture, and the guests descended upon the Terrans like a flock of brightly colored warblers.

"We understood that both Erlind and Chacarre are provinces of the same continent." The words issued from the translator box of the one called Celestinbellini. "We too have regional dialects and food-preparation rituals."

Ferro stepped back, watching the guests circulating. The two press slipped through the group like dun-colored shadows.

"He means nations," Laochristopher said.

"We take no part in local disputes," Celestinbellini said.

One of the elderly Sotirites spoke up. "What about the rumors you've given weapons technology to the Erls?"

Bird of Heaven! Ferro leaned forward, searching for the Terrans' reaction. If only their crests would move, a single hair, anything to give him a clue!

Both were silent for a long moment, silent and motionless. Ferro wondered if the translator unit had interpreted the guest's words correctly. Their eyes, with that inhuman oval shape, were shadowed and unblinking.

"Why do you ask such a question?" Laochristopher said slowly.

"We will defend ourselves," broke in Celestinbellini, "but we will not support either side."

The Terran Laochristopher turned his head toward his companion. To Ferro's mind, it looked as if he were going to speak, then changed his mind. Ferro felt a rush of heat along his crest; this was the first glimmer of understanding he'd gotten of these alien creatures.

One is superior, the other follows orders.

Ferro did not think the Terrans had given the Erls any weapons. Not yet, anyway. It was his intuitive guess, not a sure knowledge. One thing he did know, however.

They have weapons.

Chapter 4

Breathing hard, Sarah Davies pulled her way along the ladder leading to the Command deck corridor. Her hands had gone slippery after the first few rungs, but she dared not pause. She wasn't athletic enough to scramble around in near darkness by memory and feel. She reached the top, gulping stale air. As if on cue, the strip of lights flickered, then went to emergency orange.

She bent over, her vision graying. Her skin felt clammy and her stomach twisted. In a moment, the air scrubbers would kick in. They cycled alternately with the lights, but at least each worked some of the time.

Hold on, she told herself. Sure enough, with the first faint stirring of air, the feeling of suffocation passed.

Sarah straightened up and headed down the corridor. At least, she'd have a clearer head for her meeting with Hammadi.

The first reports from Bandar, as they'd dubbed the planet below in hopeful reference to the dead rising to life, had come in. Since Chris was still down on the surface, she was the closest thing to an expert they had. Sociology consultant, she mused, was not something she'd ever dreamed of becoming. She'd chosen it as her minor because she enjoyed the mental gymnastics of going back and forth between migration demographics in West Africa and calculations of the highly-excited states of transition metal ions, her doctoral thesis.

Hammadi strode down the corridor toward her, moving with a grace at odds with the thickness of his body. He wasn't fat or over-muscled, but he changed a room just by walking into it.

"Davies," he said, nodding.

"Captain," she replied. The science staff used each other's names; there had been a brief scuffle during their pre-flight training when command insisted on being called by their rank. Dr. Vera, as Dean of the Science Faculty, cheerfully reciprocated by refusing to respond except to her full title. After a few weeks of "Dean Doctor Doctor Professor Eisenstein," things settled down: one Captain, one Doctor, names for everyone else.

Hammadi slapped his palm on the lock panel of the conference room. Nothing happened.

With few exceptions, *Prometheus's* internal doors were set on universal, not personal locks. Hammadi pounded on the door. Sarah heard a muffled voice from inside, so someone was already in the room. After some shouting back and forth, it was clear that the door was locked from both sides. When Hammadi tried the palm panel again, a red warning light came on, indicating the room was unsafe to enter.

"Damned thing's hackered." Hammadi tapped the link hooked to his belt. "I need a door repair, conference room, command level."

"Sorry, sir." The answering voice was scratchy with static. "Something's screwy with the computers. Links with Engineering are down. We're having to route all communications by messenger."

"I might be able to open it manually." Sarah reached for her tool kit. Working mostly by touch, she removed the protective panel. Hammadi watched over her shoulder as if he were afraid she'd break something.

"I hope you know what you're doing."

"I worked my way through college as a Machinist Two."

"Oh? Where?"

"Mars." She caught a finger between the housing of the heat sensor unit and the steel stud, and winced. It was good her hands were small. "Can you give me a hand? Just hold the sensor unit horizontal—a little more to the right."

When she tugged, the latch slid smoothly in its groove. The door whispered open. From inside came a burst of exclamations.

Adriana Gomes, Hammadi's acting second now that Les Bellini was planetside, stood in the doorway. The muted emergency lights burnished her cheeks to bronze, her hair to coppery-black. "Thank goodness. Sir."

Hammadi said, "We had a minor difficulty with the door."

Inside the conference room, a tangle of torn cloth strips waved in front of the air vent. The lights were dim except for a spot above the table. The monitor screen behind Hammadi flickered, a square of gray-streaked brilliance. A faint crackle-hiss came from the speaker.

Sarah slid into the last empty seat. Besides Hammadi and Adriana Gomes, there was Max Elliott, Nuclear Physics head and the closest thing to a metallurgist they had, and a higher-level Engineering tech named Rhomi Calhoun. Les Bellini would be attending remotely.

"Here's our assessment in a nutshell." The speaker gave Les Bellini's voice a broken, almost warbling, quality, and the visual wasn't working. Everyone leaned forward, as if by concentrating hard enough they could wring out the answers they needed. "We've made contact with the two most industrialized provinces. We started off in Erlonn, the major city of Erlind.

They seem curious, intelligent, and excited to see us. Maybe too excited. By the time Lao got the bugs out of the translators, they were asking us far too many questions about weapons."

Adriana Gomes, sitting beside Sarah, drew in a breath.

"They're smart enough to have figured out that if we've got spaceflight, we must have bigger and better guns," Les said. "They want to make sure they get their hands on them first."

"What kind of savages are they?" Max Elliott asked under his breath. No one ventured an answer.

Prometheus was armed, after a manner of speaking. It carried an automatic system to detonate any solid space matter too small to be detected a few light minutes in advance. The hand-sized tunable laser cutters could be adapted as personal weapons; there was even a setting that would stun anything more sophisticated than a slug. The contact team carried these modified cutters.

Sarah pressed her fingers together hard enough to bend the joints backward. The pressure helped focus her thoughts. The natives' radio broadcasts suggested that these people still thought in terms of nationalist boundaries. They probably had nothing worse than chemical explosives and projectile weapons, although they didn't yet possess heavier-than-air aircraft. One of the big ship-mounted lasers, designed to vaporize a cometary fragment or chunks of proto-asteroid, would slice through primitive steel armor and stone walls like tissue.

"Interesting," Hammadi was saying. "What did you tell them?"

"I let them know we were prepared to defend ourselves if necessary," Les said. "When it comes to bargaining, we already know what they'll ask for."

"Have you verified that they have the capability to supply what we need?" Max Elliott asked, leaning forward.

"Bartov thinks so," said Les. "They're at the equivalent developmental level of our early twentieth century. But we think—Lao and I—"

Les's voice disappeared in a static burr. An instant later, the spotlight over the table flared and died, leaving the room in shadow.

"Get the link back!" Hammadi said.

Rhomi Calhoun, sitting closest to the computer console, cursed aloud. "The access is blocked. I think we're still getting a signal, but the ship's computer won't relay anything."

"This line is supposed to be priority one," Adriana snarled.

"I want this thing fixed *now*." Hammadi didn't speak louder, but deeper in pitch and slower.

"I can't get in," Rhomi said. "Someone's running a reconfig."

"Security, stat," Hammadi spoke into his link. "Find whoever's mucking with the computers and shut him down."

"I've traced the source," Rhomi said. "I don't believe this! It's coming from Medical."

"Medical?" Hammadi repeated.

Medical? Triple shit! Sarah glanced at Max Elliott and caught his shared, horrified expression. The last Sarah had seen Dr. Vera, an hour ago, she was complaining there wasn't enough designated memory to run her analyses of the "dark" hole data in less than a week and she was going to try a fancy juggling of unused computing capacity.

The next instant, the lights flashed on, air blasted from the vents, and the speakers let out a deafening squawk. Eye-searing color jazzed across the monitor, then settled into the image of Dr. Vera's face.

Hammadi leaned across the table. "What have you done to my computers?"

"What I've done to *your* computers is to straighten out the unholy mess in *your* environmental patch-up," the older woman said crisply. "One of *your* programmers apparently decided to solve *your* temperature problems by using the kitchen oven control program as a template. I've found 43 versions of it so far."

So far? Sarah thought. *She's not done yet?*

"Since the oven controller was designed to control *only* temperature and has no secondary input channel to accommodate the air scrubbers—or anything else," Dr. Vera went on, "some *other* moron got the brilliant idea of rerouting the scrubbers through the lighting system, resulting in the recent alternating deprivation torture."

"She's got some nerve, lying there with nothing to do but complain," Rhomi muttered.

"Not only that, *your* programmer replicated the same kitchen program to stabilize the star drive interaction chamber temperature and overestimated the chamber mass of the reactor by a factor of 127."

"Oh my god," Max Elliott said.

"If I hadn't repaired *your* repair, by tomorrow morning the temperature fluctuations would have cracked the wall of the main chamber and the resulting reactions would have reduced us all to interplanetary dust. That, in short, is what *I've* done to *your* ship."

By now, it had dawned on everyone in the room, not just Sarah and Max, that Dr. Vera had saved their lives.

"Oh, and you should have visuals back for your planetary link," Dr. Vera added.

"If, in the future," Hammadi said tightly, "you feel *inspired,* for whatever noble and worthy reason, to tinker with any of the vital operations of this ship, you will advise me before you begin. Is that clear?"

Sarah caught the shift in Dr. Vera's expression that meant she'd lost interest in the present topic and was already thinking about something else. Her image winked off an instant before Hammadi finished speaking.

Hammadi turned to Sarah. "Is she always like this?"

"Only when she's bored," Sarah said, keeping a straight face.

"Then you personally will see to it that she isn't bored. Find something for that woman to do! Something safe and self-contained."

"Technical developments of the mid-twentieth century? A list of inventions we can offer the natives?"

"I don't care, just so she stays out of my way." He turned to Adriana Gomes, saying, "I want the star drive and its control programs triple-checked."

"I've re-established the link to the planet," Rhomi said.

Les Bellini's image flashed on the monitor. His head and shoulders were framed by the curved gray-white walls and instrument banks of the shuttle cockpit. A shadow moved just beyond the focus, Sergei Bartov by the shape. "Excuse me, Captain. We experienced a momentary interruption in linkage."

"I know," Hammadi said dryly. "You're coming in clear now. You were saying we might stand a better chance dealing with this other province, Chacarre?"

"Yes, sir. They asked about weapons, too, but they seemed more worried about the Erls not getting them. We've met with them several times now. They appear to be reasonable."

Hammadi asked more questions, drawing out the details from Les, impressions of the city Erlonn, the police force there, and the security arrangements at the Chacarran Embassy. Max Elliott discussed technical capabilities with Sergei Bartov and came away looking relieved.

"See what the Chacarrans can provide us," Hammadi said when Les came back onscreen. "Don't do anything that could be construed as a commitment." With a few more sentences, he wrapped up the interview and broke the link.

Hammadi turned to his advisors and asked for comments.

"If we go with Chacarre, we've got two areas of concern," Adriana said, ticking off points on her fingers. "One, no matter what the Chacarran natives say, they'll be just as anxious to get their hands on our technology as the Erlinds are. We'll have to set up appropriate safeguards. Two, there's a distinct possibility that our presence will upset the balance of power. An armed conflict could be disastrous for our success."

Like others of her generation, Sarah had only an academic knowledge of warfare. Her parents had served in the United Terran Peacekeeping Command in the Mideast Buffer Zone before she was born. She remembered their stories of ethnic gangs, assassinations, duels, and bombs planted in densely populated neighborhoods.

"The last thing we need is to land in the middle of a war." Max's mouth twisted in disgust.

"We must be alert for any signs of preparations," Adriana went on, "like movement of troops or inflammatory speeches."

"We can monitor their radio," Rhomi said.

"That's assuming," Sarah said, "that they are like us. Maybe the ways they express belligerence are different from ours. We could inadvertently precipitate something we can't control. I think we should gather more information."

"A decent study would take years, decades even," said Max. "Time is a luxury we don't have."

Sarah bit her lip, realizing he was right. Even if *Prometheus* were stabilized, every day that went by without contact with *Celeste* worsened the chances of finding her crew alive.

"Then I recommend that we maintain a neutral posture and develop contacts with both groups," Sarah said. "No favoritism either way. If the teams are working in parallel, we won't lose time, but if something goes wrong at either site, we'll have a backup."

"We'll be spreading ourselves pretty thin," said Adriana. "Security will be twice as tough."

"We've stayed alive this far," Hammadi said, meaning, *We can handle a few low-technology natives.* "Can we shuttle the raw parts shipside and finish them here?"

Max said no, not for the big star drive and hull components. The natives lacked the facilities to handle massive operations. Delicate work like the lanthanide doping for the navigation focusing lasers would have to be done in the onboard labs.

"We'll split the projects and set up centers in both major cities," Hammadi said. "Erlonn and—what's the other one called?"

"Miraz," said Sarah.

"Okay. Erlonn gets the antenna project, we keep a tight hold on hand weapons, we trade civilian-applicable technology only. Got that?" He glanced at Max, who nodded. "The rest of the stuff—the star drive parts, the nav system, anything with technology capable of being applied to weapons, we'll do ourselves. For that, we'll need a self-contained center where we can work without these people breathing down our necks."

Reluctantly, Sarah spoke up. "There's the modular observatory. It's designed to be independent in space. If there's a suitable foundation, we can remove the internal framing and partition it as needed." She paused, knowing that once it was modified as a planet-side factory, it would no longer be spaceworthy. A certain amount of observational astronomy could still be done onboard, but the low-energy photon studies, the work she had come so far and sacrificed so much to do, would be impossible within the ship's magnetic and gravitational fields. On the other hand, the observatory was fitted with a high-power protective laser.

Hammadi liked the idea of a self-contained, defensible unit, especially one that could be disguised as anything they liked, a cultural research center or museum.

"People, I don't need to remind you that although this is not a military operation, our authorizing agency is the United Terran Peacekeeping Command. We come from a long and proud tradition of preventing maniacs from blowing each other up. I don't doubt we'll be able to do so here. In fact, I'm counting on you to make sure that's what happens."

Chapter 5

Miraz: WORK ON TERRAN COMPOUND BEGINS; Report by Talense.

After weeks of negotiations, work has begun on the Terran Compound in Miraz Plaza. The plaza site affords both sufficient space and easy public access to this modern miracle, a multi-story building of prefabricated panels mounted on an armature of specially hardened metal.

Once completed, the Miraz Compound will house Terran scientists and support staff. An educational and fellowship center will be open to the public following its completion.

"This is a great day for the people of Chacarre," Mayor Chelle said as he opened the ceremonies that commenced the building. The text of the Terran announcement follows.

Lexis-az-Doreth stepped from the tram car onto the smooth concrete landing. The underground station was cool as always, perhaps the only place in the city that remained comfortable during these early autumn days, except perhaps a few private wine cellars. Instead of catching a bus to the university to deliver his lecture on Diacritics in the Post-Modern Ballad, he decided to walk across the river. It would do him good. When he was on foot, Miraz came alive for him in a way it never did otherwise. Trams put too many barriers between him and the vitality of the streets.

As he walked, Lexis scanned the western hills, the buildings clustered at their feet, pale gold facades beneath roofs of brick tile weathered by centuries. The city worked its magic on him. He felt its agelessness as a physical presence, not oppressive but sustaining.

Trams lined up in their lanes like children's blocks. The stream of pedestrians crept over the hump of the bridge and down the other side toward the plaza. The flow of traffic pulled Lexis along like a tide. Lost in thought, he bumped into the person in front of him, a burly Hoolite.

The Hoolite hissed and elbowed him back. "Get back! Who do you think you are?"

Lexis set his teeth and tightened his grip on his satchel, but he kept his distance. The Hoolite looked as if he were in the early stages of polarization, capable of anything.

An hour earlier would have brought Lexis out before the heat, as well as avoiding the congestion. He'd forgotten this was the morning when many of the Clan elders came together before the statue of the first Chacarran Helm. That accounted for the density of the crowd and the shortened tempers of anyone who, like himself, just wanted to get to work.

The presence of so many polarized struck Lexis as intolerable, bordering on obscenity. Why didn't they stay home like decent people until the madness was done? At the university, it was easy to avoid contact with them. Most of the students were too young, and the faculty had finished their breeding. Lexis himself had survived as a singleton past the susceptible age. Over the years he'd found other ways of satisfying his body's urges.

As he came down the ramp of the bridge, Lexis caught sight of the Terran compound. Rising to a pointed tower, it dwarfed the statue of Carrel-az-Ondre, the first Chacarran Helm. Carrel was depicted as heavily pregnant, one hand cradling the fertile promise within his belly, the other gesturing outward to include all who passed before him.

In contrast, spikes studded the peak of the compound tower. Antennas, the news stories said. Lexis had never been inside, for tickets to the public museum were difficult to obtain. His first impression of the compound had been a tent, metallic fabric stretched into an ungainly shape. Behind the compound itself, a section of pavement had been cordoned off for the Terran shuttle. The pale pink surface was scored and blackened.

Lexis's crest rippled. Even after the Terrans were gone, the scars would remain, his city forever marked.

The shuffling crowd carried him toward the compound. Beyond it lay his destination, the underground station on the university route. The crowd spread out, some heading for the statue, others continuing on their way. Lexis worked his way toward the periphery.

A commotion from one of the side streets drew his attention. Four young people, students by their dress, rushed toward Lexis, yelling, "Peace with Erlind!"

Lexis's crest prickled. His pulse leaped in his throat. The next moment, he heard more shouting and caught sight of a streamer-decked placard. He never paid attention to student demonstrations, and it was damnably inconvenient of them to hold one on the day so many Clans came to honor the Helm. *Today, of all days!*

"Get out of my way! Let me through!" Lexis tried to push past his neighbor, but more demonstrators blocked his path.

Behind Lexis, someone snapped, "Watch where you're going!" and bumped into him hard enough to send him stumbling.

In the center of the plaza, people began chanting. Lexis heard a shouted plea for order, quickly drowned in a volley of cries. Out of the corner of one eye, Lexis spied a city warder bearing down on the crowd. He offered hasty thanks to Sotir, First Aspect of the god, whose attribute was loyalty. Help was near. They'd soon have the situation under control.

"This assembly is unlawful!" brayed the warder through his amplifier. "Remain calm! Disperse! Be on your way! Go to your homes and businesses!"

People jostled Lexis on all sides. He pushed in one direction, then another. No matter which way he turned, someone else blocked his avenue of escape. He felt desperate for the safety of his office.

"This is your last warning! Disperse now or face arrest!"

Acid filled Lexis's mouth as if he were a child, sick with a stomach ailment. Then his nausea turned to panic. Something explosive built around him, dangerous and unpredictable in the surging crowd. His crest quivered and his breath sizzled between his clenched teeth.

We'll all be arrested, he thought. *I'll end up in jail.*

His next thought—what Dim-Dim would say—was quickly washed away in a chillingly rational consideration of the effect that criminal charges, even if eventually dismissed, might have on his academic career. He thought of what being arrested would actually be *like*—a narrow gray cell—nights filled with the smell of rank, polarized bodies, their suffocating closeness—their greasy, sweating flesh rubbing against his—

Something burst open inside him. Caustic seared the line of his crest. Every hair jumped erect. A stench rose up from his own flesh, sulfur-edged.

"Let go of me!" Screaming, Lexis began swinging his satchel.

The leather collided with the shoulder of a commuter trying to wriggle past him. The commuter staggered. Eyes bulged and crest hair jutted out in all directions. Lexis caught the reek of polarization, like burnt leather.

"Stay away!" Lexis yelled. "Don't you touch me, you degenerate filth!" His words disappeared into the rising din. Around him, people shouted pleas, warnings, hoarse-voiced obscenities. Every scream, every shove fueled the building madness.

He swung again, this time striking the side of a rioter's head. The rioter howled. Blood spurted from his nose. Lexis caught only a glimpse of the rioter's fist before it smashed into his own face. Lexis's head whipped back. The joints of his neck snapped. Pain jolted through his skull. His vision went white and he couldn't breathe.

A second blow landed. His body jerked and recoiled.

Frantic energy surged through Lexis. He kicked out as hard as he could. His foot, encased in a leather shoe, shot toward the rioter's crotch. It sank into the soft mound.

Wailing sirens filled the air. Somebody shoved Lexis from behind and he fell against another body. He gasped for breath. The pain in his head throbbed with every heartbeat. All he could think of was the intolerable odiousness of the crowd.

Stinking, breeding vermin!

"Get away from me, all of you! Get away!" Lexis took hold of the satchel and began swinging again—right, left, right—screaming with each sweep, "Get away! *Get away!*" His muscles strained and his shoulder joints popped. The handle jerked in his grip, but he kept on swinging.

Once or twice, Lexis stepped on something that crunched and twisted beneath his feet. His nerves sang and his mouth filled with exhilarating bitterness. Fire raced along his limbs.

Lexis no longer felt any pain. The satchel acquired a life of its own, beyond his conscious control. Each *splat!* of hard leather against unresisting flesh sent sparks of pleasure through his bones.

Something thumped into Lexis's back. He whirled, poised to strike. In a flash, he saw a person, a fallen heap of pale, tangled mane and caramel silk. One cheek was scraped raw and already darkening into a bruise. Eyes bright with terror lifted to meet his own. Lips curved into soundless words. His gaze locked on the hands crossed over chest in the ancient, instinctive gesture of surrender.

In a single pulse beat, the howling inside Lexis's head dimmed. The fire in his belly died. Cold shot along his crest. The red fury fell away, replaced by the reflexive *need* to protect.

Trembling, sick to the marrow of his bones, hating himself and yet unable to do anything else, Lexis reached out. The fallen scrambled to his feet and threw his arms around Lexis's neck with an inarticulate cry. Through the layers of rumpled clothing, Lexis felt the softness of the body pressed against him, the curves of breasts and belly. He wanted nothing more in that instant than to thrust the other from him, smash that face with its melting sweetness into bloody splinters, batter that disgusting, fertile body to a lifeless pulp. Yet his arm tightened protectively and his voice whispered words of comfort.

A high-pitched squeal pierced the air overhead, leaving Lexis's ears ringing. Bodies jostled him on either side. He tightened his grip on the still-sobbing pregnant.

The squealing sound came again and then again. Lexis ignored it, concentrating on staying on his feet. The satchel was useless now. He couldn't defend himself while this damned breeder had a stranglehold on him.

The clamor died into patchy shouting instead of a single roar. People clutched each other and looked toward the Terran Compound. More lay sprawled on the pavement.

Chapter 6

Reporter's carry-all slung over one shoulder, Talense positioned himself near the Terran compound, watching the foot traffic stream across the plaza. The morning sun, sweet and mild, gleamed on the ancient bronze statues. People moved about their business. Flower-sellers, fruit carts, and news sheet vendors lined the plaza periphery, along with a few warders.

So far, he hadn't seen any sign of the organized demonstration scheduled by the Chacarran-Erlind Fellowship League. His mate, Jeelan, had joined the organization last year and was one of the event's planners.

"We can't go on like this, century after century of bitterness and suspicion, surely you see that," Jeelan had said as Talense prepared to leave that morning. No, not *said*—argued, announced, orated. When it came to politics, Jeelan was anything but moderate. Jeelan's family, like Talense's, were Fardites, but sometimes saw no distinction between the divine attribute of change and its inversion, insanity.

The shouting began in the center of the plaza. It sounded to Talense like slogans, but not the familiar ones. Listening carefully, he separated individual words from the general noise. He caught the refrain of *Peace with Erlind!* but also something else.

"Down with the warmongers!"

"Down with Kreste!"

Down with Kreste?

Talense's crest ruffled. What had Jeelan, in his passion for justice and good causes, gotten himself into?

More demonstrators appeared, positioning makeshift barricades to cut off the side streets. Within moments, the orderly pattern of foot traffic broke up. People shifted direction, first this way and then the other, like wild grommets at the approach of a weasel.

Talense caught the quicksilver change in the crowd. Bumping and shoving erupted into knots of violence. A scream pierced the confusion.

Reflex panic, he thought. He knew its scent, that sulfur-edged tang.

A handful of commuters rushed past him, heading toward one of the open streets. The swirling crowd parted and he glimpsed streamers, raised hands, and a striped orange tunic.

Jeelan!

Talense shoved his note pad and pen into his carry-all. He jumped down from the platform and headed for the opening.

"Clear off! Clear off!" A tall Maasite, his shoulders thickened by polarization, collided heavily with Talense. Talense stumbled, scrambled to keep his feet. The next moment, he found himself surrounded. Beside him, someone jabbed him in the ribs with an elbow. The air burst from his lungs. He tripped on something solid, a foot maybe. With a shock, his knees crashed into the stone paving. He thrust out his hands to catch himself.

A boot came down on Talense's fingers. One knuckle went *snap!* Pain lanced up his arm. He cried out, pulling his injured hand to his chest. A knee rammed into his side. He couldn't see past the rush of feet. Someone fell against him, knocking him over with the sudden impact. The strap of his carry-all dug into his neck and snapped.

He tucked his body into a ball, bringing his knees to his belly. Something hard collided with his head. Roaring filled his ears, the din of the crowd, the hammering of his own heart. He squeezed his eyes shut. More blows landed, fast and hard, raining on his back and legs. He tasted blood.

His lungs filled with the reek of heated sulfur. Fire ignited in his belly. His breath burned. It clawed at him, the need to act without thinking, to release the demanding pressure inside. He felt himself shredding under its power. Dimly he fought against it. He could not remember why or who it was that he must find, only that he must.

Someone shouted, very close. The voice sounded urgent rather than frightened. Talense raised his head. He squinted against sun. A face, blue under dead-white fur, loomed over him. A hand wrapped around his free arm.

The stranger lifted Talense to his feet. He pulled Talense close, to steady him. His body felt as solid as a tree. "Come, I will help you."

Cradling his injured hand, Talense stumbled along behind his rescuer. He couldn't think clearly. Fire smoldered in his belly. He felt sick and dizzy.

Someone rushed toward them. Talense braced for the impact. Then his new friend edged in front of him and the rioter slipped past, barely brushing Talense's sleeve. Through the milling bodies, Talense glimpsed the wall of the Terran compound. It shone like a beacon. They moved steadily toward it. With each step, a space opened in front of them.

Talense stumbled at the edge of the platform, but his rescuer caught him and pulled him up. Here, at the edge of the surging crowd, the augmenting effect lessened. His stomach felt as if he'd eaten ashes, but each passing moment left him steadier. More important, his mind was once more his own.

Jeelan! he thought, shivering, and prayed the Prophet would be at his mate's side.

"You are free of the *tal'mur* now," said the stranger. His soft voice lilted above the clamor.

Talense gestured agreement and thanks. For the first time, he took a careful look at his rescuer. The other was short and burly, dressed in the simple clothing of a farmer. His fur was a chalky white with no hint of gloss or undertint. He wore no visible clan token. Wayfolk, then. In response to Talense's inquiry, he said his name was Hayke-az-Midrien.

"Now that we're here," Talense said, his voice almost normal, "let's see if we can get a look inside." The impulse arose mostly from professional curiosity but also in small part from a lingering desire to escape the madness of the crowd.

Beyond the glass-clear doors of the compound lay the lobby and public museum. A Terran in a white uniform barred their way. He held a long metal staff as if it were a weapon. Whether it was some sort of rifle or merely a stick, Talense couldn't tell.

"Entry is forbidden," the translator unit around the Terran's neck buzzed. He raised the staff.

Talense took a deep breath and lifted his crest in his most authoritarian posture. "I demand to see the ambassador."

Hammadi shifted sideways in his chair, readjusted the angle of the monitor, and finished going over Adriana Gomes's personnel reports. With cool efficiency, she'd detailed how many people in which areas were still disabled, how many could perform limited work, and how they might best be used. Her recommendations for reassigning the science staff to technical and engineering functions, both shipside and planetside, were excellent.

Hammadi initial-coded the report and scrolled to the next item, the one with the flashing "Science Dean" insignia. Suppressing a sigh, he brought up the first page. He wished, not for the first time, he could find a way of harnessing that insatiable curiosity, that piercing intellect. Six weeks in immobilization, plus a month more of intensive physical rehab, had left Dr. Vera with far too much free time. She'd already tackled the problem of what technology to offer the natives. Her list had ranged from synthetic fibers to infrared detectors, television—hell, the natives didn't even have photography—improvements in optics, electric motors, solar-electric conversion, and high-efficiency storage batteries. He'd drawn the line at computers and heavier-than-air dynamics as having too much military potential. But she'd given him a gold mine to work with.

It hadn't kept her busy for long. He'd already turned down three further proposals and scotched two more that she'd already started. Her latest scheme glowered at him from the monitor screen, a sociological study of the natives in Chacarran capital, the idea no doubt coming from her protégée, Sarah Davies.

As he read on, he realized that she wanted to modify the neutrino particle study probes into free-standing observation modules and scatter them all over the city of Miraz. They could provide invaluable data about movement patterns across different neighborhoods. The compound had been well accepted by the natives, she pointed out. The probes, designed to withstand the stresses of outer space, should be impermeable to mechanical assault. After all, they were equipped with built-in protective systems to deflect particulate space debris.

Hammadi didn't like the idea of committing a resource for a nonessential purpose. "Sociological data" could be gathered by other, less invasive means. Let her stick to nice, non-meddlesome analyses of radio broadcast programs.

His desk speaker let out a squawk—something in the circuits still wasn't right—and he heard Gomes's voice.

"Captain, there's an emergency message coming in from Sergeant Adamson in Miraz. I'm putting him through."

With a flicker and a horizontal crackle of gray, Jon Adamson's face came onscreen. Hammadi recognized the background as the chamber above the central core, which they'd designated as Ops. Adamson's face was flushed. Behind him, one of the Engineering techs was flicking the switches to charge the capacitors for the large, roof-mounted laser.

"Sir! We've got a situation on the plaza." Adamson described the chain of events succinctly. The ordinary morning foot traffic had degenerated into what Adamson called, "chaotic traffic patterns."

"How close?" Hammadi asked.

"A few meters, sir. We haven't seen any evidence of weaponry, not even hand guns, but there are close to two thousand people out there."

A rumble came over the speaker, someone talking outside the focus cone of the compound receiver. Adamson's brows knotted. "One moment, sir." He turned away, half out of the visual field. "A what? Interagency official?"

More gabble issued from out of view. "All right, take him up to the observation deck and put a guard on him. Don't let him touch anything."

Hammadi said, "What's going on?"

"Sir, Arguilles was down on the ground level when the disorder broke out. He's admitted a government official, says the native appears to be injured."

Hammadi nodded. Providing aid to a local dignitary might give them the leverage they needed here.

"The observation deck was mostly astronomical instrumentation, sir," Adamson went on. "We stripped it except for sealed recording equipment housings. There's not much even one of our own people could assimilate and I'm keeping him under guard."

Hammadi liked the way Adamson said *I*, assuming responsibility for the situation. "Carry on," he said. "What's the current status outside?"

Adamson glanced down, consulting readouts. "It's rapidly escalating. Casualties, although we can't tell how many. We're getting unarmed fighting at the perimeter of our foundation slab."

He looked up, mouth tight. "Request permission to fire defensive laser system."

"Can you get me visuals?" Hammadi said.

"Linking now." Adamson's face winked out, replaced by the natives who looked at first glance like cheetahs given manes and turned human. In the blurred movement, they looked as if they were wearing ancient Greek war helmets. The sound came through in a static roar.

Hammadi cursed under his breath. Engineering had modified the big laser for defensive usage, but it had been designed to fire in a vacuum. No one could be sure the stun setting would be safe to use on the natives. At the same time, no mob should ever be considered unarmed. He'd learned that lesson in his early years of peacekeeping work against the terrorist gangs in Peru and Indonesia. You never let them take the initiative and you never, ever negotiated with them. And indecision was the worst possible action.

"Sir!" Adamson's voice, tinny with stress, broke his thought. "They're on our doorstep!"

"Permission granted!" Hammadi slapped the work surface with one palm. "Sweep the damned plaza, do whatever you have to in order to safeguard your position. Then make sure that government official knows we acted for their own benefit."

Chapter 7

With the farmer at his heels, Talense followed the Terran past the entrance to the public museum. His emotions were a mixture of relief and the fading effects of the mass panic reflex. He'd visited the place during a special press reception before the official opening. The displays included scale models of the orbiting ship and landing craft, as well as various Terran artifacts, clothing, a flute of blown glass, and a translator unit that the visitors could operate themselves. There were no obvious weapons and for the first time he wondered about them. Were they absent or merely hidden?

The farmer, Hayke, glanced around as they went, by the smoothness of his crest and his demeanor more curious than nervous. They paused while the Terran placed his hand flat on a shoulder-height panel outlined in red. A door hissed open and they proceeded inside, down another gray corridor, below strips of brilliant lights.

The corridor ended in a small compartment. They followed the Terran inside and a transparent panel, much like glass, slid down from the wall to form a fourth wall. A few moments later the compartment rose up, as if the floor beneath their feet had grown wings.

Talense's breath caught in his throat and he could not contain the sudden shiver along his crest. He glanced at the farmer. The bright overhead lights cast shadows from his crest, now stiffly raised, and turned his skin to a pasty gray. But the round, dark eyes measured their surroundings with calm intelligence.

The elevator came to a halt, although the glass wall did not immediately slide open. Talense and the farmer were escorted into a room like a narrow enclosed balcony, dominated by a massive window. The peculiar tangy odor of the aliens tinged the air. The room seemed eerily quiet. None of the clamor from below penetrated the glass.

"Look all you want," the Terran said. "Just don't touch anything."

Talense glanced around. A low shelf ran just inside the window, covered with box-like structures and panels. Lines like soldered seams ran vertically across the inner wall. He suspected he'd been put in a place where everything was locked away and hidden.

Talense moved to the window and looked down. From the angle of view, they must be near the top of the compound. He saw people running and uniformed warders moving in from the periphery. They looked like churning streams of color, colliding, then reforming.

The next moment, a high-pitched squeal blasted overhead. A beam of yellowish light lanced across the plaza.

Bird of Heaven! What—

"Look!" the farmer exclaimed, pointing. "See there! On the ground!"

Huge swathes had been cut in the crowd, as if they had been mowed down. Their bodies lay in haphazard jumbles. As Talense watched, another klaxon sounded and a second light beam shot out from above him. It played across the frantically milling crowd. They toppled.

Talense stared, hardly breathing. From behind him came the farmer's voice, hollow.

"Please tell me... are they dead?"

Deborah J. Ross

Chapter 8

In a daze, Lexis watched the warders pick their way through the fallen bodies. Buses with barred windows pulled up in the boulevard along the plaza. None of the people left standing looked capable of resistance, and as for the rest, they might as well be dead. Only the sound of their breathing suggested otherwise. In the distance he heard the clamor of emergency medical vans. A warder and a green-coated medical approached him.

"It's all right," the warder said soothingly, "it's over. You're safe now."

The pregnant, cowering against Lexis's side, murmured, "Safe?" Lexis caught the immediate tenderness on the faces of the warders as they noticed the curve of his belly. A nearby press watched, taking notes.

The medical held out his hand and gestured, but the pregnant drew back, whimpering and clinging to Lexis's arm. "Come on, let's get you to Old Hospital," the medical said. "They'll check you out, make sure all three of you are all right."

Lexis stumbled as he allowed himself to be guided around the clumps of bodies. Dazedly he realized that he'd been mistaken for the other's mate.

Once they got into the emergency van, the pregnant let go of Lexis's arm long enough for a medical to give him a brief examination and check the fetal heartbeat.

Originally designed as a winter palace for one of the eight dominant Chacarran clans, Old Hospital was a massive building of silvery-green stone, ornamented in the floral style that had been popular three hundred years ago. It had been turned into a place of healing after the Last Great War with Erlind.

As soon as they arrived, Lexis was taken away, questioned, and rayed and bandaged. His nose was broken, they told him, and he had a mild concussion but nothing worse. The pain medication did nothing for the soreness in his arm. The medical explained they couldn't give him anything stronger because of the concussion.

Lexis walked slowly through the hospital lobby. He still carried his satchel, now scuffed and darkened by blood. Shock was beginning to wear off and he felt shaky but determined to get out. Besides, it was clear they didn't have room for him. There were still people waiting in the intake area who hadn't been examined yet.

Lexis pushed open the heavy wood and glass door. The light outside made him squint. His nose ached under layers of bandages and his neck muscles twinged. He was hungry, for it was well past lunch time. Glancing at the knot of people gathered on the steps, he recognized them as press. He did not expect them to take notice of him, a nobody with a bandaged nose, and he was not disappointed. They swarmed past him and into the building.

Slowly Lexis climbed the steps to his parents' rooms. With every step, he discovered a new ache or bruise. He'd forgotten to take his next dose of pain medication. Where had he put the packet—in his satchel, where he carried everything of value? He searched his memory and discovered no image of opening it, only the clasp crusted with dried blood. The medication must be in his tunic pocket.

His feet came to a halt. He lifted his head and studied the shadowed top of the stairs. He wasn't at all sure he could reach it. The only thing to do was sit down right where he was. He shuddered, a quick jerk of his thin shoulders.

Sit down, right on the same step where people's filthy shoes had walked?

The stairwell lay above him, as cool and closed-in as a cellar. He ducked his head, drew in his breath, and began to climb.

As Lexis reached the last step, he heard voices coming from the apartment. Dim-Dim's voice was raised, as usual, in annoyance. Lexis couldn't make out the words, only the strident tone. His stomach clenched and he thought for a moment of going back downstairs, wobbly knees or no, going out the front door, past the bake shop, going somewhere, anywhere but here. He'd been through enough today. He deserved a respite. He'd survived that awful mess at the plaza, more by luck than any effort of his own. He saw that now, the pathetic conceit of his flailing about. It was only coincidence he hadn't been badly hurt, no thanks to that whining leech of a breeder.

But, he thought as he lifted his shoulders in an effort at resolution, people didn't always get what they deserved. He turned the latch.

"Lexie! By the Faith!" Pim-Pim leapt up from the worn sofa, bristling with nervous energy, and threw his bony arms around Lexis. Half-stifled, Lexis gulped and tasted Pim-Pim's familiar sour smell. His arms had no strength to push his parent away. Pim-Pim held him in a cage of living bars.

"Where have you been? Press have been calling us for hours!" came Dim-Dim's voice from across the room.

"I came from Old Hospital," Lexis began. "The plaza—a riot—"

"Yes, yes, we know!" Dim-Dim snapped. "It's been all over the casts."

"My poor baby," crooned Pim-Pim, crushing Lexis even harder against his slat-like ribs. "You might have been killed!"

"You should have come straight home," said Dim-Dim. "We were worried enough to be hospital cases ourselves!"

Lexis managed to free himself with an effort. There was Dim-Dim, wringing his hands, on his feet instead of sprawled in his favorite chair. His crest was combed, his clothing neat. A stranger, impeccably groomed and dressed in a richly tailored tunic, occupied the favored spot. His red embroidered emblem of J', Third Aspect, embodied taste and subtlety. Lexis watched the blue and silver tones play across the fabric with the shift in light. It was the sort of sensuous garment he could never hope to own.

"This is, oh! it's so wonderful," Pim-Pim said.

The stranger rose. "I am Ralle, assistant to Mayor Chelle."

Lexis realized he was still holding his blood-spattered suitcase. "Mayor," he repeated tonelessly. The mayor of Miraz was one of the most powerful people in Chacarre.

I must be hallucinating, he thought. *An effect of the concussion. I must take my pain medication. I must call a medical.* Neither mayors nor their assistants, no matter how lowly or insignificant—and this one clearly was not—would ever visit Dim-Dim and Pim-Pim.

"Please, you must sit down." In a single swift movement, the mayor's assistant moved to Lexis's side, gently uncurling his fingers from the handle of the satchel and leading him toward Dim-Dim's favorite chair.

As Lexis sank in the upholstery, he realized that in all his years he'd sat in that chair less than a handful of times. He noticed for the first time the places where the once-thick fabric had been worn down to the threads, the odor of sweat and body grime that clung to it. The shabbiness of the apartment struck him like a physical blow. It seemed incredible that only a few hours earlier, he'd been in the brisk open air of the plaza, screaming and swinging, more terrified and more alive than he could ever remember.

"In the riot today, you came to the aid of a pregnant." Ralle pulled up his chair and leaned forward earnestly. "You held off the mob, practically single-handedly. You risked your own safety to protect him."

Instinct kept Lexis quiet. What was this elegant bureaucrat getting at?

"You have no idea who that was, do you?" Ralle said.

Lexis made a gesture of negation. He noticed Dim-Dim's expression, the way he kept clasping and unclasping his hands, how Pim-Pim stuck his chest out, crest rippling, and strutted at Dim-Dim's side.

"The person you saved was the mayor's own partner."

Lexis blinked, not quite daring to believe what he heard.

"And," Ralle continued in a quietly dramatic voice, "his only child as well. The hospital was in such an uproar, no one realized where you'd gone or even who you were. We've been searching for you for hours."

"Well, I really—it was nothing," Lexis stammered. "Only what any decent person would have done."

"He's a *hero*," Dim-Dim said. Pim-Pim shot him a look of reflexive disapproval and as quickly smoothed his crest and juggled his features into a smile. He slipped one arm around Dim-Dim's rounded shoulders as if they were posing for a publicity photograph.

"A hero, that is what you are," Ralle said. "One of the very few in today's tragic events. The mayor intends to thank you himself."

Chapter 9

On the morning of the Miraz plaza riots, Alon-az-Thirien had fallen asleep in the overstuffed chair in his parents' bookstore in the old Westbank district. It was not the first time he'd done so. He had grown up immersed in the smells of paper and waxed-canvas bindings, had played as a child between the ranges of scrolls and board books, and later worked here after he'd finished school.

The morning was a good one for a nap, already drenched in early autumn heat. The breezes that insinuated their way through the high-set windows had barely enough energy to stir the air inside.

Alon had stayed up far too late last night, dancing and then lovemaking with Birre. Now he slept on as Birre cracked the door open and reached up to muffle the chain of porcelain bells. Birre slipped inside, past the portfolios of antique botanical prints, the round-bellied clay stove and corner desk. His eyes glinted as he bent over Alon.

Alon's head lolled against the back of the chair, one arm dangling, loose-jointed as a child. A patch of sunlight glowed on his face and highlighted the soft fur, turning it to russet over skin so pale and thin, the veins showed as a threadwork of darker blue. His flat, unformed breasts barely disturbed the folds of his tunic.

Suddenly Alon startled awake, heart pounding. His feet kicked out and the hair along his crest stiffened. His hands flailed empty space and then, unexpectedly, closed around Birre's shoulders.

Alon's vision leapt into focus. For a long, terrifying instant, Birre's face seemed utterly unfamiliar to him, as if he'd never seen it before. Yet at the same time, he seemed to be looking into a mirror. They were of an age, although Birre was taller and more slender, his crest almost burnt-colored. Yet in a heart-stopping moment, those round black eyes, so unexpectedly serious, seemed to see right through Alon to the very depths of his soul.

Alon trembled. Everywhere Birre's body touched his—hands, knee against thigh, the almost imperceptible movement of breath over hair—he trembled. But not with the shivering spasms of lust. Lust he knew well enough, a night's mutual pleasuring. This new emotion swept away everything that had come before it. He couldn't breathe, couldn't think.

Birre took a step backward, a graceless stumble. The folds of his tunic slipped through Alon's fingers.

Despite all the lingering confusion of his awakening, Alon knew in that moment that this was what he wanted for the rest of his life—to be turning, ever turning, toward Birre's sun.

Birre stood, shoulders hunched slightly, hands hugging his arms, eyes fastened on a display of children's picture books. His nostrils flared and the hairs along his neck lifted slightly. He stood so still he didn't seem to be breathing. Noises drifted in from the street outside, people laughing, the clatter of boot heels on stone and a creaking, hand-pushed cart.

Alon moved to stand behind Birre, aching to take him into his arms. He had been warned—they all had, at school, by their parents—of the dangers of such a moment. How instinctive drives could take over, overruling sense, judgment, even personal taste. Of the disasters of a pairing without intelligent choice. In times past, before Carrel-az-Ondre, the First Helm, such a union could have serious political consequences between feuding clans.

Birre's head dipped and the movement, almost timid, so unlike him, sent a rush of tenderness through Alon.

"Alon, I'm scared."

"Yes."

"I didn't... expect it so soon."

"Or with me?"

"Oh no, don't think I wouldn't want you." Birre's voice roughened with emotion. "Never think that!"

The next moment—Alon could never tell how it happened—Birre's arms were around him, hard and tight, and his heart felt as if it would explode. His breath stuttered through his throat in a half-sob. He couldn't make out Birre's murmured words and he didn't care.

Sometime later Birre drew back, pushed Alon to arm's-length and looked at him frankly, without any trace of shyness. His fingers gripped Alon's arms. "Did you have any idea this was going to happen?"

Irrational joy surged through Alon. When he found his voice, he said, "Oh yes, I stayed up all night planning it."

The familiar twinkle returned to Birre's eyes. "I *know* what you stayed up all night doing." He slipped his arm around Alon's shoulders. "We should let them know." Meaning, of course, his own family. They were an aristocratic sept of one of the eight ruling clans.

Alon thought that all his own parents had to do was look at him and they would know. They might even guess it was Birre because for the past year it had been *Birre-this* and *Birre-that*. It would come as no surprise, either; he and Birre were undoubtedly the last to realize what was going on.

56

He turned his head, found the side of Birre's neck and touched his lips to the suddenly attractive curve there. He inhaled Birre's scent.

"Be practical, Alon. We need to decide... if we're even ready to have a baby."

"We may not have much of a choice." Alon straightened up, touched Birre's breast gently. Birre shivered; the fur of his ruff rose briefly and subsided. "You see?"

Something in the tension of Birre's muscles struck Alon as fragile, although he'd always thought of Birre as being tougher, more decisive, certainly more athletic. He wanted to surround that new vulnerability with his own strength.

With an effort, he moved away. No matter how they polarized, Birre would never be a person to be protected. And Birre was right, they were too young to be having children, no matter what the biological urgencies of their bodies. Yet the longer they touched and tasted each other, the faster and deeper the physiological changes. They'd both had the classes; they both should know what they were doing.

Knowing and acting were, however, two different things.

The door bells jingled and a trio of customers, Bavarite by their azure tokens, entered the bookstore. They paused in front of the desk, apparently oblivious to the flustered expressions with which Alon and Birre jumped apart.

"Strange and wonderful to the University professors, to be sure," one said to the others, continuing their conversation, "but in the end, what have they to do with us?"

"Nothing, that's just the point! They contacted the Erls first, that's what," another one said, his crest ruffling.

"You're just corked because you couldn't get tickets to the opening of the Terran Compound Museum," the third said, and wandered off to inspect the botanical prints.

"Erls, of all people!" the second one kept on, gesturing to include Alon and Birre in his audience. "That bunch of tight-minded brigands!"

Birre managed to regain his composure. "Given the Erls as a sampling, the aliens should rightfully have decided there was no intelligent life down here and gone on to the next planet. Perhaps they aren't so superior after all."

The third customer ruffled his crest in disagreement. "You think the Erls a joke, do you? Maybe some fools would make peace with them, but others of us have better memories."

"Chacarre and Erlind have been at peace for a century." Alon made a conciliatory gesture. "But we haven't gone weak in the meanwhile. If they overstep their bounds, even with the help of these Terrans, Kreste will whip them back to where they belong."

The customer sniffed and turned to the shelves of scrolls. Alon and Birre exchanged a lingering look. The customers selected a few books, not the most expensive, and left with them, neatly wrapped.

Moments later, the door flew open, sending the bells clanging. A Wayfolk youngster rushed into the store, panting.

"Meddi and Tellem—where are they?"

"Calm down, Dennet." Alon circled around the desk and put a hand on his friend's shoulder. "They're delivering an encyclopedia to The Suzerain, that shop by the plaza."

Dennet gulped for breath and made an equivocal gesture. "The plaza—something's going on—warders everywhere. Padme sent me to make sure your parents were all right."

Alon's crest went rigid and his breath caught in his chest. There were few places in Miraz, with its long history, that had not been touched by some momentous event, often violent. Old Hospital still bore the gouges of battlestones from the clan feuds before the Helm brought the Convocation of 1053. Hundreds of years ago, the front steps of Octagon had run with blood, much of it Wayfolk.

Alon grabbed the phone behind the desk and tapped in the number of the store his parents had gone to. Heart hammering, he listened as the switches clicked and disconnected. Cursing under his breath, he tried again, this time with the same result. The circuits to the plaza district must be jammed.

"Blazes!" For an instant Alon's vision swam. He took a deep breath. More calmly, he took Dennet by the shoulders and pushed him into the chair behind the desk. "Stay here. Watch things. Come with me, Birre."

Alon swept through the door with Birre at his heels.

Outside, the air sizzled in the morning sun. They hurried south toward the nearest bridge, circling the outdoor restaurant tables with their gaily tinted sunscreens. Above them, curtains blew from open windows and the smell of cooking spices drifted on the breeze.

At this hour, a scattering of pedestrians, abroad before the midday heat, drifted across the cobblestoned street. The usual crowd had gathered around the wall where news sheets were sold and official notices posted.

What was happening across the river? It could be anything, a student demonstration, an isolated fist fight. It could be nothing—it must be nothing.

Alon grabbed Birre's hand and pulled him down the intersecting street. The door he pushed open was, like its neighbors, painted gray, a shade darker than the surrounding facade, and surmounted by a stone arch.

"We can't go in there," Birre said. "It's a private residence."

"No, it's a traverson," Alon said, pulling Birre inside and closing the door behind them.

Beyond, a shadowy corridor led through the building and on to a courtyard, open to the sky and paved with broad, age-smoothed tile. To one side, a curving staircase wound upwards in the darkness. Together they crossed the little sunlit yard and went through the door at the far end, and into an alley.

Alon felt Miraz guiding him, sustaining him, as if it were a living creature. What he couldn't feel was what was happening across the river, in the open plaza.

A few blocks later, Alon led Birre down a short flight of stairs that appeared to be the entrance to a private basement, then up a ramp and out into another alley. They turned a corner and came out on the broad street leading to the main bridge.

"How do you *do* that?" Birre said as they started across the bridge, passing the stalled motor traffic. "I've lived here all my life and I still can't tell what's a door to a private house and what's a traverson. I know only the ones everyone does, and even then I sometimes get lost. I'd be hopeless in the catacombs."

Alon's ability to navigate the city's hidden passages was a family legend. His parents still told the story of how he, a baby barely able to walk, had wandered off and was halfway to Westhill by the time a warder spotted him. He'd apparently gone the whole way by traverson. A true wandering Wayfolk, Meddi had said.

They hurried over the bridge, dodging the other pedestrians and the pedal-cyclists. From the center of the bridge, Alon glimpsed of one of the boulevards that bordered the plaza. It looked as crowded as always in midmorning. He heard muted noises in the distance and made out the vivid green lights of official vans. The warders had the street blocked off and were ordering everyone to stay clear.

Most of the crowd had gathered on the opposite end of the plaza, near the Terran Compound. The area immediately surrounding The Suzerain shop was surprisingly quiet. The slatted blinds were drawn tight and a discreet sign in the lower corner of one display window read, "Closed."

Alon rapped on the locked door. There was no answer.

"Don't give up," Birre said. "They may just be overly cautious."

Alon knocked again and called out. After a pause, the door swung open a crack and a nervous-looking clerk peered out.

"It's Alon-az-Thirien. Are my parents still here?"

"Oh yes, they're safe in back." The clerk gestured for Alon and Birre to enter.

The door closed behind them, cutting off the noise from the street.

Collaborators

Light from a Convocation ceiling lantern, more decorative than functional, gleamed on the rows of art objects, many from the land of Shardi and hundreds of years old. The faint odor of incense hung in the air.

Alon and Birre followed the clerk along the central aisle, past ceremonial urns of brass inlaid with ivory and moonstones, chests of carved, aromatic senna wood, and life-sized porcelain sculptures. A doubled gate led to a reception room of equal luxury, carpets of intricate Valadan knot-weaving, upholstery and wall tapestries glowing with silk brocades.

Meddi and Tellem sat on a low padded bench, sipping tea from cups of translucent jade. Across from them, sat the owner of The Suzerain, Shardian by his billowy white robes.

"Alon!" Meddi set his cup down on the marble table with a clatter and heaved himself to his feet. He was short for a Chacarran and had always been stocky. Sudden emotion turned his blue-tinted skin a shade darker than usual. Tellem, thin and graceful, looked up with eyes momentarily narrowed in surprise.

"You're safe!" Alon threw his arms around Meddi.

Drawing back, Alon noticed the thinning of Meddi's scalp hair, the white along his jaw line against the blue of his skin, the sagging flesh at his neck. Meddi's body, which had always felt so solid, had taken on a new, brittle quality.

He's old, Alon thought with a rush of tenderness. *He's spent his life raising me and now he's old.* And Tellem, who never seemed to change, Tellem too had aged. Or perhaps it was he, Alon, who'd changed.

"Padme called the store," Alon said. "I was so worried."

"We apologize for having entered your establishment in such an unmannerly fashion," Birre said in Shardian with a formal bow to the owner. "The message Alon received sounded urgent and we were concerned for his parents."

The owner made a dismissive gesture. "As you can see, it is nothing but an unseemly emotional display." He sniffed. "The warders will dispose of it."

"We saw only the first moment or two," Tellem said. His tone indicated that it was The Suzerain's owner who had decided the safest course was for all of them to hide in the back room, and they'd complied, rather than risk losing his future business.

"Alon... what's this?" Meddi said, glancing from Alon to Birre. "Yes, yes? It's happened? And so suddenly?"

"Isn't it always?" Tellem said. He wrapped Alon in a quick, hard embrace, then patted Birre's shoulder. Birre's crest ruffled in pleasure.

The owner made a polite noise in his throat. "I extend my wishes to you and your newfound partner for a long and happy life together."

Flushing, Alon murmured a polite reply. The sensation of heat beneath

60

his skin was new and startling. He didn't know if it was part of the pairing process or a signal of the onset of actual polarization. He'd have to ask Tellem in private or, better yet, look it up in his school health text. In unspoken rapport, Birre reached out to take his hand.

The owner rose, gathering his robes around him. "Please, stay as long as you wish. Do not discommode yourselves with the unpleasantness outside." In a swift, graceful movement, he swept through the back door.

After an uneasy moment of silence, Tellem gestured for them all to sit.

"It only happened this morning," Alon said, clasping Birre's hand between his own breasts. "Then Dennet came with the message. We haven't—" he paused, flushing darker blue, "—I mean, it's just—"

"When Tellem and I paired, my sibling Ranni thought I'd gotten a virus," Meddi said sympathetically. "I was so mad I hit him."

"You?" One corner of Tellem's mouth curled upwards.

Meddi held up his thick-boned hands. "What can I say? I was young, and newly paired."

Tellem turned to Birre. "I take it you haven't told your own family yet?"

"No," said Birre. "I just hope they're as happy about it as you are."

Alon glanced sharply at him. "Why shouldn't they be?"

"It's all right—" Tellem began, laying one hand on Alon's arm. "We understand what he means."

"Well, I don't!" Heat flared up behind Alon's eyes. He felt as if he'd been shoved into the body of a stranger. Unable to help himself, he went on in a tight voice, "What's wrong with me?"

"It's not *you*," Birre said, flushing. "It's them. They're... complicated. Traditional."

"And perhaps not overjoyed to see you paired outside the Faith?" Meddi said.

Birre's crest rippled. He lowered his gaze.

"I don't believe this!" Alon said. "These aren't the days of the purges! Nobody—not even *your* parents, Birre—cares a Flaming Feather for clan purity anymore!"

"I didn't say I agreed with them." Birre said. "Just that—I can't—"

"No matter how difficult, how utterly impossible it seems at the time," Tellem said, "if you search for the Way and let it guide you, there will always be an answer."

"But I don't follow the Way," Birre said, meeting Tellem's gaze with an expression that verged on defiance. "And that's the other half of the problem, isn't it?"

Alon struggled to keep his crest decently smooth. He'd heard all the arguments about pairing outside the Way, but he'd assumed they were superstition.

"Are you afraid Birre's going to convert me," Alon asked Tellem, "and that our children will be lost to the Way?"

Tellem's eyes flickered to Birre, standing beside Alon, and then back to Alon. "It is always a possibility. But no, I would not say we are *afraid.*"

"Then what?" Alon's hands curled into fists so hard his fingers cramped. He stared at them, astonished once again at his sudden shift in mood. Meddi reached out to stroke his shoulder.

"Alon, we have done our best to raise you in the Way. If we've failed, it's certainly too late to start now. You are an adult and free to choose. How can I tell you that it doesn't matter? That Tellem and I are not concerned what might happen? Of course we are." His face, so mobile and expressive, twisted, and Alon could not name all the emotions there. "You are our precious child, born of our love and our flesh."

"It is said of the Way," Tellem said slowly, "that each of us chooses according to our nature."

"And I have chosen Birre," Alon said defiantly.

"Or the Way has chosen you each for the other," Tellem finished. "It isn't for us to approve, only to accept."

"I hope that's what my parents will say," Birre said. "In the end, I think they will."

"Ah!" Meddi exclaimed. "To think that I should live to have Faith folk for relatives!"

"As soon as my parents get over the initial shock, they'll rush over to Octagon," Birre said, his hands moving expressively. "The priest will faint when they walk in, out of surprise to see them after all these years. Oh, they'll try their best to be open-minded about it. They'll know it's far too late to interfere, so the only thing they can do is pray. Pray to Hool and any other Aspect that will listen."

"As well they should," Meddi said with a mischievous gleam in his eyes. "Before we're through, we'll have them all dancing naked through the groves." He referred to the old stories that priests of the Faith had spread about Wayfolk during the years of persecution.

Everyone laughed, even Birre. Alon felt an absurd sense of tenderness wash over him.

As they raised their cup of tea to drink, Alon glanced at Tellem and could not miss the expression in his eyes. His parents said they respected his choice, for it was the Way to flow with adversity. The old Chacarran proverb said that individuals were but poor lost fools, and only the family could achieve true wisdom. But that didn't mean there would not be stormy times ahead for everyone.

Chapter 10

Radiocast, Miraz: RIOT IN MIRAZ PLAZA! Demonstration ends in tragedy; 12 dead, 106 injured. Details at 10.

Birre's parents invited Alon and his family to dine at their clan enclose that same night. Alon was nervous because the issue of where they would live was sure to come up. If Alon had been anyone else—anyone but Wayfolk, that is—there would have been only one answer, for Birre's family sept was not only wealthy but prestigious. In addition, there might be the question of a temple sealing, although few families performed the ancient ritual any longer. It had been used in times past to secure offspring and property to the higher-status clan. Alon knew of it only from his history classes.

Wayfolk, on the other hand, lived apart from such traditions. They taught that their clan was all Wayfolk everywhere, so what did it matter where they lived? They often lodged at their places of business or in splits, areas of small separate apartments, alongside isolated families that had fractured off or become orphaned when their clans died out.

Birre's family lived in an expensive district behind the western hills. Lacy moonflower vines covered the high wall surrounding the enclose. A bell-chain hung beside the single wooden door set into the wall. When Alon pulled, a chime sounded in the distance. Meddi smoothed his evening robes over his belly while Tellem stood, his face impassive, carrying a basket of fruit. Wine or fruit were traditional Wayfolk gifts to a dinner host, and Tellem had chosen it himself.

The door swung inward. Birre stepped out, his eyes gleaming in the light of the lanterns. Alon trembled at how beautiful Birre looked, every line of his features outlined in flame and shadow. The next moment Birre's arms went around him and his scent filled Alon's nostrils.

Birre made a gesture of formal greeting to Meddi and Tellem. "May you be welcome to this dwelling. May the peace of my clan enclose you." He took Alon's hand and let the door swing shut behind them. "I'm so glad you're here. I couldn't wait another moment."

"I can see," Meddi said to his mate in an undertone, as they followed Birre through the passageway, "that these young people are going to need quarters of their own rather quickly."

They emerged into the central courtyard. Wind harps hung from miniature flowering trees, rippling with music at the slightest breeze. Birre led Alon and his parents around the central fountain past beds of night-blooming salitz. Alon thought the garden must cost an enormous amount of money to maintain, for only a few months of pleasure each year.

The enclose itself was brightly lit from within, and its radiance streamed outward into the night. They passed through another, much shorter passageway, then a set of glassed doors and into a high-ceilinged living room.

The couple rising from the long sofa wore the same subdued colors as the carpet and walls, tones of cream and gray. The lines of their tailored tunics revealed little of their bodies, but the taller of the two had the suggestion of jowls around his rounded cheeks. Their crests were so immaculately groomed, they looked varnished into place.

"My parents, Saunde and Enellon."

Saunde, the shorter of the two, took the basket of fruit and commented on the quality of the handiwork. They all sat down, Saunde and Enellon side by side on the sofa, and Alon and his parents facing them in individual chairs. Birre, with a toss of his dark mane, sauntered over to Alon's chair and leaned against its upholstered arm.

Tellem, who managed to look poised even in the oversoft furniture, opened the conversation. "This is an awkward situation for all of us. We don't know each other, and we come from different backgrounds, with different circles of friends and associates. We don't even share the same beliefs. And yet our children have paired and here we are. Meddi and I want you to know how much we appreciate your hospitality."

As Tellem spoke, Alon glanced over at Birre's parents. They seemed like a pair of formal bookends, legs precisely parallel, crests utterly still.

"It is of course difficult to know what is best," Saunde said. "With the children, I mean. How much guidance they need, how much independence they can responsibly handle. One never knows for certain, does one? All the standards we—" with a delicate emphasis on the word *we*, "—were raised by seem to have been dispensed with as outmoded inconveniences." He lifted one eyebrow, inviting agreement.

As if on cue, Enellon added, "The young have so little respect for tradition these days."

Meddi shifted in his chair and Alon, catching the stormy expression in his parent's eyes, held his breath. Meddi had none of Tellem's talent for diplomacy.

Birre threw his head back and laughed, a cascade of merriment that sent shivers through Alon's body. "Oh, Pim, you've been saying that since the day I outgrew diapers and the world hasn't come to an end yet! If Alon and I had so little regard for your feelings, we wouldn't be here now, we'd be halfway to Valada."

"Valada?" Alon looked up at Birre with an expression of mock astonishment.

"Alon's worst marks in school were in Valad," Meddi said in a conspiratorial whisper. "His accent is so bad that a Freeporter once thought he was speaking Erlindish."

Alon loved Birre all the more for giving Meddi such a graceful opening.

A few moments later, their hosts suggested they go in to eat. In the center of the dining room, an oval scoured-stone table bore flowers and ornamental fruits in glittering crystal bowls. Saunde deftly guided them to their seats. At each place, cups of costly granna had been set out, as well as individual porcelain platters on which various delicacies had been arranged artistically. Alon picked up his cup, then set it down. Something in the way Birre's parents sat, their hands folded in front of them, made him hesitate.

"We will all give thanks," Enellon said.

Birre's head shot up, crest ruffling. He glanced at his parent with an agonized expression, but Enellon gave no sign he'd noticed. Enellon began intoning a complicated ritual, phrase after phrase of how munificent were the gifts of Hool, Fourth Aspect of the God, whose color was purple and whose attribute, fertility.

Alon sat rigid, fists in his lap and teeth clenched. At the corner of his vision, he caught the darkening of Meddi's face, the tension in Tellem's shoulders, although not a hair on either of them twitched. Like them, he must endure these few moments for Birre's sake.

Enellon lifted his cup, signaling the end of the blessing. Alon tasted his granna. The lightly fermented grape puree slid smoothly over his tongue, the very best of the season. Tellem, clearly making an effort to be civil, complimented the food.

"It would be better if the herbs were fresh," Saunde said. "I went down to the quay-side market this morning, but with that awful riot in the plaza, I turned around and came right home. What a nuisance it all was, even if the salad did turn out all right in the end."

"Your little shop is in the old district, isn't it, across Westriver from the plaza?" Enellon said to Alon's parents. Birre's clan owned a variety of businesses, located mostly in the southeastern outskirts: a mill that smelted metals for their other factories, a chemical plant, and a wool-weavery. "Did you see anything?"

"We were at the plaza, making a delivery but well away from the disturbance," Tellem said.

"The warders had the streets blocked off," said Meddi. "Traffic was horrendous, medical vans and warders all over the place."

"Ten people dead was what I heard," Alon said.

"The warders have no business arresting our own people," Birre said with a vehemence Alon had rarely heard in him. "It's the Terrans they ought to be getting after, them and their Erlind allies."

"I think the press exaggerated the situation," Saunde said. "You know how they are, always making things more dramatic."

"Ten people dead was an exaggeration?" Birre asked.

"What was it all about, anyway?" Alon said, thinking to shift the subject of conversation. It seemed that Birre was going out of his way to provoke a quarrel with his parents. What had made him so irritable?

"Who knows?" said Tellem. "One report says it was a demonstration that got out of hand, another says the whole thing was staged by Erlind sympathizers."

"Unless those demonstrators weren't so innocent," Saunde said, giving his spouse a worried look. "Unless there wasn't any other way of restoring order. A... primitive unpleasantness, you know."

"There are some things more important than order." Birre's voice was more snarl than exclamation. "Truth, for one!"

Saunde's spoon clattered to the table. The sound split the air.

"Birre, you are not to talk to your parent in that manner," Enellon said.

Birre's crest rippled like a ribbon of living silk. "I'm not a child!"

"You're not anything else so long as you live in this enclose!" Enellon snapped. "Now sit down and let us resume our discussion like civilized people!"

Birre's muscles tensed visibly. Alon caught the metallic jolt of danger in the air, but he didn't know how to quiet the confrontation.

"I'm sorry if anything I said was offensive." Birre regained control of himself with a visible struggle. "But I'm not sorry for speaking what I think."

Silence hung over the table. "The day's events have left us all upset," Tellem said quietly.

"That's right," added Saunde. "Who can be rational in times like these? We mustn't lose sight of what's truly important." He reached out to caress Birre's cheek.

Birre didn't respond, not even to jerk away. He stared fixedly at a point on the table directly in front of him.

Enellon picked up his cup. His voice sounded strained but forceful. "To our children. And their future together."

They all drank to that.

After the meal, they strolled through the courtyard and settled on a cluster of benches. Alon and Birre sat together, holding hands, the length of their thighs pressed together. Everywhere they touched, Alon felt a line of fire. His nipples tingled. If it weren't for their parents, he would have pulled Birre closer. Just at the moment when he wondered if Birre was feeling the same, Birre stroked the back of his hand with his fingertips. Alon shivered in delight.

"How very pleasant this garden is," Meddi said. "It's so tranquil, with the fountain and the night birds singing."

"Yes," Saunde sighed, "I often sit out here when my worries seem too much. I listen to the birds and look up at the stars. They remind me of the truly important things in life, the things that don't change with every passing event."

"Like today's riots?" Birre said tightly.

"Exactly." Saunde paused. "If it isn't one thing, it's another. The world has never lacked for sorrows."

"I thought we weren't going to talk about the riot," Enellon said.

"You're right as usual, my dear," Saunde said. He reached out to clasp his partner's hand. "But this does bring us to a rather difficult subject—the necessity of holding fast to things of enduring importance. You understand what I mean?"

"No," Birre said. "What *do* you mean?"

"We mean," Enellon said, "that while you cannot of course be sealed in Octagon with your chosen mate, the next generation of this family must nonetheless follow in the Faith."

"This is outrageous!" Birre leapt to his feet, shaking. "It's bad enough, insulting our guests—"

"Come now, sit down and be reasonable," Saunde said to Birre. "You are of course free to pair with anyone you wish. We are not disputing that, but—"

"You've been talking to the priest, haven't you?" Birre demanded. "What did he tell you—that the Bird of Heaven would swoop down and Burn us all forever if we didn't bring up our children in the Faith?"

"No, of course not—"

Enellon got to his feet and reached out a restraining hand. Birre jerked away and whirled to face him, knees bent, body hunched forward, fists poised.

"Curse you! Curse you both!"

"Stop this, all of you!" Meddi shouted.

Alarm shrieked along Alon's nerves. His heart pounded and his tongue went dry. He caught a whiff of something explosive, exciting and terrifying at the same time.

Then all four parents started talking again at once. Their voices rose on the night air, clashing, building... It was no use, why couldn't they see that? It was only fueling Birre's madness. Why couldn't they see what was going on?

He's polarizing!

Realization hit Alon like an icy wave. The talk of riots, of violence, then of children, and the indirect attack on Alon through his family—it had all accelerated the changes.

Birre took another step toward Saunde, who'd backed up against the chair he'd been sitting in. Saunde stumbled and grabbed on to the chair for support. Shouting, Enellon moved in on Birre.

"No!" Alon leaped to his feet and grabbed Birre's arm. Birre whirled around, one fist already swinging.

Birre's face contorted, dark and feral. He jerked up short, barely missing Alon's jaw. Alon threw himself against Birre's body. Through the fabric of Birre's tunic, he felt a rush of feverish heat and the tautness of fight-primed muscles.

"It's all right," Alon whispered. "I'm here."

"Hold me." Birre dipped his head, brushing his lips against Alon's neck. "I'll be all right just as long as you hold me."

"Well," came Saunde's voice, "now we can—"

"Just sit down," Meddi cut in, "and let the young people work it out themselves."

Alon slipped one hand around Birre's waist. He was almost afraid to look up, to see the faces of any of their parents. "Come on, let's get out of here."

They walked toward the back wing of the enclose. Behind him, Alon heard the parents' voices, murmuring, Meddi's **rumbling tones and the murmuring of the parents' voices.** Birre closed the door behind them and the sound cut off abruptly.

Alon had been to Birre's house, to the room he had lived in as a child, only once before. The chamber was twice the size of his own, still decorated with the things Birre had treasured as a child, his books and wall hangings, his awards from school.

They stood together in the middle of the room, on the round rug with its pattern of animals and winter birds, holding each other as if the world were at an end.

Chapter 11

Talense set aside his report on the plaza riot and went down to the warder headquarters building. He went at noon, which was the time an announcement would be most likely. Yellow-tinted clouds scudded across the sky, but no breeze shifted the branches of the gnarled, gray-leafed rufino trees. The air was hot and still, as if the city had been placed under a glass dome.

The warder building took up a solid block and one whole side of the square. It had once been an enclose, two stories high, weather-scarred granite flecked with black specks as if it were dusted with soot. The front doors were modern, metal and glass. A crowd had gathered outside, perhaps twenty-five or thirty in all. People stood about in groups, each clan to their own, glancing at the doors and occasionally at each other.

Talense waited beside the front steps, along with Druse, his longtime friend from the agency, and a few other press who wrote for single-clan news sheets.

For the better part of an hour, nothing happened other than a few warders going in and out of the building and others keeping the steps clear.

A mobile news vendor arrived and sold a few sheets. When a food cart came by, the aroma woke Talense's hunger. He hadn't been able to eat breakfast and couldn't remember if he'd eaten the night before, maybe a stale cheese bun while finishing the Terran interview. When he'd wandered into the communal kitchen, his cousins had fussed over him as if he'd been a child. What little interest he'd had in food had died immediately. He didn't want fussing, he wanted Jeelan.

Talense bought tea in a paper cone and peppers roasted on reed skewers for himself and Druse. The peppers were soggy and bitter, this late in the season.

Warder Chief Kallen came out on the steps in his crisp uniform. In clipped tones, he announced that processing of the prisoners was not yet complete and it would be another several hours, possibly the rest of the day, before the names would be released.

A few people cried out and pushed closer to the barriers. "I knew it!"

muttered a press from the Keshite clan sheets, who'd been standing behind Talense. "Flaming waste of time, coming here."

"Further installments of nothing, if you ask me," another agreed.

Druse gestured agreement.

As Kallen turned to go back inside, someone shouted, "They haven't done anything wrong! You've no right to keep them!"

"Charge the guilty and let the rest go!"

"Please! At least tell us who they are!"

Talense caught the faint rippling of the chief's crest, the flicker of tightly-masked emotion. Then the doors swing shut behind Kallen's back and the warders closed ranks. The crowd pressed forward.

They were right, scorch it all, Talense thought, and not just because Jeelan might be in those cells.

"That Faithless snot-brain! He could have told us something! He's got a gizzard colder than a singleton's bed." An oldster wearing a sash of Bavarite blue across his withered breasts shook one fist aloft.

Druse said, "It was like this all day yesterday. How am I going to make a story out of this? Nothing but unhappy families and empty speculations. Shall I call it CHIEF KALLEN ANNOUNCES NOTHING? Or, PRISONER RELEASE DELAYED AGAIN?"

Talense gestured, wry. Kallen was tough and hard-minded, as unbiased as anyone Talense had ever worked with. He'd never publicly worn a ribbon with his clan's colors, not even on Victory Day. Why was he stalling?

There was one thing Kallen was surely unhappy about, Talense thought, and that was the way the Terrans had interfered with the warders' handling of the riot. Talense guessed they hadn't consulted Kallen first. If he were Kallen, he'd be screaming Flaming protests to the mayor and the Helm's office. But what—here Talense's thoughts grew muddied—what did that have to do with the delay in the prisoner release?

Talense felt tired, wrung-out. One moment, he could think clearly, the next, his mind scattered from here to the Ice Sea. Bits of memory jumbled together—the embassy aide who'd let him in to see the Terrans—the farmer's dead-furred face as he pulled Talense to his feet—the image of Jeelan, cold, frightened, hurt.

Talense lifted his head, his nostrils flaring to catch a scent that no breeze blew. There was nothing more to be learned here today. Druse would let him know if anything unexpected developed. Meanwhile, he would submit his nightmare images to the exorcism of work.

The next day, the strange, breathless weather still hadn't broken. Talense phoned warder headquarters a few times, in between his own work on the Terran intervention. As before, he was met with "no information on the arrests and no knowing when we'll have any."

Talense returned to the headquarters building at noon. Even more had gathered, perhaps a hundred. He stretched the moments out, watching the others. They seemed to embody his feelings, to express them in his place. This one was pacing for Talense, this one arguing, this one standing with his shoulders hunched, crest a tattered jumble.

An hour later, when the comfort of observed misery had worn thin, a warder came out and said the first group of prisoners would be released from the south entrance.

The prisoners emerged single file, blinking as if the sun hurt their eyes. They reminded Talense of passengers arriving through Border Control—the dazed, slightly disoriented expressions, the furtive glances at uniforms.

The first prisoners rushed to their families with wordless cries. Talense's chest felt thick and heavy. Pain radiated down one arm, but he ignored it. Here now was Jeelan's striped orange tunic among the muted greens and browns, Jeelan's rumpled-looking crest, rising as he spotted Talense.

With a muffled sob, Jeelan broke from the line and hurled himself into Talense's arms. Talense grabbed him, pressed the thin body against his own. He buried his face against the curve of Jeelan's neck, inhaled his distinctive scent. The coiled knot in his belly loosened. Jeelan's fingers dug into Talense's back. He felt tauter and thinner than Talense remembered.

"Let's go home," he whispered against Jeelan's ear.

"Oh, no!" Nerve-wiry, Jeelan twisted in Talense's embrace. His crest rippled in disjointed patches and his round eyes looked almost milky. "How can I just go home and leave the others inside?"

"What good can you do here? You're exhausted, not thinking straight."

Jeelan gestured negation. "We aren't being charged at all. They've dismissed everything! Bird of Heaven, it's a nightmare!"

Talense hesitated, thinking hard. Around him, people chattered, streaming by, arms around each other, happy to be together and going home. He grasped Jeelan's hand and led him into the street, away from the worst of the crush. He felt the absence of his own enclose walls as a physical ache. *Run home, hide, be safe with your own blood,* ran like sap along his nerves.

Kallen had more than enough time to process formal charges against the people now released. So why had it taken even this long if they weren't going to be accused of anything? Why hold on to a few?

"Who is Kallen still holding? And why them?"

Jeelan's agitation calmed visibly. He moved closer into the curve of Talense's arm. Talense stroked Jeelan's crest smooth. He heard croons of comfort from the people around him, felt the shift in the very taste and texture of the air.

"Oh!" came a sharp cry from Jeelan.

Talense turned to follow his gaze and saw a cluster of black-robed Fardites standing in front of the main door, arguing with a pair of warders. The warders were as large and impassive-looking as any Talense had seen.

"I was right!" Jeelan exclaimed. "It's Rogrettemer's family. The warders refused to release him-can you help?"

"I can try."

Jeelan bounded up the steps, said a few words to the Fardites, and led them to where Talense waited. "This is my mate, Talense. He's a press with contacts in the warders, so he can help you get answers about your kin."

"May the Prophet bless you with the wisdom of change," Talense said.

The eldest of the three ruffled his age-darkened crest. "You follow in the steps of the Blessed Fard?" His eyes flickered over Talense's unadorned tunic.

Talense briefly explained that it was not customary for anyone who worked at the Interclan News Agency to wear a clan token. The Fardite elder made a gesture of mild disapproval, but the moment of suspicion had passed.

Jeelan suggested that they continue their conversation in a less public place. They headed for a restaurant up the street. The Fardite elder looked critically at the awnings hanging limp and the tables strewn halfway across the sidewalk.

Talense led them past the tables and through the shade-dark inner room. There was a garden out back, walled but open to the sky; sometimes he ate there when he was working late on a story and it was too hot to sit indoors.

Talense ordered salted toast and wine, steamed despite the weather because they were all clearly suffering from shock. The elderly Wayfolk who ran the restaurant brought both without questions and then left them alone. The wine slid down Talense's throat. Heat spread outward from his belly. Jeelan laced his fingers around his cup. He had stopped shivering.

"I thank you for the wine," the Fardite elder said with grave dignity. "But I cannot imagine what service you can do for us."

Talense hesitated. More than once Jeelan's boundless enthusiasm had drawn him into something he would rather have left alone. At the same time, he was convinced that the riot was part of a larger story, the sort of events that marked shifts in history. And these people had no one else to turn to. "I don't know for a certainty that I can," he said, "but I will try. As a press, I've had considerable experience in discovering information the authorities would rather not be known. Jeelan is correct, I do have contacts within the warders. It will cause no pain to me to ask."

"No, I suppose not," said the Fardite. "My apologies if I sounded ungrateful. This has been a most distressing sequence of events."

Talense picked up a round of toast. "I take it that you're the family of one of the League organizers?"

The elder Fardite did not respond to Talense's attempt at humor. "We cannot understand why they will not release our cousin. What happened in the plaza was terrible, but it's human nature for such things to occur from time to time. Our Rogrettemer is no more responsible than anyone else." His eyes rested on Jeelan just long enough to make his point without being overtly offensive.

Talense felt a rush of compassion. Jeelan was safe; he could see him, touch him, smell him. How might he feel if Rogrettemer were free and Jeelan still a prisoner? "Why would he be singled out? What about the others who are still being held?"

The elder looked uncomfortable. The youngest of the three said, "Because they're all from Erlind, that's why! Because they believe in peace between Erlind and Chacarre!"

As well they might, Talense thought, with family on both sides of the border. "If your cousin is an Erlind national, how does he come to be here in Miraz?"

Jeelan looked at him, shocked. "Rogrettemer's here lawfully—"

"The question is genuine, my heart," said Talense. "Not a challenge. It's one Kallen's people must ask. If I am to help your friend, should I not have all the information the warders do?"

"Rogrettemer's own parents died about ten years ago in the lung fever epidemic in Er-Albi," said the elder. "We're the closest collateral branch, so we offered to bring him into the family business, trading in wool and goat-hair cloth." He paused. "It wasn't easy for him."

"No," Jeelan said, "of course not. Think of how he must have felt! But Rogrettemer always insisted that the only way to ensure lasting peace was to eliminate the causes of war—the bitterness, the suspicion. He was already well into a leadership position when I joined the League. I remember how intense he was, how passionate about the cause."

The Fardite elder narrowed his eyes but kept his hands still. Talense guessed he didn't approve of his young relative's political opinions or the zeal with which they were expressed.

"Change isn't easy, although it is the blessing of Fard," Talense said mildly.

"May the Name be praised," the elder and the middle of the three repeated.

"Let's return to the question of why your cousin is still being held," Talense said. "Is it possible Kallen suspects he might be an agent of the Erls, that he somehow engineered the riot at their command, using the League demonstration?"

Collaborators

The Fardite elder's crest shot up, a spray of short, almost-black bristles. His ruff lifted, revealing the pale, wrinkled skin of his throat. "What are you accusing our family of?"

"Calm yourselves, please," Talense said, raising both hands in a placating gesture. "I did not accuse your cousin of anything. I'm sure he has nothing but the noblest intentions, may Fard guide his steps." He paused as they subsided, the elder on one side and Jeelan on the other. "I can't use my official press position in this matter, but I'll see what I can do."

With polite, inconsequential comments and promises to get in touch should anything new develop, they left the restaurant, and the Fardites went about their own business.

Talense and Jeelan walked slowly along the tree-lined avenue. The air was thick and heavy, although the sun had burned off the overcast. Jeelan murmured something about the unfairness of it all.

Talense's thoughts churned. Was the riot truly an accident, a chain of reflex reactions brought on by circumstance? A badly planned demonstration that got out of control? An attempt to shift public sentiment against Kreste? Or was it a diversion to draw Kreste's attention away from something else?

Although Talense had been in the midst of the riot, had seen it from the height of the Terran tower and felt its effects in the lingering bruises on his body, its meaning slipped from his grasp like smoke. The more questions he asked, the less sure he was of what he knew.

One thing, he did know. It was Fard's own blessing that the Terrans had stopped the riot when they did. If not, hundreds might have died.

Talense and Jeelan emerged from the underground station, fingers intertwined as if they were newly paired. Jeelan pressed against Talense and whispered, "Almost home."

Home. The enclose sprawled over most of a block, shaded pink and gray-white stone. Centuries ago, it had been much smaller, a single inward-looking structure. As the clan's fortunes had grown and those of its neighbors waned, adjoining buildings had been purchased and modified to create a patchwork. As a consequence, there were several smaller courtyards joined by traversons, sections of building exposed to the street, and others folded away behind layers of rooms. Jeelan would have preferred an inner suite, but Talense, who'd grown up chafing at the sense of muffled isolation, wanted a separate outside entrance. Maybe his peculiar taste had something to do with his tolerance of foreign travel or his occasional fits of reclusiveness from the rest of the family. It was the single thing he and Jeelan had seriously disagreed on, and even now there were times when he wasn't entirely sure Jeelan had forgiven him.

They went in through the door that was theirs alone. Talense took Jeelan into his arms and for the first time noticed the oily, foreign smell of a strange place and strange people on his mate's fur. Jeelan pushed away, his nostrils curling. "Bird of Heaven, I must stink of the jail!"

Talense gestured indifference. "I'll take you with the jail stink any day."

"Pervert." Laughing, Jeelan disappeared in the direction of the bathroom.

Talense went into the bedroom and stretched out on the rumpled sheets. They should have been changed last week and carried down to the enclose laundry, but neither he nor Jeelan had had the time. He was glad they hadn't. The sheets still bore the imprint of their sleeping bodies, of the private scented space between them.

The sound of water splashing lulled Talense. His knees and low back ached as they never had when he was younger. He thought back to the conversation with the Fardites, Rogrettemer's family. He should make some phone calls—to Kallen, to his contacts in the mayor's office. If Rogrettemer and the other Erls were suspected of acting as agents of Erlonn in provoking the riot, then it would not be by Kallen's orders alone they were retained and questioned.

It would be at the command of Kreste, Helm of Chacarre. Kreste, whose name had been shouted so loudly and so unexpectedly during the riot. Even now, Talense could hear the echoes of the chant, *Down with Kreste!*

Suddenly he did not think the demonstration so innocent, after all.

When Jeelan returned, Talense asked, "Is there any possibility the riot could have been provoked?"

"Provoked?" Jeelan's eyes narrowed.

Talense ran his hands over the fur on Jeelan's shoulders. "Right before the shouting started, I saw people blocking off the streets, cutting off the crowd's natural dispersal routes."

Jeelan's muscles tightened. "Not any of our people."

"Not yours, but masquerading as yours?" Talense said as soothingly as he could. Jeelan had so clearly had a difficult time of it, he needed calm and understanding, even if he was annoyingly irritable.

Jeelan flopped down on the bed, facing away. "Bird of Heaven, you're the last person I'd expect to be mouthing Erlind infiltration charges."

The League could be genuine, and still be used by the Erls, Talense thought. The only thing to be gained from saying so was another argument. A sour, weary feeling swept over him.

He nuzzled Jeelan's neck, smelling soap and damp fur and Jeelan's own dizzying odor. After a few minutes, Jeelan sighed, rolled over, and put his arms around Talense. His cheek fit exactly into the hollow of Talense's shoulder.

They held each other like the old paired couple they were, finding easy comfort in each other. Talense felt his body grow heavy as his breathing slowed. The outside world of demonstrations and light beam weapons, warders and space aliens, seemed very far away. Jeelan's eyes grew larger, engulfing him. He felt himself lost in their darkness, even as he had been so many years ago. A pulse rippled through him and he couldn't tell whose it was, where Talense left off and Jeelan began. Perhaps, after all this time, there was no difference.

Yet it seemed to Talense there was a new, shadowed corner behind Jeelan's eyes, a place where Jeelan stored thoughts and experiences that didn't include him. Slender and tenuous, perhaps the separation would fade with time. Talense shivered, remembering the feeling he'd had that if anything happened to Jeelan, he would not live long afterward. At the time, he'd dismissed it. Now, caught in the liquid essence of his mate's eyes, he knew it to be true.

Chapter 12

Ferro straightened his tunic and made his way down the hallway behind the public rooms to Dorlin's office at a properly sedate walk. He wasn't about to give the Erls the satisfaction of disturbing a single hair.

Morning sun turned the office into a tapestry of gem-like hues. Ferro took his appointed place in the green shadows near one of the planters. A short while later, the guard escorted in a heavy-set Erl and two underlings, their armed escort left outside the embassy gates. The Erl's unadorned crimson cape marked him as a minor member of the ruling House. He looked surprisingly young.

Dorlin's secretary performed the presentations. Dorlin-az-Beshre, Erl-tha-Westenpat.

Dorlin, with impeccable smoothness, extended greetings on behalf of his government and offered refreshments. If the Erl noticed the subtle implication of the substitution of Chacarran wine for the usual Erlind shallan, he gave no sign.

"Let me be forthright, as we Erls pride ourselves," Westenpat said, brushing aside preliminary courtesies. "We both know I have not come here on a purely social errand."

Dorlin set his wine glass down on the porcelain tray without a sound. "We are listening."

"I've come here to lodge a formal protest—the most severe and strenuous protest—against the recent behavior of your government."

Dorlin blinked, his face reflecting the most inoffensive of expressions. "I must beg your indulgence. I know of no action by my government that could be construed as an outrage to Erlind. Nor anything whatsoever to do with your nation, as a matter of fact."

"Every Flamehead in Erlonn knows about the demonstrations yesterday and how your Helm used them as a pretext for the illegal and atrocious abuse of innocent Erlind citizens."

"I will of course convey your message to my government, as is my duty," Dorlin said. "To the best of my knowledge, yesterday's events were purely domestic and in no way involved any interest of the nation of Erlind."

Collaborators

The Erl tensed in his chair, and Ferro could almost hear him thinking, *Then you have the brains of a moldy callet!* "The victims of yesterday's action," he said, biting off each word, "were heroes in the struggle for peace between our two nations. Many of these are of Erlind citizenship and now rest in the hands of the city warders. Most notably, Erl-tha-Rogrettemer, the founder and head of the noble Erlind-Chacarran Fellowship League."

"Ah," said Dorlin. "*That* Rogrettemer. I thought the name sounded Erlindish."

By his tone, Dorlin also very much doubted that the Undersecretary would refer to Rogrettemer with honorifics under normal circumstances.

The Erl leaned forward and the hairs of his ruff lifted slightly. "In the name of the August and Stalwart Realm of Erlind, I *demand* the immediate release of this unjustly detained political prisoner."

"I wish I could oblige you," Dorlin said, "but I have no jurisdiction over domestic concerns. This is a matter for the Miraz authorities."

The Erl made a vigorous gesture of negation. "This is an incident of international terrorism! We demand his immediate release!"

"You have made your point quite clear." Dorlin's voice was still quiet, but sharper in tone. "I have duly registered the complaint."

"This isn't the last of the affair, you understand? My government will not rest until our hostage is freed." The Erl gathered the folds of his cloak and stood up, scraping the legs of the chair across the floor.

"I wish you a pleasant day, then," said Dorlin, remaining in his seat.

After the secretary had left, Ferro said, "What do you suppose the Erls were really after, sending that buffoon?"

"Kesh knows." Dorlin ran one hand over his crest as if it ached from being forcibly held still. "It's not out of concern for this Rogrettemer. The Erls are undoubtedly looking for a way to embarrass us in front of the Terrans."

"I wonder.." Ferro moved restlessly in front of the desk. A feeling like electricity crept along his crest. In his mind, he heard the words of the Terran Laochristopher, as clear as if they'd just been spoken. The Terrans had insisted they would not involve themselves in local affairs, yet they had acted swiftly and decisively to end the plaza riot. There were some circumstances in which they *would* intervene. If Kreste were manipulated into harsh measures to maintain civil order...

He could see Kreste now, sitting in the Miraz offices where they'd met so many times. If Miraz embodied the best of Chacarran tradition, Kreste had often said, it also represented the worst. There were too many reminders of the very history he as Helm stood in opposition to, the facades scarred by battlestones, walled encloses with the austere isolation of besieged fortresses, the rubbled remains of clan toll barriers.

Erlind, that's where Kreste's attention would be focused. He'd be thinking what the Erls would try next. A border skirmish, perhaps at Demmerle. They claimed that stretch since it was ceded to them after the Last Great War. Kreste had already begun to reinforce the area. He didn't think the Erls would be stupid enough to initiate a war. An armed and vigilant Chacarre would not be easy prey. If anything, an all-out assault would result in the loss of even more Erlind territory and the fall of the ruling House.

"Then what are they after?" Ferro muttered under his breath. Were they hoping to enlist Terran alliance—and Terran weapons?

Chapter 13

As the sun cleared the horizon, turning the night into broken shadows, the train to Demmerle wound its way westward between the steepening hills. With every incline, it slowed, straining, as if weary or in some way still tethered to the city so many miles behind.

Hayke swayed in his seat and stared out the window. He'd come to Miraz on what should have been a routine paperwork errand and gotten caught up in the riot, then been taken inside the Terran compound. Nothing in his previous life had prepared him for those events. Objectively he knew that he was still in shock. As a farmer he'd seen death before—old people when their bodies had worn out, children from illness, adults from accident or infection. When it was necessary, he'd killed predators who'd stalked his animals. He had nursed Rosen, watching him grow weaker and weaker until he himself was too sick to do more. His fur had turned as dull and white as bone from his own illness.

But never in his life had Hayke experienced anything like the moment he looked down at the crowd and saw the people fallen as if they were stalks of grain, waiting to be gathered into sheaves. No sound had penetrated the glass wall of the compound, no touch of wind or sun. In memory, he heard the Terran's flat, translated words of reassurance.

Hayke shivered, his crest ruffling as he struggled to calm himself. The plaza, the screams, the bloodstains, the light beams were hundreds of miles away, he told himself. His body rocked to the train's soothing rhythm. On the other side of the aisle, an old couple had fallen asleep, one crumpled forward, the other leaning against him, both snoring gently.

I saw them dead.

The vision carried no taint of ill-wishing, of thinking the worst of the Terran aliens. If anything, it had the flavor of a premonition.

Premonition?

It is not the Way to feed such fears, Hayke reminded himself. *Through the darkness, a path will open.*

The traditional phrases brought no comfort.

Collaborators

The platform was no more than a deck of weathered boards with a sign bearing the name of the village. Torrey and Felde waited with Torrey's friend Adso and his parent, Verne, who'd taken care of Hayke's children while he was in Miraz. Felde jumped into Hayke's arms and wrapped skinny legs around his waist. He smelled of sunshine and wild sinthe.

"A moment, youngsters." Hayke set down his packs, heavy with his city purchases—clothing and shoes for the children, books and art supplies. He carried the documents—the transfer of ownership of the farm and a stack of legal papers he'd filed in Miraz for his neighbors—in an inner pocket of his tunic.

When Felde wriggled to the ground, Hayke didn't want to let him go. Something of the vitality of the supple young body steadied him, the touch of his child's lips against his cheek, the small fingers clasping the back of his neck. Hayke grabbed Torrey with one hand and pulled him close.

Verne gestured a greeting. "Was it very bad in Miraz?"

"I was there in the plaza," Hayke said.

Torrey's eyes grew even rounder. Hayke glanced at Verne with an expression that said, *We will talk more of this. Privately, without the children.* He and Verne picked up the heavy packs and stowed them in the back of Verne's truck.

"Then what happened?" Adso said breathlessly as they clambered into the cab of the truck. Hayke held Felde on his lap, while Torrey and Adso folded into the narrow second seat.

Felde leaned back in Hayke's arms. "Were you scared, Dimmie?"

"Yes," Hayke said slowly. "I was frightened. Everyone was shouting and pushing, deep into madness. I couldn't see a way out. But then... then I saw someone worse off than I was. He was down on the ground, helpless. Bleeding where people had kicked him."

Hands clutching the steering bar as he guided the truck along the dirt road, Verne made a sound of revulsion deep in his throat.

"And when I stopped thinking only of myself, the Way opened before me," Hayke continued, his voice rising to the lilting rhythms of the traditional teaching stories as he finished his tale.

"Now," Hayke said to the children, "you must tell me what you've been up to while I was gone."

"Torrey's black chicken laid three eggs," Felde said. "And I made a new song for my flute, and Iannen baked spiral buns for when we all get back." Felde loved spiral buns, sweet dough twisted with chopped spiced fruit.

"Grub!" Torrey scowled and jabbed Felde with his elbow. "That was supposed to be a secret!"

"I'll forget," Hayke said. "Verne, any news in the village? It feels like I've been gone a year."

"Just the usual. Coremeth leased his place to the co-op and went back to Erlind. Most of his family's there, so it wasn't a complete surprise."

"I thought his oldest was close to pairing with Egren's Geller," Hayke said. "It certainly looked that way to me."

"People will be gossiping about it all winter. Geller's very upset and even talking about going after them. Egren, of course, won't hear of it. Not with the border patrols so jumpy."

The children took advantage of the pause in the conversation to pepper Hayke with questions until they pulled up at the farm that was now, officially, Hayke's alone. Verne helped Hayke carry the luggage across the yard.

Iannen came out on the weathered porch and wanted to hear everything all over again. He and Verne owned the neighboring farm and had looked after it and the children while Hayke was in Miraz.

While the children were enjoying the spiral buns, Hayke and Verne strolled out to the truck. "You'll be repeating that story a thousand times," Verne said.

"It will not change with the telling," Hayke answered. They'd walked far enough so the bright chatter of the children grew muffled, distant. "For a terrible moment, I thought those people on the plaza were dead. That vision still torments me."

For a long moment, Verne remained silent. The sunlight accented the wrinkles that time and weather had etched into the skin beneath his creamy fur. "Hayke, we all loved Rosen. We all miss him. He was the kindest, gentlest... And then you were so sick, you very nearly died, too. No one would blame you for thinking—for remembering, every time you look in a mirror. The trip to Miraz—well, it couldn't have been easy, getting his name taken off the tax records, erasing another piece of his life."

Hayke shivered, running his fingers over his face. The fur felt dried-out, brittle. Perhaps he was imagining dire portents in the events of the day, which were already sufficiently terrible in themselves. Perhaps the grief in his heart was a festering sore, oozing poison.

Perhaps not.

Chapter 14

Sarah straightened up from spreading quick-hardening ceramic gel around the base of the observation probe. The bullet-shaped unit housed a range of sensors, visual, sound, infrared and radio wave, behind panels of ultradur plastic that looked and resisted attack as if they were hardened steel. Despite the bright sun, the day was crisp, chill-edged as the hemisphere tilted into autumn.

She arched her cramping back and took a deep breath. The air smelled wonderful, the tangy river breeze mixed with the subtly evocative scents of growing things. The trees that grew thick and lush along every major avenue had started to turn from blue-green to orange and purple. Westriver Bridge rose behind her in a graceful arch of age-satined gray stone. She'd never lived in a city with such beautiful architecture or so many trees, and on a day like this, it was hard to concentrate on her work.

Gosem, the Bandari engineer assigned to help her, prodded the edge of the ceramic square with one foot. Standing so close to him, Sarah caught his pleasant, faintly spicy body odor. He was slightly taller than she. Sparse ebony fur covered his face and arms, showing pearly skin beneath. A cascade of denser hair fell over his shoulders and upper back. Sarah couldn't see much of his shape under his flowing knee-length garment, except that he was slender. She presumed Gosem was male. The tapes indicated three distinct sexes, but the bio and medical people weren't sure about the androgynous hermaphroditic state, except that it didn't seem to be fertile. The translators didn't give coherent answers to the questions about gender, either. When asked, "Are you male or female?" the alien would usually reply, "No."

"And now you will *enliven* this unfortunately unaesthetic device?" Gosem asked.

"I'll activate it, yes."

The Bandari engineer watched her closely, bending his head to peer at her equipment. The remote flashed that the systems self-check had been completed and everything was functional. Sarah tapped her link to Compound Ops and verified that they were receiving signals. Now for the final step. She stepped on the hardened gel and placed both hands on the one significant external feature of the probe, a raised ring. Her fingertips found the groove switches, located an arm's-length apart. She pressed hard and the ring lifted slightly. In five seconds, the unit would be armed, the ring generating a static electricity charge of sufficient magnitude to give any would-be vandal a nasty shock.

Gosem reached out one hand, oddly long and narrow with its three fingers. "Don't touch it," she said. He turned to stare at her with his round, slightly bulging eyes. She couldn't read his expression; to her eyes, the aliens all looked serene. His hands moved in a curious gesture; the hairs along the central ridge of his skull fluttered in an unseen breeze.

"They use hand signs," Jon Adamson had told her during orientation, "but we haven't figured out how to translate them yet. When a native speaks to you, listen to the actual sounds, not just the translations. Chris Lao over in Erlonn swears it's a tonal language like Chinese."

Gosem suggested that they cut across the plaza and south toward the railcar station and get something to eat. Sarah had only a dim recollection of a hastily gobbled snack around noon. A number of local foods had been passed as safe to eat, particularly fruit, grains, and their products. As long as she stayed away from cheeses and anything leafy, she should be safe.

She'd also been warned not to drink the local wine. It wasn't the familiar fermented grape juice, but a sort of cider made from something that looked like crab apples and needed a long growing season. Samples were contaminated by tree pollen that contained analogs of psychoactive alkaloids. Relaxed was one thing, but roaring mean drunk was quite another; she'd skip the wine in favor of grape puree or water. In Erlonn, Chris had tried the local specialty, a flower-scented honey mead called shallan, and found it overpoweringly sweet.

No wine, then. But bread or those wonderful succulent pitfruit sounded lovely. Her mouth watered.

Sarah followed Gosem down the boulevard to the plaza. As they crossed the expanse of pink-gray paving, they came close to the massive bronze statues. She was particularly struck by the central statue of a heavily pregnant woman wearing a long, flowing robe. It made sense that these people revered fertility, since by Dr. Vera's initial data, their birth rate was low, barely above replacement level. Maybe they regulated their growth by the percentage of neuter births. The emphasis on clan and extended family made sense, a cluster of working adults supporting and protecting those few who bore children.

She couldn't make out Gosem's gestures, but he seemed to be saying that Carol or Carrel had saved Chacarre from destruction and brought about the present system or order.

The local version of The Mother of Her Country. Sarah found it vaguely annoying the way the translator kept using the masculine pronoun to refer to someone so obviously female. The sooner she learned the native language, the better.

They had just moved away from the statue when a commotion attracted Sarah's attention. She heard raised voices, too far to be within the translator's pick-up zone.

The group must have been a couple of dozen, milling around, arms waving, crests raised like a flock of exotic birds. A handful of uniformed police waded into the group. They carried short black sticks. She saw one come down across the shoulders of a civilian, heard the piercing cry. Her belly clenched and her pulse thundered in her ears.

She'd grown up on the stories her parents told when they thought she couldn't listen - the chaos that wracked the Mideast Buffer Zone during their time in the United Terran Peacekeeping Command. For years, even in her early adulthood on Mars, she'd had nightmares of people she loved being caught up in riots and bombings, while she watched helplessly.

When Sarah took a step toward the police, Gosem grabbed her arm. She ignored him and kept on going. Ahead of her, two police officers shoved a civilian and sent him stumbling toward the nearest street. A high, keening cry came from his huddled body. No one stopped to help him.

No one.

"Do something!" she screamed at Gosem.

"Please, do not be interfering!" His words came through the translator. "We must not go near."

"But they're beating people up!" Outrage shot through her, leaving her breathless. "We can't just stand here!"

"The warders do not intend injury. They only use what force they must to break up the—" The next few words came through as unintelligible syllables. Gently Gosem pulled Sarah back.

"I don't understand." She glanced back to where the group was now dispersing. One of the people who'd been thrown free still lay curled on the ground. A warder came up and knelt beside him.

"There were too many of them. That is why we must not approach too closely, or we would add—" she thought the translator must have missed the word, "—to the reaction."

Sarah's stomach went cold. "They got beaten up for meeting in a public place?"

"Yes."

"But that's terrible! Don't you—" She cut herself off in midsentence. If this were indeed a police state, with citizens forbidden to assemble peacefully, then they would hardly enjoy free speech. Gosem might get into trouble for talking with her about it. She'd thought from the orientation materials that this society was considerably more open.

"It is a cumulative effect, since the riot," said Gosem. "It is necessary for the warders to do this."

"You mean the police crack-down on meetings?"

He gestured, then added, "Yes."

Sarah didn't trust herself to say any more. She set her lips together. If anything, she was even more furious than before. Her fingers curled into fists at her sides and she forced them open.

"It is the Helm himself who has ordered this," he said. "It is necessary."

Necessary? For what? Sarah remembered that the analysis of the riot intervention had made reference to the demonstration that apparently touched it off. *He's suppressing criticism of his regime.*

With an effort, she wrestled her feelings under control. Stupid, stupid, to apply human standards to this alien society, no matter how familiar it might seem.

Have faith in the ability of people to work through their own problems once they stop shooting at each other, her father had always said. Okay, she told herself, they aren't shooting.

The crowd had scattered, as had the police. Warders, Gosem called them. *Wardens, more likely.*

Shadows lengthened and the breeze turned chill. The tightly woven synthetic fabric of her uniform kept out the worst of the wind, but she felt it on her face. During the winter, it would slice across this open space with a blizzard's edge.

We're supporting a tyrant, she thought angrily. She told herself that meddling was stupid and ill-founded, not to mention dangerous. They had neither the resources nor the training to involve themselves.

Maybe she couldn't stop the Miraz police from beating people up. There had to be some other way.

She thought back to the stories her parents had told her, of failed interventions and protracted police occupations. "Nothing you can do from the outside," her father had said, "can match what the people themselves can accomplish."

... what the people themselves can accomplish...

Maybe all they needed was the awareness that they didn't have to put up with the situation any longer.

Aboard *Prometheus*, Hammadi sat for a long time, staring at the notes he'd taken. He found something reassuring in the anachronism of his own written scrawl, loops and bars of black across the whiteness. He ran his fingers over the words and thought curses in the language of his childhood.

Sergei Bartov had just called him on their most highly encrypted link. A personal laser was missing. His staff had repeatedly searched the building complex in Erlonn; they'd used short-range radar and magnetometers, on the chance it had slipped behind a piece of equipment or fallen out of sight, and they'd done everything but tear the place apart, molecule by molecule. The location of every handheld laser had been accounted for during the last three days.

All except one.

It had taken a day or so for its absence to be noted, a typical bungle of two people thinking the other had it or that it had simply been replaced in the wrong locker slot. No one had seen it leave the building. No one had seen any Erl handle it.

He had to assume the worst and be prepared for it.

Given two distasteful tasks, Hammadi preferred to tackle the more daunting one first. He called Dr. Vera, scrambling the shipside link.

She was alone in her laboratory. A small stuffed animal had been propped up in the corner at the far end of the shelf, next to the work station belonging to Sarah Davies.

Dr. Vera shifted from one computer touchpad to another. Complex equations scrolled across the two oversized, partitioned monitors within view; a third showed an anatomical diagram of a humanoid body. Hammadi could see right away that she hadn't wasted any energy resenting his orders keeping her from going planetside. She was, Davies had told him, too busy to waste energy on grudges.

Dr. Vera looked up, one eyebrow arched quizzically.

"Suppose one of the natives got hold of a modified personal laser," he said without preliminary.

Her eyes widened.

"I want to know everything they could figure out from it," he continued, now that he had her full attention. "If they take it apart, can they figure out how it works? Build another one? A bigger one?"

"I'm supposed to deduce this from what we know of their technological development," she said, "their level of scientific understanding, and their general intelligence and inventiveness?"

"You got it."

Slowly she smiled. He had a flickering image of something predatory and carnivorous, a shark perhaps. "From which site was it stolen?"

Hammadi hesitated only an instant before he told her, "Erlonn." He didn't know how far he could trust her, but he wanted the best she could give him. She had little enough to go on as it was.

"How long have they had it?"

He told her that, too.

"Give me a couple of hours," she said.

"Fine." Hammadi cut the link and decided, after a moment's reflection, to have all her planetside calls recorded. He tapped in another scrambled link, this time to Miraz on the high priority channel. Within moments, Les Bellini's features appeared on the monitor.

Hammadi didn't like the idea of pulling his second out of Miraz and sending him to Erlonn. The mission was vital; repairing *Prometheus* took precedence over antenna construction. The orbit wasn't stable and as things stood, it would take the better part of a year to complete the repairs to their own ship, whereas *Celeste*, by Dr. Vera's own calculations, might never emerge from the gravity loop, or might come out a thousand light-years distant. Bellini was one of his most competent officers, which was exactly why he was the best choice to send to Erlonn.

Bellini listened with the intent, professional quiet that Hammadi valued so much in him, while Hammadi outlined the situation. He nodded slightly when he received his orders. Hammadi knew there'd be no excuses and no second weapon lost.

Chapter 15

Miraz: FACE-TO-FACE; Part One: AS THE TERRANS SEE US, special report by Talense.

Miraz: FACE-TO-FACE; Part Two: EMBRACING THE FUTURE, special report by Talense.

Miraz: INTERCLAN PRESS NAMED TO TERRAN LIAISON COMMITTEE, report by Druse.

Talense-az-Mestre, longtime respected press for the Interclan News Agency, has been appointed to the newly formed Terran-Chacarran Liaison Committee, a speaker for the mayor's office announced this morning.

"In regard for his unparalleled record of impartial, insightful reporting, most notably his coverage of the arrival of the Terran aliens in Erlonn and his superb story on the Terran role in halting the plaza riots, it is our pleasure to include Talense in this historic landmark panel." It is to be hoped, the speaker added, that the Terran-Chacarran Liaison Committee will open a new era of cooperation and communication between our two peoples.

As autumn deepened toward winter, the trees that lined the Eastriver quays blazed with color, sulfur yellow and orange as fierce and hot as if they'd been set on fire. As they rippled in the river breeze, the branches blew upwards to reveal the purple undersides of the leaves.

Collaborators

Talense turned away from the river and strode up a broad avenue. His destination was a large, gracefully proportioned building. It could have been the residence of a rich family or a foreign embassy, but no clan emblem or national pennons adorned the gabled doorway. Instead, it bore a discreet sign, Chacarran lettering chiseled into satiny black marble read, "Terran-Chacarran Liaison Committee."

Once such a committee would have been beyond his wildest imagination. Now he wasn't sure what to think of it. People needed time to adjust to the recent political shifts, but events kept moving faster and faster. The only thing he was sure of was that life would never be the same.

Up a flight of stairs and halfway down a wide carpeted hallway, lined with narrow planters and benches upholstered with antique brocades, Talense found the appointed meeting room, spacious and long, the wall hangings dark with age. The table in the center was so highly polished, it reflected the crystal cups and carafe of water as if it were a mirror. Two white-clad human figures stood at the far windows, gazing over the rooftops and the rows of burning-color trees. Talense recognized the familiar shoulder-heavy polarized shape of Conradoarguilles; the other was a stranger. They turned as he came in, shifting out of the window's glare.

"It's Talense, the press I was telling you about," said Conradoarguilles. "Talense, this is Sarahdavies. She's the one responsible for installing the observation modules."

Sarahdavies held out his hand, Terran-style. Talense took it, marveling at the feel of so many fingers, the softness of the flesh.

"I'm pleased to meet you," Sarahdavies said, showing white-yellow teeth. His voice was light and higher in pitch than Talense was accustomed to hearing from the Terrans and he spoke Chacarran without a translator device. "I've been greatly impressed by your writing, most particularly your sensitivity to the implicit issues."

Talense murmured a polite reply. He could not keep his eyes off the Terran's bald face. The skin had a texture like satin. Intellectually, Talense knew that despite the evidence of his eyes—the rounded hips, the full breasts, the contours of cheek and belly—that this Terran, this Sarahdavies, was in fact *not* pregnant. Nonetheless, the natural desire to protect roused in him. He murmured a prayer to Fard the Prophet to shield him from the demonic inversion of such insanity.

Ralle from the mayor's office walked in, followed by Ossen, the Helm representative. They all sat down. A few moments later, Kallen entered in the company of the Terran subcommander, Jonadamson. Commander, Talense corrected himself, since Celestinbellini had gone, presumably back to Erlonn and on unspecified business. Talense gestured a polite greeting to Kallen.

Ossem had given Talense the background on the continuing discussion.

Since the plaza disturbance, Kallen's warders had been spread thin. They'd managed to prevent a handful of spawn-off reactions, but the constant vigilance took a heavy toll. The city had "magnanimously granted"—that was Ralle's expression—the Terrans permission to install their units for the purpose of scientific research. Everyone knew that records were being made, using mechanical devices in place of people who might get tired or hungry or distracted. The Terrans had indicated their willingness to grant the warders access to this information, in exchange for other concessions that were still being discussed. It would be a temporary measure, until the residual crowd reactivity had died down. By the spring, things would be back to normal again.

The problem was that the records were in the form of visual likenesses. Someone would have to look at them to observe the behavior of the surrounding people. Talense had seen some of the Terran's static images. The Terrans had offered a process called *photograficts* as part of their technology exchange, and the Helm's representative sent samples to the news agency to see if anyone had any interest in it. Talense found the flattened patterns repellant, with their frozen crests and lightless eyes. The priesthood of Octagon, representing all Eight Aspects, had undertaken to determine if such images were permissible, whether they, like the statues in the plaza, showed properly the multi-dimensionality of living, god-graced beings.

Sarahdavies suggested that if what Kallen was interested in was crowd density, that information could be obtained by using counters instead of direct observation. "You could set the counters to trigger an alarm at the concentration you pre-set." He—no, Talense corrected himself—*she* leaned forward as she spoke, her breasts pressed against the fabric of her garment. "The counters won't give you any information about what people are doing, only where and how many they are. You'll still have to deploy your men to evaluate the situation."

Men? Talense ruffled his crest quizzically.

"You must do something about the appearance of observation units," Ralle said, when the topic shifted.

"I'm sorry," said Conradoarguilles, "they're not edible."

"Check your translator, Con," said Sarahdavies. "The verb is second-tone, not third."

"They're.." Ossen paused, gesturing as if searching for a diplomatic phrase.

"Aesthetically deficient," Ralle said.

"They're supposed to be culture-neutral." Sarahdavies said.

"That may be true onboard your own ship," Ralle said. "But here they're—they're... To begin with, they sit on the street corners like deformed metal mushrooms that have somehow sprouted in the wrong place."

Sarahdavies smothered a sputtering sound with one hand. "So bad?"

Talense shifted uneasily in his chair, thinking that the Terrans could well begin with eliminating these she-males from public contact. It was strange enough dealing with Terrans like Conradoarguilles, who appeared so strongly polarized, but Sarahdavies's pregnant appearance—real or not—was impossible to ignore.

"What you must understand," Ralle said, "is that Miraz is a thousand years old, and many of our families have lived here for almost that long. Some claim lineage dating back to even more ancient settlements on this same site. Our city is the heart of all Chacarre. But even the most ardent followers of the Prophet can't adapt that quickly to change, especially when it means one of your giant metal mushrooms in front of their family enclose."

"I suppose we could decorate the exteriors with textured plast," Sarahdavies said. "That might make them harmonize better with your architecture."

"Ugliness isn't the only problem with the units. You told us they were *safe*." Talense saw the opening he'd been waiting for. He reached into his satchel and drew out a sheaf of papers. "These are hospital reports of children who've been shocked by the so-called protective rings. So far, the only injuries have been burns and tremors. One of these times, the medicals tell me, someone with a bad heart is going to stumble into one."

"Couldn't we just remove them from high traffic areas?" Ralle asked.

"We've only now achieved the optimal distribution." Narrow brows drew together across Sarahdavies's naked face.

Conradoarguilles said, "Can we put protective railings around them?"

"The railings had better be substantial," Talense said, "or the children will just take them as a challenge. I would have, anyway."

"Well, if it's just kids, we only have to discourage them until the novelty wears off," said Conradoarguilles.

"Ralle, can your office handle installing the railings," Ossen said, "and combine it with the redecoration?"

"How about getting a local celebrity to unveil the completed units?" Sarahdavies asked Talense.

"An interesting concept," Talense said. "The added publicity would do a great deal to spread the warnings."

She looked at him overlong, even for a Terran. "The press can be a powerful educational tool."

"You remember that poetry professor who came out of the riots as a hero?" Ralle broke in. "People thought he was wonderful."

"Is he still at the University?" Talense said.

"No, we've got him over at Internal Affairs," Ralle said. "Giving speeches to junior schools, that kind of thing."

"Ah, yes." Talense remembered Lexis at the award ceremony, thin and stooped and dull-haired, plodding through his prepared statement, remembered his barely contained excitement and how his eyes gleamed as the audience burst into applause. "By the Prophet, he's perfect."

Chapter 16

The wind blew from the north, damp and razor-edged from the Ice Sea. Sarah pulled the folds of her loose-cut coat around her shoulders. The coat was a gift from her engineer friend, Gosem, hand-woven in his family's mills, the wool brushed to feathery softness and dyed gold-green-gray that reminded her of sunlight over fields of sage and heather.

On the street, just outside the doors, stood an armed Terran, someone Sarah knew from Environmental; they'd worked together on the repair crews. Hammadi had started using technical staff to supplement his own people. The guard raised his hand laser in greeting.

At least, Sarah thought as she started down the street, there hadn't been any theft problems with the lasers here in Miraz. Dr. Vera had told her about the one missing in Erlonn. Maybe the observation units had something to do with it. Recordings had already helped the local police solve a number of crimes.

The wind gusted, burning-cold on Sarah's face. It smelled of snow and the faint moist tang of the river. She lifted the hood over her head and heard her name spoken. Gosem stood there, with that odd expression that meant a smile. He'd wound his knitted scarf around his neck, leaving his crest free. The hairs lifted in a delicate ebony spray. Sarah smiled in return.

They'd worked closely together, first on the installation of the observation probes and then on the construction of the refracting furnaces for refining the lanthanide ores. The furnaces had finally extracted enough combined rare-earth elements to begin the crucial process of separating them. While the chemistry staff performed the differential, Sarah put in long days assaying the samples, identifying and quantifying contaminants, then working with the chemists to refine the process. What other time she had went to consulting with the Liaison Committee. These last weeks she and Gosem had each been too busy to do more than gesture in passing. She'd been looking forward to spending some leisure time with him and in the process gather more information about the native culture.

"It's too cold to stand out here talking," Gosem said.

"Any of these places decent?" The Chacarran word for *decency* came closer to the Terran *fertility*.

"The bar on the corner."

Warmth and orange-tinted incandescent light greeted them, people talking, laughing, a trio of bass-harps twanging out a dance tune in the corner, couples hop-stepping in the open space between the tables. The room smelled of cloves, steamed wine, and the familiar, almost-citrus odor of the natives.

Tables filled two-thirds of the room. As Sarah followed Gosem down the cramped aisle, she spotted a group of her own people in white uniforms.

Sarah shrugged out of her coat and folded it over the back of her chair. A server came over. Gosem ordered steamed spiced wine. Sarah's mouth watered at the thought. Regretfully, she asked for hot citron-water. The server's crest quivered as he turned away.

"It's a drink for little children," Gosem explained. "Ones who have eaten too many honeycakes. We adults are supposed to have more self-control."

Sarah sighed and looked out over the room. Her shoulder muscles ached. She could have used wine to relax after today, but it would have to be the real thing, not the Chacarran version with its unpredictable effects on human physiology. Ned Hankins had drunk half a glass and gone running for the toilets, where he spent the next hour puking his guts out. Another woman in their party attacked Sergei Bartov with her bare hands, claiming he had shaved her dog and she'd get even with him if it was the last thing she ever did. It took six of them to hold her down. After that, Sarah decided not to find out what Chacarran wine would do to her.

It was clearly too noisy for conversation, but Gosem gestured toward the dancing couples. "Okay," she said. "I'll give it a try."

Gosem took Sarah's hands, turning them so that hers rested on his palms, his fingers curled loosely over hers.

The bass-harps shifted to a minor key. Dancers in twos and threes moved through slow, graceful figures, bending their knees in a dipping movement. The music hung in the air, each note liquid, suspended. Sarah imagined herself floating on each rippling phrase. She startled, realizing that Gosem had been leading her over the floor, their path intertwined with that of another couple. Taking a deep breath, she felt the tension fall away from her shoulders. Gosem circled her as if they revolved one around the other.

"You're a good partner," she said, "to make it seem so easy."

"At home, I help to teach the youngsters. Our clan dances often—to celebrate, to mourn, for the days sacred to our Aspect. It's a necessary skill. But," with a slight hesitation, "here in public, I dance only the steps everyone knows."

Glide... glide... dip...

Sarah blinked and her heart speeded up. Neither she nor Dr. Vera had suspected dance might be a private language with each clan having its own distinct variations.

They had not been dancing long when a third partner joined them, clearly someone Gosem knew well. Hands linked, the three of them stepped through the same pattern as before. Sarah's body responded with a sureness and a grace she hadn't known was in her.

Glide... glide... dip... The dance carried them on.

Part of Sarah felt like an outsider and interloper, and yet another part was joined to the other two. Gosem no longer looked at her, but at his friend. They mirrored each other, their differences sharpening in a way that completed a whole. Some were physical, but the more powerful changes she sensed rather than observed—a quickness balanced by a slowness, an advance answered by a subtle yielding, question and response, light and darkness, air and fire. The strange vitality came from neither one individually, but from the interplay between them.

Sarah felt suddenly weak and breathless. Excusing herself, she returned to her chair, recognizing it by the folded coat over the back, and sat down. A gulp of cooling citron-water, heavily sweetened with honey, helped to steady her. She held the crockery cup between both hands.

"Hey there," a voice said. A male voice, rough around the edges.

She looked up to see a man in a white uniform standing beside her. It took her a moment to realize that he was speaking to her in Terran. She recognized him as one of the Hydroponics technicians. He'd been injured during the flight from the "dark" hole—his knee, as she remembered. She'd almost crashed into him in the corridor outside Medical. Another time, they'd sipped coffee and joked about it. She remembered him as sweet-natured and slightly awed by her scientific expertise.

"Didn't see you come in." He placed one hand on the table beside her and leaned close, like a conspirator. His voice slurred the words. "Thought you might appreciate your own kind of company."

Something in Sarah came alert. "Is that wine I smell? *Chacarran* wine?"

"Look," he said, "we're off-duty and we're all above the legal drinking age. Let's loosen up and have a good time. Just you—" he ran one hand over her shoulder and down her arm, his fingers brushing her breast, "and me and our friends back there. Unless you wanna make it just a twosome."

Sarah's muscles went rigid. After the delicacy of Gosem's touch, the caress seemed unbearably coarse.

"Take your hand off my breast," she said.

"Come on, we're not on the ship. No need to be all formal. Shit, we've been through hell together, why shouldn't we celebrate? Not askin' you to marry me, fercry. 'S just a friendly—"

The next moment she was on her feet, the chair clattering to the floor behind her. The tech stumbled back a step. His eyes flashed and his cheeks went even darker.

The music fell silent. The voices dropped to a few hushed exclamations. Sarah's heart pounded in her ears. Her stomach went cold.

What's wrong with me?

"Sarah?" Gosem stood at her side.

"Oh, so that's it?" An unmistakable sneer laced the tech's voice. "You're too good for your own kind now?"

Sarah stared at him. "You're drunk, mister."

The tech threw back his head and laughed, a raucous blare. "Not so drunk I can't see what's in front of me! And what if I am? I'm still a real man. I can still give you what any real woman needs."

He grabbed Sarah by the shoulders. He was taller than she and surprisingly strong. As his mouth covered hers, she felt herself suffocating. She threw herself backward with all her weight. His grasp released a fraction.

"How dare you? Let me go!" Sarah lashed out, slapping him hard enough to spin his head around.

"Bitch!" Staggering, the tech let her go. "Frigging bitch!"

What's happening to me? Sarah had never in her adult life struck another human being, let alone a shipmate. Her hands flew to her face. Her cheeks felt as if they'd been scalded.

The tech's mouth contorted and his eyes narrowed. She couldn't see any white in them. His lips thinned into a grimace. His body hunched, one shoulder dipping. Too late to react, she saw the fist aimed at her face.

Before Sarah could cry out, two pairs of hands grabbed the tech's arm. It was the other men from the table. They wrestled him into an arm lock.

"Clear it, Svi," one of them said.

A Terran woman came up behind them. "Don't waste your air. He can't hear you." Sarah knew her, Command, a friend of Adriana Gomes. "Sorry, Davies. He's had a bit too much to drink."

"He shouldn't—" The blood pounding through Sarah's skull sounded more distant now. She gulped a breath. "He shouldn't have been drinking at all. Not wine, anyway."

"Yeah." The woman tightened her grasp on the tech's arm and turned him toward the door. From the slur in her voice, she'd had her share. "That's what they always say. Nothin' wrong with a little recreational now and then."

Especially after what we've been through. Sarah finished the thought in her mind. She watched them half-carry the tech out of the bar. *You can't expect people to keep going under those conditions, month after month, without any letdown.*

Someone had straightened Sarah's chair. She lowered herself into it. The music started up again and the room filled once more with the sound of voices. Gosem sat down beside her.

"Is that how your people polarize?" he asked. His crest had come fully erect, each strand standing stiffly separate.

Sarah couldn't think straight. All she wanted was to get the hell out of there and back to the dormitory at the Point Seryene factory where the scientific and technical staff were housed.

She struggled to frame a reasonable answer. *Polarization* meant mating, that much she remembered.

Mating! she thought, suppressing a scornful snort. "No, just making a fool out of himself." She picked up her coat. Its soft weight in her hands felt both familiar and alien. "I'm going now. Thank you for the dance."

"I regret the evening ended as it did."

"So do I. But there will be others, I hope."

"I, too."

Outside, the wind rasped along her skin. The cold felt clean, simple. It helped clear her head. The street was almost clear of traffic, except for an occasional pedal-cycle. A tightly-bundled Chacarran passed her without a gesture. A short way up the block, she spotted the tech between two of his friends, the three of them weaving through the shadows of the line of trees.

"You all right, Davies?" Turning, Sarah noticed the woman from Command approaching from the direction of the bar. "He didn't mean anything by it, you know. He's really a nice kid."

Sarah pulled her coat closer around her body. "We were all warned about the wine—"

"What are you, some kind of self-appointed morals cop?" The woman put her hands on her hips. "What else is Svi—or any of us—gonna do at night? Sit around playing chess?"

Sarah stared at her.

"Look, the rest of us may not be top brains, but we're not stupid. Or undisciplined, either. We've trained hard for this mission and worked our asses off getting this far. But we have needs, too, needs that can only be put off so long. It's even harder on the men. Most of us women already have partners. In case you hadn't noticed, there isn't exactly a sex district around here. So what else is there to do except get drunk?"

"I don't know." *I don't care. I just want to get out of here.* The nearest underground station was a couple of blocks away. Not wasting anymore words, she headed for it.

"Wait!" The Command woman grabbed Sarah's arm. "I'll walk you to barracks."

"What for?"

"You don't think it's dangerous to go walking alone and after dark in an alien city?"

Collaborators

Sarah jerked her arm free. "I think it's a hell of a lot safer out here alone than it was in there with Svi and your other friends." Not waiting for a response, she pulled the hood over her head, turned, and strode into the darkened street.

Chapter 17

Miraz: FELLOWSHIP LEADERS CHARGE DEATH THREAT, CALL FOR TERRAN INTERVENTION. Report by Druse.

Following last week's bombing of the Northhill office of the Chacarran-Erlind Fellowship League, Rogrettemer revealed that in recent weeks the organization has received a number of unsigned threatening letters. Some, he claimed, were directed against the League's activities, others against himself personally.

According to warders, no report of such threats was ever recorded. "We would have investigated thoroughly if the matter had been brought to our attention," warder chief Kallen said earlier today, in answer to why no action had been taken to safeguard the premises.

"We didn't take the first letters seriously," Rogrettemer said this morning as he stood in front of the heavily damaged office. "But now it's clear there are powerful forces at work here, forces that cannot tolerate the end of our centuries-old feud with our Erlind neighbors. Ask yourselves who stands to lose from true, lasting peace, and you will find the perpetrators of this outrage."

When asked if he implied that the Kreste administration was in some way responsible for the bombing, Rogrettemer said, "I'll let you draw your own conclusions to that question. Has Kreste tried to stop the attacks? Where was he when hundreds of peaceful citizens were injured during the infamous Miraz Plaza Riot? Where is he today, when honest people cannot speak their opinions without putting their very lives in danger?"

"I have a message for all those who stand against us. You can bomb our buildings, you can burn our homes, you can batter our bodies, but our spirits will fight on! For the first time in our history, we have powerful allies, allies who are committed to the cause of peace!

"I call on the United Terran Peacekeeping Force to establish a protected area in Miraz, to do what the Helm faction and its corrupt, self-serving accomplices, the Mirazan warders, are either unwilling or unable to do—ensure a safe city for all our inhabitants!"

Miraz (newscast): KRESTE PREPARING FOR WAR, CHARGES FELLOWSHIP. PROTEST IN MIRAZ PLAZA DRAWS CROWD; 100 CHARGED; INDICTMENTS TO FOLLOW.

The teapot was Jeelan's favorite and, in a peculiar way, it reminded Talense of his mate, with its generous curves, so soothing to the contours of his hand, the rough surface of the chip in the spout, the fragile-looking handle. Steam wafted upwards from the places where the lid didn't fit quite right. The pot sat in the middle of the low table in the central room. The outside windows had been shuttered against the ice-tipped night.

Talense had come in after a harrowing day, most of it spent on Liaison Committee business, to find Jeelan not home. He'd brewed Jeelan's special tea, too strongly flavored with chiroseth for his own taste, but a peace offering, a gesture to bridge all the times these last weeks when they both had been too exhausted for even companionship.

Now Talense sat alone in smothering silence. Most of the time, he appreciated having this suite of rooms with its separate entrance, away from the evening bustle, the clatter of the children released for a precious hour of play after dinner, the hum of adults catching up on the day's news. Tonight, he felt isolated.

"Jeelan?" Talense turned at the sound of the door latch.

His voice trailed off as the door swung open to reveal Jeelan standing on the threshold. Talense knew right away that something was wrong. He had not seen Jeelan's crest in such disarray since the arrests following the plaza riot. Then Talense saw who stood beside him.

Sweet Bird of Heaven, what has Jeelan done now?

Perrin-az-Mestre, the eldest living member of the clan, shuffled into the central room, steadying himself with Jeelan's elbow. He walked with difficulty these days and spoke little, but what he did say carried the authority of the entire clan.

"Grandparent," Talense murmured, coming forward. When he embraced Perrin, he had to stoop, as if to a child.

"Come," Talense took Perrin's other hand, "sit down." He settled Perrin in the most comfortable chair and served him with the first pouring of tea, striving to curb his anxiety over this unexpected visit. Jeelan took the second. Talense sat beside his mate on the sofa.

Perrin sipped his tea once, muttered, "Chiroseth," and set the cup down. His eyes, glossy as obsidian, met Talense's gaze steadily. "This is not a tea-and-crumbcake visit, Grandchild."

Talense glanced at Jeelan, who was sitting, eyes lowered, fingers tucked between the pillow and his thighs. "This is a clan matter, then?"

Jeelan pulled his hands free and knotted them in his lap. Talense wanted to take Jeelan in his arms, smooth his fur, stroke the tension from his body.

"I speak now for the clan," Perrin said. His voice lost its quaver and he sat taller in his chair. "We have for some time now been concerned about the repercussions of Jeelan's political activities upon the family. Under normal circumstances, we would have nothing to say except that we prefer our talents to be offered first to the clan and secondly to the outside world."

"I would never do anything to endanger the clan," Jeelan said in a tight voice.

Talense took Jeelan's hand. "We know that, heart. I, more than anyone, know that." He looked back at Perrin. "But these aren't ordinary times, are they?"

Perrin gestured negation, a sharp, decisive chop. "Certain actions have attracted the attention of the Miraz City warders."

"The arrests following the plaza riots—" Talense said.

"Were only the beginning. Jeelan has been followed on more than one occasion."

Talense glanced at Jeelan, stung that his mate had made no mention of it.

"Yesterday," Perrin said, "Trenne and Mared were taken into custody."

Talense startled. Trenne and Mared were family; he'd known them since they were children. "This is terrible!"

Perrin went on, "They were subjected to questioning, and held overnight. Our advocat staff effected their release this morning."

"I didn't hear of the arrest," Talense said, suppressing his alarm. "Not even through my sources. Why did it happen? Why would the warders want to question them? Neither of them is political."

Perrin's steady gaze went to Jeelan. Jeelan's crest lifted. Perrin waited.

"Because of me," Jeelan's voice sounded strained and distant. "They assumed that if I were involved in... *questionable* activities, my family must be, also." He glanced at Perrin. "I have been asked—on behalf of the Mestre clan—to withdraw from the League. I have been asked to stop endangering my family by subjecting them to hostile warder attention. I have agreed."

"But—" Talense said, then bit off the rest. He would only add to Jeelan's pain by arguing. Jeelan's life was his own, the work he had chosen.

He would rage against giving in to intimidation.

It made no difference that Mestre was the clan Jeelan had paired into, and not that of his birth. He had made his choice with what dignity and grace he could summon. Perrin had come with him, hobbling the long corridor from the common rooms, not as an agent of discipline, but as a demonstration of Jeelan's enduring place in the clan.

Talense's chest throbbed, sending pain down one arm, and he felt a sick, cold sweat break out. He stood, unable to speak, as Perrin rose and took one slow, halting step after another. When the door had closed behind him, Talense sat watching Jeelan. Almost imperceptibly, Jeelan's crest fell and his neck ruff flattened. Talense had never seen him more miserable, not even after his miscarriage.

"Each of us does what we can," Talense said gently.

"And I can do no more."

"You can talk to me."

"You? You've never been interested in the League. Not even when Rogrettemer's family appealed to you—you were only after a story!"

Talense had not suspected that Jeelan harbored such bitterness. Perhaps it was better that it come out now than linger, festering. Perhaps it was the source of the distance he felt between them on those long cold nights when he lay awake, unable to sleep, afraid to turn over for fear he'd wake Jeelan.

He kept his voice soft. "What you—and the League—have to say is vital to Chacarre. Of course you must act to protect the clan. But your voice must not be lost."

Jeelan stared at him for a long moment, round eyes unblinking. "What can you do? Write a story about this—no, not even *you* would dare to make such a thing public."

Talense took a deep breath. "I can make sure the truth is told—*all* the truth. I'm more than a single press now, no matter how well-regarded. I'm an advisor to the Liaison Committee—no," at Jeelan's gesture of scorn, "hear me out. I've been talking with the Terran Sarahdavies. She has a vision of the news media, sheets and casts both, as a way to—to educate the people of Miraz. To make sure they have all the facts and hear all sides of a dispute. *Free speech*, she calls it."

Jeelan blinked. "Why should she care?"

"For the same reason I work for Interclan and not the Mestre sheet. Oh yes, I could have done so, and been considerably less travel-worn as a result. But sometimes we must rise above our own immediate interests and act not as Bavarites or Hoolites or Followers of the Prophet, but as Chacarrans. The news sheets are the key, or at least Sarahdavies thinks they can be. We've been talking about forming a Department of Information Services, perhaps under the mayor's office or even the Terran Command, for greater neutrality."

Jeelan untwisted his fingers. "And you—you are willing to tell the League's side of the story? To stand against the war propaganda of Kreste and his fawns?"

Talense took Jeelan's hand in both of his. The downy fur felt soft as a baby's. "I promise it."

Chapter 18

Half-frozen rain sheeted down the slanting roofs. Snow lay in sodden piles along the wide downtown street. Sidestepping puddles of slush, Lexis drew his scarf tighter around his neck with one hand and clutched his satchel with the other, the stem of his umbrella clamped against his side.

No snow covered the Terran observation unit. Its metal gleamed, pristine, as if mere weather could not touch it. The units were all over the city now and a special group of Fardite priests of unimpeachable moral rectitude had been granted permission to view the visual images. Not everyone thought the units or their recordings were a good thing, however. Two minor clans had filed protests with the mayor's office.

Lexis himself had no objection. He did not think a mechanical device could endanger his spiritual welfare and as for the recordings themselves, what had any law-abiding citizen to fear?

People hurried past, their collars drawn up. Nobody recognized Lexis any longer and certainly no verses had been penned in his honor. He was no longer the famous Lexis, but just another minor official.

At least he had escaped from the pointless work of teaching, work for which he was—he saw it clearly now—inherently unsuited. He'd been granted a chance to make an impact on his world, as well as the freedom to write his own poetry. He had his own quarters—he mustn't think about the silence when he'd told his parents he'd found his own apartment in the splits—and his own office.

In contrast to the gleaming metal of the Terran structure, the weather-smoothed walls looked dingy, in need of a decent scrubbing. The sign, letters carved and then painted in blue, discretely identified the Bureau of Internal Affairs.

Beyond lay a narrow, over-heated lobby, its charcoal-colored walls papered with official notices. A warder stood inside the door and a bored-looking clerk sat behind a slab desk.

The door at the top of the stairs opened to the communal working area. Light and heat struck Lexis full in the face and he found himself sweating profusely. He drew in a breath and smelled tea, something sugary—a confectioner's box sitting open on the edge of a table—and the musty odor of paper and dust that marked every office he'd known.

The room glittered with movement—people spreading maps and diagrams on the tables, aides rushing about with sheaves of documents or bottles of ink, a messenger carrying a double armful of flowers. A group of officials wearing sanitation badges hurrying by, sipping their tea.

Still clutching his satchel, Lexis made his way to his office. It was, even by University standards, little bigger than a closet, meant to be neither comfortable nor inviting, merely a place to store his umbrella, take a private phone call, or compose his thoughts for the real work outside.

Several sheets of paper sat neatly in the center of the desk. The schedule was empty except for a visit to a junior school. The remaining papers were the text of the speech he was to deliver. He scanned it, one triviality after another.

What had he expected, anyway?

Lexis stalked to the window and looked out. It wasn't much of a view, just the street below, the piled, half-melted snow, the tops of heads and umbrellas hurrying past, trees like wire sculptures.

Innovation and initiative. That's what he thought was expected of him when he'd first taken this job. Now it seemed the mayor didn't want him acting independently, only reading someone else's boring speeches.

The phone on his desk jangled. "Yes?"

"Lexis! Bird of Heaven, I finally got through to you!"

For a moment, Lexis couldn't identify the caller, for the voice was distorted by emotion. Recognition sparked—it was the University Dean, who'd been so unctuous about his leaving. Lexis had always thought him an odious person, even if he was from another branch of the same Sotirite clan.

"Lexis, we've got an emergency here." Lexis heard fear in the Dean's voice. "Another riot."

"Then call the warders—"

"You don't understand! The warders are *part* of it!" The Dean paused, breathing hard. "The students had planned another demonstration. They're always upset about one thing or another. This time it was Kreste's new restrictions on the Fellowship League. You can imagine what they said about *that*. Or rather, screamed about it."

"'Censorship, unlawful arrest and detention'. All the things they always say." Lexis found himself gesturing in dark amusement. "If we didn't provide them with something to protest, they'd invent it."

"More students gathered than we expected. We called the warders as a matter of routine, mostly to comply with the new regulations since the plaza misfortune. A few minutes ago, the students started moving toward the Administration Complex."

Lexis waited. The Dean drew a deep breath. "The warders were *expecting* trouble." His voice regained its frenzied edge. "I tried to reason with them, but nobody listened. There's got to be a way to stop it. The whole thing's gone crazy! It's out of control! Lexis, can't *you* do something for us?"

Memory rose up to cloud Lexis's senses—the screams, the exhilaration pulsing along his nerves, the ecstatic music of his own pulse, the feel and weight of the satchel as he swung it again and again.

"I'll get help for you," Lexis said. "By Sotir, the First Aspect, whose attribute is loyalty, I promise you." He hung up and let the phone rest in its cradle for a moment. Then he dialed the clerk's desk.

"I want to talk to the Terrans. No subordinates, direct to Jonadamson."

"That may be difficult—"

"I don't want excuses, I want action!" He heard the clerk's indrawn breath. A burst of something hot and satisfying raced through him. "*Now!*"

Then he made two more phone calls, one to the Interclan news agency and the other to a hired-car dispatcher.

Miraz: STUDENT DEMONSTRATION HALTED BY TERRANS; WARDER INTERVENTION FAILS. Report by Talense.

Earlier today, students at Miraz University campus protested the continuing governmental suppression of the Erlind-Chacarre Fellowship Council. Speakers claimed that Kreste's administration has unethically interfered with their free speech. The gathering escalated rapidly from its peaceful beginning. A few demonstrators, possibly outside agitators, hurled rocks at faculty and by-standers.

The warders had been called in to supervise the event and prevent any catalyzed distress reaction when Lexis, the renowned hero of the Miraz Plaza Riot and former Professor of Poetics at the University, arrived on the scene.

Exactly what happened in the next few minutes is still unclear. What we do know is that the Terrans arrived in a shuttle aircraft. Hovering over the campus, they sprayed the entire quadrangle with the same type of light beams that contained the Plaza Riot. Within minutes, the entire crowd had either fallen, stunned, or had dispersed.

No warning was issued, nor were any instructions to disband given. After the disturbance was contained, a number of students were taken to Eastbank Hospital, although it is not clear whether they were injured as a result of the stun beams or the violence earlier during the demonstration. No deaths have been reported. The names of the injured students have been withheld at the request of the University.

MIRAZ: HOOLITE NEIGHBORHOOD BARRICADES BLOCKED BY CHALLENGE FROM KESHITES. CLAN LEADERS CLASH IN COURT BATTLE.

Chapter 19

Alon paused on the steps of the apartment his parents had found for him and Birre. He fumbled for the key, juggling his satchel, two long loaves of bread, and a cluster of star-eye daisies. The flowers were an extravagance in this season, but they'd caught his eye as he crossed the plaza, one fresh bunch surrounded by buckets of wilting hothouse lillettes. These days, his attention seemed as flighty as a sparrow's. He wondered what he'd forgotten. Chances were, it was something essential and unromantic, like toilet paper.

The lock clicked open and Alon shoved the door with one rounded hip. His stomach rumbled; it seemed he was hungry all the time now. He'd stood in the bakery and devoured three cheese buns before buying the loaves. Humming, he cut a piece of bread and nibbled on it while he searched the cupboards for a vase.

Alon put the pot of bean stew on the stove to heat. Steam carried the smells of herbs and garlic into the air. He smiled, thinking how Birre teased about how domestic he was becoming. "Nesting behavior," Birre called it, as if Alon were an exotic bird. Privately, Alon thought it was the influence of the apartment's cozy, lived-in feeling. The owners of the apartment were only a few years younger than his parents, Wayfolk of course, and longtime friends.

Birre came home late, looking more tired than usual, but strong, broader in the shoulders and more muscular than he had been, classic signs of polarization. Seeing him walk through the door made Alon's heart beat faster. His breasts tingled, touched by fire.

Birre put down his book-crammed case and took Alon into his arms. His body felt hard against Alon's, warm through the fabric of his coat.

"You smell so good," Birre murmured. His breath stirred the hair on Alon's neck.

Alon pulled away so he could meet Birre's eyes. For a long moment, all they could do was gaze at each other. Alon took a breath and said firmly, "I know what you're thinking, but it won't work. You've got to finish your advocat training."

"What's the use? I can't concentrate." Birre threw the coat on the nearest piece of furniture and turned back to Alon. "It's the polarization. Our bodies want what they want."

Alon gathered himself together with an effort. Right now, all he wanted was to lead Birre off to bed, although what he wanted to do there wasn't nearly so simple. He forced himself to say, "The teachers will let you repeat what you need to, you said so yourself. We won't *always* be this crazy."

"Faith, I hope not—"

"And meanwhile, you're building a future for both of us, for our children."

"You're right—as usual," Birre said, his eyes softening. "You're so good for me. To me." His crest lowered to lie smoothly along his skull. "I don't mean to sound overly practical, but... is there anything to eat?"

After dinner, Alon and Birre curled up in the window seat, looking out on the courtyard between their apartment building and the next. The strip of garden was dry and withered. Alon's cooking herbs stood out as isolated sprigs of green. A single tree, almost bare, cast shadows of black-on-gray from the city lights.

Birre's lips moved against Alon's hair. Alon closed his eyes, feeling every place their bodies touched. Deep in his own belly, in a place he hadn't known existed, he felt a building pressure—a need, a longing, a fullness. Intellectually, he understood terms like *egg ripeness factor* and *fertility readiness signals*, but what he felt was like nothing he'd ever imagined.

Alon set his cup of tea down and put his arms around Birre. His breasts, taut and aching, pressed against Birre's chest.

His skin became an organ of perception; he felt Birre everywhere. He sensed the egg, ripened within Birre's body, as clearly as if it glowed with visible light. He could see the ripples of desire and readiness, echoed and intensified by his own.

"Our bodies want what they want."

Birre trembled as Alon led him into the bedroom. Alon pulled off his own clothing and then Birre's. Instead of artificial fabric, he would enclose Birre in his own living flesh.

The room was chill, but neither of them minded. Birre lay back and closed his eyes, his breath coming in catches. His head fell back in the valley between the two pillows. A pulse leapt in his throat; Alon felt absurdly moved by his vulnerability, his surrender. He ran his hands over Birre's body, stroked the genital nub now swollen with the egg he would take into his own body and fertilize. Birre stiffened and cried out.

Birre's skin tasted like honey and herbs. A new, driving energy overshadowed Alon's rush of arousal. He slid his body over Birre's. Birre reached around Alon's waist and caressed his buttocks, gently pulling them apart. The tip of Birre's nub rested against Alon's slit; they seemed to pulsate against each other in a single pounding rhythm.

A surge of pleasure shook Alon as Birre flexed his hips upward. Alon felt as if he were teetering on the brink of an abyss. He had only to shift his weight to bring Birre inside his body. Once there, he sensed there would be no controlling what happened next, no turning back. The same reflexes would drive both of them—Birre's to release the ripened egg, his to flood it with seed.

His body ached with wanting it, his heart ached with longing for oneness with his mate, and yet part of him hesitated. The act was irrevocable. Even more than the moment of their pairing, this would change their lives forever. They would create a new person, where none had been before. All his life, he had been able to retreat from his decisions, correct his mistakes, choose his Way.

Sometimes we do not choose the Way, Meddi had once said. *Sometimes it chooses us.*

Alon closed his eyes. His legs quivered. Birre slid into him, filled him in ways he hadn't known he was empty. His body arched, straining; his hips moved of their own accord, driving him deeper around Birre. His belly resonated with the rhythm; something inside clenched tighter and tighter, tension mounting, muscles threatening spasm.

Below him, Birre moaned and twisted, his fingers digging into Alon's shoulders. Birre cried out, a sound of elemental pleasure.

A flood of relief, of opulent fullness surged through Alon's body, cool against the fire that had raged through him a moment before. His head snapped back, his muscles jerked. For a long moment he couldn't breathe, couldn't hear, couldn't see.

Half-sobbing, Alon collapsed on Birre's chest. He lay there, listening to Birre's heartbeat gradually slowing, an echo to his own. His exposed skin turned icy as the last of the day's warmth seeped from the room. Birre pulled the covers over both of them.

With the Year's-Turn Gathering only a week away, Alon hung the bookstore with traditional greenery and placed a bowl of clove-studded citrons on the desk. The odors brought smiles to Wayfolk customers, who recognized the twin elements of fertility and preservation. There were few enough of them, as travel across Chacarre's borders was much reduced this winter.

The round-bellied stove filled the store with gentle warmth. Alon settled in the chair behind the desk and propped his feet up on the stool Meddi had brought for him. His belly was still firm, for the baby wouldn't start to round it out for another month. The changes were more felt than seen—the texture of his body, the dreamy haze that so often drifted across his vision, the pervading sense of contentment. Birre accused him of being intoxicated on pregnancy hormones.

The door bells chimed. Icy, moisture-laden air gusted into the room. An impeccably dressed customer walked in—no, no customer this, but Birre's parent, Enellon. Alon's crest quivered nervously as he slowly got to his feet. He hadn't spoken to Enellon since that fateful dinner last autumn, although he'd seen him a few times in the old city, at a distance.

"Can I help you?" The words, so many times repeated, came easily to Alon's mouth.

"I would like to.." Enellon paused. "To talk with you."

Alon gestured to the two armchairs drawn up around the stove. Enellon's silk scarf and tailored coat, of beautifully woven wool bordered by an intricate pattern of leather cording dyed to match, looked out of place next to the threadbare upholstery of the chairs.

Enellon declined Alon's offer of a hot drink. Alon sat down in the other chair and waited, noting the runnels of age in Enellon's face. It came to him that Enellon's visit was in itself an overture, a gesture of good will. For Birre's sake—for the baby's sake—could he afford to do any less?

"Meddi always says there's nothing harder than starting over again," Alon said.

Enellon lifted his hands as if in gesture, then lowered them. "Your Meddi is a person of surprising wisdom. I had a speech all planned out, but everything I was going to say sounds foolish now."

"Oh yes," Alon said, "very foolish." Enellon frowned and Alon hastened to add, "Birre always thinks it's entertaining to agree with me when I say things like that. I'm sorry, I'm just nervous."

Enellon ran his fingers over the fringed edges of his scarf. "No matter who Birre has chosen, he is still our child. It is not the teaching of Hool, Fourth Aspect of the god, to forsake the people we love when they need us most. But Saunde and I—we think Birre chose well."

Alon sat, unable to speak, and stared at Enellon.

"It's time—" Enellon began, just as Alon burst out, "We never meant—" They both broke off, laughed.

Enellon continued, "It's time we found a way through this problem. We realize now—Saunde and I—that your family must feel as strongly about your beliefs as we do about ours."

"We never meant to create a rift between you and Birre."

"We know that now," Enellon said with unexpected gentleness.

116

"Perhaps it took a time of separation, of realizing what it might mean to never know our grandchild, to make us see the true cost of our stubbornness."

Alon's head shot up. His hands went protectively around his belly. "Oh, no, we would never have—"

"Perhaps not." Enellon smiled. "But let's not put it to the test, shall we? Saunde and I—we want to help you two as much as we—no, as much as *you and Birre* will permit us. Money, medical fees, housing—your own quarters, of course, safe in a clan-patrolled neighborhood. For the time being, anyway. We thought of setting up a trust fund that you could draw on when you wished. We certainly have the funds available. We've just leased two of our warehouses to the Terrans and—"

"Please!" Alon held up his hands. "This is too much, and it's Birre who should be hearing it, too!" He reached out with one hand to touch Enellon's arm and stumbled on, "I can't tell you how much—it's wonderful—that means more than money, more than anything. Birre will be so happy!" Alon's last few words came out in a sob. He ducked his head, combed the fingers of one hand through his crest. "I'm sorry, I'm just... I don't know, so *emotional*, these days."

Enellon smiled again and patted Alon's knee. There was something in the spontaneous gesture that Alon found inexpressibly comforting.

"I'll tell you a secret," Enellon said, "just between the two of us. When I was pregnant with Birre, so was I."

Chapter 20

The Gathering took place at Padme's restaurant, for Alon's parents' apartment would have been far too small to hold their many friends. The private back room rang with laughter-punctuated babble. Warmth and sweet smells filled the air. Tables had been arranged in a open U shape and set with platters of preserved fruit and candles wreathed with dried flowers, according to Wayfolk tradition. The walls were lined with pegs holding winter coats, hats, and umbrellas, decorated with more dried flowers.

Alon and Birre were hugged and patted, then led to the last two empty places. Meddi and Tellem, and Enellon and Saunde were already seated, scattered around the table. Alon recognized many of the guests, some he hadn't seen since he was a child.

Padme, as host of the Gathering, sang the blessing of opening. It was the one part of the Wayfolk tradition that had never been translated into any modern language, yet every Wayfolk child knew its meaning.

> *"Through the dark times,*
> *The Way will guide us,*
> *Like water, ever to the sea."*

Without any formal signal, people began passing around beakers of spiced wine, to even the children, and began reaching for pieces of fruit. Alon took a sliver of honeyed peach and popped it into Birre's mouth.

"Remember," Alon said, his eyes twinkling at Birre's astonishment, "you're not allowed to feed yourself, and no one can leave until it's all finished."

"Let's see how much you can chew, then!" Birre said, reaching for the nearest platter. "One for you, one for the baby, one for you. What about the wine, do I get to pour that down your throat?"

Alon struggled to speak with his mouth filled with dried apple twists. "Not mine—your own!"

His stomach was pleasurably full when the last pieces of fruit vanished from the platters. The room fell silent, expectant. This was Alon's favorite part of all the Wayfolk ceremonies. The Inviting, it was called, waiting for the Way to open inside each of them. Sometimes the Way was silent and people would sit until they felt moved to go home. Other times, people burst into song or danced wildly about the room. Rising to speak, as Meddi was now, was a fairly conventional beginning.

"We welcome new friends," Meddi said, holding out his hands to Birre and his parents. Scattered around the circle as they were, the gesture included the entire room. A murmur rippled around the table and a few people smiled. "We welcome a new spirit, a new teacher, a new comrade on the Way." He paused, and Alon heard his unspoken words, *My grandchild.*

Someone else got up as soon as Meddi sat down. Alon remembered him from festivities years ago; he was a distant cousin of Tellem's. His own children were grown and he'd given Alon many wonderful outgrown books and toys. He reminisced about Alon as a small child, some incidents Alon had forgotten and others he wished he had, and ended up saying it was Meddi who was supposed to ramble on, not making sense, and he who was supposed to come up with something short and direct.

"So, Alon, in recompense for having forced you to listen to the most boring Gathering speech in the history of Miraz, not to mention the most embarrassing, I gift you with six evenings of baby-care, in order that your intellect may not disintegrate in like fashion for want of social stimulation."

Everyone cheered as he sat down. Alon choked on his laughter. Birre slapped him between the shoulder blades with one hand and signaled to the speaker with the other, "We accept!"

A handful of guests stood up in rapid succession, some offering gifts, others stories; one a lullaby about a grommet and his three boisterous offspring, each more inventive than the one before in its reason for staying awake *just a little longer.* The entire room hummed along with the final chorus.

> *"Sleepy time, sleepy time,*
> *Dreamy time has come.*
> *Starry skies will light your Way,*
> *And love will make us One."*

The circle began to quiet down, settling again into the pleasant state of anticipation.

"Open up in there! Warders!"

The inner door flew open and a dozen warders armed with riot sticks burst into the room. Three or four restaurant workers came clattering on their heels, pale-eyed and distraught. The warders spread out inside the door.

Alon's muscles tensed instinctively, but he held himself still, as he'd been taught long ago. *Like a grommet when the eagle soars above,* Meddi had once said. *Listen and watch. Wait for the Way to open.*

Padme got to his feet, hands open and away from his body. "The restaurant is closed, friends," he said in a calm voice. "This is a private Gathering."

A warder stepped forward, looking unhappy but grim. "As of sunset tonight, all meetings of more than five people are banned. You are to clear the premises immediately."

"By whose orders?" Enellon's voice carried an edge of warning. The set of his shoulders and the aggressive thrust of his chin reminded Alon of Birre that night when he was first polarizing. On the other side of the table, Saunde's crest lifted in indignation.

"Kreste's declared a civil emergency!" barked the officer. "If you don't like it, complain directly to him. For now, don't give us any trouble."

Birre thrust himself between Alon and the nearest warder. "We've done nothing wrong! We have every right to be here."

The officer thumped Birre's chest with the end of his baton, hard enough so Alon could hear the sound. "You can go on home to your nice warm beds, or you can spend the night in a jail cell. It's all the same to me."

Alon felt the sudden leap of tension in Birre's body, the temptation to smash his fist into the warder's arrogant face. Polarization and outrage spurred him on.

"It is a lawful order," Padme said.

People shrugged into their coats and embraced each other, murmuring a word or two of blessing. But Birre had not grown up with the Wayfolk custom of avoiding direct confrontation with force. He would not understand; he would see mindless docility, not resilience.

"Come on," Alon put his arm around Birre and pulled him after them.

"You can't be serious!" Birre jerked away, but not very hard. "You're just going home—doing whatever they say—"

"Outside!" Tellem, behind them, hissed.

The warder stood by as they filed through the restaurant and out the front door. Alon had never seen the street so deserted, not so early after dark. He glanced back to see Meddi and Birre's parents in earnest conversation.

"Go on home. There's nothing more any of us can do here," Tellem said.

"But—" Birre protested.

"But nothing! Your baby needs rest and safety."

Alon recognized Tellem's peremptory tone of voice. He grabbed Birre's hand and hurried down the street. For once, Birre didn't argue. They slowed only when they reached the underground station. A warder stood at the entrance.

Wind howled through the station, beneath the low, arched ceiling. A few passengers waited, heavily swathed in coat and scarf. No one spoke or looked up for more than a blink.

The railcar burst into the station with a roaring whoosh. Once they'd settled in the almost empty compartment, Alon leaned toward Birre. "Tellem was right, you know. There was no point in provoking an incident. It's not the first time something like this has happened. Our histories tell of much worse. And it isn't our Way to fight force with force."

Birre looked startled. "I was only standing up for my rights."

Alon gestured in disagreement. "That may be what you intended, but look at what would have happened. You'd take a punch at that warder, he'd hit you with his stick, we'd all end up in jail with smashed heads. All that would accomplish is a much harder time for the next Gathering. The warders won't even give them a warning, the way they did us. They'll just break in, swinging. Do you want to be responsible?"

"That's crazy."

When Alon heard the stories of Wayfolk blood on the steps of Octagon, he'd thought them tales invented to frighten disobedient children. He hadn't realized how easily they could become real. "We have somewhat differing views of Chacarran history."

"Well, it's not going to happen here. Not now." Birre pulled away, hands curled into fists on his thighs.

A bell tone signaled the next stop. Alon shuffled through the sliding doors, weary down to the marrow of his bones. The joy he'd felt amid the love of his family seemed a century, not an hour, ago. He could barely remember getting up that morning.

At the top of the underground entrance, Alon paused, leaning on the rail. It took a few moments for him to catch his breath, while Birre stood at his side and looked around nervously. The cobblestones gleamed with night moisture. There were no warders here, only a few pedestrians. One hurried toward the station, a parcel under one arm. Birre called a greeting at him, a neighbor they knew slightly. He ran a small pharmacy on the next street.

"Is the underground still running?" the neighbor asked.

"It was a minute ago," said Birre.

"Thank all Eight Names at once! I was afraid they'd shut it down." He indicated his package. "Heart medicine for my old cousin—I should have gone an hour ago, but who could have foreseen this? What are you young people doing on the streets? This is no time to be abroad."

"The warders kicked us out of a private meeting," Birre said hotly. "There'll be protests in the streets tomorrow, I can tell you. Whatever caused Kreste to issue orders like that?"

"Then you haven't heard?" The neighbor ducked his head, eyes shadowed. "Mayor Chelle's been killed. Assassinated, they say. Kreste's declared a national emergency. Last time we had anything like this was when we almost went to war with Erlind fifteen years ago. By the protection of Sotir, what am I doing, standing here babbling? You children get home where it's safe!" He disappeared down the station stairs.

Birre wrapped one arm around Alon. "Good advice. Come on, there will be more news on the caster."

Alon's body responded automatically to Birre's touch, but his thoughts tumbled uneasily. *What kind of world am I bringing this child into? One with a real future, or one that repeats the worst of the past?*

Miraz: CHELLE, 3 OTHERS KILLED IN EXPLOSION; LEXIS NAMED MAYOR. Report by Talense.

An explosion ripped through the offices of Mayor Chelle late yesterday afternoon, instantly killing the mayor, his assistant Ralle, and two senior officials. Five other city employees were injured by the blast and taken to Old Hospital, where two of them remain in critical condition.

Within hours, Kreste authorized emergency regulations, including a ban on all public meetings of more than five individuals, a night curfew, and authorization for warders to use pellet guns. Citizens are urged to carry identification at all times, as warders are empowered to detain anyone without it.

Chief Kallen immediately launched an investigation of the bombing, and late yesterday hinted that his laboratories have detected evidence of the origin and manufacture of the bomb. Further details are being withheld, pending the arrest of suspects. Kallen, meanwhile, has assigned additional patrols throughout the city.

"We must all do our utmost to maintain order during these difficult times," Kallen said in a brief interview.

This morning, the Bureau of Internal Affairs, at the request of the Terran-Chacarran Liaison Committee, named Lexis-az-Doreth to the post of mayor of Miraz. Lexis, known for his heroic actions during last spring's Miraz Plaza riots and for his tireless work on the city's Bureau of Internal Affairs, was hailed as the ideal successor.

"He's a person of integrity and vision, a true hero of our times," said Chelle's sobbing widow. "Now, more than ever, we need someone to lead us with courage and determination. If anyone can find out who did this terrible thing and make sure they're prosecuted to the bitter end, it's our

Lexis."

Lexis himself spoke briefly to reporters on the steps of City Hall. Looking haggard from a night of emergency meetings, he promised to personally supervise the investigation of what he called "the most heinous crimes of the century." Preliminary public opinion polls indicate strong support for Lexis's new administration.

Miraz: KRESTE CHARGES ERLIND CONSPIRACY, OUTLAWS FELLOWSHIP; PROTESTS CONTINUE OUTSIDE CITY JAIL.

PART II

Chapter 21

Felde burst through the front door of the farmhouse and into the kitchen just as Hayke patted the last loaf into shape and slipped the pans into the oven. That morning, he and Torrey had gone to gather winter-pears, succulent fruit that ripened after the first frost.

"Dimmie! Dimmie!" Felde's body, under layers of winter clothing, quivered with excitement, his eyes so round that they bulged in their sockets. "They're coming! They're coming!"

"Calm down, little one." Hayke straightened up and wiped his floury hands on his apron. "Now, then. Who's coming?"

Felde struggled to catch his breath. Hayke could almost feel his heart fluttering. "Trucks, people in uniforms!"

The hair over Hayke's spine prickled. The orchards lay to the east, toward the Erlind border. Was this the invasion they had all dreaded?

"*Where's Torrey?*"

Crest fluttering, Felde hopped from one foot to the other. "He ran to tell Adso."

At least Torrey had the sense not to linger and watch—whatever was happening. Torrey wouldn't have sent Felde running back if he'd recognized whoever it was.

Hayke jerked the pans of bread from the oven and set them on top of the stove where they wouldn't burn. In the mud room, he kicked off his house shoes, shoved his feet into snow boots, and threw on his coat. Felde at his heels, he rushed to the shed where he parked his ancient truck. Felde slipped into the passenger side without a word.

Hayke pumped the fuel lines; the engine caught and sputtered. *Should have gotten the cables replaced last fall, should have—*

"Come *on!*"

The engine died.

With the lines flooded, he'd have to wait to try again. A minute or two, nothing more. Struggling for calm, Hayke pressed his forehead to the steering bar. It felt cool and hard. His heart pounded and sweat dampened his face, not all of it from the morning's baking.

Maybe the children had seen something completely innocent—neighbors, tourists, a study team from the University. But neither Felde nor Torrey were fools. Country-wise, they knew every regular traveler in the area.

Past the orchards. East. Towards Erlind.

With an effort, Hayke got his thoughts under control. He saw how Felde sat huddled, curled in on himself.

I dare not him with me, in case... But he's so little, so scared.

He reached out and took one of Felde's hands in his. "It will be all right. Whatever it is, it will be all right. Now, little grommet, I must go check this out for myself. That way I will know the best thing to do. Torrey's safe at Adso's right? And *you* will be snug here at home."

Felde nodded, still round-eyed. The soothing words softened the edge of tension in his body.

"I'll be back as soon as I can," Hayke said. "Are you big enough to finish the baking all by yourself?"

Felde hesitated, eyes darting to the house where the bread that he had never before been allowed to tend by himself waited. Delight lit his face. He jerked open the car door and bolted for the kitchen.

Hayke tried the truck again. This time, he got it started. He drove slowly along a road that was hardly more than a trail. The snowfall had been light and the children's footsteps dotted the path. They'd been following each other's tracks, just as he'd taught them, taking turns breaking through the snow to save their strength. Here and there, smaller prints left the trail—Felde after a new treasure or scampering free for the joy of it. Hayke imagined their voices ringing through the crisp air.

The land rose in gentle pleats to the groves of winter-pear. The branches of the trees made delicate patterns against the white of hill and sky. Rosen had planted them far enough apart to allow for growth, and now it seemed to Hayke that they were reaching out for one another, reaching but never quite embracing.

Beyond the orchard lay a narrow gap, a slice in the steepening hills. The truck slowed, laboring. Above the noise, Hayke caught a different sound, a thrumming, a racking. A sound of big machinery, military transports. The children had been right to run for help. Alarm spread like a veil of ice over him. He was not at all prepared to encounter an Erlind invasion force on a rural road.

He turned the truck around and slammed the throttle open. The truck leapt back down the main road, bouncing and juddering. The bar nearly jerked from his grasp. The truck's gears clashed and whined, but it kept on

128

going. Past the edge of the orchard, he veered off into a narrow gully. He took the truck far enough so he was sure it couldn't be seen from the road.

Hayke sat there for a moment, heart pounding, crest moving in reflexive quivers. Every instinct urged him to stay still, hidden like a grommet in the shadow of a hawk—but he had to look.

He slipped out of the car and scrambled up the side of the gully. At the top, he crouched behind tangled leafless brush, watching. A wind, dry and cold, cut through his hair and shivered along his skin.

The noise of the other engines deepened, grinding to a rumble. A huge armored transport rolled through the narrow gap, its treads slicing deep into the snow. Hayke stared at the red Erlind pennons attached to its frontal gun turret. More transports followed. There must be fifty of them. He pictured the convoy as a beast, huge and ponderous, difficult to stop and even more difficult to get going again. They inched closer and closer until he could feel the faint vibrations through the ground and smell their exhaust fumes.

As they emerged from the cleft, the transports had fanned out on both sides of the road and into the sloping orchard. Young trees went down beneath their treads. Hayke wasn't sure if he actually heard the sound of splintering wood or felt it in his bones.

Hayke felt a pang of loss. He had strolled with Rosen through these same hills, picking flowers and resting in the shade of those same trees.

How dare these Erls destroy Rosen's trees? How dare they march across his land like this, frightening his children, tearing through his earth?

Hayke's fingers curled into claws. Hot breath hissed between his clenched teeth. His body moved without his thinking, rising up, hands raised, eyes judging the steepness of the slope before him, the distance to the convoy.

Tal'deh... The word sounded dim and distant, as if thought by someone else. *Tal'deh*, the madness of rage.

But he was already catapulting down the hill, screaming curses, stumbling, catching his balance. His feet plunged through the thin crust of snow, sometimes sliding but always finding traction on the hard earth beneath.

The lead transport had slowed to a crawl. A door opened and an Erl in military clothing leaned out. He shouted something, his voice distorted over the rumble of the engines behind him.

Panting, Hayke reached the bottom of the slope and skidded to a halt directly in front of the first transport. Without a crowd to fuel its madness, *tal'deh* faded. The red haze lifted from his eyes. The fiery tumult in his belly eased. He faced the transport, hands empty at his sides. Strangely, he felt no fear, as if the stillness of the hills had seeped into him and the winter's cold now flowed through his veins.

Collaborators

It came to him that *tal'spirë*, surrender, was but a heartbeat from *tal'deh*, that madness and grace were but two sides of the same passion.

The ground beneath Hayke's feet vibrated and he felt the heat of the lead transport's engines on his face, smelled the reek of its exhaust. Under his knitted cap, his crest lay as smooth as a skein of fine silk. His heart beat slowly and drum-steady.

The transport creaked as it drew to a stop just feet away from Hayke.

The Erl jumped down, scattering loose snow under his boots. He wore a padded crimson jacket over tight pants, a bandolier across his chest. A leather holster hung from his belt. He waved his arms and shouted in Chacarran, "Are you deaf or simply too stupid to understand! Move aside, I said!"

Hayke pitched his voice to cut through the rumble of the transports. "This is my land. Your army may not pass."

"You stupid cropper! This is rightfully Erlind land, and by tomorrow will be so once more!"

Ignoring him, Hayke pointed towards the line of transports. "Go back where you belong."

The Erl reached for the holster at his hip and began unfastening the flap.

"What are you going to do," Hayke said. "Shoot me? Kill a single unarmed farmer? *That* will certainly win you the gratitude of all Demmerle."

"Stop this!" A voice boomed out from the lead transport. An instant later, a second figure clambered out on the snow, an officer by his plumed helmet. Hayke remembered seeing him before. He'd been in the market square, wearing civilian clothes. He couldn't recall the Erl's name, only that he had family on both sides of the border.

"Stop this at once!" the officer shouted in Erlindish. "There will be no assaults upon civilians! Tomorrow these will be Erlind lands. We don't want the farmers resenting us."

"It's no use explaining things," the first Erl said. "He's Wayfolk. We have them in Erlind, too. They're like vermin, you can never get rid of them. Or talk them out of whatever they've got in their obstinate, Egg-sized minds."

"Nevertheless, we have better ways of handling those who will soon be our subjects."

"As you command, sir." The first Erl saluted and climbed back in the transport.

The Erlind officer took something shaped like a slender egg from a hidden pocket in his belt. Sun flashed on metal as he raised it and pointed at Hayke.

Hayke stared. All he could think of was the beam of light in the plaza and the fallen bodies. There was nowhere to run, even if he could have overcome his reflexive paralysis. He was too dismayed to feel afraid.

Felde... Torrey... Remember how I loved you.

"This won't harm you," the officer said as yellow-tinted light washed away Hayke's sight.

Hayke dimly heard the sound of something heavy falling on the snow.

Cold, he was so cold. Rosen must have kicked the blankets off during the night again. Hayke flailed with one hand, felt nothing, curled back on himself. Part of him wanted nothing more than to drift back into the lazy warmth of sleep, but a voice in the back of his mind shrilled at him, *Get up! Get up!*

"All right, Rosen," he murmured. His tongue moved sluggishly in his mouth. "I'm awake."

Hayke squinted his eyes open. Sun flooded through him. His stomach clenched and his mouth filled with sour-tasting saliva.

Whatever had possessed him to lie down in the snow like that? His hat and one of his gloves were gone. Ice crystals encrusted his fur.

Slowly the gray cleared from his vision and his belly settled. Brushing the powdery snow from his clothing, he got to his feet. He'd been lying partway up a steep slope and between the two hills, where once a narrow truck road had been, now a swathe of muddy slush.

Memory stirred—the convoy, the Erl pointing the metal egg, a glimpse of light that was yellow like the beams that had swept the plaza during the riot.

If the Terrans had armed the Erls...

Hayke's eyes scanned the horizon in the direction of his neighbor's farm. His breath caught in his throat. He must have been too dazed to notice it before, that smudge on the brightness of the sky. Smoke, coming from the direction of Verne's farm.

Verne's farm... where Torrey had gone.

Vera Eisenstein sat in her laboratory, eyes closed, listening to a radio broadcast from Miraz, and tried to ignore the pain in her back. The standardized ergonomic chair wasn't meant for a spine that had been broken in six places. Even after the fractures had healed, even after two solid months of electrodynamic therapy, sitting straight hurt. She often ended up half-twisted in the chair, one hip forward and the other foot tucked under her.

As she listened, she held her conscious thoughts in abeyance, deliberately suppressing any impulse to translate familiar words, sinking instead into the rhythm and texture of the language, letting the back of her mind sort out its internal logic. At times, Chacarran reminded her of syncopated atonal music. At others, it disintegrated into a jumble of noises. And at others—still all too rare—something came together and she understood not just the individual phrases but the world behind them. For an instant, she could see through alien eyes. It was only a first tentative step. When she dreamed in Chacarran, then she could begin to truly understand.

A raucous blare jarred Vera out of her reverie. She cut the broadcast and stared at the data displays on her screens. There—that sudden spike on the high-gain interferometer array that she'd fine-tuned to the signature frequency of the hand lasers. Someone on the planet's surface had fired one.

The peaks on the screen scrolled off. The image faded from her retinas, to be replaced with a steady background jibble.

"Again," she muttered, as if by force of will she could make it repeat.

Nothing.

Vera's fingers darted over the touchpad, accessing the records of the last few minutes. A touch froze the crucial moment. She stared at the distinctive pattern. Another spurt of commands to the computer brought up coordinates where the hand-held laser had been discharged, as well as a map of the region. Demmerle was a border province, even as she'd suspected. She turned the name over in her mind. She thought it was not a truly Chacarran word, but not Erlindish either. She wished Sarah were here, or Chris Lao with his talent for languages.

She tapped a link to Hammadi. In a few terse words, she told him of the signal and its location.

"We've got them now!" he said.

"For all of 0.742 seconds, we did," she said.

"The shuttle can be there from Erlonn in less than half an hour." From his tone, Hammadi didn't care if the burst represented an accidental discharge, a child playing with the device, or a brief, devastating attack. He meant to move on it with full force.

"We don't know how the Erls will react—" she began.

"If they're military, I already know how they think."

Vera recognized the conviction in Hammadi's voice. Nothing would be gained by lecturing him. It didn't matter if the enemy were human, Bandari, or jellyfish, Hammadi would see the same underlying principles of motivation. And he would believe in his judgment utterly.

As a young officer, Hammadi led an elite Peacekeeping squad during the bloody, protracted civil mess in Peru. He'd dealt with terrorists and factionalists alike with ruthless finality, depending on his own instincts in the Andes and again in the aftermath of the gravity loop. His decisive action had saved all their lives, hers included.

And now? She didn't know. The planetside reports depicted the Erls as a hierarchical society, deeply respectful of authority. Leadership in such cultures—human ones, at least—was often based on superior force.

There was so much she needed to see for herself, not guess second-hand. Her own ignorance rose up before her like an unscalable wall. She wanted to shriek aloud in frustration. Caged here on *Prometheus*, she felt deaf and blind.

The only way down to the planet was by Hammadi's orders, by convincing him that he needed what she could learn there. If she couldn't control him, she must resort to persuasion.

"The laser was fired in Chacarran territory," she pointed out. "The Chacarrans will react to the invasion. Sarah's reports strongly suggest their leader is preparing for war. He might well use this incident as an excuse."

"We'll be ready to defend ourselves if he does," Hammadi said. "Even if that means suppressing local conflict."

"The pro-war position doesn't appear to be popularly supported," Vera went on. "The Miraz probes have recorded a number of instances of suppression of anti-war activities. Sarah's opinion is that the Chacarran people would support another leader, one who wants peace."

"Thanks for the information. I'll count on you for more in the days to come."

He broke the link. Vera sat staring at the map, letting the frustration jitters settle down. She couldn't feel her way through this, the way she could through a problem in chaotic dynamics or quantum theory.

She turned the broadcast back on. It was a musical program now, a single medium-pitched voice accompanied by harp and something stringed, like a viola. She tapped out the rapidly changing rhythms—five-eight, five-eight, seven-eight, five-eight, then faster, eleven-sixteen, she thought, back to five-eight. The melody line broke apart, new patterns emerged, then reformed. Something moved in her, not the familiar response to beautiful music, but subtle, cutting across the very edge of her esthetic sensibilities, or perhaps deeper than she expected, as if the singer touched a part of her she hadn't known existed. She shivered to think of a Terran shuttle, armed with wide-beam lasers, bearing down on a farm village.

I'm thinking human and that's dangerous in itself! she thought. *What I need is a Rosetta stone, something to hold in my hands, a key to understanding these people. While Hammadi will listen to me before it's too late.*

Chapter 22

Sliding and scrambling, Hayke dashed up the slope. Yes, there was his truck, right where he'd left it. It looked undamaged.

Somehow, Hayke got the engine started. The truck lumbered over ridges of hard-packed snow; its cleated tires dug, slipped, caught hold again. He sweated until the hills flattened into rolling farmland. At the crossroads, the track toward his own farm ran in one direction, while the avenue of churned slush continued straight toward Verne's. A lone milker stood in the field, bawling plaintively.

He saw the smoke more clearly now, hanging in the air like a curtain of sooty gauze.

Let the Way open before you. The words sounded hollow, a mockery. He clung to them as to a lifeline. *Tal'mur*—panic waited beyond the next heartbeat with its own madness.

Above the sound of the motor, his ears caught an echo, sharp like gunfire. A few minutes later, the farm came into view, the dark outlines of house, barn, and silo. Two transports and several lighter vehicles were spread out over the yard and surrounding fields. Figures darted here and there. Puffs of smoke erupted from turrets atop the transports.

Hayke slid the truck to a halt and crawled onto the roof for a better look. The barn was gone, daylight glimmering between the blackened timbers. The house still smoldered.

Torrey! Verne—the others!

Gunfire sputtered, quieted for a few moments, then erupted again. Hayke knew nothing of battles, had never wanted to know anything about them. But he knew better than to go charging forward now. He'd be killed for certain and be of no help to anyone. Wherever Torrey and the others were, they had sense enough to stay there. And if they were already dead— his heart stuttered—there was nothing he could do for them.

Hayke searched the yard, trying to sort out the firing. At first, the transports looked alike. It seemed to him, though, that one of them was pitted against the other and the lighter vehicles. The single transport must be the Chacarran patrol Verne had seen. Hayke felt a fool not to have realized it immediately.

Show me the Way.

The words might be empty, but this time their familiar cadence brought a certain calm. There was nothing he could do except wait for the battle to be over.

The firing continued in its strangely accented rhythm.

Then Hayke saw one of the lighter vehicles wheel about and start in his direction. Though small beside the transport, it was massive compared to his own truck. And it was armed.

Something whizzed by one ear. Hayke shoved the truck into gear, spun it around, and took off across the field. He'd never driven so fast. The truck bounced and skittered, then hit a rock buried in the snow. It rebounded, springs screeching, and tilted wildly. The wheels on the far side spun without traction. Hayke threw his body toward the uplifted side. Shots whistled by the opened window.

Something exploded under the truck. The truck jerked and dropped flat on to the driver's side. Hayke's body slammed into the door underneath. The engine emitted a high-pitched wail. Then it died.

Hayke's vision whirled as if he'd hit his head on the inside of the cab. A moment later, he was able to unlatch the topside door. It was surprisingly heavy. He cursed as he shoved it open.

The light vehicle was still coming at him. He could see the form of the driver and another in Erlind red leaning out the side, firing. Beyond them, back in the direction of the farm, a bright disc surged across the sky like a piece of the sun gone *tal'mur*. It was like nothing he'd ever seen, brilliant as fire, unbelievably silent and swift.

A Terran space ship. It must be. How could anything else move so fast?

Hayke wavered between the safety of the truck and the need to keep running. Run—here? The forest sent out a tongue of brush. Yes, he could run that far. But to leave Torrey—

Yellow rays streamed from the space craft to the farm yard.

Boom!

Hayke's vision went flat gray. He squinted, his eyes watering. The moment of blindness passed in an instant. Where the farm buildings had stood, snow boiled. Bits of wood and stone were hurled outward as tongues of flame leapt and died. Hayke covered his face with his hands. His fingers were numb, icy.

They couldn't have been in the house. It wasn't possible. Verne would surely have taken the children away.

But only if Verne had known. Only if he'd had a choice. What if something had happened to him? What if he'd taken them down into the root cellar, thinking it would be safe, and that too had been destroyed?

Meanwhile, the light vehicle slowed and turned away, back toward the farm yard. Hayke's body moved of its own accord, scrambling toward the tongue of woody copse. He ran like a terrified grommet. His feet churned the snow. He slipped and stumbled as the ground rose up in hidden mounds. Icy crust sliced his hands as he struggled up again.

Boom!

Another blast enveloped him, smaller and nearer than the first. He dove into the nearest drift. More by instinct than volition, he burrowed, throwing snow over his back. An instant later he froze, except for the heaving of his chest. He heard the distant, fading whine of the space ship.

Moments passed, fading one into the other. Hayke's breath melted the snow, and droplets trickled down the walls of the air pocket. He strained his ears, half dreading what he might hear. Once or twice, he caught a whirring sound, muted with distance. No voices came to him, or rumble of engines. He waited.

His breath slowed to normal and the snow turned damp around him. Sweat dripped down his sides under his jacket. Slowly his crest subsided.

How long had it been, a minute, an hour? No, surely not that long.

Show me the Way.

The Way to survival? The Way to truth? The Way to the moment when he'd find Torrey's charred body back at the farm house?

Torrey... Ah no, not Torrey. The words wailed through his mind, clawed at his heart.

He waited, measuring time by the insidious chill along his fingers, the cramp in the muscles of his back, the pressure of his knee against a rock. His feet tingled and went numb. He listened to the silence. He heard no sign of life from the farm yard, no rumble of engines, no voices.

Torrey...

One kind of terror overcame another. Hayke lifted his head. The snow gave way, resisted, then broke into ice-crusted fragments. He paused. No sound.

He got his feet under him and stood up. Where his truck had stood, or near enough to where he remembered it, he saw only a pile of rumpled snow and a hole in the earth like a great wound, blocking his view of the farm house.

Hayke walked to the rubble. He recognized pieces of truck, twisted metal and seat fabric, splotches of machine oil that smoked slightly. The recalcitrant thing would never start again and he missed it already.

Step by step, he approached the farm yard. In place of the buildings, a circle of churned mud spread out before him. Most of the house had lain within that circle; only a tangle of wall and roof fragments remained. Nothing moved in the eerie silence.

Gone, all of it gone. Farm house, transports, border patrol, soldiers—Erls and Chacarrans alike—wiped from the earth.

The barn had fared no better than the house. Hayke bent to pick up a piece of straw. Feathers clung to it. He saw no blood. Not yet, anyway.

But there might be hope. Every farm house had an underground chamber for storing root vegetables, cheeses, and wine. Something might have survived there, sheltered from the worst of the blast.

Hayke paced the twisted foundations, scanned the ground. Just as he took another step, his foot plunged through the floor. He staggered, arms wheeling, and caught his balance. Kneeling, he brushed away the snow and debris. Wood splintered under his fingers. He'd found the cellar door, damaged but intact.

"Verne!" he called out. "Iannen! Torrey! I'm here!"

Hayke yanked chunks of door away, the planks shredding even as he grabbed them. Below lay brick stairs and a gaping black hole. The air flowing from it had been chilled by ground frozen during long winter nights. Hayke patted his pockets, but wasn't surprised when he found neither matches nor battery light. It didn't matter. As soon as he had cleared enough space, he scrambled down the stairs.

The light from above was enough to show him the tumbled shelves, the splintered glass jars. Apple bins had tipped over, but their sealed lids had held firm. He called out again, but the frozen dirt walls gave back no answer.

Slowly Hayke felt his way along the wall to the next chamber, where wine would be kept. Here the light was dimmer, but enough to show wooden racks tilted wildly, rows of bottles reduced to glittering shards dripping dark ooze that smelled of brandy, plums, and rose-honey.

At the back of the wine room, Hayke found still another door, more by feel than by vision. A rack of bottles had fallen at a crazy angle. The smell of pear wine hung heavy on the air. The cross-bars, shattered, stuck out like a spray of splinters. Beyond it, he glimpsed a low opening, like a horizontal, dirt-lined mine shaft.

His heartbeat quickened and his crest moved in ripples. Some of these old farm houses, especially those owned by Wayfolk, had escape tunnels. Even those of the Faith had dug them during the last great war with Erlind.

Hayke could barely see the opening in the dim light. Moving with care, he got down on his knees and ran his fingers over the edges, wincing whenever he brushed against a shard of glass or a wooden sliver.

Only a few inches beyond the entrance, his probing fingers met the pitted hardness of brick. He inched as far as he could and reached out, tracing the rough-edged contours. He grasped the edge of one chunk and tugged. Nothing happened. His hand came away covered with eye-stinging dust. He tried another piece, a smaller one this time. With a grating sound, the brick budged enough to shift everything above it. A low rumbling sound made him look up. Lumps of brick and mortar dust rained down on him. Hacking and coughing, he crawled away from the opening. It was no good continuing the search in that direction. It took a few moments before he could see again.

Hayke sat back on his heels. No inspiration rose to his mind, no sense of the Way opening before him. He'd have to make this decision for himself, where to go from here. His thoughts plodded on, one slow step at a time.

Perhaps a branch of the tunnel led to the barn, but that was no help now. Where then? There was only one place that would offer any kind of real shelter, and that was the spit of woodland. He would check there first, and if he was wrong, he would go back to his own farm for lantern and shovel and try the tunnel again.

Hayke headed for the nearest copse at the fastest pace he could sustain. He'd been in shock, he realized, and now it was wearing off. The sun moved overhead; brilliance sheeted off the snow.

He reached the first stragglers of brush and rock, thrust out through the smooth white surface. A little way beyond, the snow layer thinned and the earth broke through in patches of mottled brown. The air carried the sharpness of wet, moldy leaves.

Hayke cast about for anything that might hide the tunnel exit, but found nothing. He called out, but only silence answered him. The cold wore on him. His feet turned into knobs of unfeeling flesh that he thrust through the snow again and again. He thought of Torrey, hiding and frightened, thought of Felde waiting back at the farm house, not knowing what had happened. His heart contracted around an icy spike.

He came to a standstill. His breath burst from his lungs in cloudy puffs that blew away in an instant. He felt the woods around him as a presence. Trees seemed to lean toward him, a mixture of scraggly old growth, too twisted to be of any use but firewood, and newer, straighter trees not yet marked for the axe.

A few paces away, a grommet sat on its haunches on a rocky outcropping. Its cup-shaped ears flared in his direction, slit nostrils quivering as it tested his scent. The movement of its breathing sent iridescent ripples across its pale winter coat. Hayke could almost hear the tapping of its heart against the delicate cage of its ribs. He dared not move, not even a finger, lest he send it scampering away. The little animal reminded him of Felde's favorite story of the grommet who sang such wonderful music to the stars that when he died, they could not bear to lose him.

Behind Hayke, snow slipped from a tree branch to the ground, the faintest of noises, no more than a whisper. Yet when he looked back at the rock face, the grommet was gone.

When he could draw breath, he called out again.

"Verne! Torrey! Iannen! It's Hayke!"

This time, he heard a muffled response.

Chapter 23

A figure stepped from behind the nearest boulder, for a moment shadowed against the whitened sky. In silhouette, it lifted a firearm up to aiming position. Hayke recognized it as a pellet rifle, like the one Rosen had kept for frightening off scavengers or killing livestock that were too sick to heal.

"Verne! It's me!" Hayke stumbled forward.

"Dimmie, Dimmie!" Torrey's voice pierced the air like the cry of a bird.

Hayke tripped, landed on his knees, tried to heave himself to his feet. Suddenly, his legs wouldn't move. Torrey collided with Hayke and threw his arms around his neck.

Hayke gasped for breath. He couldn't think, could only feel the trembling of the child's body against his. He closed his eyes. After a moment, he stood up, holding Torrey tight against his side.

Verne walked toward him, carrying the rifle. Greasy soot clumped the fur on his cheeks. His crest jutted out in all directions. A few paces behind came Adso and the other children, eerily silent. Verne's partner, Iannen, held the youngest in his arms. There was too much white in his eyes.

Still holding Torrey by the hand, Hayke went to Verne and put his arm around him, then Iannen. Even through the thick layers of clothing, their bodies felt like eggshell bound together by wire. When they'd been children together, Iannen had been the best athlete; even after bearing three of their four children, he was strongly-built and agile. Now he seemed withered, a winter tree.

"The farm," Verne said in a rusty voice, "what about the farm?"

Hayke's crest rippled and Iannen, seeing it, made a small, strangled sound. Hayke held out his hands and said, "You'd better come back to my house."

"I want to see," said Verne.

Hayke thought of offering to take the children around the long way, but there was something in Verne's tone, in the very texture of his body as he began trudging back toward the farm, that kept him silent.

We all need to see. To understand what's happened, to make real what we've lost.

They made their way along the spit of woodland, following Hayke's track. Verne nodded when Hayke told him what the Erls had said, about taking back the border territory they thought of as theirs.

Verne told the story of their escape in terse, emotionless phrases. When Torrey had come rushing up with the warning, Verne had not believed him. Only when they heard the transports did Iannen bundle the children up in their warmest clothing and rush them down into the cellar. Verne had taken the rifle, his only weapon, and climbed to the top of the barn. He'd seen not only the Erlind caravan but a Chacarran border patrol.

"Why did they have to fight *here*? Why couldn't they just have moved—over to one of the pastures, the road, anywhere?" His eyes, bleak as the treeless fields, searched Hayke's.

"The Erls didn't blow up the farm," Iannen broke in. "Why would the Terrans do such a thing—turn on their own allies?"

"We thought," Hayke said slowly, "they were human like us."

Torrey clung to Hayke as they paced the hole gouged by the Terran weapon. No one spoke, but once in a while the children whimpered or someone picked up and then let fall a shard of wood. One of the barnfowl had miraculously survived to scratch in the rubble.

"There's nothing to be done here," Hayke said as gently as he could. "Come away, to my place. In a day or two, we can fetch the supplies from the cellar."

"The Terrans—how could they do such a thing?" Iannen asked again. His hands moved, twisting the ends of his scarf. "We might have been in the house! The children.."

After a moment, Verne said, "I think I know why the Terrans destroyed the farm. They wanted no witnesses."

A vision rose up in Hayke's mind, the plaza in Miraz strewn with bodies like stalks of mown hay, like carelessly scattered toys. His crest shivered right down to his spine.

The first thing was to get to the village. They must be warned and a message sent to Nantaz, the regional capital. The truck was gone. Hayke had another one in the barn, although it needed repair. The tractor would be slow and he'd have to keep to the main road. On the old pony, he could take the shortcut, following milker trails along the hillsides. The beast would be no faster than walking, but it could carry more, food and spare clothing.

The thought of being separated even overnight, from Felde and Torrey sent a jolt of physical pain through Hayke. If something happened here while he was gone, if the Terrans came back, could he do any more than Verne?

Verne was more likely to shoot. Perhaps in these days, that was not a bad thing.

Against the Erls, yes, Hayke answered himself, but what good would a pellet rifle be against Terran weapons? He imagined himself with the rifle, aiming it at another person, firing. He pictured blood pooling around splintered bone. Pictured the wounded earth that had been Verne's farmyard.

He felt as if part of his soul were bleeding away into the snow.

Felde had spent the rest of the morning finishing the baking. The house was warm and fragrant with the aroma of new-baked bread. The familiar smells enveloped Hayke as he moved around the kitchen, making hot brew for everyone. Still clutching the rifle, Verne lowered himself to a bench.

"Please, let me help," Iannen said. He detached himself from his two youngest children, wrapped one of Rosen's old aprons around his waist, and began slicing up the still-warm loaves. A few moments later, every child in the house was contentedly munching bread smeared with honey and brambleberry jam.

Hayke poured two mugs of root brew and sat down beside Verne. "It will be dark soon."

Verne's head jerked up. He took the offered mug, but did not let go of the rifle.

Hayke felt the house around him, the fragile stillness of the yard outside. Was any place safe? Was anything permanent?

They could have come here instead of Verne's farm. I could have lost this place that Rosen and I shared, gone in an instant.

He reached out to take Verne's hand and was surprised how cold it felt. "You and Iannen cannot leave the children. Someone must tell the village, and it must be me."

Iannen's eyes softened. "We will take care of Torrey and Felde. They are as dear to us as our own."

The hard part, Hayke thought, would be convincing the children to stay behind.

The three of them cuddled together on the big bed, Felde burying his head against Hayke's chest. "I have to go away, little one."

"I don't want you to go," Felde said.

"I don't want to leave. But sometimes even we big people have to do things we don't want to do."

Torrey, curled against Hayke's other side, trembled. "It's because of the Terrans and what they did to Adso's farm."

Hayke held his breath for a long moment. "Yes. That."

Felde pushed himself up on one elbow. His eyes glittered. "Why did the Terrans blow up Adso's farm?"

"I don't know," Hayke said. "Perhaps they didn't think of the people who would be hurt."

Torrey, for once, said nothing. Felde thought for a moment. "Then you must tell them, Dimmie. About how sad Adso is, and all the animals that have no home. You must ask them not to do it again."

If only they would believe me. If only it were that simple.

"Don't be stupid, grub," said Torrey, his lip curling. "If Dim goes to the Terran place, it won't be to ask them for anything. It'll be to *make* them stop."

Felde looked up at Hayke and said in a troubled voice, "You're going to fight the Terrans, Dimmie?"

"No, no." Hayke stroked the child's fur. "I like your idea much better."

"But, Dimmie!" Torrey cried. "That won't work! They'll just laugh at you!"

Hayke suppressed a smile. If being thought a fool could turn back the Erls or stop the Terrans from blowing up someone else's farm, he'd gladly make a fool of himself.

"I don't intend to fight anyone," he said. "It's not our Way. And besides—" remembering the fallen bodies at the plaza and the gaping hole where Verne's house had stood, "—I'm not sure it would be any use."

Chapter 24

Three days later, Hayke returned from the village. The pony quickened its pace as the farmyard came into view. In the inner pasture, a herd of milkers stood at the hayricks, lowing plaintively. The blue-black hides of Verne's beasts alternated with Hayke's own duns. The older children must have been up early, rounding them up. Hayke noticed that the pasture gate had been mended.

Felde, playing in the yard with one of Verne's middle children, saw Hayke first, gave a shriek and came running toward him. Torrey and Adso emerged from the barn, followed by Verne, a moment later. Machine grease covered Verne's hands and he wore a tool belt. He'd already begun work on the old truck.

Hayke hugged all the children in turn and clasped Verne's shoulder. "How's everyone?"

"A bit calmer. Iannen's in the kitchen with the little ones."

Hayke nodded, watching Torrey and Adso lead the pony off to the barn. Home lessons were another sign of life's ordinary rhythms re-establishing themselves.

"What's the news from town?" Verne asked.

Hayke wrapped one arm around Felde and walked toward the house. "Everyone's concerned about you. They're setting up their own patrol."

"For all the good it will do," Verne said.

Once inside, Hayke told the rest of his story. When he'd notified the police in Nantaz, he had been met with skepticism. No one had called him an outright liar, but no one else had seen the convoy. The warder chief suggested that the Erls had made a foray for their own domestic political reasons and then had returned home. At Hayke's insistence, however, the chief agreed to investigate and then send word to Miraz. Everyone was talking about the recent bombing deaths in Miraz, the mayor among them, and that news overshadowed Hayke's report.

"If those fools in the village won't believe you, let them all Burn," Verne said. "Them and the Erls and the demon Terrans with them!"

Verne stomped off to the barn, where he and Hayke spent the

afternoon, until the light failed them, working on the truck.

Hayke arose before sunup the next morning, feet lashing out in panic, heart pounding, the fur along his neck ruffling. His eyes darted about the room. The house seemed undisturbed. Torrey and Felde, who'd slept in the big bed with him, lay curled together, breathing quietly.

For a moment Hayke's vision went blank and he saw only the fading images of his dream. Once again he looked down at the plaza in Miraz, awed and sickened by the sight of so many fallen bodies.

Miraz.

Hayke sat up, blinking, ears straining. It came again, the faint noise that had woken him. Someone was moving about in the kitchen. Moving slowly so as not to disturb the children. Hayke slipped out of bed. At the hallway, he paused, listening. He recognized the muffled thump of the oven door closing. A yeasty smell wafted through the air.

In the kitchen, Iannen looked up from a sinkful of soapy water. He wore one of Rosen's old aprons, dusted with flour. A dozen loaves, beautifully browned, sat cooling on the table. Each top was scored in a delicate wheat-grain pattern, quite different from Hayke's unadorned, utilitarian baking.

"I made enough, I think," Iannen said.

"What we have is yours," Hayke said, repeating the old Wayfolk hospitality proverb.

Thanks to Verne's mechanical ingenuity, the old truck was drivable by midday. Hayke and Verne set out for the farm. Iannen stayed behind, keeping the older children at their lessons once their chores were done. Hayke said nothing, for it would not harm the children and it might do Iannen good.

All through the morning and the slow drive to Verne's farm, Hayke could not dispel the memory of his waking dream. He did not want to believe his Way led back to Miraz. He most emphatically did not want to leave Felde and Torrey, nor could he see any way to bring them with him.

Retrieving the salvageable food from the cellar proved more difficult than any of them anticipated. Last night's snowfall blanketed every familiar trace. Only the gaping entrance to the root cellar broke the smooth white surface.

"It's as if we had never lived here," Verne whispered.

In the cellar, they found that much of the food that had spilled from broken containers had frozen overnight and could be repacked.

The two adults carried load after load up to the truck. Hayke had just climbed out of the cellar with a crate of redroots when he noticed what

Torrey and Adso were doing. They'd taken a break from hauling cheeses and had set up a target range, snowballs piled one on the other into towers. Torrey placed a stone in his leather sling and began circling it.

"*Jow!*" The topmost snowball exploded under the impact.

"Die, Terran demon!" Adso cried.

As Torrey turned toward his friend, Hayke noted the crest raised in a central ridge, the curve of the cheek under its downy winter fur, the set of the shoulders, the fingers loosely, almost carelessly reaching for another bit of rubble.

"Don't worry," Torrey told Adso, "we'll get them. We'll get them all."

Hayke's arms froze around the crate and his feet rooted to the stone step. Part of him wanted to rush over to his child, this child he had carried within his own body, who had once been one with his own flesh, wanted to make him realize what he was saying, forbid him to ever speak of killing, explain to him this was never the Way—

Violence had burst upon their lives; hatred prowled but a step behind. There was no escape now, no matter what he said, what rules or instructions he handed down.

Maybe Felde had the right idea. Maybe I should just go to the Terrans and ask them to stop.

They saw the soldiers from a distance, three carriers of them surrounding the farmyard. Even though Chacarran pennons flew in plain view, Hayke felt a sudden dread. From the back seat, Torrey and Adso pointed and cried out. Verne drew in his breath, but said nothing beyond, "Hurry."

The old truck wheezed and strained under its load. Hayke felt the tires slipping, cut back the speed. Verne's hand closed around his shoulder.

Soldiers moved to block their way. They held their rifles ready, to be noticed, to be used. Hayke's crest shivered and his mouth went dry.

"There's nothing to be afraid of," Verne said, as if trying to convince himself. "They're our own people."

As they drew closer, Hayke noticed the white sashes tied around the arms of many of the soldiers, although he knew they might not be from the same clan. Many professional soldiers changed their religious affiliation to Oni, Seventh Aspect of the god and once thought to be Ultimate, before Fard the Prophet was incorporated as the Eighth. The older attribute of Oni had been vitality, but now was victory, a suitable blessing for a soldier. An image flickered through Hayke's mind, the white of victory pitted against the black of the Prophet's change. Black for change, black for insanity.

But, he reminded himself, in the ways of the Faith, the inversion of victory was blindness.

Hayke brought the truck to a halt. "I live here," he told the one who challenged him. "You trespass unasked on my land."

"Hayke? Hayke-az-Midrien?" Before Hayke could do more than gesture acknowledgement, the soldiers bustled him out of the truck and into the house. Not through the back door to the kitchen, which had been the center of warmth and activity when Rosen was alive, but the draftier front room. He heard Verne's shouted protest at being kept behind.

Hayke took in the scene like a museum tableau. The officer standing in the center, uniform pressed into crisp lines, white sash shimmering in the indoor light, eyes narrowed as he turned to face the disturbance. Iannen sat in a chair from the kitchen, crest standing out in clumps, hands grasping the seat of the chair as if to keep himself upright. The children piled on the old sofa, holding on to each other. The soldiers standing at the doors to the kitchen and hallway. The light reflected on the metal barrels of their rifles. The house smelled wrong—the sweat of strangers, pellet explosive, and leather polish—things that did not belong there.

Felde scrambled to his feet and bolted for Hayke. Hayke shoved aside the nearest soldier, stooped and caught Felde, held the whip-taut body tight against him. His heart shuddered behind his breasts; bitterness flooded his mouth.

The officer snapped out a question. One of his soldiers said, "It's the one who saw the bombing. He just got back from the village—"

"How dare you break into my home, frighten my children and my neighbors?"

Hayke screamed, hardly knowing what he was saying. *Tal'deh* crept like fire along his nerves. His vision swam with its heat. "Haven't they been through enough? I won't have you making things any worse for them! You have no right to be here! Get out!"

"Calm down," the officer said, raising both hands in a conciliatory gesture. "We aren't here to hurt anyone. There's been a misunderstanding—"

"No misunderstanding at all!" Hayke's pulse hammered in his skull, each beat a fiery throb.

Tal'spirë, he prayed, though the words slipped through his mind like water, *surrender to grace*.

"I'm telling you—all of you—get out of my house and off my land!"

"We're here for your protection—"

"Protection be torched!" Hayke put Felde down and pulled the child behind him as he took a step toward the officer. "You're worse than the Erls, marching in here, terrifying our children, harassing the very people you're supposed to defend! We want nothing more to do with any of you!"

"Be reasonable, friend. We're not going anywhere, not until we've done what we came here for. Our mission is the safety of everyone. We had a report phoned in last night from your village, a very alarming report, and we need to know what happened yesterday at your neighbor's farm. Were you a witness? Can you tell us what you saw?"

The words reached Hayke even through his bone-shaking fury. What the officer asked wasn't unreasonable. Hayke smoothed his crest back with one hand. His hair felt like ice.

"I'll talk to you," he said. "But I want my people safe first. I want you and your soldiers out of my house."

The officer gave a series of orders and immediately the soldiers began filing out.

Hayke turned to the officer. "We can talk in the barn or one of your carriers, I don't care. I just can't—" he hesitated, stumbling over the words. "I want it to be over."

"Friend," the officer said in a surprisingly gentle voice, "this war is far from over. It's only now beginning. Maybe what you tell us may help us win it. Remember whose side we're on."

Whose side you're on? Hayke shuddered as he followed the officer outside. *Or whose side I'm on?*

Whatever the officer did with the information, it would be for military purposes only. No one would go to the Terrans and ask them not to frighten children. No one would count the cost of Torrey's innocence. No one would bear witness to what had happened here, or that it had been the Chacarran army spattering blood on the snow in Verne's yard, not just the Erls and the alien Terrans.

No one... unless he did it himself. But who would he go to? Who would listen, who would care?

Hayke saw himself once more in the plaza at Miraz. His memories were of summer's gentle heat. It would be different now, the trees bleak against the frozen sky.

Tal'spirë, he had prayed for. *Surrender. Grace.*

The Way had opened up before him. He could not doubt that now. The repeated visions of the plaza had been harbingers of the call. The terror and grief of the last few days, standing before the Erlind convoy, hiding in the snow, searching the ruined farm yard, all of these seemed like pale ghosts of fears. For the first time, Hayke was deeply, bone-shakingly afraid.

Chapter 25

At the end of the day, Ferro left the embassy for his favorite bar. The wind blustered and the sky had gone thick and gray. Inside the embassy itself, a clammy chill seeped through stone and layers of wool clothing. By late afternoon, Ferro wanted nothing more than to curl up with a mug of hot spiced wine. The bar was congenial and conveniently located, as well as the place where he checked for coded messages from Miraz. He'd received only a few of these and didn't expect one today.

So it was a surprise when he found the message tucked between his wine mug and the thick crockery saucer used in Erlind restaurants. As he brought the mug to his mouth, he folded the note into his pocket. The bar grew more crowded as Erls, mostly clerks and a few professionals, dropped by to exchange gossip and fortify themselves for the journey home.

Ferro sauntered back to the ill-lit washroom. In damp weather, as now, it smelled faintly of mildew. He turned on the faucet—it didn't matter which one, as they both dispensed only cold water—and read the note. It was in code, of course, based on an ancient Chacarran epic poem, yet from the syntax and nuances, it clearly had come from Kreste himself. For long moments, he stood there, while the water splashed in the basin, holding the piece of paper in both hands. He had known this would come. He had just not expected it to be so sudden.

Situation critical. Return at once.

Ferro shredded the note and flushed it down the bowl. The tone of the note disturbed him as much as its contents. In all the years Ferro had known him, Kreste had never acted rashly, never done anything without careful consideration. He was, if anything, too cautious.

The street outside looked reassuringly normal, revealing no sign of impending cataclysm. It had started raining again. Half-frozen drops fell in spurts, blown by a gusting wind. People hurried along, heads lowered, faces hidden under hoods and umbrellas. Ferro pulled up his collar and tucked his satchel under his arm. He would return to his quarters at the embassy, pick up the currency he'd left in Dorlin's safe, pack a satchel of clothing, and be on a railcar to Miraz by dinnertime.

Collaborators

With his head bowed against the pelting rain, Ferro could see only a short distance in front of him. When the pedestrian in front of him, a worker in a heavy woolen coat, stopped suddenly, Ferro bumped into him. They were half a block away from the embassy and a marshall van blocked the street just ahead, disrupting both foot and motor traffic.

Crest ruffling, Ferro elbowed his way forward. He was stopped by an Erlonn marshall a few yards from the entrance to the embassy. The next moment, the iron gates were flung open and a handful of marshalls rushed through. They wore the crimson badges of the ruling House of Ar.

Ferro stared in shock. The marshalls half-dragged, half-carried someone in their midst. It was Ambassador Dorlin. He wore only his indoor clothing and his wrists were manacled together. He was shouting in outrage, demanding diplomatic immunity. The marshalls paid no attention as they shoved him into the van.

Other marshalls pushed the crowd back, separating them into smaller groups, deftly isolating anyone who showed signs of contagious panic. A portable loudspeaker blared out for people to stay clear of the area. Under the mute obedience, Ferro sensed confusion and uneasiness, but no taint of *tal'deh*.

Just inside the gates, a Chacarran guard lay curled on his side, whether dead or unconscious, Ferro couldn't tell. He caught a glimpse of the secretary as he was dragged away, along with the young aide. The secretary stumbled along with a bewildered expression, glancing around as if appealing for help. Instinct sent Ferro dodging back into the crowd before he could be recognized.

It was all Ferro could do to keep himself from bolting outright, but that would only draw attention. He clung to that thought, the need to appear calm. His crest hairs pushed against his heavy knitted scarf. As he forced himself to walk at the same pace as the others, to blend in, he caught bits of conversation, mild curiosity. This was only a small item of excitement to mark an otherwise dreary day. He told himself, *This is how I should appear to react.*

Ma, he intoned silently to evoke the holy presence of the Sixth Aspect. All the while, he struggled to make sense of what he'd seen. Something had happened, something dire enough to cause the Erlind authorities to seize the embassy, against all international custom. It was only chance and a taste for spiced wine that had kept him free.

Ferro scanned the news sheets displayed under the vendors' awnings, but the headlines had not changed since the morning. Local news, an exhibit at the Erlonn Terran Compound museum, the pairing between members of two large mercantile families in Erseth, more accusations of suppression of free speech in Chacarre.

Keeping to the smaller streets, he headed toward the railcar station. He dared not go back, not even to the bar. He had to get out of Erlonn as quickly as possible. Nor could he depend on anyone else; anyone willing to help him might be incriminated by that very act.

His resources were limited to what he had with him. He did a quick mental inventory as he hurried along. He carried his passport with him everywhere, safe in the inner buttoned pocket of his coat. His clothing passed well enough in the city, but outside, even in the towns, he would stand out. It would be better if he could change it for Erlind garments.

He had some money, for which he fervently blessed Maas, for money was worth a great deal more than charisma. Perhaps it would be enough to get him to the border. If the worst had happened, if Erlind was on the brink of war, then the Chacarran border would be doubly guarded and anyone attempting to pass it would have to show his passport. If his name showed up on any list of people to be held and questioned...

It was dangerous to dwell too long on that possibility.

Ferro took a measure of comfort in the anonymity of the Erlonn railcar station. Huge and modern, it served as a hub of transportation throughout Erlind. Now more than ever, everything in it struck Ferro as glossy and over-bright, from the glass-paneled entrance to the abstract mosaic murals, metallic turnstiles, and tile flooring. Every sound seemed magnified and distorted, individual voices unrecognizable. At this hour, commuters from nearby towns jammed the platforms. The faces around Ferro looked tired in the shadows cast by the blue-white overhead lights. Few of his neighbors met his eyes or appeared to take any interest in him. So far, he'd made the right choice.

He paused to read the boards announcing international destinations. Although he was expecting it, it was still a shock to see all the routes to Chacarre canceled. Keeping his crest lowered, he took his place in the line for domestic routes. Around him, voices and footsteps blended with the blare of the announcing system. His head twanged with the racket, and a distant throbbing began at the base of his skull.

The person in front of him shuffled forward, pushing a battered suitcase along the mud-tracked floor with one foot. Behind him, two traders from Joosten attempted a conversation, their voices loud enough for Ferro to overhear their complaints about the Erlind railcar service.

He had enough money to purchase a ticket to Er-Anvers, near the Joosten border. He knew the area slightly; he'd vacationed in Joosten as a child, mostly in Gallivar along the Ice Sea, where fishing ships plied the narrow channel to the Empty Isles. The country around Er-Anvers, called simply Anvers on the other side of the border, was wooded and hilly. With any luck, he could find a way of getting across the border unseen and then to Gallivar, the Joosten capital, where Chacarre maintained a consulate.

Ferro spent another two hours in the Erlonn station while waiting for the railcar to Er-Anvers, hours slumped in a bench well away from the stream of the traffic, hiding his features and attempting to appear half asleep.

Wait, Ferro told himself for the hundredth time. *There's nothing to be done now except wait.*

He found his seat on the railcar in a compartment that was at least twenty years old but scrupulously clean, next to a stern-faced oldster in a hooded coat, Anvers style, neatly patched and worn to shininess at the seams. Blue bands encircled the sleeves, marking him as Bavarite. Many of his countryfolk followed the Fifth Aspect for protection against the demonic inversion of natural disaster, living as they did in the Drowned Lands.

Ferro murmured an apology as he took his seat beside the window. The oldster's crest relaxed. "You are Chacarran, then?"

For a moment Ferro feared he'd absent-mindedly lapsed into Chacarran, but no, they were both speaking Erlindish. The Anversian had picked up his faint accent. Bird of Heaven, he'd have to keep his mouth shut. Or was he simply overreacting to a chance comment?

The railcar soon filled with Erls and a sprinkling of people from various of the Joosten cities—Talinn as well as Anvers and Gallivar. The smells of wet wool and the ubiquitous boiled callet hung in the air. Outside, a horn blared once, then again.

Ferro glanced at his companion, but the Anversian had taken out a much-worn book and held it up a few inches from his nose. He wondered if it were a wise decision to go through Joosten. Chacarrans were not always treated warmly by Joosteners. The province of Anvers had been annexed by Erlind in one of its expansionist phases and its residents had looked to Chacarre for help. After the Last Great War ground to a halt, the province had been split as part of the peace treaty, and the old city renamed. Some Anversians regarded Chacarre as a betrayer rather than an ally and all of them wanted nothing more to do with Chacarran-Erlind politics. They would, however, gladly trade with either of their neighbors if there were sufficient profit to be made.

The railcar began to move, at first in starts and bumps as it threaded its way along criss-crossing rails, out of the station, and past factories that looked even dingier than usual under the heavy gray skies. Then it picked up smoothness and speed, leaving the industrial areas for outlying storehouses and scattered residential areas that were once villages.

The railcar glided clear of the city, moving through flat farmland. Slush-drenched stubble, mulch from last autumn's harvest, covered the earth. Farmhouses stood out in stark relief against the day's last light, huddling in on themselves underneath clusters of leafless trees.

Ferro surrendered to the swaying movement of the railcar and rested his head against the seat back. The noise of the other passengers subsided as the journey got underway in earnest and darkness settled on the countryside. The Anversian switched on the lamp and every few minutes would turn a page with a whispery sound.

Unexpectedly, Ferro remembered being a child, curled up in bed next to his own parent, listening to the same slow rhythm of pages turning, the movement of fingers tracing the lines of print, a voice murmuring a phrase here and there. He would fight to stay awake as long as he could but then, as now, his eyelids fluttered closed, his thoughts began to drift.

Ferro woke up sometime later as the Anversian stood up. The railcar was slowing, jerking and rocking, the brakes screeching. Snow fell in a light dusting, brilliant against the velvet darkness in the lights of the station ahead. He could barely make out the ghostly shapes of buildings.

"Where are we?" he asked.

"Er-Anvers," said the oldster, gathering up the wicker hamper stowed below his seat. "May Bavar preserve it."

Ferro nodded. He trudged off, following the general direction of the other passengers. The station here was small, with low ceilings and antiquated light fixtures, but the age-cracked tile floors were freshly scrubbed. Despite the late hour, food booths did a brisk business. After visiting the washroom, Ferro spent a few coins on hot tea and the local specialty, a flat wheaten bun stuffed with apples and onions. The buns were lukewarm and the apples mealy, but he ate three of them.

Ferro found a local street map tacked to a post beside a railcar schedule. Northeast lay the border itself, with main crossings marked at the railcar tracks and the major road. What he needed was a secondary road, maybe a dirt trail, where he could slip through. He worked out a likely route and decided to start for it, using what was left of the night as a cover, rather than wait until day and try to trade his Chacarran coat for something less noticeable. Once he was in Joosten, it wouldn't matter. He headed for the street exit, passing the red-uniformed guard standing just inside the door.

Snow drifted from the night sky, coating the slush that had piled up around the twin fountains. Ferro remembered seeing those same fountains in summer, the sprays of water dancing in the clear northern light, surrounded by beds of sky-on-the-ground. Now the fountains stood lifeless, like weirdly shadowed sculptures.

"Hallo there! Ferro!"

Ferro turned slowly, half-afraid the voice had come from the marshalls at the gate. The person striding toward him, face shadowed against the lights, wore ordinary clothing, Erlind cut but of good quality. He carried an expensive-looking satchel.

"It *is* Ferro, isn't it?"

Ferro still couldn't place the voice. Then the stranger moved so the street lights fell full on his features. Instantly Ferro recognized Ysanomeret, one of the sub-directors of the Erlind Academy of Science. He'd been present at the reception when Ferro had gotten his first introduction to the Terrans.

"What are you doing here? I thought you were in Erlonn!" Ferro cried, at the same moment Ysanomeret said very much the same thing.

The Erl laughed and clapped Ferro on the shoulder. "I just got in from Gallivar, a scientific presentation at their university. What a trip, the weather was terrible!"

"Yes, very bad for this time of year," Ferro said. Out of the corner of his eye, he noticed the marshalls had stepped through the door and seemed to be watching him. His crest rose in jagged ripples, quickly masked. "That's all very interesting, but if you'll excuse me now, I'm quite tired from my journey."

"Then you must spend the night with me. I'm breaking my own journey here and I often bring home guests from Erlonn."

"This really isn't necessary. I had already made plans to stay in a hotel," Ferro lied.

"No, no, I must insist." The Erl drew closer and lowered his voice. "Besides, the hotels here are not the best. I could not allow you to inflict one upon yourself, when I might have the honor of hosting you. I'm sure that were our circumstances reversed, you would do the same."

The Erl took Ferro's arm firmly and led him toward the curb, where a private car had just pulled up. It would be impossible now for Ferro to free himself without attracting attention. He could feel the eyes of the red-uniformed marshalls, taking in his every move, alert for suspicious behavior.

Images burst upon Ferro's memory. The fountains were no longer draped in silent snow, but splashed beneath a cloud-misted sky. Passengers in loose pastel robes strolled between them, scattering crumbs for the water doves. Ferro had been twelve, on a holiday trip with his parents. He didn't remember the exact circumstances, only the sudden appearance of angry-sounding people in crimson uniforms. He had forgotten the experience, but now it all came flooding back, the questions, shot at him in a language he barely understood and could not speak, the way their crests had stood straight up, knife-edged, making them seem even larger and more terrifying.

He remembered, too, the shrill sound of his parents' voices and their faces as they were dragged away from him, the sulfur-edged reek of reflex terror in the air, the long ride to the station, the hours waiting, not knowing what had happened to them. Years later, his parents had told him that a child of one of the wealthy families, perhaps even Ysanomeret's own, had been kidnapped by a rival House and later found dead.

Even as his body moved in the unconscious creation of a role, an innocent traveler, friend to this well-placed Erl, Ferro thought, *I am no longer a child. I am an adult, and no longer subject to a child's fears.*

He had a great deal more to be afraid of now than he had then.

"My thanks for your hospitality," he said as he slid into the rear of the car. The Erl sat beside him and gestured the driver to move on. They made their way down a street that had been swept clean of snow. "I didn't know your family lived in Er-Anvers. Somehow I'd gotten the impression you were Erlonn natives."

Ysanomeret leaned back in the upholstered seat, gesturing expansively. "Yes, I can see how you'd think that. I've always thought of Erlonn as my second home. This branch divided about forty years ago. I visit whenever I'm able."

Ferro noticed that the Erl hadn't mentioned his exact business here, or asked Ferro what he was doing so far from Erlonn.

"Winter travel is so dreary and exhausting. Are you going on tomorrow or can you spare a few days with us?" The Erl seemed to be looking out the window. They were rapidly leaving the center of the town.

Ferro kept his crest tight against his skull. "I'm afraid I must be leaving first thing tomorrow morning."

"Ah, well. At least, you'll have a good night's rest."

They drove on, passing through the outlying suburbs. The clustered buildings of the city gave way to estates surrounded by fields, softly luminous with the snow. The land rose into sloping hills, broken occasionally by patches of conifer forest. A pungent, ice-edged smell filled the car. By Ferro's sense of direction, they headed due north, bringing him closer to the border. His coat, warm enough by city standards, would be barely adequate here. His shoes would not hold out for long.

A short time later, the driver turned off the main road and up a winding path. Even from the distance, the enclose reminded Ferro of a fortress. The architectural style was clearly Erlind, the snow-dusted carvings, the slope of the roof and placement of the gables, the proportions of the high narrow windows, like archers' slits. By its newness, it had been built since the formal annexation of this area a century ago. A sallyport, large enough for a medium-sized van, pierced one wall. Tire tracks marked the snow, although no other cars were in sight.

They emerged from the tunnel into a brightly-lit courtyard. A gate, barred like a portcullis, slid across the opening behind them. Ferro shivered at the sound. A couple, swathed in animal furs, came out of the central door and gestured their greetings.

Ysanomeret introduced the couple as distant cousins of his parents. Ferro followed as they bustled Ysanomeret inside.

In all the times Ferro had visited Erlonn, he'd never been inside an enclose. Inns, apartments, government buildings, museums, the living quarters at the embassy, yes, but never a private family residence.

The central hall blazed with light and heat from an enormous fireplace. Enough food for a dozen sat on chafing trays. It was clear to Ferro that the old couple had been waiting for their young cousin to arrive, to fuss over him and ply him with questions about the rest of the family.

Claiming fatigue from his journey, Ferro excused himself. Ysanomeret insisted on ushering Ferro to his room, up two flights of stairs and along a complicated series of corridors.

When Ysanomeret left, the door clicked shut, and Ferro wondered if he were locked in. The room was small, its ceiling angled under the steeply gabled roof. It had the smell of a place that hadn't been used much, although it was clean.

Ferro checked the door and found it opened easily. Then he removed his outer clothing, tucked his passport and what was left of his money into his undershirt, and slid under the thick quilt. Through the walls, he could hear distant voices, but outside the window lay a dense, brooding quiet.

Chapter 26

Ferro opened his eyes. Moonlight glimmered in silver bars through gaps in the shuttered windows. It was so quiet, he could hear the individual pulsations of his heart, yet something had awakened him.

He pulled on his clothes and tried the door latch. It wouldn't open. He lifted the handle more firmly, but something blocked it from the outside.

How could he have been such a fool, to let himself be taken prisoner? A dozen clues should have warned him.

But why? What could Ysanomeret, an official with the Science Academy, want with him? Why lock him in?

The window was high and narrow, shuttered from the outside. If he were desperate enough, he might be able to reach it, but he wasn't sure he could work his way through. Even with the sheets as a rope, the drop to the ground would be tricky.

He switched on the bedside lamp and carried it to the door, bending to examine the latch more closely. From the amount of play in the lever, he guessed that an object had been used to jam it from the other side. Memory suggested several chairs, stiff and unused-looking, along the corridor.

In the morning, they would come for him. Red uniforms like the ones who dragged away Dorlin. Red uniforms like—

He was no longer a child, Ferro told himself, subject to a child's fearful memories. Silently he appealed to Maas, although perhaps Kesh's endurance or the victory promised by Oni might be more useful.

Ferro ran both hands over his crest, forcibly smoothing it. There *had* to be a way out. The room wasn't intended as a prison; he was supposed to be an unsuspecting guest. Ysanomeret had been surprised to see him so far from Erlonn. Then something had happened in the middle of the night—a phone call perhaps, news of the arrests in Erlonn—and Ysanomeret had decided to make sure Ferro stayed where he was.

Ferro was not going to be there in the morning. He was going to be halfway to Joosten, even if it meant prying the Faithless door off its hinges with his teeth.

He took the lamp back to the door for another look. As he guessed, the hinges were on the inside. It would be possible, although not easy, to remove them. If he wasn't careful, the door might fall on him with enough noise to raise the household. As he studied the door, another possibility occurred to him. The latch itself was attached by four screws.

What could he use as a tool? Papers in his satchel... pens... the passport and money in his undershirt?

He shook out the collection of metal currency on the bed. The silver coins were clearly too thick, the coppers too soft, but he had two nickel-alloys. The screw resisted for a moment, then creaked, slowly turning. His fingers smarted with the pressure, but he kept on, one screw after the other. The last one was the hardest. It felt as if it were rusted to the latch plate. Twice, the edge of the coin slipped from the groove.

He took a deep breath, grasped the coin as firmly as he could, and twisted hard. The screw came unstuck with a jerk. A moment later, he had the entire latch free. He opened the door, catching the chair that had wedged the latch.

Ferro made his way along the dimly illuminated stairs. He didn't know what he would say if Ysanomeret suddenly appeared and demanded to know what he was doing, prowling around in the middle of the night, fully dressed. He halted at the entrance to the living room. The fire had died down, but the embers gave off a gentle warmth. A table had been drawn up, set with mugs and the remains of a braided fruit bread. Seeing it, Ferro's mouth watered. It had been too many hours since he'd eaten those three wheaten buns at the railcar station. He tiptoed over.

Beside the tray lay a news sheet in Erlindish, this evening's. The headline stood out, even in the orange light of the embers.

CHACARRE DECLARES WAR!

For a long moment, Ferro stared, unbreathing, at the news sheet. Then he picked it up, straining for the details of the story. Through the censored account, he gathered that Erlind troops had penetrated Chacarre's eastern border and destroyed a patrol that resisted them. Kreste had taken the invasion as an act of war and had reciprocated.

That's exactly what Kreste would do, and the Erls knew it. Did they think they could take Demmerle without a fight?

The authorities in Erlonn denied any such encroachment and accused the Chacarran military with fabricating the story. They formally challenged the Chacarrans to produce evidence to corroborate their story.

He had to get out of this house. Even a single night might make a crucial difference. He imagined Ysanomeret calling his superiors, *I've got a very suspicious-acting Chacarran as my guest here. From the embassy at Erlonn. No luggage, no good reason to be out here. Yes, yes, I'll hold him until you come.*

Ferro wrapped the rest of the bread in a napkin and shoved it into his pocket. Then he tried the doors. The luck of Maas was with him, for, a few minutes later, he found the room where his own coat hung beside the heavier, Erlind-styled garments of his hosts. He took one that fit him reasonably well, along with a pair of fur-lined boots. He would have taken money, too, had he known where to look for it.

The door at the far end of the cloak room was bolted from the inside, but its hinges were well-greased. It opened without a sound. As he'd hoped, he came out on the side away from the sallyport. Against the wall, he found an assortment of sheds, none of them locked. In one of them he found an old pedal-cycle with heavy-treaded tires for country use. The leather seat was cracked and hard, and rust laced the handlebars, but he now had transportation.

Ferro pedaled through the night, always heading north and east. The road curved through the hills, rising and then falling. The cycle's lamp, run by a generator hooked to the wheels, cast a wavering light. More than once he skidded on a patch of ice and went down, scrambling up again in fear that the cycle might be damaged.

He sweated and panted, but kept going. His legs ached and then burned. A dozen times he felt too tired to go on, and then he would think of a transport filled with red-uniformed soldiers, rumbling up the road after him.

It worked for a while. Hours passed, and cold deepened. The snowy hills muffled the sound of his passage. Overhead, a hunting rawl spread its wings, silhouetted briefly against the larger moon, then melted into darkness.

He reached the border shortly before dawn. It was nothing more than a gate across the road, with a wire fence on either side. The place appeared deserted. A chain and lock fastened the weathered gate. He slipped between the strands of the wire fence and pulled the cycle after him.

Surely there should have been something more—armed guards, trucks with blaring klaxons, pennons and explosions. Not this lonely country crossing. The trip had been too easy.

By the time the sun cleared the horizon, Ferro reached one of the little villages in Old Anvers. He stopped at a news vendor to change the last of his Erlind currency. The sheets carried the same story he'd already seen, the disputed invasion and declaration of war. He wavered on his feet. Every muscle from his hips downward seemed to be on fire. His lungs ached with cold. He wanted nothing more than to find a corner in which to collapse. But he couldn't rest, not yet.

"Crazy, this business." Beside Ferro, a Joosten merchant dressed in Ice Sea seal furs pointed to the posted sheets and muttered to his comrade. "Next thing you know, they'll be wanting *us* to take sides."

"I say to Blazes with both of them," the other muttered.

Ferro watched the two Joosteners trudge off, then continued toward the post office, where he hoped to find a public phone. When he finally purchased a token for the single phone and took his turn, it was difficult to hear because of the background noise. The operator informed him that due to the war situation, only priority usage could be allowed.

"All right then," he said, "connect me with the Chacarran consulate in Gallivar." He'd met the head of the Gallivaran unit once or twice and remembered him as a person of steady temperament and little imagination, not a bad combination of qualities for a diplomat posted to the Drowned Lands.

"You can connect that line directly," the operator said tartly and hung up.

Ferro replaced the receiver, silently cursing the unreasonable, self-absorbed, recalcitrance of Joosteners. From the public phone, as in both Chacarre and Erlind, he could make only local calls directly and he had no more tokens. The customer behind him nudged his shoulder and asked if he were finished.

Joosteners, having few natural resources of their own, were consummate traders. Ferro was able to sell the pedal-cycle for enough to pay his passage on a truck hauling household goods to Gallivar. The Erlind coat he traded for one of lesser quality but Joosten styling, there being nothing like Chacarran clothing available.

At first Ferro thought the truck driver had let him off in the wrong part of Gallivar. It was late afternoon, already growing dark beneath a lowering sky. The earlier sunshine had given way to swollen clouds, boding another winter storm on its way from the Ice Sea. Then he caught sight of the small plaque beside the door. Like all other structures in Gallivar, it was part of a continuous building that formed the entire block, distinguished only by its street number.

The Chacarran guard at the door came alert as Ferro approached. Ferro knew what he must look like, with his eyes red and his crest uncombed, wearing shabby clothing. At least, it wasn't the stolen Erlind coat.

The guard examined his documents carefully before admitting him. Even then, Ferro was required to leave his coat behind. Anxious-looking

Chacarrans filled the reception area, mostly business travelers trying to get home. A disquieting, burnt-sulfur smell tinged the air. There was not an unruffled hair in the room. Ferro presented his passport to the harried-looked receptionist.

"You'll have to wait your turn like everyone else." The receptionist looked like he hadn't slept all night. "We simply aren't equipped to cope with a situation like this."

"I ask only that you convey my name to the consul," Ferro replied.

"Wait here with the others."

There were no available seats, so Ferro stood beside the nearest wall, trying to ignore the glares of those who'd been waiting longer. A few minutes later, the receptionist returned, looking somewhat less hostile.

Ferro found himself ushered into an office decorated in subdued Chacarran taste. The small blaze in the fireplace scented the air with burning resin. The consul stood and gestured a greeting.

"Ferro—of course I remember you. Kreste himself introduced us. But I never expected to see you this far from home." Beneath the surface calm of his immaculately groomed crest and tailored dress, the small movements of Menore's eyes and hands gave him away.

Ferro took the proffered seat beside the desk. "I've been in Erlonn. I need a reliable assessment of events at home."

"Yes, things are very difficult these days." Menore paused for a moment, his eyes narrowing. "Our position here is somewhat equivocal, you see. Kreste may have declared war on Erlind, but he is no longer Helm of Chacarre."

Sweet holy Name of Maas! Ferro controlled the immediate impulse to spring out of his chair. "What's happened?"

"He's been removed from power and a caretaker government instituted until elections can be held."

"Removed?" Ferro echoed, stunned. "*By whom?*"

"The United Terran Peacekeeping Force."

"But that's—that can't be legal!" He must be imagining this, he must be still pedaling along in the dark, his feet moving in endless circles, the road hypnotic before him.

"Doubtless." Menore sat back in his chair. "But you can appreciate the, ah... delicacy of our position here. We are representatives of the nation of Chacarre, and exactly who that might be is now unclear."

Ferro steadied his thoughts. "The courts, the rest of the government, the Miraz city leaders—surely they have challenged the Terran action?"

"Not so far, and I think it unlikely. Given the risk of another war with Erlind, or a peace in which neither side holds the other an advantage, which would you choose? Besides, the Terrans do not propose to rule Chacarre for themselves. The Terran-Chacarran Liaison Committee is now the Governing Council. There are some Terrans on it, true, the local base commander and his advisors, but also representatives from the offices of the Miraz mayor and the Helm—although I shouldn't wonder if he's removed as he's Ondre clan like Kreste—"

"I thought you were loyal to Kreste!"

The Consul's crest did not quiver. "I am loyal to *Chacarre*."

Yes, that was the truth. Kreste was replaceable, *would be* replaced naturally in the course of time. The institution of the Helm, the enduring spirit of Chacarre, those were what truly mattered.

The army would take no action in the internal struggle, for the very same reason. Their intervention would lead to one of two things: outright warfare between rival clans, or the ascendancy of a single clan, backed by military power. Chacarre would become a second Erlind, dominated by one powerful family.

Kreste sent me to Erlonn to make sure the Terrans did not become Erlind partisans.

All his efforts in Erlonn had come to nothing. He should have made it clear to the Terrans, he should have—

He should be doing something, not sitting here wallowing in self-recriminations.

"You see," Menore said after a moment. "The advantages are great. The Terrans have promised 'free elections' once order is restored."

"Elections? What are those but a contest to see which clan can form the biggest alliance? They negate everything we've worked for!"

"We must let events take their course."

"And the Terrans? What if their goal all along was to take over Chacarre? What if this Governing Council is just a ruse, and we're giving our country to them with all this *waiting*, with all this *letting events take their course?*"

Menore's eyes sparked in the reflected firelight. His crest rippled visibly. "What would you have us do, then? Fight the Terrans ourselves?"

If we have to, Ferro thought furiously. *If we have to.*

Chapter 27

The bus crawled through Joosten on a circuitous path, along roads like smears of charcoal, past piled slush and groves of leafless trees under a sky that changed little from morning to dusk. The interior smelled of machine oil, wet wool clothing, and stale cheese, but Ferro was grateful to have a place on it nonetheless. The bus was the best transportation the consulate could arrange for him. The few places available on the airship flights had been sold out at the first rumors of war. Ferro, crowded up against a window, shared a seat for much of the way with an oldster and his three grandchildren.

Once past the Chacarran border, with no more than a routine passport check, the bus stopped less frequently and took on fewer passengers. One passenger expressed relief that the war with Erlind had been averted, another was rushing home—the automatic reaction of seeking the safety of the Clan. Someone remarked about the price of leather goods, wondering if the war scare would result in an increase.

The bus rumbled on through the night toward Miraz. At one point, Ferro startled awake from a doze to see a sleek white oval speed across the night sky.

Morning came, and the bus stopped long enough for Ferro to buy a cheese bun and a cup of tea at the town depot. The vendor looked less inhospitable once Ferro spoke to him in Chacarran.

"I've been in Gallivar on family business," Ferro said, sipping the tea and wincing at its bitter taste. "It was colder than a singleton's bed! What's the story about the Terrans taking over Miraz?"

The vendor handed another customer a crunch cake wrapped in a paper. "Everybody'd got a different opinion—it's good because they stopped the war with Erlind, it's terrible because the Erls will find a way to take advantage of the situation, these Terrans have no right to mess with a Chacarran Helm, but once we have these what-are-they-called? *elections*, we'll get Kreste back, so what's the difference? At least the army's got the sense to stay clear of it. It's Hool's own blessing they remember their job is to defend Chacarre, not rule it."

"Nobody's doing anything about the takeover?"

"Oh sure, the students will protest, not that *they* need any excuse," the vendor said. "A few troublemakers will end up in jail. But I guess most people are just going about their business like you and me, waiting to see what comes next."

The vendor turned away from Ferro and bent to smear butter over horn rolls. "Meanwhile, everyone is either telling me or asking me, as if I were some kind of Faithless news service. You want the latest, you buy a sheet."

Past dusk, the bus neared the outskirts of Miraz. Towns sprawled together into suburbs, and buildings lost their country styling. Ferro noticed the heavier traffic moving in both directions. Ahead, a roadblock sat haloed by portable lights. The bus slowed, creaking.

The passenger beside him hawked and swallowed. "Another Flaming identity check." He began rummaging through the layers of his clothing.

Ferro's passport was safe in the inner buttoned pocket of his coat, along with the little money he'd changed in Gallivar. It would show he'd entered, but not departed, Erlind, and come recently from Joosten to Chacarre. He hadn't counted on having to show it, not here in Chacarre. He eyed the handful of papers that his neighbor brought out. They looked like the census records. He had a set himself, somewhere in his family's enclose. He'd never needed any form of identification within Chacarre.

As the bus drew to a halt, the passengers began shuffling toward the front. The bus was not crowded, but the line moved slowly. Ferro sat where he was, watching the others inch by. Something in their posture, in the texture of their murmurs, fueled his sense of unease. He hadn't been away that long, he thought, just half a year. But something had changed.

Ferro got in line near the end. As he drew near the doors, he saw the passengers standing below him, lit by the glaring lamps, caught the glimmer of a uniform, white like the snow before the road dirt crusted it.

A train attendant in the usual dark uniform stood, crest covered by a knitted hood, checking papers by the light of a hand-held lamp. He was flanked to one side by a white-garbed Terran. Ferro had learned to read the alien's expressions a little in Erlonn, but he couldn't surmise much of this one.

"Papers." The train attendant held out his hand to Ferro but didn't meet his eyes.

"What's all this about?" Ferro offered his passport.

"I need to see your identity papers. I don't know what to do with this."

Ferro gestured a question. The Terran lifted his weapon and moved closer. The translator box on his chest rumbled, "Is there a malfunction in some nearby place?"

"I'm sorry, I don't understand," Ferro said in a carefully inoffensive tone. "I've been away, traveling."

The train attendant shoved the passport back at him.

"If I were you, I'd remember to carry my census records. Next time, you might not be so lucky. You'll end up with a night in jail instead of a warning."

Ferro's hands shook as he put the passport away. For the first time, he heard the complex layering of fear beneath the attendant's words.

I've come home to an occupied country.

Ferro nodded and climbed back on the bus along with the other passengers. His seat had disappeared, his neighbor was now jammed against a back corner next to a young farmer, and he had to stand the rest of the way into Miraz.

Ferro rode the bus through the business district to its final terminal, got off, and pondered his next move. All the long trip back, he'd clung to the promise of home, safe and familiar. He pictured Miraz, the way the dawn light reflected rose and gold from the facades of the buildings along the rivers, the scented green shade beneath the trees along the avenues, the aromas from the bakeshops, and music curling down the cobbled streets of the Old Quarter, the cups of creamy tea sipped in open-air cafés.

But that had been in summer. Now snow clumped against stone walls. The sky pressed down on the city like a suffocating veil. Terrans in their white uniforms ghosted through the streets, and squat metallic shapes sat brooding at every corner. People hurried past them, bent over as if clutching secrets to their breasts.

For an eerie moment, standing at the entrance to the underground, Ferro saw two cities, their images overlapping. Which was real, he wondered, and which existed only in his imagination? And would he ever see the city of his summer vision again?

Ferro spent most of his remaining currency on a token for the underground railcar. He waited on the platform heading for the Eastbank district where his family's enclose lay. At this hour, commuters jammed the station. Their voices echoed in the enclosed space, a jumble of chopped-off phrases. The air was heavy with the smells of mud and damp fur.

Ferro scooped up a discarded news sheet from a trash bin moments before his tram pulled in. The press of bodies carried him aboard. The few empty seats were quickly taken.

As the car moved off, Ferro leafed through the news sheet. It was filled with stories about how the Terrans had brought an end to centuries of warfare and ushered in a new age of political freedom and responsibility. Scanning, he caught a reference to the suspension of Kreste's administration.

"Pending free and democratic elections," he muttered, keeping his voice low against the rushing noise of the car moving on its single rail. "What the Blazes does that mean?"

With the Terran Compound sitting in the plaza and its light ray weapons capable of immobilizing an entire crowd, it meant whatever the Terrans wanted it to mean.

He should have found a way to make them understand. He had no Terran contacts here, no one he could rely on, nothing he could use to make them listen.

He thought of the message Kreste had sent. His first assumption had been that it was a warning to him, for his own welfare. But what if it were something else—a cry for help? Kreste had trusted him with a mission and he had failed.

He would not fail again.

Ferro emerged from the underground several blocks from his family's enclose. It was full dark now and the cold nipped at him after the closeness below. Street lamps shone flat against the carved porticos; leafless branches mirrored the patterns of the balcony railings. The lace-ivy covering the stone walls was no more than a tracery of dry tendrils that in summer would form a perfumed mat. Then he noticed that the windows were shuttered tight, even in the absence of a storm.

He hurried onward, thinking of a hot meal, a bath, his own bed. Half a block from home, his footsteps faltered to a halt. In front of his family's enclose, in the shadow of an observation unit, two Terrans were stopping pedestrians while a Miraz warder watched from across the street.

Ferro's crest jerked upright. The fur around his neck quivered. His passport would mean nothing here. He looked disheveled, little better than a vagrant with his mussed hair and stained clothing. He whirled, almost colliding with the person behind him, and turned down a side street.

A few minutes later, he had worked his way around to the other side of the block. He silently blessed Maas, Sixth Aspect of the god, who could have any attribute it desired as long as it kept bestowing such luck. There were none of the Terran spy mushrooms on this street.

Ferro pushed open the door leading to the traverson. It was narrow but well lighted, for the families who owned the encloses on both sides were prosperous. A row of trash receptacles lined one side. Ferro tried the latch on the private door, but it wouldn't open. He'd left his keys back at his embassy quarters in Erlonn. For a moment, he wavered between frustration and hilarity—another locked door!—then pulled the bell cord.

The door swung open a few moments later. One of Ferro's favorite cousins stood there, blinking in surprise. He held an open notebook in one hand and behind him peeked two preschool children.

"By the Sacred Bird of Heaven and all its Incandescent Droppings! It's Ferro! You're frozen through!" Corred bundled Ferro inside. "Let's get you something hot to eat—I'll let your parents know—everyone will be anxious to hear what's happened." Corred taught plant physiology at the University's agriculture facility and was always bringing home his unsuccessful experiments to nurse back to health. "We thought you were in Erlonn!"

"I was, but—"

Corred gestured the younger children back inside and closed the door. "Off with you! Back to your play time!" To Ferro he said, "You go right on up, then, and I'll bring you something from the kitchen. You can tell us all about it later."

Ferro trudged upstairs to the suite of rooms he shared with his widowed parent. This arm of the enclose was quiet. The youngsters were mainly in the communal study, doing their lessons, and most of the adults were still out. He found his own room musty, not from lack of cleaning but from simply not being lived in. He lowered himself to the bed, not sure what he wanted to do most—sink into a tub of hot soapy water or curl up on the bed in his filthy clothes. He was home, safe, with warmth and safety and people who loved him.

It isn't over, not until Kreste is back in office and the Terrans have left Chacarre.

He washed first, measuring the time he allowed himself. Oil, added to the water, left his body fur sleek and lightly scented. He'd forgotten how wonderful it was to be clean. When he got out, he discovered a tray of soup, thin-sliced bread, and cheese. He wrapped himself in a towel and ate it all. His pile of discarded clothing had disappeared and he hoped Corred had thrown it out, rather than have whoever was on laundry shift try to clean the layers of sweat and travel soil. He found a winter-weight knitted tunic and leggings in his closet and was surprised how well they fit. It had been less than a week since he'd left Erlonn.

The enclose had been built two hundred years ago and followed the traditional Clan-era style, windows facing inward except for slit-like defensive apertures. During the day, clerestory windows filled the large central room with oblique light, heightening the rosy beige of the carpets and tapestries. Isarre, Ferro's birth parent, had designed the artificial lighting to recreate the same effect.

Ferro found a good portion of the adult members of the family, plus the school-agers, waiting for him. He remembered a time when nothing of the outside world could reach within these walls. This was family. This was home. This was the soul of everything Chacarre stood for.

"May the peace of the clan enfold you." Isarre came forward and embraced Ferro in formal manner, one adult to another. As Ferro passed from one set of arms to the next, repeating the ritual phrases, the reminders of fidelity, he noticed changes in the assembly—one cousin newly pregnant, another just graduated from the nursery.

They settled down to hear his story, the adults on chairs and the youngsters on the floor. Ferro was reminded of the many family meetings he'd attended here in the past, announcements of pairings, business decisions that affected everyone, resolutions of major arguments, assessments of financial shares. He felt their curiosity and concern, their apprehension of the events that had just transpired in the outer world.

They listened as he told an edited version of his adventures. "I don't know what my status is, here in Miraz," Ferro concluded, meaning his role as Kreste's agent. "I don't want to involve anyone else in the family in case there's trouble.

"Hardly seems likely, does it, given that no one knows you've even left Erlind," one of the grandparents said.

Isarre gestured impatiently. "What does it matter what they think? He's home now. He's safe with us."

"We must all draw together, like in the old days," one of the school-agers piped up. "We must depend only on ourselves. That's right, isn't it?"

A century ago there would have been no choice, no Helm, only the demanding loyalty of family and clan. Instinct and tradition tugged at him.

One of the grandparents got to his feet, moving stiffly because of his arthritis. "Ferro's story is now declared a family matter. No mention, even of its existence, goes beyond these enclose walls. Agreed and sworn?"

"Agreed and sworn," the murmur filled the room.

"We will continue. Ferro, Isarre, Corred, the elders," the grandparent went on. "The rest of you, back about your work."

A few of the younger school-agers grumbled as they returned to their studies. Their tutors would keep them inside for the next few days, until the first fervor died down. Fortunately, the family was large enough to have its own internal school.

"The less time I spend here, the less risk for everyone," Ferro told the remaining circle of elders. "If there is advantage in surprise, I must act immediately. No one knows I'm back. I know Miraz, I can go anywhere, talk to people, organize meetings. Maybe more. I hope more." He paused. "Any talk on what the Terrans intend for Kreste?"

"Oh, they say they're keeping him safe," said Setty. "As if there were assassins lurking at every corner. Some folk out there even believe them."

"Or they're too Flaming impressed with all those Terran contraptions," Isarre said sourly. He had been a mechanical engineer before managing one of the smaller family businesses, a factory that made lighting fixtures. "Nothing but a collection of fancy mushroom towers and light beam gadgets."

"There's enough who think stopping the war with Erlind was worth any price," said the grandparent.

"But is the war really ended?" Ferro said. "Or only our ability to defend ourselves? Without Kreste, what chance do we stand if the Erls attack in force? We know how well they keep their treaties!"

"He's right," said Setty. "Without Carrel-az-Ondre to bring them together, the Clans would have lost the Last Great War. If the Erls march on Miraz tomorrow, who would lead the fight against them? These *aliens*?"

The assembly murmured in general agreement. As he listened, Ferro's thoughts sharpened. The more he considered the matter, the more clearly he saw Kreste poised between powerful forces. Even aside from his position as Helm, Kreste commanded enormous personal loyalty.

Sooner or later, the Terrans would recognize Kreste as a threat and take steps to neutralize it. Neutralize *him*. Which was what Ferro himself would do, were he in their situation.

They must not have that chance.

Chapter 28

M IRAZ: GOVERNING COUNCIL CREATES DEPARTMENT OF
INFORMATION SERVICES. (Statement by Sarahdavies, Terran
Representative to the Governing Council, translated into Chacarran by
Talense; to be printed in all Miraz news sheets, from all agencies)

Chacarre has just emerged from the first stage of its most desperate
modern crisis. Thanks to the leadership of the Terran-Chacarran Liaison
Committee and the speedy intervention of our Terran allies, a devastating
war with Erlind has been averted.

Now we enter into an even more challenging phase, that of
consolidating our gains and ensuring the tranquil progression from the old
order to the new, the bridge from the glories of the past to the bright
promise of the future. This transition will require all our resources—
intelligence, wisdom, and courage.

Vital decisions loom ahead of us, decisions that cannot be made on the
basis of ignorance, prejudice, and fear. In order to ensure that all
Chacarrans have free access to the facts, presented in an unbiased and
balanced way, the Governing Council has established a Department of
Information Services, which will oversee all articles appearing in all major
news sheets.

The Council proudly announces the appointment of Talense-az-
Mestre, formerly of the Interclan News Agency, to be Director of
Information Services. He brings to this post a lifetime of distinguished
service and unequalled impartiality. Together with the Terran consultant,
Sarahdavies, he will create a new era in objective, informative reporting,
the basis of an informed and participating electorate.

MIRAZ: ERLIND ADMITS DEMMERLE INVASION, OFFERS FORMAL

APOLOGY! Report by Druse. Cleared by the Department of Information Services.

In a startling development early this morning, the government of Erlind has admitted that it violated Chacarran territory in an unprovoked attack on the border region of Demmerle. Speaking through his ambassador in Miraz, the Erlking tendered formal apologies to the people of Chacarre for the incident that he described as, "a lamentable mistake."

According to a statement from the Chacarran military, a border patrol engaged a battalion of Erlind troops several miles within Chacarran territory. Only swift Terran intervention prevented a bloody battle from ensuing. No civilian casualties were reported and the nearby village was apparently undamaged.

A representative of the United Terran Peacekeeping Command stated, "We have the situation under control and call on all men [sic] of good will to remain calm. The precipitous declaration of war would have served only to needlessly escalate the situation."

North from Miraz, the suburbs lining Westriver's placid banks gave way to broad, sweeping meadows and groves of rufino and tress, their branches now stark and leafless in winter. The bus slowed as it passed the great clan estates, though there was little to see beyond the public landscaping, muddy brown under patches of melting slush. Behind their sheltering walls, the residences faced inward, each toward its own private courtyard. One such building was set farther back than the others, hidden by unusually high walls.

Ferro signaled the bus to stop and walked to the side entrance to the Helm Residence. The gates were guarded by two armed Terrans, and one of the metallic surveillance units sat a short distance away. He shoved his hands deeper into his pockets, rounded his shoulders forward, and let his feet drag on the paving. Doing his best to ignore the Terrans, he reached for the bell cord.

One of the Terrans barred his way. "This is private property." The translator sounded harsh, like the bray of a goat. "No lobbying allowed."

"I've got work inside," Ferro mumbled.

The Terrans exchanged glances. "What work?"

"Gardening." Ferro shuffled his feet and tried to look as if he did manual labor.

"You are not the habitual gardener."

For a moment Ferro wondered if he might claim to be a substitute, but decided it was too risky. "He asked me to give him a hand. Getting in the bulbs for the spring." He let a whine creep into his voice. "Times are hard. This is the only work I've had in weeks."

One of the Terrans yanked the cord. A few minutes later, one of the family cousins who worked in the garden appeared, a heavy-set, round-cheeked person that Ferro knew. The gardener's fur rippled in surprise, but the Terrans didn't seem to notice. They let Ferro pass and closed the gate behind him.

Ferro hurried on the gardener's heels through the outer walks, the winter-bare hedges and empty borders. They paused by a grove of evergreens, thick enough to block the view from the house.

"What are you doing here?" the gardener whispered.

"I just got back from Erlonn," Ferro said. "Kreste sent for me. Can you get me in to see him?"

The gardener grasped Ferro's arm. "He isn't here." Ferro's crest jerked upright. "They've taken him to the city. The sheets are calling it 'protective custody.' I think they got the phrase from the Terrans."

"But—" Ferro smoothed his crest with one hand. Of course, the Terrans couldn't leave Kreste with all the trappings of power. "Where?"

"I heard the name and it went right through me." He gestured apologetically. "Maybe the other cousins remember."

The Helm's Residence had always struck Ferro as never still, never sleeping. Kreste had carried with him a sense of inexhaustible energy. Something was always going on, a meeting, a member of his personal staff working late into the night. Now it seemed deserted, forlorn.

The kitchen, however, retained its former brightness and bustle. Sunlight streamed through the windows, warming the air. Potted plants hung from the rafters beside strings of garlic and dried herbs. The gardener strolled in and helped himself to the pastries cooling on racks. Kreste might be gone, but the rest of the family needed to eat.

The baker remembered Ferro and offered him a hot drink. His sibling, the head cook, had accompanied Kreste to the Helm's town house. The baker, stretching back in his chair with his own mug of tea, sniffed, his expression indicating that he'd rather cook for grats than for Terrans.

"No greens, no cheese, no wine," he grumbled. "No wonder they're as cheerless as a singleton's bed."

Ferro was familiar with the Helm's town house. He'd attended social gatherings there and knew some of the staff, hired rather than family.

"It's thick with warders. No Terrans, though," the baker answered Ferro's question. "Kreste wouldn't have 'em."

"Well, I don't like it, them moving Kreste around this way. Sounds like a nice way to set up one of those *accidents*, if you know what I mean," the gardener replied.

"I need to see Kreste," Ferro said. "Can you get me in without attracting any attention?"

The baker smiled.

Ferro entered Kreste's town house by the servants' entrance. The door was unlocked by the head cook, who'd been alerted to look for him. Carrying a leather satchel, Ferro traced his way along the back hallways. He tapped lightly on the door that the cook indicated, waited a pause, and went in.

The room was long and high-ceilinged. One wall bore a faded geometric progression on the color red and the tone *san*, sacred to the Name of J'. Kreste sat at a desk beside the single window, his back to the door. The contours of his shoulder muscles showed through the fabric of his tunic. Sunlight gleamed on the streak that ran like a silver ribbon through his dark crest.

"No tea, I said," Kreste said without raising his head. For a heartbeat, Ferro couldn't move. He imagined the entire room quivering, as if an elemental power surged just below the surface, waiting only a whisper for release.

He tried to speak. No sound came, nor breath to his lungs. The air in the room turned to glass. The mural blurred in his sight, the repeated pattern of the divine attribute of joy. The satchel slipped from his nerveless fingers to land with a soft *phlump!*

Kreste's head jerked up, crest fanning upward. He turned and pushed himself away from the desk. Papers spilled to the carpet. He had lost weight since Ferro had last seen him, gone to bone and wire-taut muscle. His eyes were shadowed, as if he hadn't slept.

"Thank all the Names you're safe," Kreste exclaimed. "Dorlin said you'd disappeared. I feared the worst."

"I left Erlonn as soon as I got your note." Ferro stepped forward, unsure. All the fear and fury and despair he'd suppressed during his journey from Erlonn came boiling up in him at once. His knees turned to powder. He was afraid if he said anything more, he'd collapse in sobs.

Kreste crossed the pale red carpet in a single flowing stride. When he took Ferro's hand, his touch was like an anchor. "But you are well? Unhurt?"

Ferro felt dizzy and sober all at once. He raised his free hand, but no gesture came, only meaningless movement.

"We're all still in shock."

"I know," Ferro said in a strangely rusty voice. "I've been talking to people, watching, listening. Already there are demonstrations protesting your removal."

"Students, ah yes." Kreste's voice smiled. He dropped Ferro's hand and moved away. "Can you imagine them staying quiet about anything for long? They're a barometer, annoying but vital. They point the way, even though they cannot lead."

"Neither can you, from here."

"Then I must find a way. Since I am captive here, it will be difficult."

"It will be impossible. The Terran occupiers will see to that."

Kreste looked toward the window and the city beyond it. The whiteness of the winter sky washed the color from the walls. His body took on a new stillness, a quality of listening. "What are you suggesting? That I abandon Chacarre?"

"Not *abandon*—lead our people from a place where your voice can be heard."

"I can still lead from here, on our own soil. Here in Chacarre with my people. It's where I'm needed."

"What can you do, penned up here?" Ferro said, his crest rippling with fervor. And fear—fear that Kreste's devotion to Chacarre would get him silenced permanently. "Will you wait for the Terrans to invent so many lies that's all the people know? That's happening already."

"Surely there is resistance, those courageous enough to speak out. The press—"

"Haven't you seen the news sheets? This new Department of Information Services now controls everything."

Ferro's heart thundered in his ears. Sparks danced along his nerves. He drew a shuddering breath and wrestled his desperation under control. Argument was useless; he must speak from his heart. He took Kreste by the shoulders and turned him around so their eyes met. "There is no other Helm to bring the clans together. The god would not ask it of anyone lesser."

In an instant, Kreste's face changed. His hands sketched a gesture of capitulation. "What would you have me do, then? Save my own life at the cost of Chacarran freedom?"

"I came here to get you away. No matter how dangerous an escape might be, to stay will only mean your death."

"You are right, my dearest friend, but these things take planning."

"Fortunately, planning is one thing I know how to do." Ferro picked up the satchel. "How would you like to join the Miraz city warders? Unofficially, of course?"

The city warder uniforms were genuine, borrowed from their legitimate owners by way of Ferro's family-run cleaners. Ferro timed their escape to take advantage of the changing shifts. They emerged through the side entrance just at the moment when the nearest pair of guards were halfway down the street. Ferro's fear was that even at a distance, Kreste would be recognized. By the blessing of the Sixth God, whose attribute is hope, the other guards just sketched a wave, unquestioning of the warders' uniforms. From there, Ferro and Kreste made their way to an apartment in the splits, well away from the family enclose. Here they changed again and picked up the money Ferro had hidden after renting the place.

"What did you do, rob a clan bank?" Kreste joked as he fastened the money belt around his waist.

"No, I emptied the discretionary account you set up for me. This escape is being financed by the government of Chacarre."

Kreste shrugged into the worn coat and cap that Ferro provided. "What about census records?"

Ferro reached into his pocket and held up two sets of papers, pocket-creased and slightly grimy. "We are now Morren and spouse. I'm short enough to be Morren, although I've just lost thirty pounds or so; my mate is shy and doesn't say much. Your voice, you know, is distinctive. The farther we get from Miraz, the less chance of meeting someone who can recognize you."

"Is there a real Morren?"

"Of course there is. He's just earned his children's University tuition, too. Don't worry, he's resourceful enough to acquire duplicates." Ferro did not add that the advocat students were already forging identity papers.

Kreste resisted leaving Chacarre entirely. He argued for Tallin on the Joosten border, one of the southern towns near Shardi. Ferro was adamant that remaining within the reach of the Terrans was the worst choice. The Empty Isles, despite their name, were not uninhabited. They were cold and desolate, but scattered with towns that occasionally sent students to the University in Miraz. The Isles had once been part of the far-flung trading empire of the Freeport Cities, long since abandoned to only the most hardy, stubbornly independent settlers, hence the designation, "Empty." They were as safe as any place, for the Islanders were notoriously resistant to outside influence. While the Islanders might not actively help Kreste's cause, they would take a perverse delight in his making as much trouble as possible for the Terrans.

The Terrans could undoubtedly conquer the Isles, given sufficient incentive, but Ferro thought that even then it would be almost impossible to capture one single person who didn't want to be found. As for communication with the mainland, radio casts were possible, and fishing or trader boats plied the strait in all but the worst weather.

In the end, Ferro was able to persuade Kreste that the Empty Isles were the best place from which to launch a resistance movement.

They were able to catch a railcar headed northwest for Avallaz. The warder at the station yawned as he glanced at their papers. Ferro bought sandwiches, a half-round of cheese, and a bag of wrinkled apples. He put them, along with a bottle of pear wine, in the satchel he'd used to carry the uniforms.

The trip to the coast was as nerve-shredding as anything Ferro had yet been through. If he could have talked to Kreste, he might have been able to relieve the tension. There was so much he wanted to say and even more he wanted to ask.

For his part, Kreste was a poised and undemanding traveling companion, in a way that did not call attention to himself, yet clearly alert to his surroundings. Once they had settled on a plan, he did not bring up the subject where strangers could eavesdrop.

At one of the short stops, Ferro picked up an evening news sheet. It carried local news and articles from the Miraz news services. Most of it was the same *Welcome Our Terran Friends* and *Terrans Bring A New Era of Peace* that he'd seen before. The article at the bottom of the first page described a vicious criminal at large, disguised as the former Helm, Kreste.

Ferro folded the sheet, tucked it under his arm, and returned to his seat. He kept his head down, hardly daring to breathe. The muscles in his shoulders ached.

"What's wrong?" Kreste said once they were underway again. He had been writing in his journal.

"You're not supposed to talk!" Ferro hissed.

Kreste's fur rippled, then stilled. He closed the journal and put it in the inner pocket of his coat. "Something's upset you." Silently Ferro handed him the sheet.

Kreste studied the sheet before placing it on the seat between them. He looked out the window, apparently absorbed by the passing mud-gray fields, the bare-branched orchards, the feed racks with their herds of dun milkers.

"I should have seen it coming, I should have known," Kreste said in a low voice. "But I was so... obsessed with this Fellowship conspiracy, I thought that was our only threat. May Sotir preserve me from the inversion of blindness, I even declared a state of martial law to stop the protests." His crest rippled and his mouth tightened. "We could get rid of Erlind tomorrow—erase it from the face of the world—and not be any better off."

They spent the night at an inn in a small town a few miles outside of Avallaz, where either the news reports had not yet reached or were, after the fashion of country folk, blithely ignored. The inn was smoky but very quiet. The only other guests were a Wayfolk pair who kept to themselves.

The next morning, Ferro changed some of his coins at a Wayfolk bank in the village and located an old car for hire. He bought more food, the warmest outer clothing he could find, rain gear, and boots. He loaded it in the car, picked up Kreste at the inn, and drove west. The road hugged the coast, rocky cliffs falling away to restless, gray-green water. Every so often, it dipped to a crescent of pale sand, a little bay or inlet where boats moored beside sprawling, driftwood-colored houses.

Days later, they came to the narrow strait that separated the mainland from The Empty Isles. Ferro hoped to find a boat he could charter to take them across.

On their third day of searching, they found a fisher named Joxel, who was willing to take them across. His boat looked sound and his price was reasonable. Ferro paid him half in advance, with the balance when they arrived. The fisher agreed, the tide being right. He and his mate stood on deck and watched with flattened, expressionless crests as Ferro pushed the rented car into the sea.

As they clambered aboard the rickety plank, the fisher's mate lifted his face, testing the wind. Ice-edged, it whipped the clouds to a bright froth across the horizon. "Storm coming."

"Nothing we haven't seen before." Joxel squinted at Ferro and Kreste. "Not that *they* have any choice."

Ferro turned away, leaning on the railing, but Kreste put one hand on the fisher's arm and caught his gaze. "We are not criminals."

The fisher blinked. His crest softened. "If I thought you were," he said in a very different tone, almost reverent, "I wouldn't be taking you. Rest now. It won't be an easy passage, but we've come through worse."

When Ferro asked if the two of them were enough to handle the boat in a storm, the fishers laughed at him.

Chapter 29

The boat, although seaworthy, stank of fish and sealing tar. Ferro recognized equipment for the catching, sorting, and storing of oil-rich Ice Sea jackfish. A dinghy stood upside down on a cradle over a midship hatch in front of the deck house. Through the heavy-paned windows, Ferro glimpsed a steering wheel and radio equipment. Everything from the fittings to the cabin interior looked functional, uncomfortable, and ugly.

The cabin below was little more than a hole lit by a single salt-crusted porthole. Two built-in bunks lined opposite walls, along with storage cabinets, a fold-down table, and sanitary bowl, everything latched into place.

Ferro set the packs down and came back on deck. He half-expected to see a line of warder cars screeching along the road, or a Terran space ship whizzing through the sky, but the only things in the air were the jade-colored sea herons, whistling as they wheeled and dove.

Only a few minutes past the breakwater, Ferro began to feel ill. The boat rocked up and down, with his stomach always a half-second behind. There didn't seem to be a point in the sky, sea, or ship that wasn't in constant motion. He leaned over the nearest side and spewed forth his breakfast.

Joxel made a cackling sound. "More food for the fishies!"

Kreste slapped Ferro across the shoulders. The rising wind ruffled his fur, showing the pale skin beneath. The silver streak in his crest fanned out like a pennon. "Take deep breaths and keep your eyes on the horizon. You'll be better in no time."

Ferro groaned and stumbled off toward the cabin.

"You'll regret it," Kreste called after him, laughing.

After the brisk sea air, the cabin was narrow and stuffy, not to mention dingy. Ferro threw himself down on a bunk, closed his eyes, and fervently wished for unconsciousness. The entire universe swayed and rolled. He gritted his teeth and concentrated on taking one breath after another. Sour-tasting saliva filled his mouth. Finally he admitted to himself that Kreste had been right.

Ferro grasped the deck railing in both hands, spread his legs wide for balance, and kept his eyes on the far horizon. They were now in open sea, surrounded by water the color of pewter. Waves swelled, crashed against the boat's sides, and sprayed into the air, lacing the wind with icy droplets. All color had bled from the sky, chased by clouds that boiled up, dark and thick, before Ferro's eyes. There was no sight of land in any direction.

Kreste stepped out from behind the deck house, following Joxel. He gestured as he asked questions, pointed to different pieces of equipment. He moved confidently, with easy balance.

"How are you doing?" Kreste asked. "Better, out here?"

In the few minutes he'd been on deck, Ferro's face had gone numb with cold.

"I love this," Kreste went on. "All through my childhood, my family owned a boat that we sailed out of Cimembo. We'd sometimes be out for weeks at a time. Of course it was warmer there." Leaning against the railing, head thrown back, he seemed to absorb vitality from the wind, the surging waters. "There's something about being on a boat in the middle of so much ocean. All your problems get sorted into perspective. You discover that half of them aren't nearly as important as you thought they were. No, make that nine-tenths."

As they stood at the rail, the wind increased. The motion of the boat shifted from rolling to more violent pitching. The sky turned even darker.

Joxel ambled over to them, surefooted on the tilting deck. "You two had better get below," he shouted.

Ferro started making his way toward the cabin hatch. The boat shuddered beneath him as a particularly forceful wave smacked against it. He staggered, grabbing the rail for balance.

Kreste glanced back at the fisher. "Need any help?"

"Naw, we've been through worse, and brought in a day's catch, too. But you don't want to join them fishies now, do you?"

Kreste laughed and followed Ferro down into the cabin. It was quieter here, darker than before, as if night had already fallen. The shadows intensified the boat's motion.

Ferro huddled on the nearest bunk and tried to compose himself. They'd gotten out of Erlind, past the border, and back to Miraz. Kreste was free and on his way to neutral ground. Surely the worst was behind them. But what if they'd overestimated the Terran threat? What if something disastrous happened—the ship capsizing, sinking?

"It's all right, it's just a storm." Kreste sat down beside Ferro. "Fishers go out in worse all the time."

What if I lose him now? Ferro thought.

They sailed on. Every time Ferro was sure the storm had gotten as bad as possible, it seemed to get worse. Kreste kept talking about their plans, about the people they might reach back home, about who would support them and who could not be trusted.

A splash of brilliance lit the single window and was as quickly gone. Ferro stared for a moment, not quite sure he had seen it; then his ears caught the *crackle-boom!* of thunder. Although muted against the racket of the storm winds, it sounded directly overhead.

A deafening *snap!* shivered the air. The boat staggered as if it had struck an ice floe. A metallic odor stung Ferro's nostrils. Without thinking, he jumped to his feet.

Against the murky cabin light, a tongue of yellowish flame burst into life. Tiny flickers caught the oiled wood of the cabin's interior and flared.

Without a moment's hesitation, Kreste gathered up the blanket on the bunk. Ferro joined him, covering the fire with the heavy woolen folds. A few moments later, it was out.

The hatch swung open. A sheet of icy water sprayed down on them. Kreste caught most of it, but Ferro got a faceful. He gasped in the cold. Salt stung his eyes.

Kreste scrambled up the stairs, Ferro at his heels. Thunder crackled through the air. Water burst over the prow and sluiced off the deck. The boat steadied momentarily, then rolled. Another wave hit the side, spraying upwards.

Ferro clutched the rail. He could hardly see through the sleeting rain.

His ears caught a new sound, the shrieking of wood bent to the breaking point, then a crashing. He and Kreste scrambled after Joxel, around to the other side of the deck house.

Ferro skidded to a halt, horrified. The cradle structure holding the dinghy was now a blackened mass of splinters. The last surge of water had broken the dinghy loose on one end. The pointed nose had been driven through the wall of the deck house. Through the shattered boards, Ferro could see the fisher's mate wrestling with the steering wheel, struggling to free it from fragments of wood.

Ferro grabbed the nearest edge of the dinghy, and found it slick as glass. He heaved with all his strength but nothing moved. Rain sleeted over his eyes, momentarily blinding him. Thunder boomed above the howling wind, and spurts of brightness shot through the sky. Beneath him, the boat pitched like a wild thing.

Maas, Sixth Aspect—Ferro broke off his prayer. What good would charisma, merely personal power, do now?

"Come on!" Kreste's voice broke through the din of the storm. He pointed to the tackling gear.

Ferro slipped and scrambled on the tilting deck. An arm shot out, caught him. Joxel shoved a heavy leather belt into Ferro's hands and gestured that he should put it on. Ferro fumbled with the buckle and somehow got it fastened. The fisher clasped on a length of rope and attached the other end to a bolt set in the deck. Kreste had already secured his own belt.

Ferro wasn't sure he felt any safer, though he told himself the fishers must know what they were doing in a storm. A wave caught him unexpectedly. It sent him to his knees. Joxel hooked one hand under Ferro's armpit and hauled him up. He shoved Ferro in the direction of the deck house.

The wind tore away the fisher's words, but Ferro understood. He saw Kreste making his way toward the block and tackle, ready to pull the dinghy away as soon as it was freed.

Ferro and Joxel began pulling the shards of wood away from the deck house wall. Splinters dug into Ferro's hands. On the other side of the dinghy, the mate yelled orders at Kreste. The craft was stuck fast.

Suddenly there came a break in the storm. The boat seemed to steady itself. The rain paused.

"Now!" Joxel shouted.

Ferro spun around to see Kreste hauling on the ropes of the tackling gear. Kreste's face contorted, his whole body knotted with the effort.

The prow of the dinghy came loose with a crash. It swayed, slamming into Ferro's hips. Ferro scrambled for traction, but the deck was too slick. He couldn't stop. For a terrifying moment, he was certain he'd go skidding overboard. He tried to scream, but no sound came out.

Desperately he grabbed for something—*anything*—to hold on to. His fingers curled around the rope tied to his belt, but it was loose, he hadn't reached the end of it. Then one outstretched foot struck the upright bar of the rail, caught, and miraculously held.

Shaking as much with fright as cold, Ferro got to his feet. The fisher bent over the dinghy prow, attaching a rope to pull it back to maneuverable position. Kreste stood by the tackle. The gap in the railing framed his body against the gray of the sea.

Suddenly the waves fell away beneath the fishing boat as if a chasm had opened up. Ferro's stomach lurched. He staggered and caught himself. The boat shuddered. Wind whipped the rain to icy needles.

A wall of white-frothed sea slammed against the far side of the boat, right where Kreste stood.

Ferro screamed out a warning, but the wind tore away his voice. He couldn't see Kreste behind the curtains of water, sea rising, rain plummeting, white and gray, up and down and sideways all at once. Without thinking, he hurled himself across the width of the ship, skirting the rounded bulk of the dinghy hull.

An instant later, he saw Kreste slip through the unrailed gap.

Ferro swerved and grabbed the edge of the rail with one hand. He reached out with the other.

Kreste disappeared beneath the waves.

The water looked all white, except for isolated patches of darkness. An instant later, Kreste's head broke the surface.

Ferro threw himself flat and stretched out his hand as far as he could. For a moment, it seemed he could actually touch Kreste's upheld arm. But the distance was too great, the movement of waves and boat too erratic.

Beside Ferro's feet, the rope to Kreste's belt drew taut, then held. Ferro grabbed for it. Crouching, he braced one foot against the rail and pulled. The rope sliced into his splintered palms, but he kept pulling. From below he heard Kreste's voice. He felt a fierce, sudden resistance, a weight far beyond his strength to hold. His back muscles spasmed and his finger joints popped and cramped, but still he held on. Leaning over, he could see Kreste bobbing against the side of the boat.

The rope tore through Ferro's hands as the next wave swept Kreste away.

Ferro screamed. Kreste was a powerful swimmer, that much Ferro knew, but the weight of his sodden winter clothes would surely pull him down.

A wave, more wind-lashed froth than water, surged over Kreste's head. An instant later it subsided, leaving no trace of him.

Chapter 30

Ferro sprinted across the deck. He grabbed Joxel, who was still struggling with the prow of the dinghy. Pointing, he screamed, "Overboard!" For an instant, he feared the fisher hadn't understood, the wind so twisted his speech.

Joxel rushed back across the deck, never slipping or pausing. He braced himself against the edge of the railing, swaying with the pitching of the boat. His eyes scanned the water.

"There!"

The back of Kreste's head broke the surface, his hair wet and tangled like seaweed. He lifted his face, mouth gaping wide. One arm curved upward in a swimming stroke.

Something hot and bright burst inside Ferro. He wanted to shout, to hurl himself into the water, to cry out loud for sheer relief.

Joxel gestured for Ferro to pick up the rope and pull it in. Under the traction, Kreste floated closer and closer to the side of the boat.

"Easy, easy—" Joxel lowered himself to the deck, leaning far out but still not reaching.

What was wrong with him? Why did he wait? Didn't he *realize*—

Ferro forced his attention back to the rope, keeping the tension steady, drawing Kreste in. He watched how the waves carried Kreste closer and higher, then back against the rope. It seemed to him that Kreste's strokes were growing weaker and the times when the water completely covered him longer.

"Now!" Joxel shouted.

Suddenly the water rose up, lifting Kreste higher than before. The awful drag on the rope lightened. Ferro pulled and kept pulling, hand over hand, sobbing, straining, hauling with all his strength. The coarse fibers of the rope bit into his skin, deep enough to draw blood; the rope slipped, tearing his palms. Salt water flooded over his hands, burning like caustic.

In a sudden, powerful movement, Joxel reached out and grabbed Kreste's wrist. Kreste hooked one elbow over the side of the boat, then one knee, then he lay gasping on the deck.

Ferro threw his arms around Kreste, taking in the solidness of his body, the convulsive movements of his breathing. Kreste's skin had gone ashy gray beneath his water-slick fur.

*He needs dry clothing—warmth—*Ferro pulled Kreste to his feet and lurched toward the cabin hatch.

Joxel grabbed Ferro's arm before he'd gone a second step. "The dinghy!"

Ferro tightened his hold on Kreste's drenched jacket. He glared at the fisher. *You don't know who he is. He's more important than a hundred fishing boats.*

"Scorch you," the fisher yelled, "d'you want us *all* to die? How long d'you think we'll last out here—with that thing loose on deck?"

"He's right." The words came in a croak from Kreste's mouth. He could hardly stand, but somehow he managed to push away from Ferro and stumble toward the cabin hatch.

Ferro's body had gone numb in the freezing rain and he hardly felt the shredded skin on his palms. Cursing and straining, the two of them rolled the dinghy close enough to secure the ropes. Once the dinghy was in position, the tackling gear gave them leverage, making it easier to handle. The fisher hauled on the tackle while Ferro guided the other end. Finally they lashed the dinghy in place.

The fisher disappeared into the deck house, presumably to finish clearing the debris. Ferro, for a moment without direct orders, bolted for the cabin hatch.

Kreste lay in a heap at the bottom of the stairs. With the boat pitching under them, Ferro helped him into dry clothes, the warmest in the pack. He wrapped Kreste in the blankets from both bunks, but it didn't seem to help. Kreste's skin felt like ice. Shivers shook his entire body. There must be a way of getting him warm from the inside, hot tea perhaps.

Ferro didn't see anything like a stove on which to heat water. He fumbled in the shadows for a light switch, found something that felt like one, and turned it on. Nothing happened. He cursed under his breath. The lightning must have burned out the boat's electrical system.

Ferro stumbled back to the bunk. Without lifting his head, Kreste broke into a fit of coughing.

"Are you all right?" Ferro asked as the spasm passed.

"I got a lungful of water out there, that's all." Kreste's voice sounded reedy, strained. "B-Blazes, it's cold. I just can't seem t-to—to stop shivering."

"I'll get something to warm you up."

Back on deck, Ferro could feel the difference in the boat's movement; although it still pitched, it now held to a steady course.

The fisher's mate looked up. Cold reddened his exposed skin, except for the white of his knuckles, clenched around the bars of the steering wheel.

"We're an hour still from land. Can't be sure 'til we know how far off-course we are. Radio's out. Should be all right, though. Your friend okay?"

"He's colder than a singleton's bed. I've got him all wrapped up, but it doesn't seem to help. I want to make him a hot drink."

"No heating nothing. Not in this weather, with the electrical system out." The fisher paused, squinting ahead through the water-dotted window. He went on in a more conversational tone. "Tell you, the best way to warm a person is to strip both of you naked and get under as many covers as you've got. Your own body heat, y'know. Better'n any stove."

Back in the cabin, Kreste had begun coughing again, a hollow racking sound that intensified Ferro's desperation. "There's no hot water," Ferro said. "I think you're so chilled, through and through, you cannot warm itself." He hesitated—how to put this?—then chided himself. Kreste's *life* was at stake. "I can warm you with my own body, but only if we are skin-to-skin."

"My dear friend," Kreste said between coughs. "You—of all people—need not ask whether it is proper. In all the long years—we have known each other—you have brought me nothing but good."

Ferro pulled off Kreste's clothing, then his own, then piled all the blankets and climbed under them next to Kreste.

Kreste curled up facing the wall, his knees drawn up and arms wrapped tightly across his chest. Ferro positioned himself behind Kreste and put his arms around his waist.

"I'm s-s-still so cold," Kreste whimpered. His shivering rippled through Ferro's body.

"It's going to be all right," Ferro murmured. "I'll keep you warm." He stretched his arms further around Kreste's shoulders and pulled him closer. He nestled his face against the back of Kreste's neck.

By slow degrees, the shivering grew slower, then sporadic, then stopped entirely. Although Kreste still coughed from time to time, his breathing seemed easier.

Ferro became aware of all the places their bodies touched—the long smooth curves of Kreste's thighs and the roundness of his hips, the graceful tapering of his waist. Ferro's arm was around Kreste's torso. It would be a simple thing, perhaps no more than an accidental movement in time to the boat's rocking, to shift his hand upwards and brush against Kreste's breast.

Ferro's lips unconsciously moved across the nape of Kreste's neck. His tongue met salt, sweat, Kreste's personal taste. His heart pounded and he felt a growing, insistent pressure low in his own body.

They had never been lovers, for all the love that had grown over the years between them. Both were past the critical age when biological urges resulted in permanent bonding. Now the heart must be the motive force. If something happened to Kreste—if he died of exposure or was captured by the Terrans—now there would be no chance. Not ever again.

If he had wanted it, surely he would have asked, said one part of Ferro's mind. *There were chances enough.*

He would want it to be offered freely, for himself and not his office.

"Kreste," he whispered, running his fingers delicately up the center of Kreste's chest, feeling the swell of the small, perfectly shaped breasts. There was no response and after a moment, he realized why. Kreste's breathing had gone soft and slow, his muscles soft as butter. Ferro lowered his own head and closed his eyes.

Ferro woke sweating and clawing at the blankets. For a startled second, he could not remember where he was—on the train to Gallivar, in a hospital somewhere, or in his quarters in Erlonn. Instead, he looked out at a dark, close, fish-stinking prison. From above, voices rang clear. Beside him, Kreste's body radiated heat like a stove. Even as Ferro sat up and reached for his clothing, racking coughs shook Kreste's chest. Praying he was wrong, that the warmth was the result of the heavy blankets, Ferro laid the back of one hand along Kreste's temple.

Kreste burned.

Gently, Ferro shook Kreste's shoulder. Kreste murmured a few unintelligible syllables. His lids half-opened to show only crescents of white.

Ferro climbed up on deck. The sea was smooth except for a line of white-topped swells, the sky a wash of gray upon gray. Charcoal-green hills rose above the northern horizon and sea birds wheeled overhead, their whistling cries piercing the wind.

Joxel stood at the prow of the ship. He ambled toward Ferro, his reddened eyes moving over the deck. "Here we are, safe and hearty. Just as I told you. Quick as a singleton's broken promise, you'll be back on dry land."

Ferro squinted toward shore, but could see no sign of habitation on the silhouetted hills. "Where are we?"

The fisher winked, then spat off the side of the boat. "That's Banish-Care, near as we can tell. Not much of a town, sure, but nothing on the Isles is. Not even Haven."

"My friend's sick. He's got a fever and he's coughing. He needs medical attention. Does this Banish-Care have a hospital?"

The fisher's crest ruffled sympathetically. "Sounds like pneumonia to me. No wonder, after the dunking he took. As for Banish-Care, there should be someone who knows herbs. The Islanders may not be much for city learning, but they won't turn away someone in need."

Ferro shut his mouth, unable to think what to say next. Haranguing the fisher would not get Kreste proper care.

"Come on," said Joxel. "I'll make him some powdered broth with hot pepper juice. That's good for almost anything that ails you."

They were met at the Banish-Care harbor by a group of wary-eyed Islanders, who grumbled what the Blazes was a ship out of Chacarre doing in this part of the Isles and who was lunatic enough to go out in a storm in this season? As soon as they learned of the damage and the presence of a sick person aboard, their manner changed so drastically, Ferro could hardly tell they were the same people. Some brought out tools to repair the deck house, dinghy cradle, and radio. Others came on board and made a chair carry for Kreste, who was still too feverish to realize what was happening to him.

"Come you with us," one said to Ferro as they hurried away. "He'll want for a friendly face when he's himself again."

The village was little more than a scattering of thatched-roof cottages nestled in the pocket of the hills. In the misting rain, everything looked damp and slightly mossy, a tapestry of green from muted to brilliant with only a hint of brown here and there. Even the Island fishers' coats were green, as well as their intricately knit caps and sweaters. Ferro found their accents hard to understand at first, but their gestures were clear enough.

The villagers carried Kreste to one of the larger cottages, a two-story structure with half-timbered walls, bordered by pungent creepers. The healer came to the door. Short and slightly built, he wore a tunic of unshorn sheepskin. Without any mention of their names or purpose, Ferro explained his friend had been swept overboard.

The healer took one look at Kreste and hustled them inside. The room at the top of the stairs smelled close and tangy, a mixture of herbs and unbleached wool.

"You have how long been like this?" the healer asked, bending over Kreste. "The fever, the cough?"

"Sometime last night," Kreste said weakly. "I couldn't get warm—"

"We did everything we could," Ferro said.

"Sure I am that you did," the healer replied mildly. "Now, the rest of you, back to your work. I'll send word when more there is to be done."

The villagers withdrew but Ferro lingered. The healer listened to Kreste's breathing, touched Kreste's temples and the pulse-points at his wrists and neck. "Come here," the healer said to Ferro. "I be needing help in getting his clothing off and himself undercover."

"Are you a medical?" Ferro asked, pulling off Kreste's boots.

The healer shook his head. "I worked as an aide in Haven, but most I learned from my own teachers here." He paused, resuming his accent. "Know you, yes, that your mate is very ill?"

"It's pneumonia, isn't it? But that's something you can surely treat. Anti-infectives, lung cleansers, oxygen—you must have them here."

The healer smoothed the covers over Kreste's shoulders and stood up. Kreste was already asleep, his breathing audible. The healer took Ferro's arm in his knobby fingers, drew him into the hallway and closed the door behind them.

"No ordinary pneumonia this, to come on so quick and so strong. The sea water, it damages the lungs, do you see, faster than the body can clear. Infection follows, but also an allergic reaction to the body's own secretions. Very serious."

Ferro's heart froze. "You can help him, can't you? There is something you can do?"

"Very little, I fear. Medicines I have, yes. I'll try them. His own body must heal him now."

The air turned thick in Ferro's throat. He could hardly breathe. For a moment the doorway swam in his vision worse than anything at sea. "He can't die."

"He very well may."

But if I hadn't brought him here, he'd still be safe and well in Miraz. If only I'd waited for the storm to pass or gotten him out of the water sooner...

"He must not die. If you can't treat him properly here, I'll have him moved to Haven."

"All I can do for him, that I will. I have nursed my own through worse and seen them live." The healer's eyes were bright and direct, his voice crisply confident. "If better you seek in Haven, you are mistaken. The pneumonia *may* finish him or may not, but the travel, at this season and in this weather, certain will. You can do nothing except wait and pray to whatever Name you call upon. Meanwhile, come with me, down into the kitchen. I will fix you some hot tea and also a cot in his room."

Hours later, while the healer attended to other patients, Ferro sat in the kitchen, drinking tea and staring out the window at the unceasing gray drizzle. Through the thick, distorting glass, he saw a stretch of street leading down to the harbor. The cobblestones were slick with reddish mud. Framed between the rows of houses, the ocean took on a sheen like unpolished jade.

The fishing boat lay tied to the pier, waiting for the completion of the repairs. Or maybe for the fisher and his mate to finish drinking up their passage fee, Ferro didn't know. When the fisher had carried their bags up to the healer's house, he gave Ferro a few words of encouragement, though they sounded empty to Ferro's ears.

Through the long afternoon, Ferro waited, paced, looked in on Kreste, and followed the healer around the little medicine-room until the healer ordered him out of sight. Eventually the healer went out on his rounds, to see villagers too ill to come to him, and Ferro was left alone with the sound of the dripping rain.

Ferro dumped the last of the tea, now cold and sour, into the sink and went upstairs. He opened the door a slit and stood watching Kreste. For a long moment, he could see no movement, could hear no labored breath. Kreste's body seemed to have fallen in on itself beneath the weight of the blankets.

Only yesterday they were battling the storm together. Kreste had been so strong...

Ferro crossed the room and sat on the bed. He touched Kreste's face with one hand. The skin felt hot and dry. Ferro's heart trembled with an emotion he could not name—part tenderness, part pain, part desperation.

And part anger, that Kreste, for all his greatness, was as mortal, as fallible as anyone.

Kreste's body shuddered and then lay still for a long moment before he took another breath. Listening, Ferro was struck by a sense of quiet fatality. His thoughts, confused and desperate only a few minutes before, came pitilessly clear.

Ferro bent and nuzzled Kreste's dry forehead. He ran his lips over the bony crest in a lover's caress. There was no response, nor did he expect one. He made a silent promise, a parting gift.

The dream of a free Chacarre shall not die with you.

When the healer came back from his village rounds, he found Ferro still sitting beside Kreste. The healer glanced from the cooling, motionless body to Ferro's face.

Ferro said, "There's nothing more either of us can do for him now."

"Gone he is, then." The healer crossed to the bed, touched the side of Kreste's neck. "Will you be wanting to take the body on to Haven or burn it here?"

The strangeness of the Isles washed over Ferro like a wave of fire. They *burned* their dead. Protest flared within him, but he pressed his lips together and kept his fur smooth and unreadable. What difference did it make to Kreste if his body were burned or buried or cast into the sea?

And yet... the thought snaked through Ferro's mind, *maybe it was not such a bad idea.* Buried bodies could be dug up, their identities established.

"This is as good a place as any, and fire as good an end," he said. "I'd be grateful if you'd help arrange it. Then—" he took a deep breath and straightened his spine, "then I must go on to Haven as quickly as possible and meet with your elders. Or whoever else might be willing to support a free Chacarre."

The healer's crest rippled. "Misread you I did for ordinary travelers, petty criminals perhaps."

"Doubtless the Terran invaders have already branded me as *criminal,* but neither petty nor ordinary," Ferro said. "I am Kreste, Helm of Chacarre, and I have fled to these Isles to establish a government in exile."

PART III

Chapter 31

These days, with the baby rounding his belly into softness, Alon felt dreamily content. He drifted from the apartment to the bookstore and back again. Even the spy mushrooms on the street corners took on a pastel sheen in his eyes. Sometimes, when Birre came home later or went out again in the evening, Alon would fall asleep on the sofa, swaddled in the comforter. If he thought about Birre's behavior at all, he supposed that Birre was finally settling down to his class work.

Eventually, Alon pieced together the clues—snatches of conversations, names mentioned in passing—on the surface, ordinary-sounding. When he'd confronted Birre, he learned the truth, that Birre was part of a group of students and advocats meeting secretly to oppose the Terran intervention. "Occupation," they called it. So far, their only action was to file a court suit to reinstate Kreste.

"That's what we've done... *publicly*," Birre had said. "Are you sure you want to know more?"

"What you do affects me, too," Alon replied. They'd been sitting at the dining table, facing one another over a meal that was rapidly growing cold. Alon's hands curled around his belly. "What about our child? What will we do while you're off saving Chacarre?"

"If I don't, what kind of future will he have?"

Alon wanted to run around the table, grab Birre, shake him, scream at him. The skin beneath his neck ruff burned. He managed to say, "Birre, if you have joined the resistance, then I must, also."

"Alon.." Birre's eyes gentled. He sounded more like himself again, the Birre that Alon loved and trusted. "The warders are putting people in jail under the emergency provisions and some of them aren't coming out again. I don't want to place you in danger."

"I'm already in danger. How could I go on, alone, if anything should happen to you? Or will you give up this cause."

"You know I can't surrender my principles."

"Then neither can I. Let me share the risk, the way we share everything else."

Collaborators

A few nights later, Birre came home particularly late. Alon, napping on the sofa, startled awake at the gust of frigid wind and the slamming apartment door. As he sat up, he couldn't tell what time it was, only that it was late. Droplets of rain dusted Birre's crest and the yoke of his heavy wool coat. Chill clung to him. He carried a parcel the size of a dictionary, wrapped in green oiled cloth. Something fey glinted behind his eyes.

More secrets?

Birre tugged his coat off and threw it across the back of the sofa. Rain water soaked into the fabric. When he put both hands on Alon's shoulders, Alon felt the slight quiver in his muscles, the quickness of his breath.

"You said you wanted to be part of the resistance," Birre said.

Alon's mouth dropped open. A wave of heat prickled through him. "What do you want me to do?"

Birre picked up the oiled cloth package. "Keep this at the bookstore for a few days. Someone named Timas will come for it."

Alon hesitated. He would gladly share Birre's danger, but he could not expect Meddi and Tellem to do so. He could not ask them to hide a weapon...

"Go ahead," Birre said. "Take a look."

Alon unfolded the cloth to reveal a sheaf of papers tied together with string. They looked like a child's attempt at a news sheet, run off on an old screening machine and stapled along the top. Cheap paper, available at any stationer's. Line after line of closely-spaced type, detailing arrests, beatings, how to avoid the new identity-paper rules. As for the writing itself, Alon cringed as he skimmed the first article.

"It won't win any literature awards," Birre said, "but it's the truth that counts."

"None of this appears in the regular sheets."

"What else, with Talense heading the censorship bureau?" Birre's mouth twisted. "They call it the Department of Information Services, but we all know what Talense does. He's been a favorite with the Terrans since they arrived. And he's very good. He could almost persuade you he's right. That's why the underground press is so important."

"Only if people can stand to read it!"

"So we'll get someone who can write better. Will you take it?"

Alon rewrapped the bundle. "It's already done."

As he made his way to the bookstore the next morning, Alon reflected that Miraz had become a melding of the familiar and the exotic. Trams still ran, and the first migrant birds fluttered from tree to tree along the major boulevards. Flower sellers plied their wares, late snow lilies, joy-of-the-ground, and exuberant spring daffies. Even the patches of bare soil beneath the budding trees exhaled a moist, confident smell. The news sheets were full of stories about the help the Terrans had given to Chacarran law enforcement and medicine. Terrans walked the streets. A whole new barrage of jokes had grown out of what sometimes came out of their translator units.

The ban on meetings—including Wayfolk Gatherings—continued. Some of the richer families had relocated to their country estates.

Alon carried the bundle that Birre had given him beneath his spring cloak, sandwiched in between his lunch and yesterday's news sheets. No one stopped him or asked for his identity papers, although at the square in front of Octagon Temple, a Terran soldier whistled and called out. The metal spy mushrooms were everywhere.

At the bookstore, Alon stoked the little round stove into warmth. Noises from the street were muffled. The sunlit dust took on a quality of timeless calm.

He kept the door locked while he wrapped the parcel in gray paper and marked it, "For Timas. Paid in Full." He put the parcel with the other special orders and opened the store.

A couple of old people came in, browsed through the tables and, after much debate, selected an illustrated second edition of children's adventures.

"It's a gift for our grandchild," said one. Alon found something strangely touching in the way the oldster counted out the money. He thought of small coins hoarded, bruised vegetables carefully pared, clothes worn just one more season, all balanced against a child's delight in these bright pages.

"I'm sure he'll enjoy it," Alon murmured.

"I remember this story from my own childhood," said the other oldster.

He broke off as the door bells jangled. A pair of Terrans walked in. They wore jumpsuits of pale quilted fabric, with strange devices attached to their belts. Light reflected dully on their bare faces.

The faces of the two oldsters went stony; expression fled from their eyes.

Alon handed the wrapped book to them and stepped around the desk. He'd never been this close to a Terran before. He hadn't realized how large they were, how broad-shouldered, polarized but with a difference. Alon, recoiling, sniffed the salty, alien smell of their bodies.

The two old people scurried out the door. Alon felt a twist of panic, an impulse to call out to them, *No! Stay!*

Ridiculous. This was his own store, his own city.

"Can I help you?" he forced himself to say.

"We came in to look around, mizz. What position in the city is this?" The Terran spoke through a translator device. His strangely oval eyes lingered on Alon's body.

Alon patted the folds of his tunic over his breasts to emphasize his pregnancy. The gesture made him feel safer.

"We sell books, mostly antique and collector's items. We also specialize in children's literature." He went over to the display table, picked up a beginning reader and held it out toward the Terran.

The Terran took it and carelessly flipped through the pages. "Too bad we can't read your writing. It'd make a nice souvenir."

The other Terran bared his teeth. "Hey, pretty thing, how about you showing us around the town?"

"Stuff it," said the first Terran. "You know the rules."

The second Terran waved his hands in the air, an incomprehensible gesture. "Just trying to be friendly. She's the first native that hasn't looked like some Flaming unpolarized mechanical device."

The next moment both Terrans sauntered out the door. It banged shut behind them. Alon lowered himself into the chair behind the desk and wrapped his arms around his belly. He told himself this uneasiness was rooted in the hormonal changes of pregnancy. No harm had come to him, nor even any threat of harm.

Alon forced himself to get up and perform a routine task to soothe his nerves, like dusting already-clean shelves or unpacking the latest shipment of picture scrolls. He couldn't keep his mind on even the simplest job. Longing for Birre left him aching and restless. Finally he decided there was nothing for it but to close up the shop. Meddi and Tellem would understand. Most pregnants didn't work this much; now Alon knew why.

He found Birre, as expected, in the library of the advocacy school. Birre looked up, his crest rippling in pleasured surprise. There was a little whispered teasing between them before another group of students in the nearest corner, J'ites by their badges, gestured at them to keep quiet.

A few blocks from the school building, they found a bakery. The warm, sweet smells of honey, citrus, and freshly baked bread filled the shop. From the back came the soft thump of dough being kneaded, the clink of pans and shaping blades. They sat down with their paper cups of tea and a plate of nut-studded flatcakes.

"I think it's time for you to stop working," Birre said after Alon had blurted out the story of the Terrans' visit.

"And stay at home, with nothing to do but wait for you? No, I don't want that."

"I need to know you'll be in a safe place."

Alon's crest jumped erect at the tone hidden behind Birre's words. "What—what do you mean?"

"I didn't want to say anything until we were sure." Birre smoothed back his crest with both hands, as if trying to restrain it, but the stiff hairs jumped up again. He glanced around the eating area, watched the couple at the nearest table get up and leave. He lowered his voice. "It won't be for long, I hope. A few days, a week."

Alon blinked. His thoughts felt doughy. He wasn't going to like what Birre said next.

"I'm going away," Birre went on. "Leaving Miraz."

"Leaving me? Leaving me *now*?"

"Keep your voice down!" Birre gestured, a hard, strong movement. "Do you think this is easy for me? Do you think I'd do it if there were any other way?"

After a heartbeat, Alon began to breathe again. From the kitchen came the sound of oven doors closing.

"We have lost our Helm," Birre said. "This committee the Terrans have put in his place is a fraud and we all know it. What will we lose next? We— the people I've told you about—are going to organize a series of public demonstrations."

"C-couldn't you do it here in Miraz?"

Birre gestured negation. "The Terrans are too strong, too allied to the mayor and the city warders. That's why we have to go to other cities—Briaz, Avallaz, Nantaz. That's where I've agreed to go."

"Where?"

"Nantaz."

He reached out, touched Alon's hand. "I can't leave it to others, not if I want our child to grow up in a free Chacarre."

Alon swallowed. His heart beat like a caged bird's. He knew better than to try to talk Birre out of it. He knew that mood, that reckless determination. "Then I must go with you."

The light in Birre's black eyes softened in response. Alon felt himself melting into them. How could he let Birre go? He could as easily cut out his own heart and throw it away.

"If anything happens to you—" Alon said.

"Shhh." Birre shifted, but his eyes didn't change. "I have to go, and the only way I can is knowing you're safe." His words were slow, deliberate. Gently he placed one hand on Alon's belly. "Our future is worth fighting for."

"*Dying for*," Alon corrected.

Birre nodded, his eyes still locked on Alon's. "In these times, who can promise more?"

"You can promise me you won't participate in violence. You won't harm anyone."

"How can I promise that? If I'm attacked, I'll defend myself. But if it makes you feel any better, I won't be the one to start it."

Alon covered Birre's hand with his own. He imagined the baby growing inside his body, the tiny hands, each finger exquisitely delicate, the eyes like polished riverstone, the swirls of downy fur, dark now with fluid but holding hidden lights of sun-touched platinum.

If anything happens to Birre, you are all I have.

Alon struggled to his feet and into Birre's arms. They held on to each other in a fierce, passionless calm. Finally, when he could bear it no longer, he pulled away and said in a strangled voice, "When will you leave?"

"I can't tell you that," Birre said. "Only that I won't see you again until I get back. You understand, don't you? The less you know, the less risk for you."

Alon raised both hands in a half-formed gesture. His strength had become a tattered rag. "Go, then. Please."

"I'm sorry, I just—"

"Go!" Alon was shocked at the vehemence in his own voice. Desperately he argued with himself, was *this* the way he wanted to say goodbye to Birre? "I can't—Just go and come back and do whatever you have to!"

Chapter 32

MIRAZ FREE PRESS: KRESTE REACHES SANCTUARY IN HAVEN; GOVERNMENT IN EXILE BRINGS NEW HOPE TO CHACARRE'S FREEDOM STRUGGLE.

Kreste the Helm was unlawfully removed from his position of Authority and Responsibility that he had been granted by tradition and by the People of Chacarre. Despite reports from the Puppet Press to the contrary, he became a prisoner in his own Residence for many months.

Kreste did not Capitulate to the Terran Tyrants. Even now, he continues to inspire us with the Spirit of Freedom and Rebellion. True Patriots throughout the land render him Secret Aid. One of these Heroes of Chacarre discovered a Dastardly Plot to

ASSASSINATE OUR VALIANT LEADER!

The Terran Tyrants and their allies, the Erls, could no longer tolerate our Beloved Leader, Kreste. As long as he lives, the People will never accept their Lies or the presence of Terran "Enforcers" on our Sacred Soil. Through their Dupes and Puppets, they conceived a Vile and Loathsome Plot to make it appear that Kreste had taken his own life and Thus to demoralize and disable the growing Resistance Movement.

In a Desperate midnight escape, Kreste and Trusted Confederates escaped from the Helm residence and fled in secret. Now safely beyond Chacarran borders, Kreste has established a Chacarran Government-in-exile. Together we will join forces to Defeat the Terran Tyrants and to Restore Freedom and Justice to all Chacarre.

LONG LIVE THE REBELLION! DEATH TO TERRAN TYRANTS!

Collaborators

Later that week, Alon prepared dinner for himself alone in the apartment. The casserole of beans and onions, flavored with garlic and chiroseth, which was supposed to be good for the baby's blood, was a traditional Wayfolk dish. He forced himself to eat, although he could not taste it. When the phone sounded, he jumped up and ran to it. It was Enellon, demanding to know where Birre was, and he sounded as if he were preparing to lecture a disobedient child.

Irritation rippled along Alon's spine. "Birre isn't here and I can't be sure when he'll be back."

"You said that yesterday." Enellon's voice crackled along the phone lines. "Didn't he come home last night? Or maybe he doesn't realize how serious the situation is. The Bureau of Internal Affairs has begun investigating illegal student associations. I know Birre's involved in one of them. He never could resist joining something forbidden, not even when he was a child. If he won't talk to me, then *you've* got to make him listen. This is no puerile escapade. Even with our business dealings with the Terrans, the family won't be able to help him if he gets himself into this kind of trouble. Do you understand what I'm saying? Do you? Why don't you answer me?"

"I'm sure everything's all right," Alon said as calmly as he could. "He's busy with his studies, that's all." It took an effort not to add that the benefits of leasing the Point Seryene factory and living quarters to the Terrans were considerable. Enellon must be desperate not to compromise that advantage.

Enellon said, "How can you know so little of what he's doing? You're paired, aren't you?"

Alon abandoned the attempt to hold his temper. "How dare you say that! You have no right!" He slammed the phone down, strode across the living room to the sofa and sat down, shaking. A few moments later the phone rang again. He glared at it until it stopped.

The emptiness of the apartment turned unbearable. The hours of not-knowing and not being able to talk about it to anyone had built into an almost palpable weight. When Timas had come by the bookstore and picked up the packet of news sheets, he'd been taciturn almost to the point of hostility.

Alon pulled on a jacket and slipped his census papers into its pocket.

The jacket was a gift from Tellem, who had worn it during his own pregnancy. The fine wool was dyed a muted gold, reinforced with green and brown embroidery on the cuffs and collar. It buttoned up the front, enhancing the curves of Alon's breasts and hips.

He had no clear idea where he was going when he left the apartment. It was past dusk but not yet curfew. The weather had been warmer the past few days, sending more people abroad.

A short time later, Alon's muscles warmed up and he felt better. He searched his pockets, found a little money, and went into the nearest bar. Stepping through the door was like slipping back in time, before the Terrans came. Warmth and subdued laughter swirled around him; inhaling, he smelled wine and toasted bread.

One or two gestured to Alon in a friendly way. Alon recognized them from the neighborhood. He seated himself on a high-backed stool. The keeper came over and asked what he'd like. Alon settled on spiced milk, although he would have preferred wine. The keeper smiled and added a spoonful of shallan, "for the baby."

The owner of a pedal-cycle repair shop on the corner by the bakery came over and asked how Alon did, how his parents did, how business was at the bookstore.

"They're still traveling, but not so much as before," Alon said, thinking of Meddi's comments of how difficult their book-searching expeditions had become.

"Aye, it's hard times for everyone. Soon they'll have reason enough to stay home, eh? Baby-sitting!"

A few of the customers close enough to overhear the comment laughed. Alon's crest rippled with pleasure. "You're saying I should enjoy my freedom while I still can?"

"I remember those last few months," the other said. "I thought I'd burst. Couldn't get comfortable in bed, could hardly waddle around the block. An hour into my hard rushes, I was all set to change my mind and stay pregnant for a while longer—" the eavesdroppers chuckled again "—but after two weeks of no sleep and all those diapers, I was looking for some way to put the little one *back*!"

Alon laughed so hard he had to set the cup of milk down on the bar or risk spilling it. Tension lifted from him. It felt good to sit here in the warmth and soft orange light, making jokes about babies.

"Be careful out there," the repair shop owner said as Alon paid his bill. "You don't want to get caught after curfew."

"What about you?"

"Me? Who cares if I end up in Kallen's basement, a tough old shoe like me?"

Alon laughed and patted the other's arm. The other reached out, caught his hand. Round eyes gleamed under shaggy ridges. "May Bavar, Fifth Aspect of the god, whose attribute is hope, guide and protect you."

Outside, there was little traffic to disturb the brooding quiet of the street, no light except for the dim radiance of the bar and the bluish strip lights. The cobblestones, polished by the years, looked wet. Alon walked slowly, his body relaxed in the combined warmth of milk and shallan. His thoughts drifted pleasantly.

"Hi there, gorgeous. Looking for some fun?"

Alon startled, looked around. He'd just passed the underground entrance where two Terrans emerged, one still on the stairs, the other striding toward him.

"Oh, you are a sight for sore eyes, did you know that?" The Terran hooked Alon's arm and drew him close. Alon flinched and pulled back, surprised by the strength of the alien's grasp.

"What do you—" Alon began.

"All these damned boy-dolls, what's a real man supposed to do?" The Terran bent his head toward Alon's, lips spread wide to bare his teeth. His naked skin glimmered in the street light; his breath was sweet with wine and something Alon couldn't place.

"Don't hog her," said the other. He switched to Terran, but Alon understood it well enough.

The Terran clutched Alon around the waist. "Let's all of us have a nice friendly party."

Alon pulled away. What could have possessed them to behave in this way? Couldn't they see he was pregnant? Even in the dim light, they should be able to make out his prominent breasts.

His voice came out high and squeaky. "Take your hands off me!"

The Terran stumbled, flailing for balance with his free hand and laughing raucously.

"Guess you shouldn't of had those last five drinks, huh?" said the first Terran.

"Shee-it, I can still get it up." The other Terran jerked Alon around and covered Alon's mouth with his. He slid his wet lips over Alon's, pushing Alon's teeth apart with his tongue. Alon gagged, too horrified to struggle. The Terran jerked open the top of Alon's jacket, popping buttons, and squeezed his breast.

Alon's vision went white. Along his back, he felt the muscled bulk of a polarized body. The salty reek of the alien filled his nostrils. Fingers dug into his buttocks. The hand on his breast kneaded, pinched his nipple. Alon cried aloud. The Terran laughed.

"Whoo-ee, is she hot, or what?"

"Stop! Stop it now! How dare you touch me like this!" Alon stumbled, trying to find words in Terran. "I'm pregnant! Can't you see? *I'm pregnant!*"

The second Terran gave Alon's breast another squeeze. "A pretty woman out alone, after dark, dressed like that, means only one thing."

"Shit, half the whores in Marspex got buns in the oven," said the other.

"Let me go!" Alon screamed and hurled his body backwards. He thrashed, brought up one knee to kick. His foot collided with something firm. He felt the grip loosen on one side. He jerked sideways.

Something smashed into his face. Red exploded, blanketing his vision. His body crumpled, nerveless, to the ground.

Voices rumbled above him; he couldn't understand what they were saying.

"—done it now—"

"—what she asked for—"

"—we deserve *something*—"

"—who's to know?—"

"—over there, in the alley—"

"Yeah, quick and dirty." Rough hands slipped under Alon's armpits. He struggled, flailing weakly with his feet. His head throbbed and he couldn't see clearly. He felt himself being lifted, carried. He cried out and something hit him again on the face. Cold stone slammed against his back.

One of the Terrans knelt over him. "She won't give us any more trouble."

Somehow Alon's long robe had gotten shoved up around his waist and his leggings wadded around his ankles, leaving his legs bare. He moaned, tried to sit up. He had to get away, get home...

He couldn't think straight, couldn't imagine what they wanted. To rob him—to kill him?

The baby! Panic-fueled, Alon punched at the Terran above him. His fist collided with something hard. The Terran pulled back, cursing. Kicking wildly, Alon struck out again. He struggled to roll over—

Fingers clamped around Alon's throat. His vision went dark. The Terran's heavy body pinned him to the ground. Hands tore at his underclothes, knees forced his legs apart—

Something thrust against his slit, something huge and rounded, many times larger than Birre's polarized nub—

Pain lanced up through his belly, intense and sudden. Screams filled his ears, his spine arched convulsively. Hot liquid flooded between his legs.

"Christ, she's bleedin' like a faucet!"

"Get the fuck out of here—"

The screaming went on, one throat-shredding howl after another. Agony lanced through Alon's belly. He tried to move, but his muscles wouldn't obey him. Dimly, as if it no longer belonged to him, he sensed his breath high and light, the spasms wrenching his belly again and again—

A voice called out; footsteps pattered in the distance, far and then near. Someone bent over him, said something; his only thought was that the voice was Chacarran, not Terran. Then the darkness whirled around him and he felt nothing at all.

Chapter 33

L ight and movement. Pain deep in his belly, spreading upward.
"We're almost there," a voice said.

A safe voice, a Chacarran voice.

He awoke to a flood of brilliance. Pale green walls leapt into focus, metallic instruments, tubes and bandages. He tried to move his arms.

"He's coming around," someone said.

A face appeared in his field of vision, unfamiliar, white-robed. "Don't try to talk. The anesthetic will leave you groggy for a while yet. You're in Riverview Hospital and you're going to be all right."

Alon moved his lips; they were dry and his mouth felt scummy. *Hospital?* His thoughts moved thickly. Nausea hovered at the edges of his consciousness. His body felt like a lump of half-fired clay, without sensation.

For some time, Alon drifted, neither awake nor truly sleep. Gradually he surfaced. He became aware of the dull, insistent throbbing in his belly, the burning in his genitals. Bits of memory flashed through his mind. A medical gave him an injection and the world went dark again.

He could not tell how much time had passed when he drifted back into consciousness. People brought him food and iced juices. The green room assumed a dreary familiarity. A senior medical came in, introduced himself. Alon moaned when he pulled away the covers and pressed his belly.

"You're very lucky to be alive," said the medical. "A few more minutes and you would have bled to death."

Alon started shivering. He couldn't think of the right words.

"I've never seen such damage before; your internal organs were lacerated." Was it Alon's imagination, or did the medical sound shaken? "It must have been caused by a hard, blunt weapon. Unfortunately, your placenta had implanted very low and the attachment was torn loose. You could very well have died."

Alon's hands flew to his belly. It still felt softly round. "You were able to save the baby, weren't you?"

The medical stared at Alon. Slowly his crest subsided.

Alon rolled away, his hands digging into the soft flesh of his face. His body curled in on itself. Pain juddered up his spine. Every hair in his crest felt like a tiny molten needle. He couldn't breathe.

The medical placed one hand on Alon's back. "It's difficult, I know. It will take time to absorb the shock and yet more time to recover. Even then, I'm not sure we ever get over the loss of a child. But you have your family and the blessing of the god in every Aspect to sustain you."

He paused, then his voice resumed its previous briskness. "Your parents are waiting to see you. I've explained the situation to them. When you're feeling a little better, the warders want to talk to you, also."

Alon felt the medical's departure as a swirl of empty air and a momentary silence. Another hand brushed his shoulder, the touch undemanding. The bed gave slightly as someone sat down at his side. He turned and found Meddi's arms around him. Familiar scents filled him— book paper, fresh air, soap. Something inside of him gave way and a strange, molten darkness came boiling up. His chest shuddered as if his heart were tearing itself apart. He heard a noise, like that of tormented animal, rasping through his throat.

Meddi rocked him gently, murmuring unintelligible words of comfort. Tellem stood near, bending over, one arm around both of them.

"I'm so sorry, so sorry.."

Meddi stayed with Alon during the interview. The two warders didn't seem very happy about Meddi being there, but the medical insisted that, given the trauma of losing a child, the presence of family was essential. Alon sat up in the hospital bed, clasping Meddi's hand.

The older warder took out a note case and pen. "You stated that you were attacked?"

"Yes. On my way home from a bar—"

"Let's start at the beginning, shall we? You were admitted half an hour after curfew, which means you were abroad very close to that time. You'd been drinking at a bar?"

"Spiced milk, not wine." Alon's breath caught in his throat. "I was on my way down the hill. And then I stopped and had a cup of milk and headed back home."

"Which was how far away?"

"I don't know, halfway up Northhill—"

"So you would have broken curfew no matter what?"

Meddi gestured, a cutting motion. "You're acting as if Alon had done something wrong."

"I'm trying to establish the facts in the matter. Now then, you were headed back home after drinking at a bar, almost curfew, and then what happened?"

"Two Terrans came up and put their hands on me. I told them I was pregnant. They wouldn't stop. They hit me and one of them—on the ground—" Memories of the alley flooded back, the stone under his back, the impact of the Terran's fist, sound of underclothes tearing.

A giant hand closed around Alon's chest. Darkness surged up within him once again. He tried to draw a breath. The room whirled.

"It's too much for him, can't you see that?" Meddi cried. "They attacked him in the most disgusting and horrible manner, almost killed him, *did* kill his unborn child, and here you are, harassing him about details. *Details!* You want details, you ask the medical who treated him."

"We *did* interview the medical," said the second warder. "He says he can't be sure what inflicted the internal injuries. Some kind of stick—"

"No!" Alon cried. "It was his nub—he tried to—as if we were—"

The warders glanced at each other, eyes incredulous. "This Terran tried to *mate* with you? Even though you were pregnant?"

"He must have been insane," said Meddi.

"Also monstrously deformed," the second warder said. "Not to mention—"

"They're not like us," the first said with a hushing gesture. "Maybe being permanently polarized does things to their brains as well as their bodies, I don't know." He turned back to Alon. "There were no surveillance devices in the area. Can you identify this Terran?"

"Th-there were two of them." Alon searched his memory for a vision of a face. He saw uniforms, pale against the night, smelled the mixture of wine and something else on the Terran's mouth, felt the fingers digging into his breasts. His heart beat raggedly and he trembled harder. But nowhere in the darkness could he find an image of a face.

When Alon woke the next morning, he found Tellem sitting at the bedside. Alon lifted his head and blinked. The light was too bright, the bed too hard. Nothing was in its proper place.

"Meddi and I will trade off staying with you," Tellem said. "You shouldn't be alone."

"Uhh." Alon stretched, started to sit up. He gasped and froze. The medication from last night had worn off and even a small movement sent needles of pain through him.

Tellem slipped one hand behind Alon's head and lowered him back down. He raised the head of the bed and moved the breakfast tray closer. "Eat something, but don't move around. You're not supposed to get up for another day or two."

"I don't want to stay in bed," Alon said, poking at the fruit and boiled grain like a petulant child. "I want to go home."

Home? Home without Birre? Home without the baby? From the back of his mind, Alon heard a faint keening. Something deep inside him ached, ached without hope of ending.

"In a few days," Tellem said soothingly. He stroked the hair on Alon's face. "We've tried to contact Birre, to let him know. His parents don't know where he is. They said he hasn't attended class all this week. Alon... there isn't trouble between you, is there?"

Nantaz. He's gone to Nantaz. The words lay like a lump of metal in Alon's chest, crushing him, pressing in on him. How easy it would be, a few words only, to have that secret lifted from him.

"If you can't tell us where he is," Tellem said gently, "perhaps there is a person we can contact, to send a message."

"Birre didn't want me to know too much." Alon thought for a moment. "There was someone named Timas."

"Timas of the package?"

"Yes. I have no idea how to find him. Or if he can help."

"You would be surprised," Tellem said, patting Alon's hand, "how many people wander through a bookstore and how many Ways open from its doors. In times of peace, it is a center of learning; in times of trouble, a source of strength."

"Birre will be so upset." Alon tried to sit up again. His head whirled and his lower body twinged in protest. He lay back quickly, heart pounding. "Tellem, what's wrong with me?"

"I told you not to get up," Tellem said, his voice regaining its usual crispness. "You need time for the surgery to heal, that's all."

"Surgery?"

"Well, yes. The medical felt you shouldn't be told so soon after losing the baby. But I don't believe in keeping this kind of secret."

"Something else? You mean more than what's already happened to me? What could be more?"

"They had to repair the damage from the forced—penetration." Tellem stumbled on the word, but his eyes did not waver. "Although they can't be sure yet how well the tissues will heal, they're certain there will be residual scarring." He took a deep breath and went on in a lowered voice. "There's a chance you will still be able to produce and implant an egg. But you should not expect... they don't think you'll be able to carry another child."

Alon lay back against the pillows, propped up on the elevated bed. The nightmare wasn't over; he wasn't safe. He would never be safe. He would carry this with him wherever he went, invisible, this thing that changed him forever.

Tellem laid one hand on Alon's. His touch was light, more warmth than pressure. "I can't know what you're going through," he said softly. "I can only say how my heart grieves with you."

Alon stared ahead, unblinking. His crest shivered. The dryness in his eyes made them feel cold.

Tellem's voice came in a whisper. "Time, it will take a long time."

Alon's days assumed an order according to the schedules of the hospital staff. He ate when they placed food before him, slept when their medications made him drowsy, answered their questions about his bodily pains, and lay motionless in bed in between times. Tellem and Meddi traded off watches, but neither urged him to talk. Flowers arrived, a basket of fruit, letters from friends.

Enellon and Saunde came to the hospital the morning of Alon's discharge. Saunde immediately went to Alon, who was sitting on the edge of the bed, fastening his tunic. Alon's breasts had already begun to lose their fullness, and the flesh over his hipbones sagged.

"We're so very, very sorry," Saunde said as he took Alon into his arms. Alon felt fragile, all bones against Saunde's bulk. "We wish we could have come to you before this. Those awful hospital regulations, you know. Tell me," holding Alon at arm's length and looking into his eyes, "what can we do to help?"

"I don't need—" Alon began, then cut himself off. He took a deep breath. He tried to sound reasonable. "I don't know what I need. I'll call you if I think of anything."

"I'm sorry I said those things about you and Birre," Enellon said. "I should have realized that if Birre wasn't with you, and you couldn't say where he was, there must be a good reason for it. I have—" he paused, mouth working, crest leaping in jagged ripples, "—I have strong feelings about what he may be doing. These are not times when it's safe to play at secrets and conspiracies. Even the appearance of insurrection—"

"Stop it!" Alon's voice sounded shrill to his own ears. "Take your damned politics somewhere else!"

Saunde blinked, startled. "Oh my dear, we didn't mean to distress you."

Birre burst into the room. His hair was disheveled, his clothes rumpled as if he'd slept in them for days, and a fiery abrasion scarred one cheek. He pushed past his parents and caught Alon in his arms.

Alon gasped for air, crushed against Birre's chest. Unfamiliar smells enveloped him—machine oil and soot, dried blood and fresh air and underneath them, the familiar scent of Birre's body.

"I came as soon as I could," Birre murmured, low and close to Alon's ear.

The next moment, when Birre relaxed his grip on Alon's shoulders, Enellon said, "Where have you been? Whatever induced you to leave Alon alone at a time like this?"

Birre drew Alon to his side in a protective gesture and faced his parent with level eyes. "Do you really want me to answer that question?"

"Enellon—" Saunde put out a hand to Enellon, who'd started toward Birre, fists clenched. "What does it matter now? He's here, back where he belongs."

"Yes, but for how long?" Enellon demanded, his eyes still fixed on Birre.

Alon shrank back against Birre's strength. Strange how he should feel so much more fragile with Birre here. "Stop," he said, his voice almost a whisper. "I just want to go home."

"We're getting out of here," Birre told his parents. "When you're ready to listen as well as talk, you know where we'll be!" Before the door swung closed behind them, Alon heard Saunde's troubled voice, but could not make out the words.

Birre brought his mug of tea to sit beside Alon. "The message from Timas said to come home. Nothing about what had happened. I didn't even know it was from you. I—I had no idea." He paused, gathered himself. "I wish I could help you."

His sight blurring, Alon slid into Birre's arms. They rocked together. Birre stroked his hair and murmured nonsense.

"I need time, I think. Time and you being here." Alon's throat ached. "What do you need?"

Birre glanced out the window, eyes opaque. "I need to find the demons who did this. I need to make them pay."

Chapter 34

Ferro couldn't see the ocean from his office window, only a tangle of dead branches from a tree so misshapen that, had it dared to grow in a proper Miraz garden, it would have been cut down years ago. The sky hovered like a dense grayish smudge beyond the second-story walls and roofs. The mixed odors of smoke and fish hung in the air, broken only by fitful breezes from the sea. On days like this, Ferro's homesickness pressed on him. His memories of Miraz took on a dreamy glamour—the graceful lines of the buildings, the beauty and variety of the flowers, the rivers sparkling in the sun, the music and laughter that filled the streets. Haven's ugliness was due more to poverty than design, but the thought brought no comfort.

And, he thought with a sigh, there was nothing he could do about it, any more than there was anything constructive he could do about this darkly claustrophobic closet masquerading as an office. The Islanders had been as generous as they could. The town leaders wouldn't accept payment of rent, half in sympathy for his loss, half out of respect for the Helm of Chacarre, not even when the funds smuggled in from Avallaz permitted it.

Ferro sat down behind his desk, facing the door as he had trained himself to do. Here he created letters and essays that might—no, he corrected himself, *would*—change the world. Articles for the burgeoning underground press in Miraz, letters of appeal to Valada, the Delta States, and Freeport Cities, encoded correspondence with supporters at home, to be carried south to the mainland and mailed from various locations within Chacarre. In his earlier life, he would never have suspected himself of such prodigious energy. Now the words leapt from his mind, charged with a vision that seemed to come from somewhere else, to seize him, devour him, flow through him. Kreste himself could not have done more.

I am Kreste now.

Ferro took out a clean piece of paper and began to write in a sloping script that was now so like Kreste's. When he was no more than a couple of paragraphs into the letter, a tap sounded at the door. He looked up, crest ruffling in puzzlement. He'd sent his aide, an idealistic youngster from one of the fishing towns along the Ice Sea, on an errand, and the aide couldn't have returned yet.

"Come in," he called.

The door swung open and two people entered. The first, an Islander, worked dockside, keeping watch on the sprinkling of new arrivals and making sure none of them found Kreste before their loyalties were certain. And the second—

"Na-chee-nal!" Ferro sprang to his feet. "I haven't seen you since that reception in Erlonn right after the Terrans landed. What are you doing here?"

The burly Valad enveloped Ferro in a breath-squeezing hug. "I should have known that any place I sought Kreste, you would be there, also! By the Blood, he's well hidden! I had to exert considerable *pressure* on your sentinel here to find you."

The dock worker looked puzzled at this interchange between the person he believed to be Kreste and this Valad barbarian, then shrugged as if to say the dealings of foreigners were beyond understanding. Ferro, who had witnessed Na-chee-nal's powers of persuasion against far more experienced resistance, gestured reassurance, adding, "I'll continue the interview in private."

Na-chee-nal waited until the door had closed firmly. "My friend, it is good to see you. Although, truth be told, I would rather it had been under different circumstances."

"Come, sit down. How did you happen to leave Erlonn?"

Na-chee-nal perched upon the chair. "I was called back to Ah-rhee-koh-nah-tee. The Herdmasters had gotten a letter—a highly *urgent* letter—from Kreste and they dared not withdraw their official Chacarran diplomats to answer it."

As Ferro sat back at his desk, gesturing, *I understand.* Such a move would surely attract Terran suspicions.

"I assume you're here in person in answer to the appeal?" Ferro asked.

"I came here to see Kreste." Na-chee-nal's bright eyes rested on Ferro's. Neither of them moved.

Ferro realized too late that he had let the silence drag on. *By the Sixth Aspect of the god and its inversion that is apathy, he knows! Or if he didn't, he does now. The question remains, what will he do about it?*

Na-chee-nal's thick fur fluttered in an imaginary wind. "So," he said, his voice husky, "what happened? Did the Terrans assassinate him after all?"

"It was the Channel crossing," Ferro said. "Pneumonia from aspirating the sea water. It was over very quickly. But we'd gone through so much together, I couldn't—"

"You owe me no explanations," Na-chee-nal said. "All I need to know is that I am speaking to the person who wrote that letter."

After a long moment, Ferro gestured assent.

The Valad shifted sideways in his chair, as if trying to adjust his frame to its austere contours. "Officially, Valada cannot become involved in a dispute between Chacarre and any other nation, not even Erlind. In the absence of any clear threat to Valada's own welfare, we have no choice but to preserve our neutrality in this affair."

"'Absence of any clear threat'?" Ferro's crest shot upright. "Na-chee-nal, you're neither blind nor stupid. Unless we stop the Terrans while we still have something to defend, there will be no future for any of us. Or would it be in the best interest of Valada to wait until you face the combined strength of Chacarre and Erlind, armed with Terran weapons?"

"Very aptly put. Your passion does you honor and your rhetoric has improved greatly since our nights together in Ah-rhee-koh-nah-tee." Na-chee-nal's hands moved in the gesture of peacemaking. "I did not say these words came from my own mouth, only those of my Herdmasters."

Ferro's crest settled once more against his skull. "Is there a difference?"

The Valad threw his head back and laughed. "Even better—I came to help you! Me, Na-chee-nal of the line of heroes and fire-eaters!" He leapt to his feet, sending the chair rocking. "I'm worth a thousand bureaucratic water-bloods! My ancestors conquered the plains and pounded into dust anyone who stood in their way! I'll show you how to rout the Terrans and everyone else who stands in your way! Together we will sweep across the landscape, rekindle the flames of glory, and bring justice to Chacarre!"

"Please," Ferro said as soon as he found his voice again, "sit down. Let's talk about this sensibly."

"Sensibly! This is the time for bold action, not an academic symposium!"

"Of course I welcome your help, but you must understand the nature of the struggle. This is not an heroic conquest, the stuff of legends and epic poetry. The Terrans have weaponry far superior to ours. We cannot meet them in force against force."

"Then what?" Na-chee-nal placed both fists in the center of Ferro's desk and leaned forward. An indigo-tinted flush covered his skin and his round eyes bulged slightly. "Are you going to sit here writing *letters*," he made the word sound obscene, "while your country lies bleeding under the invader's scimitar? Do you have any idea how to plan a battle, stage an invasion, ambush a supply convoy? Have you ever attacked and then as quickly melted into the countryside? Do you know how to make every rock, every snowflake, every alleyway your ally, how to strike again and again until the maddened beast turns at last upon itself? Do you have even the most rudimentary understanding of what you face?"

"Do *you*?" Ferro drew himself up. The fur around his neck stirred to life. "What you're proposing is slaughter. *Ours.* The Terrans are more powerful than anything our world has ever seen. We cannot win this war as we've won others, by force of arms."

"I tell you," Na-chee-nal said, refusing to withdraw, "we cannot win it any other way. If not by direct confrontation, than by attrition, by sabotage, by extortion and terror. Whatever means we must."

"Sit down," Ferro said, "and we will talk."

MIRAZ FREE PRESS: TERRAN NEST DESTROYED! DEATH TO THE OPPRESSORS!

The Chacarran Freedom Movement struck a Mighty Blow for Liberation when our valiant Fighters destroyed the Terran barracks in the Point Seryene district. Over one hundred Enforcers met their Just Doom in the ensuing fire. The owners of the building, Traitors to the Chacarran Cause, have been warned that their continued cooperation with the Terran Oppressors will not be tolerated. They, and all who collaborate, will be Targeted for Destruction!

The Terran Barracks was selected as our first demonstration of Revolutionary Power when it became known that among its Tenants were the Perpetrators of the most Ghastly and Inhuman Crimes against the Chacarran people. Following the refusal of the Puppet Warders to take action against these Heinous Criminals, the Chacarran Freedom Movement vowed to Dedicate ourselves to the Swift and Sure Administration of Justice. The Cleansing of the Terran Nest is only the beginning!

DEATH TO OPPRESSORS!

FREEDOM FOR CHACARRE!

Miraz: FIRE ENGULFS DORMITORY BUILDING; 5 DEAD, 25 INJURED IN MASSIVE BLAZE; TERRAN LABORATORIES DAMAGED; ARSON SUSPECTED. Report by Ambrom. (Cleared by the Department of Information Services).

Early this morning, the quiet district of Point Seryene was torn from sleep by an enormous explosion and deadly structure fire. The building, once a warehouse, had been converted into factory, laboratory, and living quarters for the Terran Peacekeeping scientists. Blasts rocked the building and huge flames burst from the windows, scattering sparks into the surrounding streets. Within moments, the combined forces of the city fire control services and the Terrans were at work combating the blaze. Oxygen-depleting foams, applied by Terran hovercraft, amplified the effects of the ground-based Mirazan efforts.

Five people are known to have died in the fire, four of them Terrans. One Chacarran employed as a janitor succumbed to smoke inhalation.

Due to the suddenness and extent of the fire, arson was an immediate possibility. Miraz officials have already begun their investigation under the supervision of Terran specialists. Using the superior science of the Terrans, the perpetrators of this horrendous outrage will soon be apprehended and brought to trial.

Mayor Lexis arrived on the scene in mid-morning and inspected the still-smoldering ruins. "This is a terrible tragedy," he told a gathered crowd, "and an affront to Chacarran decency." The Chacarran Liberation Movement claimed that it had set fire to the building to protest the refusal to prosecute Terran soldiers accused of crimes against Mirazan citizens.

"We are a nation of laws, not outlaws!" Lexis proclaimed. "We will not be intimidated by such bullying tactics. Along with our Terran allies, we will defeat all who stand in the way of a decent and civilized society. I call on all loyal Chacarrans to root out this new evil! Strike the traitors wherever they may hide! Together we will prevail and bring Chacarre to a new and glorious future!"

Chapter 35

It was strange, after so much impatience and waiting and scheming, to be planetside at last. Vera Eisenstein picked through the charred splinters of the factory complex, pausing often to take a deep breath. The roof of the sleeping area was gone, the furnishings a heap of slag. She knew the chemicals used, the temperatures attained, and the force of the explosion. Before leaving *Prometheus*, she'd read the clinical reports on the injuries of the survivors. She'd spent a moment staring at the list of those who'd been killed, while her vision swam and her heart seemed to be beating inside someone else. By the time she set foot on Bandar, she was fully prepared to deal with the site investigation with calm, professional detachment.

What she wasn't prepared for was the smell. The words "burned blood" rose to her mind, although she'd never smelled it. The next moment, her nose wrinkled with more ordinary odors, soot and charcoal, half-charred wool, and overheated grease, all overlaid with something she couldn't identify. She'd been prepared to deal with sights and sounds, numbers and concepts, not the more primitive olfactory realities.

Her eyes felt wet. Disliking the sensation, she forced herself to think of the waters she carried within each cell of her body, the ocean of her own evolutionary heritage; the ionized salts, the soluble and fibrous proteins. She took a step.

Glucose, esterified fatty acids. Her heart beat steadier. *Enzymes, hormones. Mucopolysaccharides.* The ache behind her sternum eased.

Vera stepped carefully over the charred, splintered beams, her bodyguard a pace behind. She would not find human remains; these had all been shuttled up to *Prometheus* for cryostorage.

She paused to inspect a section of wooden board. One surface had turned to charcoal, the other still flat and honey-colored under its bubbled varnish. Part of a dresser, she thought, surely too delicate for a headboard or a chest. It had covered a heap of ashes. Her toe brushed them and sent the top layer billowing. There was something else in the mound. It felt soft. It was the little stuffed animal that Sarah had kept at her work station on *Prometheus*. Even then, it had been so worn, Vera had not been able to tell what it represented—a panda bear or a tiger, some creature the children of this planet had never known.

I can't have distractions like this, she thought. *I have too much work to do.*

But the image leapt to mind of the first time she'd met Sarah as a young undergraduate—the piercing quality of her questions, the way her hands moved when she was excited.

Vera remembered thinking, *This is someone who understands. This is someone to whom I can pass my legacy, the child of my mind and my dreams.*

She had never said any of this to Sarah. There had always been more urgent things that required discussion—the equipment for this experiment, the analysis of that one, a new idea or solution.

We talked about everything but ourselves.

She remembered waking up in Medical and seeing, through the muzzy waves of sedatives and anesthetic, Sarah's smiling, soot-grimed face. She remembered the touch of Sarah's fingers.

All that promise, all that bright young enthusiasm, gone. Snuffed in an instant. *And for what? One massive cultural misunderstanding after another.*

Vera turned back to one of her bodyguards—he was from Command, for Hammadi would not trust her safety to less than his best—and handed him the toy. "See this gets put in storage with the other personal effects." The guard took it with a blank expression.

Apart from the human loss, the physical damage was extensive. The incendiary device had been planted in the laboratory section. It was, in Hammadi's words, "a mess." He'd sent her down after the Engineering techs had thrown up their hands and said the place was unsalvageable, there was nothing to do but raze the rubble and start over from the beginning. Instead, Hammadi had sent Vera to work a miracle.

Vera poked and prodded, testing the blackened walls of the furnace and evaluating what was left of the laboratory glassware. She examined the bins of processed ore, assessing the damage.

The ceramic tiles of the furnace were crazed from the explosion. They'd have to be replaced with new ones. It would take months to build a replacement furnace and extract more lanthanides. They hadn't had time to separate enough of the individual elements they needed.

Maybe, Vera thought, kicking up ashes as she paced, that was the wrong way to think of the problem. Maybe the answer was to redesign the navigation focusing lasers to use what they had already purified. If she tried a different cavity geometry... An etalon-like structure without the cavity modes? A thin-film active medium, total internal reflection at one face, flat mirrors?

It might work. Her pulse speeded up and a thrill, like a fine current of electricity, dazzled up her spine. She'd have to check the pump absorption figures...

"Stop right there!" one of the guards shouted. A few meters away, a native paused, framed by the still-standing side beams of a doorway. Back-lit, he looked almost like a man.

Prereproductive polarization, Vera thought.

The native gestured, a graceful movement of one hand. The stiff hairs along the sagittal axis of his skull rose and fell in patterned ripples.

They communicate with crest movement and gesture as well as words. She moved closer. The guard, his hand laser drawn, stayed between them.

The native's words hummed through the transceiver element hooked over her ear. The translator gave them an emotionally flat tone. "I am Gosem. I am engineer. I was friend to Sarah Davies."

"Gosem, yes. She spoke of you with respect."

Vera felt a flash of irritation at the awkwardness of the translator. She switched it off. If she was going to make mistakes, she'd make her own. Her command of spoken Chacarran wasn't perfect, but it was a hell of a lot better than this stilted rendition.

The guard hovered, scowling. "Oh, get out of the way!" she snapped. "Do something useful!"

He held his ground. "I'm protecting you, Dr. Eisenstein."

"Then do it from over there!"

The guard took one step back. Vera walked up to the native and held out her hand. Slowly, enunciating each Chacarran word with care, she said, "My name is Vera Eisenstein. I was Sarah's teacher."

Hesitantly, the native placed his hand, three narrow fingers and an opposable thumb almost as long, in hers. The palm was leathery and devoid of hair. This close, she could see the subtle whorls of downy facial hair, the pearly, almost translucent quality of the skin beneath, the corded border of the jacket yoke, the position and movement of his larynx as he spoke. He said, "Sarah has spoken to me of you as well."

"You were working together on the—" she hesitated, searching for the Chacarran technical terms, finally gave up and lapsed into Terran, "—*lanthanide extraction* project?"

A pause, more rippling of the crest hairs. Vera watched, struck by the subtlety of the movement. "I am not working now. My mate will be pregnant very soon. If not for that, I could have been one of the damaged or killed in this place. I tell you that I too mourn the death of your cousin, Sarah."

She is not my cousin, Vera started to say. She could only guess what the Chacarran word meant within its own cultural context. Perhaps *successor* or *apprentice* or even, *beloved younger person,* all of which were true.

"Doctor Eisenstein," the guard said, touching the portable link hooked to his belt, "the car is ready."

Les Bellini had asked her, in her role as consultant, to sit in on his meeting with the Mirazan mayor. She very much doubted the local investigation had turned up anything of significance, since they hadn't been able to identify the explosives used without Terran help. But there were future security issues to be discussed as well.

Be careful, Vera Elizabeth, she said to herself. *Hammadi thinks he has the military situation well in hand. But things here are not as he supposes. For all its beauty, this is a treacherous place. There are forces here that can suck us up in one breath and spit us out the next.*

When she opened her mouth to say more, Gosem had already sidled toward the door frame. Just beyond, she caught sight of another native, his fur velvety black, but with richly feminine curves showing through the form-fitting jacket. Then both were gone, melted back into the city.

The guard escorted her to the entrance of the compound. Here more Command staff waited, their eyes wary. They were armed with both hand lasers and narrow-beam rifles.

"Commander Bellini sends his compliments, ma'am, and asks you to join him in his office," one of the guards said.

A large and very comfortable-looking native chair had been placed facing the desk. Les Bellini stood behind the desk, arranging flowers in a clear plastic cylinder.

"Flowers?" she said.

He stood back, brows knotting. "The mayor's been sending them every day. People here look on flowers as very serious business. If you don't display them prominently, it amounts to a personal insult. I'm not very good at arranging them."

It was a simple problem in topology. With a few deft movements, Vera rotated the blue flowers so that their heads nodded outward, a cascade rising to the single white spray with the thick green stalks forming a central pillar.

"If you can solve the nav laser problem that easily, my day will be perfect," Bellini said.

Vera lowered herself into the native chair, which felt even better than it looked. The cushioning caught her low back at the proper angle to give support. If Hammadi had something like this, she thought, it would do wonders for his temper.

"I have ideas of how to salvage what remains." She rubbed her hands together. A layer of soot clung to her fingers, ashes from the pile in which she'd found Sarah's stuffed toy.

The link buzzed. A voice said, "He's here, sir."

The mayor swept into the room, followed by an aide who took up a position just inside the door. The aide held himself stiffly, reminding Vera of someone who belonged in uniform. He wore a cloak that could have hidden a variety of weapons in its ample folds.

This whole business is turning me paranoid. Not good, as suspicion distorted the problem-solving process.

Lexis was shorter than she'd pictured him, and he wore what looked like traditional academic robes in deep purple satin. He'd been an unknown poetry professor, then a local hero after the first civil disturbance, the one for which Hammadi had authorized the use of the lasers. *Now he's in a position of power, with money enough to buy expensive clothes. I wonder what his poetry makes of that?*

Bellini welcomed the mayor with a formal bow. If it had been directed toward herself, Vera would have called it arrogance. She wondered if it meant anything at all to the alien.

Bellini was Hammadi's golden boy, the one who had commanded the first contact and later beat the Erls into that humiliating capitulation over the border attack. He didn't like to lose, not even to a gift of flowers.

They spoke Chacarran, opening with the equivalent of meaningless comments about the weather and each other's health. Vera noticed that the entire conversation, both direct and translated, was being recorded. Bellini referred to her as "our most distinguished scientist." The aide was introduced by name, Ambyntet, but not title; his name struck Vera as odd, having more syllables than usual for Chacarran.

She felt as if she had just stepped into an apparently smooth lake, only to find turbulent currents beneath.

Lexis opened discussion on the progress of the police investigation. Vera watched him carefully, noticing the constant rippling and fluffing of his crest.

"We've got a number of suspects in custody already," Lexis said. "People we've been watching for some time, people we think might have been involved in previous terrorist acts."

"You said you'd uncovered evidence of a conspiracy," Bellini said. "Precisely what have you found?"

"Just a few days ago, we caught someone trying to reach one of our important officers at the Department of Information Services. This person could give no good account of his motives, but he's Wayfolk and we have reason to think his real purpose in Miraz was assassination."

Vera watched Bellini's face, the minute narrowing of his eyes, the tightening of his mouth. He shifted in his seat.

"Your technical facilities have been invaluable," Lexis went on. "They're far beyond our own capabilities." He gestured with both hands. "I feel quite confident that together we will soon have the situation under control. For now."

"That's the real question, isn't it?" said Bellini. "To make sure this kind of atrocity never happens again."

"I've given the most thorough consideration to your proposal," said Lexis. "Under normal circumstances, of course, our own warders would be sufficient. We both know these are not normal circumstances."

Even if she could redesign the navigational laser circuits and nothing else went wrong, *Prometheus* would be captive here for months to come. If not, it could be years.

We can't police the city ourselves, Hammadi had told Vera before he'd sent her down. *And we're not about to arm the locals with hand lasers. They put their best security on the factory project and still this happened.*

Hammadi had authorized Bellini to negotiate with the Erls to supply additional police troops. Using the protocols of Peacekeeping recruitment as a model, they would be hand-picked, highly trained, and fluently bilingual. More importantly, they would be under Terran command.

"I understand your concerns," Bellini told Lexis. "If I were in your position, I would be asking questions, too."

"It's not merely a matter of questions, but of hoping, of daring, of dreaming," Lexis said. "The world is changing in directions none of my people could have possibly imagined. You tell me of the Peacekeepers of your own world, where sworn enemies come together to stop an even greater violence. It is as if you have presented me with a poem in the form of a comet."

He stopped, as if the moment had outstripped his words. His hands paused in front of his breasts, and Vera did not need to know the precise meaning to read the eloquence of his gesture. She found it strangely affecting.

"Maybe it's just as well it's you talking to us now and not a career politician," she said gently. "Someone so rooted in bureaucracy that he can't see the possibilities of the future."

"Yes! That's exactly right! 'The possibilities of the future.' In a situation like this, when people are so frightened, we must introduce these changes gradually. We cannot march Erlind soldiers down the streets of Miraz!" Lexis's crest flared to new height.

Bellini had worked with Erlind commanders after the aborted Demmerle invasion, as he now reminded Lexis. The Erls knew the consequences of provoking further retaliation. Their tradition of blind obedience to orders made them perfect for this task. Where their leaders commanded, they would follow without hesitation. Now their leaders would take their orders through the chain of command from Hammadi.

Lexis hunched forward. "This is what we must do, then. Create a special branch of the Miraz city warders, small units for specially chosen assignments. We'll put them in our uniforms to avoid any suspicion. Unlike the real warders, they will be under my direct orders."

"We won't allow transfer of command," Bellini said.

"Oh, no! I don't mean to suggest you relinquish anything! You would, of course, retain full control. It can't be official, do you see? This way, Kallen, the real Warder Chief, won't have any authority. People will eventually realize they aren't Chacarran—the accent will give them away, if nothing else. I don't see this as a permanent solution, only a way to gain additional time while we continue with our educational efforts."

"Ah yes," said Bellini. "The Department of Information Services."

"Is under capable direction. The tragic death of your liaison, Sarahdavies, will not interrupt this vital work. I assure you, it will continue. Then it's only a matter of time before we reach a new condition of tolerance."

And so, Sarah becomes just another footnote in history. The air seemed suddenly too bright.

Lexis rose to his feet; Bellini followed his lead.

"My people will be forever grateful for your assistance," Lexis said. His vocal tone shifted. "I wonder if you would take dinner with me one evening."

Vera caught the slight arching of Bellini's brow, the tension at the corner of his mouth. Bellini said, "Perhaps. When we have time for such pleasantries."

"I look forward to that eventuality." With the same sweeping movements, Lexis left the room, his police attendant in tow.

Bellini leaned back in his chair and clasped his hands behind his head. "Quite a smooth talker for someone who was an underpaid teacher this time last year."

"He needs us." Vera kept her voice even. Something in Bellini's attitude, a trace of the arrogance she'd suspected earlier, irritated her.

"That he does. He's full of ideas and enthusiasm. But the question remains, can he deliver?"

Vera studied Bellini, the smoothly confident half-smile, the tautness of jaw and neck, the hint of suppressed emotion in the corner of his mouth. *Hammadi's golden boy*, she thought again.

"That depends," she said quietly, "upon what it is we want delivered."

Chapter 36

The cell had been designed for two people and now housed six. They took turns sleeping on the twin bunks, the single cot, and the pads on the floor. Hayke always took the floor. The resulting stiffness of his body gave him something to focus on, a lens through which to see the Way during the lonely nights. Besides, it seemed a small enough kindness.

The newest prisoner, clad like the rest of them in a shapeless gray tunic over baggy leggings, shook the barred door. "Hey! Guards! Where's our breakfast?"

"No use shouting," another prisoner grumbled from the upper bunk. "They'll feed you when they get around to it."

The newcomer squinted up at him. "What're *you* in for?"

"Har!" said the lower-bunk occupant. "What you're in for and what you've actually *done* aren't necessarily the same thing."

"What does it matter?" someone else said. "We're all here because the Terrans, may Kesh curse them forever with putrid malignancies, need someone else to blame for their own stupidities."

Hayke folded the sleeping mat and shoved it in the corner. Some of his cell mates had been charged with breaking the peace or conspiracy to commit sedition. Others, like himself, had simply been arrested without any formal proceedings. He explained he'd come to Miraz to see an acquaintance.

Name? the warder interrogators asked.

Hayke told them, *Talense, a press with the Interclan News Agency.* From their immediate reaction, he knew he'd made a mistake, that it would be useless to insist on his innocence. After a while, they'd stopped asking questions. No one would tell him when he might be released or formally charged.

Keys rattled in the door at the end of the corridor and the prisoners lifted their heads. Stomachs gurgled hopefully. The door swung open. Two guards entered, half-dragging a prisoner, while a third waited by the door, his rifle in plain sight.

The prisoner stumbled, so Hayke could see nothing of his features, only the dark mane falling like a veil across his face, his torn garments, and a swath of livid bruises.

One of Hayke's cell mates let out a breath and another grunted in agreement. They all complained about their treatment, the food, the crowding, the lack of contact with the outside, as a recreation, a diversion from the endless boredom. None of them had been beaten.

The guard with the rifle nodded toward Hayke's cell. "Only six here, seven in all the others. He won't make any trouble."

Hayke and his cell mates shuffled to the far end of the cell while the door was unlocked and the prisoner was hurled inside. He crumpled to the floor and lay there, motionless except for the faint, soft movement of his chest. Dried blood darkened his lips. He looked very young.

Hayke slipped his hands under the new prisoner's shoulders and straightened him out as gently as he could. The prisoner moaned, head rolling from side to side. Hayke said to the others, "Help me get him on the mat."

"Where will *I* sleep?" one prisoner grumbled.

Hayke loosened the new prisoner's clothing and began examining his injuries.

"Blazes." The prisoner scratched behind one shoulder. "Is he hurt bad?"

"Nothing seems broken," Hayke answered, "but he might have a cracked rib. I can't tell about internal injuries... He belongs in a hospital, not a jail cell."

The young prisoner moaned again and opened his eyes. He ran the tip of his tongue over his split lower lip. One of the other prisoners handed Hayke a scrap of towel moistened from the faucet. It wasn't clean, but Hayke pressed it against the purpling bruises.

"I must be still alive," the young prisoner murmured. "It couldn't hurt this much if I were dead."

"Faith and Burning Feathers," one of the prisoners leaned over Hayke's shoulder and muttered, "what'd *you* do?"

"What the warders *say* I did was blow up the Terran barracks. They think I'm part of the Resistance, but they can't prove a thing." The young prisoner tried to sit up, caught his breath and stiffened, then slowly lay back.

"What hurts?" said Hayke.

"Everything." He squinted up. "You a medical?"

"No, just a farmer." Hayke touched the young prisoner's hand. "I'm Hayke."

"Birre." The answering touch was firm. "What are you in here for?"

"Him, he's crazy," said one of the others.

Birre grimaced as he shifted to his side. "I was in Nantaz a few weeks ago. There was a protest, fighting in the streets. The news sheets said five hundred died before the Terrans came in. That wasn't true, it was only sixty or seventy. The Terrans sprayed the crowds with their light beam weapons."

One of the prisoners gestured expressively. A hush rippled through the cell and they all drew closer around Birre. The prisoners in the nearby cells leaned forward, listening. Some of them had been there as long as Hayke had, and the Nantaz riots were news to them.

"I thought those light rays only stunned," said one of the prisoners.

Hayke shivered inside. Memory rose up in him—the crumpled bodies across Miraz Plaza and that terrifying moment as he looked down at them from the Terran Compound and thought they were all dead.

"We rushed them again and again," Birre went on, his voice on the edge of breaking. "We didn't know—we thought they were only stunning us." He broke off suddenly.

"The Terrans say they want peace," someone said.

"It's one thing to fight the Erls," another prisoner said. "They're as human as we are."

"Yar, how do we know this story isn't some warder trick?"

Birre's head lifted, his crest jerking upright and one hand curling in a fist. "Are you naming me liar?"

"Put that Fire out!" someone said.

Hayke touched Birre's shoulder. "Who is the enemy here? The Terrans? The Erls? Or perhaps our own fear, that creates enemies where there were none?"

Crest flaring, Birre shrugged off Hayke's hand. "Wayfolk platitudes are no protection when the Terrans come after you. We have to fight them in the only way they understand."

A few of the prisoners muttered agreement. The one who'd complained about breakfast grumbled that Birre and his sort were to blame for inciting a Terran backlash. Another shook his head and said he didn't care about Terrans, but he'd personally disembowel any Erl who dared set foot on Chacarran soil.

Hayke thought of the families in his village, the ones who had cousins on both sides of the border. It had been so long since he'd left the farm, so long since he'd held his children. What were they thinking, so far away? That something had happened to him, yes, surely they must think that. He imagined Verne torn between coming after him and staying behind to guard both families. He saw Felde crying himself to sleep every night, Torrey growing hard and silent.

Talk went on around him, Birre and the others arguing about Terrans and weapons and criminal charges. Hayke barely heard them. He felt sick to the very core of his being.

Hayke awoke an hour before dawn, a habit from a lifetime of early rising.

The cell had no outside windows, but he could feel the coming day like a stillness hanging over the city.

Around him sleepers snored, a blanket made a whispery sound as one of the prisoners rolled over. Hayke's eyes adjusted to the light from the overhead fixture in the corridor. His spine cracked as he stretched and got to his feet. Stepping around the other sleepers, he made his way to the sanitary facility on the far side of the cell and washed. Then he returned to his place and sat down.

The concrete where he'd slept still retained a little warmth. He folded his legs and let his hands rest, loose and open, on his knees. A few slow breaths took him into a meditative trance. During those first terrifying days of imprisonment, it had been difficult to feel his Way. He'd felt himself drowning, flailing, losing himself. So he'd begun the practice his own parents had taught him, relaxing his body, calming his mind, unbinding himself from the day's anxieties.

He imagined himself singing Felde's favorite song, one Rosen had taught him from his own childhood, about the grommet who climbed up into the mountains because he wanted to talk to the stars. During the night, the little animal froze in the snow. The stars shed their sorrow on him and his body became lighter and more radiant until he floated up into the sky, a new star.

The melody rolled through Hayke's mind, bringing an inexpressible feeling of comfort. He sensed the presence of his children and his dead mate.

The trance faded and Hayke became aware of someone watching him. He opened his eyes, which had been half-closed, to see Birre. Birre lay on his side, head propped up on one hand.

"How are you this morning?" Hayke asked. His knees popped as he straightened them.

Birre sat up. "What you were doing—that's a Wayfolk thing, isn't it?"

Hayke looked at him, considering. With his heightened sensitivities, he caught a resonance of anguish behind Birre's words. Birre was clearly not a seeker of the Way, yet surely he deserved compassion.

"It is," Hayke said. "An ancient one, not often practiced today, except by a few traditionalists. I find it useful to bring calm to my mind when there's nothing else I can do. Is this something you wish to learn?"

Birre gestured negation. "I've never understood why you people just submit when the warders do outrageous things—why you won't stand up and defend yourselves."

It's not me he's talking to.

"The answer lies in our history, friend. There have been many times when our very existence depended on not attracting the attention of the ruling clans. We survived with a somewhat different understanding of things."

"So you sit and stare at the walls while we go out and do your fighting for you!"

"Shhh, the others are sleeping. No, you do not fight for me. Perhaps there is someone else you fight for?"

Birre drew his knees to his chest. "I have no use for pacifist scruples. The weak are the first to get—" he swallowed hard, "—hurt."

Hayke felt Birre's bitterness as an aching in his own heart. Sadness swept through him. Impulsively, he reached one hand toward Birre's shoulder. "I'm sorry."

"It's none of your doing." Shrugging off Hayke's touch, Birre got to his feet. "You Wayfolk sometimes act as if you're sorry for the whole world." He took a few steps toward the sanitary facility, then paused. "I don't mean to argue with you. You've been kind to me. In these days, we don't need kindness, we need courage."

"Is there not more than one kind of courage?"

"I don't mean word play. I mean action."

A quartet of guards marched down the corridor. Their shoes clattered on the stone floor. The prisoners, now all awake, looked up. This was no ordinary breakfast delivery.

They halted before Hayke's cell. While two of the guards kept their rifles trained on the prisoners, one opened the door. The fourth pointed at Birre. "You, on your feet."

Birre rose from the floor mat where he'd been sitting. He limped as he obeyed.

"Where are you taking him?" Hayke asked.

One of the guards laughed and another said, "Nowhere *you'd* want to go."

The other prisoners returned to their own private thoughts, but Hayke stayed at the bars, watching until the guards closed the corridor door behind them. Something in Birre's pain had touched him, a shading of darkness, as if foreshadowing a terrible fate.

I saw the people lying dead on the plaza. What do I see for him?

The mayor's private office was in reality a suite of luxuriously furnished rooms in the Residence. A staircase of opalescent marble led from the spacious main room, suitable for the most elegant receptions, to offices and

233

Lexis's own bedroom. Once he could not have imagined having access to such a place. Now he could not imagine sharing it. Not with his parents, certainly. He saw them only when he pleased, which was seldom.

Lexis leaned back in his upholstered desk chair, running his fingers over his tunic, skimming over the roll of fat that now thickened his waist. The fabric, napped plush, yielded under his touch. It reminded him of the young Bavarite, a cousin of the late mayor, who'd attended so assiduously to his pleasure the evening before. For one night only, of course. Lexis took care against any possible entanglements; he dared not risk initiating the physiological changes that led to pairing.

Sighing, he picked up the nearest report, Kallen's continuing investigation of the barracks bombing and the arrests that followed. The promised Erlind troops had arrived and been uniformed as Mirazan warders. Working with Celestinbellini was turning out to be even more rewarding than Lexis had anticipated. In a fundamental, wordless way, he understood the Terran Commander. It remained to be seen, perhaps at the dinner tonight, whether he understood Celestinbellini in other ways as well.

Lexis's suggestion for the Erlind squad's first assignment, "a special police action," had been approved. In a single, masterful stroke, it would eliminate a nest of traitors, at the same time terrifying their sympathizers into submission. Such things had been done before, the prime example being the Cleansing of the Wayfolk on the steps of the Octagon right here in Miraz centuries ago; as a student, Lexis memorized the *Elegia* of the great poet Nazr'-az-Tirith. Perhaps his own verses would be remembered through the years, in memory of this day.

A buzz on the intercom interrupted Lexis's musings. He put down the report and tapped the button. "Yes?"

"There's a person to see you," said his clerk. Lexis had brought Rurrick with him from Internal Affairs, much to the consternation of his other mayoral aides. "His name's Alon-az-Thirien. He doesn't have an appointment, but he's very insistent."

"Tell him to go away."

Rurrick lowered his voice, half-whisper. "He's the one who lost his baby. You know, that awful incident.."

There'd been some unpleasantness with a couple of drunken Terrans. Kallen's people had done a good job keeping the matter quiet, as ordered. Still, the loss of a pregnancy might become a sentimental rallying point.

The clerk swung the door open and Alon entered the room. Lexis's first impression was timidity and then, as Alon raised his eyes, a piercing, almost fragile beauty. Only traces of his recent pregnancy remained, the slenderness of the waist, the downy softness of the facial hair over skin that was so clear it almost glowed, the gentle rounding of the cheek and lips. Lexis imagined those lips playing over his own body, sucking and caressing, those fingers stroking him...

Alon stood just inside the door, shifting his weight from one foot to the other.

"Come in and tell me what I can do for you," Lexis said in his silkiest voice. "The mayor's office is always open to our citizens."

Alon took the seat closest to the desk. "I didn't know where else to go for help." In his voice, Lexis heard a charming vulnerability. "It's about Birre-az-Austre, my mate. He's been arrested for the fire in the Terran barracks. The warders took him away two days ago and they won't tell me anything. They won't let him see anyone—not an advocat, not even me."

Lexis said nothing for a moment, deliberately heightening the tension. He found Alon's distress stimulating. "I can certainly look into the matter for you. Of course, I can't promise anything. It isn't for me to decide your mate's guilt."

"Oh, but he couldn't have done it! Not Birre!"

"There are dark potentialities in all of us," Lexis said. He flared his crest and then let it subside. "You might be surprised by what you yourself are capable of."

"He couldn't have done it," Alon repeated.

"If he can prove that he was elsewhere at the time, then he has nothing to fear. It will come out at the trial."

"I just *know*."

"Of course, in a case like this, a mate's testimony is suspect, but even then something can be done, given the right connections, to... shall we say, mitigate the circumstances?"

Lexis leaned back in his chair, letting one hand trail over his own breast. He prolonged the gesture, a slow circling of his nipple, to make sure Alon saw it. "Perhaps we might discuss the matter... privately. And see exactly what it is that we might be able to do... for each other."

Alon looked up and his eyes no longer looked quite so innocent. Lexis saw the familiar, automatic flicker of denial, then the softening as Alon weighed his choices. What would he do to save his mate? How far would he be willing to go?

Lexis felt a familiar glow deep within his belly. It would be particularly satisfying to have this young Chacarran eager to pleasure him. That, of course, would take some doing, but he could afford to wait, to create the proper conditions.

He slicked his crest back into a stern expression. "There is nothing I can do for you at this time. These matters require investigation. Perhaps you'll want to reconsider. When you are ready, call my clerk for an appointment."

Alon's face whitened under his russet fur as he got to his feet. Lexis thought he might have said something, offered a promise to return, but there was nothing, not even a parting glance from those gloriously melting eyes. For a few minutes, Lexis allowed himself the enjoyment of imagining what he would demand in the end.

Slowly Lexis brought himself back to reality. If he wasn't careful, he might be lured into unwise action. Young Alon's distress might be a skillful act designed to seduce and entrap. Attractive as he might be, Alon was probably too much of a risk. Better to be rid of the temptation. As for this Birre-az-Austre, he was no doubt as guilty as the rest of them.

With the Erlind soldiers ready, command routed through his authority, and the cells of traitors waiting, all the elements of Lexis's plan were ready, awaiting only his orders. He'd set up his trusted, ruthless Ambyntet to supervise the action. Kallen and his own lieutenants would learn of it after it was all over.

He picked up the phone, the one with the direct outside line. After this morning, no one would again dare to wreak such destruction in *his* Miraz. And the Terrans would have even more reason to rely on him.

Chapter 37

An hour later, there was still no sign of breakfast. The prisoners began to grumble. The guards came back, this time headed by an unfamiliar officer, who counted out the number of prisoners in each cell as he went along.

"... Eighteen, twenty-four, thirty.." He halted in front of Hayke's cell. "Thirty-five with this lot. With the fifteen from the holding cells, that does it." He gestured for the door to be unlocked. "Bring them."

"All right, you," snapped one of the guards. The door opened. "Hands behind your heads, single file. Move!"

Hayke's cell mates looked around, puzzled. The guards held their rifles ready, their eyes shifting nervously.

"Step along! Quickly now! No talking!"

The guards took them through a maze of locked doors and out—past the prison walls to the street. They did not go through the main gates but by a side entrance. The prisoners blinked in the unexpectedly bright day.

The street opened into a square enclosed by old-fashioned apartment buildings. Expanses of brick wall, mended over the years in different shades of mortar, alternated with shop windows and doors. To the east, the sky darkened as if a storm were brewing.

A crowd had gathered in the square, people on their normal morning rounds perhaps, or drawn by curiosity. The prisoners clustered together. Armed warders blocked off the area. They wore red striped arm bands in place of clan tokens. Red was the color of J', Third Aspect, but warders, like military soldiers, were specifically forbidden to display clan insignia.

The jail guards halted in front of one of the red-banded warders. "This makes fifty in all."

"We'll take over now," the other said in heavily accented Chacarran.

Muttering, the jail guards headed back to the prison building. A couple of them glanced over their shoulders. The warder officer watched them go, then motioned toward the rest of his force. "Get them all together."

The warders herded the prisoners against the largest expanse of wall. One of the prisoners, standing at the periphery of the group, broke free and darted for the nearest street. The nearest warder lifted his rifle and, without a moment's hesitation, fired.

Dust spurted up from the pavement in front of the prisoner's feet. He swerved. An instant later, a second shot caught him squarely in the chest. He folded to the ground.

At the sound of the first shot, the watching people flinched, gasped. Someone cried out in alarm.

The warder officer turned to the crowd and raised both hands for attention. "Two weeks ago, the Terran barracks at Point Seryene were destroyed in an act of deliberate arson." His voice, resonant with polarization, boomed across the square.

"The group that claims to have executed this barbarous outrage is the very same that has fomented insurrection and discord in Chacarre. We believe they are also those who engineered the Miraz Plaza Riots."

The crowd hushed, and the prisoners crowded together, pressing in on Hayke from either side. Their fright was almost suffocating.

"Terror cannot give rise to anything but more terror!" the warder went on, his voice rising. "It has no place in a civilized society. Therefore, on the decision of the Provisional Governing Council of Chacarre, I hereby authorize the following demonstration. Anyone who has sympathy for the terrorists, take heed and consider the consequences of your actions!"

"Fard shield us!" a prisoner behind Hayke exclaimed.

The officer brought down both arms in a decisive gesture. The next thing Hayke saw was the warders raising their rifles in his direction.

Shots barked, echoing off the stone walls. Prisoners screamed. They milled about, searching for a way out through the cordon. A few of them fell and lay still.

The rifles fired again and again, peeling off the prisoners on the outside.

Then someone in the street began to scream and the next instant, other voices punctured the air, shrieks of horror and anguished wailing. A few surged forward, to be held back by the red-banded warders.

Hayke, standing near the center of the group, froze like a cornered grommet. Some prisoners tried to break free, thinning the group even further. One or two fell to their knees, praying loudly to their Aspect. Hayke could see the faces of the warders now, their crests jagged.

He had only a few moments left before he was fully exposed. His fur stood on end. His heart pounded raggedly. The acrid stench of burnt-sulfur stung his nostrils. *Tal'mur*, the madness of fear, raced like quicksilver through his veins.

One of the remaining prisoners grabbed Hayke by the shoulders, using him as a shield. Hayke stumbled along, too frightened to resist. Together they headed for the nearest street. A warder brought his rifle around to aim at directly at Hayke.

Hayke tripped on a fallen body, jerking his captor off balance. The prisoner let go of Hayke as they both scrambled for footing. The shot missed Hayke's shoulder by a hairsbreadth.

Hayke struggled to his feet. The prisoner, cursing, bolted for the shelter of the nearest corner. Infected by the same frenzied energy, Hayke raced after him.

The next shot caught the other prisoner. He went down. Hayke vaulted over him.

Stone walls and a row of horror-stricken faces blurred before his eyes. An opening appeared before him, a glimpse of the street. He sprinted for it.

A warder in a red arm band, crest flaring, stepped from the crowd. As if in slow motion, Hayke saw the black bore of his rifle as it swung around to aim at his heart. His stride faltered and his arms rose in instinctive surrender, hands crossed over his chest. The gun barrel wavered.

Hayke heard voices yelling behind him, the crowd surging and belling like a frenzied herd of woolies. He kept going. His legs churned faster than ever before, even in the woods near Verne's farm. Here there was no snow to slow him down. His boots flew over the pavement. His lungs sucked in fire.

Behind Hayke, rifles fired in a peppering of shots. A sudden breeze tore at the side of his shirt, sending a ribbon of ice across his ribs.

Ignoring the pain, Hayke rounded the corner and pelted down one street, up an alley, then down another. There were people on the streets, morning traffic. He tried to dodge and swerve, but was moving too fast. He slammed into a pedestrian, then a second. Others scattered before him, their faces reflecting surprise.

At the end of the fourth street, or maybe the sixth, he forced himself to slow down and think. He could not escape by running. He was wearing prison clothing, easily identifiable. Blood and sweat trickled down his body. His ribs burned as if touched by a molten brand. He pressed his hand to his side and it came away slick. A wave of dizziness shook him. The world swayed sickeningly.

Shelter...

He had to get off the street. He might have only a few moments before the warders found him again. The buildings here were two or three stories tall, small shops or business offices on street level, apartments above. Hayke spotted a door between two shops, partly open. He slipped through and closed the door behind him.

Hayke found himself in a dimly lit, low-ceilinged corridor. Just inside the door stood several metal receptacles that gave off the odor of overripe food scraps. A staircase spiraled up into the bulk of the building.

Holding his side, Hayke crept down the corridor. It was cool and slightly damp, like a cave. The stone floor was age-worn smooth. At the far end, he spotted a door.

Feet pattered down the staircase. Hayke flattened himself against the wall. He hardly dared to breathe. The far door opened. Hayke caught a glimpse of the intruder, slender and young, a student perhaps. Light and sound streamed in from the street before the door swung shut again. It sounded like ordinary street noise, although in his condition Hayke couldn't be sure. He saw no trace of blood on the floor, but that did not mean he had not left a trail outside. He gathered himself and hurried through the corridor.

The far end was not, as he'd thought, a second door, but the landing to another stairway. This one led downward. Metal bars formed a gate, its lock encrusted with rust, across the top step. The stairs looked very old, their corners touched with cobwebs. They led most likely to a basement, probably locked, but right now what Hayke needed was a place to hide, even if it was the bottom of a stairwell, a place to stop trembling and plan what he must do next. He clambered over the gate and went down.

The steps were steep and narrow, turning back on themselves at the first landing. Legs shaking, Hayke climbed down another range and came to a wooden door. He could barely see it, the light here was so dim. When he touched the door, his fingertips met peeling paint. The wood beneath had gone spongy with rot.

He tried the latch. For a moment it resisted him. Then, as he pressed against the door with his good shoulder, the door frame gave way. The gap was barely wide enough to sidle through. On the other side lay velvety blackness.

Hayke had never been afraid of the dark, not even as a little child, and it welcomed him now. He closed his eyes to better sense his Way. The surrendering of his vision, like a fleeting moment of *tal'spirë*, brought certainty.

He closed the door behind him, settling it to appear undisturbed to a casual glance. He went on, one hand feeling his way on the rough stone wall.

Stairs led down, at such an angle and so sharply wedge-shaped they were barely wide enough for his feet. He felt his way to each step.

The stairs leveled out into another landing. The air tasted dank and stale. Something glimmered ahead, a patch of luminescence on the wall. A tunnel opened to one side, below the glowing patch.

I must have wandered into the catacombs.

Hayke sat down on the landing, his back against the wall. He'd read about the catacombs, how most of the stone for the original city had been quarried here. In later ages, criminals and outcasts had taken refuge, more often than not, permanently. Wayfolk had hidden during the religious wars. He'd thought all the entrances blocked, and was glad to be mistaken.

Hayke's muscles gradually stopped shaking and his heartbeat slowed. The air was chilly, but no colder than three seasons of the year at home. He was in no danger of frostbite, and he could keep himself warm by walking. The wound in his side had stopped bleeding, although vigorous movement might open it again.

As he went on, Hayke stopped frequently to catch his breath and ease the pain in his side. His body felt increasingly heavy, as the oppressive dankness of the air seeped into his flesh. Cold and shock made a bad combination.

Keep moving, he reminded himself. *But to where?*

He could not go long without water. He must wait a reasonable length of time and then go back up. But he would emerge only a few blocks from where he'd started, and he didn't think the warders would give up the search easily. The Terran surveillance units were everywhere. Anyone dressed as he was, in tunic and leggings of prison gray, blood-stained or not, would be noticed.

On the other hand, he could follow the tunnel in the hope that it would eventually lead back upward. Once on the surface, his most immediate need would be for a disguise. Perhaps he could take some clothing from an unattended laundry line and find a sheet to bandage his side. He disliked the idea of stealing, but saw no other choice.

Next would come food and a way out of the city. He might be able to get a ride east with one of the farmers who trucked their produce to the open air markets.

After resting, Hayke felt calmer, refreshed. He got up, stretched gingerly, and headed down the tunnel.

The catacomb tunnel ran on. Overhead, luminescent patches on the low ceilings shed a wan light over the occasional branchings. Hayke had no way to mark his trail, so he chose the one that led straight ahead. If that proved to lead nowhere, he decided, he would have to backtrack and devise another plan. For now, he continued, despite the weakness that swept through him in waves. Whenever he stopped, the chill of the tunnel bit into his bones.

Silence and pitchy darkness pressed in on him, yet he found a peacefulness to the tunnel, a sense of eternal repose. Despite his efforts, he might lose his way and perish of thirst or hunger. He might fall down a pit. These were natural perils, ones he could face with serenity.

Quite different were the dangers he'd witnessed above. He thought of the prisoners, their screams, their frantic attempts to escape, the burnt-sulfur whiff of *tal'mur*. He felt no anger at the prisoner who'd grabbed him for a shield. Yet who were these warders, who could cut down a mass of unarmed people?

As Hayke shuffled down the tunnel, something in the stillness of the underground seeped into his thoughts, bringing an eerie sense of calm. Perhaps, he realized, a more proper question would be, how could anyone, when faced with such savagery, remain sane?

Several times Hayke sat down to rest, his back against the rough-cut stone wall, but never for more than a few minutes. Thirst roughened his throat. Despite the dampness of the tunnel, he'd come across nothing like drinkable water and, being a farmer, his definition of *drinkable* was fairly broad. His stomach rumbled, reminding him that he hadn't eaten since the afternoon before. The searing pain in his side muted to a throb.

A sound whispered down the tunnel. Hayke froze, holding his breath. His ears strained for more. Carefully, he advanced a few steps, paused and listened again. Echoes from the rock distorted the sound, but there was no mistaking its source—a voice.

Hayke went on, more quickly now. Ahead, the tunnel curved and a brighter illumination reflected off the far wall. He made out several voices, talking in hushed tones.

"*An execution* they're calling it.."

"... reprisal.."

"... unrealistic. How can we expect... put their families at risk... stand up to.."

"... take into account... planning our next step.."

Hayke inched forward, toward the voices and the light. The lights winked out.

"Hallo? Friends?" he called. "I'm lost in the tunnels. Can you help me?"

He pushed on, fingertips of one hand brushing the wall. Silence answered him. "I'm unarmed," he said. "Please, is anyone there?"

Brilliance blinded him, a hand-light shining directly into his eyes. He squinted into it.

"Who are you?" a voice called out, urgent. "What are you doing in the catacombs?"

"At the moment, I'm lost." The brightness shifted, no longer directly in Hayke's eyes. After a moment of graying vision, he made out faces, three or four of them, wearing grim expressions.

"I need water," he went on, "and ordinary clothing and a way out of the city. Can you help me?"

"You know who we are?"

"I think you might be the resistance, hiding down here," Hayke said. "There was one prisoner brought in yesterday—Birre was his name—he said the warders suspected him of being part of such a group."

One of the shadowy figures rushed forward, thin with a haggard, intense face and fever-bright eyes. "Birre-az-Austre! What's happened to him? Slaughtered with the others?"

"No, no, he looked well enough the last time I saw him," Hayke said quickly. "But he wasn't with us in the square. They took him away earlier, I don't know where."

A second stepped forward. The lantern showed a slab jaw and curled lip, pale fur so thick it looked matted. "How come *you're* still alive? How do we know you're not a spy planted by the warders?"

Hayke, moving slowly and carefully, lifted his arms over his head. Wincing, he turned so the light fell directly on his side. A stab of pain told him that the wound had broken open. Wetness trickled down his skin. Shivering, he lowered his arms.

"He didn't do that to himself," one of them drawled. "What's your name, friend, and where are you from?"

The first rebel, the one who'd asked about Birre, laid a gentle hand on Hayke's shoulder. "I'm Lorne, and that's Timas, Orsen," the suspicious one, "and Evers. We'll do what we can for you, although it isn't much. The Flaming spy huts are everywhere and people are afraid to help. We can offer you food, bandages, and a safe place to stay for a few days."

Something in the other's voice, the rough blend of tension and kindness, stirred Hayke unexpectedly.

"Leaving the city won't be easy," said Timas. "Without Birre, it'll be a lot harder to get fake identity papers."

"I must go home," Hayke said. His voice came in a half-sob. He put one hand against the side of the tunnel to steady himself. "My children.."

Hayke couldn't go on. His legs gave way under him. The impact knocked the air out of his lungs and he lay there gasping.

"Leave him alone." Lorne knelt beside Hayke. "He's hurt and exhausted. You can yammer at him all you like later. Let's go."

Timas grunted assent. Lorne and one of the others helped Hayke to his feet and supported him as they moved along the tunnel, carrying their hand-lights.

"The entrance is close by," said Lorne. "We don't go far into the catacombs. There are no maps, and it's easy to get lost."

Hayke glanced up, for the first time noticing the stripe of sooty black running along the tunnel ceiling. Clusters of dots marked an intersection.

"Handy guides, those," Lorne said. "We don't know who made them, but they're at least five hundred years old. Kesh alone, whose aspect is divine endurance, knows how many people they've guided over the centuries."

"Are you a student of history?" Hayke asked, leaning his weight on the others.

Lorne snorted. "Hardly. I was the last of an orphaned sept and couldn't qualify for a University scholarship from the city, not after the trouble I'd gotten into as a youngster. They trained me to fix cars and so I do, when there's enough work."

"When you aren't getting into even more trouble," said the fourth. "Hayke, what skills do you have?"

"Farming," said Hayke. "Wheat, beans, winter-pears, cheese."

"Mmm, winter-pears," said Lorne. "Maybe when this is all over, we'll raid your orchard."

"Do you see an end to it, then?" Hayke asked.

"How else do you think we keep going?" said Orsen, the suspicious one.

They came to a well, a rope ladder hanging along the side. Lorne looked hard at Hayke. "Can you climb?"

Hayke took hold of the rope ladder. This wouldn't be the first time he had to find strength beyond his own. Getting a harvest in before the rains, birthing Torrey... tending Rosen through the long nights until he was too sick to sit up.

He took a breath, tightened his grasp on the ropes, and began to climb.

Chapter 38

Alon stumbled down the steps from the mayor's office, hardly seeing the street before him. He had been a fool to believe those eloquent words about how eager Lexis was to help any citizen in need. He'd been taken in by the stories of Lexis's heroism during the Miraz Plaza riots. He could hardly believe that the person who looked at him with such lascivious appetite, who hinted of favors given and received, could be the same one who'd stood between the mob and a helpless, pregnant stranger.

Alon stormed across the square with such single-mindedness that pedal-cyclists and pedestrians swerved to avoid him. There was a lesson to be learned from all of this, he told himself savagely. He'd come to Lexis from Enellon's business office, where he'd asked, no—*begged*—for help after he'd heard of Birre's arrest.

"You *know* Birre," he had pleaded. "He couldn't have done it!"

Enellon had risen from behind his desk, its surface glittering with inlaid moon-wood. His voice was low with anger. "Whatever Birre has become, he's no longer any concern of ours. Not after he showed himself willing to sacrifice anything and any one—you, Saunde, me, even your unborn child— to this political obsession of his. Clan and family come before everything else, that's how it's always been, how it always *must be.*"

Alon had flinched when Enellon put both hands on his shoulders.

"Of course we still love Birre, but the only way we can truly help him is to separate ourselves from his mistakes. That, and pray to Hool, Sacred Aspect of the god, that he sees the truth while there is still time."

So Enellon was of no help, and without him, Saunde would never act. Meddi and Tellem had no influence or power. Anything they did would surely put them at risk, and Alon wasn't willing to do that, at least not yet. Lexis—the very thought of following through on his unspoken offer made Alon feel sick. The press? Other than the cheaply printed underground sheets, the news was controlled by the Department of Information Services.

One thing was clear, nobody else was going to help Birre. Alon would have to do it himself. When he'd tried the jail earlier, the warders wouldn't let him see Birre. He would ask a hundred times a day if he had to. He would sleep on their front steps until they let him in. He would go to the law students, to an advocat, to Timas, to anyone... He would find a way.

A knot of people had gathered around the square that fronted the jail. The ban on public gatherings was still in force; he couldn't think what it could be, unless traffic was blocked off. A sharp, barking sound penetrated the street noise.

Alon elbowed his way through the crowd, but before he could get a clear view of the square, he heard screaming. He paused, his crest ruffling. Then everything went wild—more screams, people struggling in all directions, some pressing forward, others turning to flee.

Another noise punctuated the air, a shot. He was sure of it now. The crowd surged. Alon, near the center, found himself unable to move in any direction. The first screams had died down and people around him were murmuring, reeling. From the center of the square, he caught scattered phrases.

"... no place in a civilized society... acts of violence... the Provisional Governing Council of Chacarre... hereby authorized to execute.."

"Holy Bavar, protect us!" someone cried out in a voice reedy with shock.

"Sweet Bird of Heaven, no!"

Alon's mouth went cottony. His muscles took on a sudden, frenetic strength. He shoved the person in front of him aside, an oldster with a couple of paper-wrapped loaves under one arm. People stumbled as he pushed them out of his way, running toward the gunfire.

Finally Alon stood, panting, at the edge of the crowd. In front of him, a big, heavy-shouldered warder wearing a red striped arm band held back the bystanders. A pile of bodies lay against the wall that formed one side of the square, all dressed alike in rumpled gray jail tunics. A few still twitched, but most lay in the stillness of death. From this distance, Alon couldn't make out their faces.

A circle of warders began moving in on those prisoners who were left standing. They leaned forward as if eager for the kill. Other warders stood at a distance, eyes scanning the crowd, rifles held ready, crests at grim angles.

Alon's pulse, which had been thundering in his ears, stuttered, and then for an awful moment went silent. His legs crumpled underneath him. He staggered and someone caught his arm, steadied him.

A warder officer raised his hands to the crowd and spoke. "Thus will we put an end to violence and deal with all enemies of the Chacarran people!" His words blew past Alon like dried leaves.

"Clear the street!" bellowed the nearest warder.

Dimly Alon heard the command to disperse. The person supporting him lingered for a few moments.

"Will you be all right?"

Alon turned, blinked, seeing the other for the first time. Fur grizzled with age, a laborer's felt cap, eyes sunken and red-rimmed. Did he have a mate out there, a child, a cousin? Alon couldn't speak. Taking Alon's silence for agreement, the other hurried off.

Like a magnet, the mound of bodies caught and held Alon's gaze. He couldn't look away. It pulled at him with an awful fascination. He had to see, to know.

A burly arm caught Alon across the chest. It was one of the warders who'd held back the crowd.

"Go out of here," said the warder. His speech was heavily accented. "All to go out of here."

"What about the families?" said a person by Alon's shoulder. "They'll want to—"

"These were worst of criminals," the warder barked. "Anyone who asks will be arrest as sympathizer."

Alon backed away and broke into a run. Streets sped by in a blur, buildings and café tables, stands of flowers and spring fruits, housewares and piles of iced river-fish, boards with tacked-on news sheets, windows reflecting brilliant blue.

He crossed the pedestrian bridge over Westriver. Here he paused, staring down at the water. Who could have done such a thing? Who could have given the orders?

He remembered the words of the officer in the square, *The Provisional Governing Council.*

Birre's words flickered through his mind. *"The Helm is gone. This committee the Terrans have put in his place.."*

The Terrans. The same Terrans who had done things to him that he could not bear to remember.

He did not want to die. He wanted to live, no matter what the cost, and to make the Terrans pay.

It was exactly what Birre had said, after the baby died.

Alon was still shaking with fury when he reached the bookstore. He had no intention of opening it up for business although this was his day to open it, Meddi and Tellem being gone for a week of book-buying in Avallaz.

A chill wind blew in before he slammed the door behind him. Familiar smells enveloped him, book paper, ink, and the faint, resinous smoke of the pinecones Meddi burned in the evenings. Sunlight streamed through the eastward-facing windows, but Alon took no warmth from it. He'd never be warm again.

Mechanically, Alon prepared himself a mug of tea and stirred in a spoonful of honey. He lowered himself into the chair behind the desk—the very chair he'd woken in on the day he and Birre bonded to each other.

Sitting in the store, surrounded by memories of his childhood, Alon had never before felt so alone. So desperately, hopelessly alone. No new life budded within him, no second half of his heart waited at the end of the day. How could he bear it, the emptiness inside? Meddi would say to let the Way open before him but where was the comfort in that? There was no answering peace within his soul.

I will hold on for this moment, and the one after that. Moment by moment, I will survive.

For something to do, Alon began slitting open the morning mail with a single-edged knife. The door chimed open. Alon glanced up and gasped. A Terran walked in, moving with the strutting gait of polarization.

"Go away. We're closed."

"Looks to me like you're open." The Terran's bare face was unreadable. He took a couple of steps towards Alon. "I just want to look around a bit. I won't be any trouble."

Alon got to his feet. "We're closed," he repeated.

The Terran kept coming, closer and closer with each step until he stood on the other side of the desk.

Alon's muscles tensed, then began trembling violently. The fur along his neck puffed out. His eyes stretched wide; he tried to turn away, but couldn't look at anything but the looming, inhuman face.

"You're no more than a frightened rabbit, just like the rest of them," said the Terran. "What the hell is going on in this city, anyway?"

"Don't you know?" Alon demanded, outrage unlocking his voice. "Don't you know what happened this morning?"

"Listen, lady, I heard there was some ruckus with local authorities, but I wasn't even there. I don't know any more than you do."

Cold fire flared up inside Alon. He burned with it, but he no longer trembled. He picked up the knife used as a letter-opener from the desk. The hilt slipped into his palm as if it belonged there.

"Go away," he said again.

"Now, is that any way to act? We come down here and put our goddamn *asses* on the line for you people." The Terran pointed one stubby finger at Alon, as if he were aiming a weapon. For a long moment they stared at each other. The only sounds in the shop were the ticking of the ancient clock, the one that had been in Meddi's family for three generations, and the Terran's heavy breathing.

The Terran strolled over to the nearest book rack. "My buddy told me about this place, said it had some interesting stuff. I just wanted to have a look around, maybe pick up a souvenir." He took a book from the rack, an illustrated collection of children's poetry.

"Put it back! You've taken enough from me already!" Alon tensed, gripping the knife. He didn't know if he could use it. He didn't want to think about what might be coming.

The Terran paused, book in hand, his peculiar oval eyes fixed on Alon. "Just take it easy—"

Something broke loose in Alon. He lunged at the Terran with the knife upraised. The Terran reached out one hand to fend him off. Alon swiped at him with the knife.

The Terran jumped back. His body arched away from the sweeping blade. He stumbled. The wooden edge of a display table caught him at hip level. He reeled, off balance. Alon lunged at him again.

Alon could never be sure what happened next. He saw the Terran's face, pasty pale, mouth gaping wide, saw the muscled body spinning. Arms flailed, and then there was a sickening *crack!* and the Terran lay unmoving on the floor.

Panting, Alon approached the Terran. Had the alien hit his head on the table? On the floor? Had he stabbed him without knowing it? He couldn't remember, he couldn't think straight. He stared at the knife in his hand. Bits of paper fuzz clung to the sharpened edge. The metal glinted, unstained.

The Terran lay still, his arms flung out and legs in a graceless tangle. Alon knelt and touched his neck with one finger. The bare skin felt warm and elastic. He had no idea where to check for a pulse, or if the creature even had one. How could he tell if the Terran was dead?

Alon straightened up. The cold fire in his belly subsided, leaving an almost crystalline clarity.

Neither the Terrans nor their warder puppets will believe it was an accident.

He briefly considered disposing of the body, pretending the Terran had never come into the shop. But someone might have seen him.

The risk was too great, not for his own sake but for Meddi and Tellem's. Innocent or not, alibi or not, the warders would surely arrest them, even as they had arrested Birre.

Savagely, Alon cut off the thought. He must not think about the pile of bodies outside the jail.

If I run, if I disappear, they might blame me alone.

Alon glanced around the store. There was no time to return to the Northhill apartment. With regret, he emptied the cash drawer, hiding the larger bills in his inner tunic pocket.

The papers! The packet for Padme was still in the pile to be delivered. He'd meant to do it days ago, but had forgotten in his desperation over

Birre's arrest. He would take them now. They would lead him to Timas and his Freedom Movement.

Alon stopped at a public phone to call his parents in Avallaz. They always stayed at the same hotel. The line to their room buzzed, and for a moment Alon feared they were out. He dared not leave a message. Then the line cleared and he heard Meddi's voice, his wheezing breath.

Quickly Alon sketched what had happened—the fight, the fall, his decision to join the resistance. Meddi listened in silence, then:

"You have seen it—this is the Way?"

Alon wanted to slam the phone back into its holder. "What choice do I have? It's my only chance to get back at them for what they've done. I'm going to call the warders now, so you'll be out of the city when they discover the body. I just wanted to warn you."

"Tellem and I must discuss our return to Miraz. I'm reluctant to abandon what we've built up when there might be another solution. The Way isn't clear, but neither of us will go rushing off soul-blind. Perhaps we'll stay a little longer here in Avallaz. Our love goes with you, Alon. May the Way open before you."

Alon went on foot to Padme's restaurant, keeping to the traversons whenever possible. The corridors and alleyways gave him an unexpected sense of comfort, as if Miraz itself had become his ally.

I can disappear in this city. I can go anywhere I want, and the Terrans can't stop me.

Outside the restaurant, tables and chairs sprawled across the sidewalk. The interior smelled of Padme's special blend of garlic and herbs. Padme himself came out from the kitchen, wiping his hands on a towel, his round-cheeked face flushed with heat. He smiled when he saw Alon. "It's good to see you again. How are your parents?"

Alon held out the wrapped parcel. "I brought a book on cooking, for your collection."

Nodding seriously, Padme took the parcel.

Alon hesitated. There were no customers inside, but the doors were open and anything he said openly might be overheard. This was the way life was going to be from now on, a web of deception and secrets. He put his arms around Padme, Wayfolk style, and spoke in a half whisper.

"I want to join the movement."

Chapter 39

Gradually Hayke's vision cleared. He looked around, strangely unsurprised that one moment he should be lying in bed shivering and the next standing at the top of the Terran Compound, looking down at the crowd below. The curved window had disappeared and he felt the warmth of the sun. A gentle breeze tousled his fur. Below him, people milled around, their voices like the rustle of forest leaves.

Hayke leaned over the railing and tried to shout, to warn them. But the air had turned so thick, he could hardly draw it into his lungs. From above, the yellow light beams shot out, playing over the crowd. Bodies tumbled to the pavement, like stalks of grain waiting to be gathered into sheaves.

Beside him, someone said, "They're only sleeping," but Hayke knew that something had gone terribly wrong. What he'd feared most had come true and the people lying on the plaza ground were dead. A silent keening rose behind his throat.

Then, as if given wings, he found himself floating down to stand upon the plaza. Slowly, the people lying at his feet began to stir, to lift their heads and look around. They blinked as if the sun were suddenly too bright for their eyes. Hayke moved toward the nearest, thinking to embrace him, but something held him back. Then he realized that to these people he was invisible, incorporeal. He could pass right through this solid-seeming world and be utterly untouched by it. Yet as he moved through the crowd, he saw that wherever he went, people rose up like flowers turning toward the sun.

He went faster and faster, anxious to reach as many as he could. There must be no one left behind. In the ancient teachings, each one represented a world encompassed in a single spirit, a unique guide to the Way; he had never seen this so clearly before. It didn't matter who they were or what they'd believed, he could not bear to part with a single one of them.

The next moment Hayke was sitting up in bed in a strange room, his chest heaving as if he'd just run halfway home. He remembered everything that had happened to him, the executions outside the jail, being wounded, wandering in the catacombs, finding the resistance. His side throbbed under layers of bandage.

The dream had been so vivid, so real.

Someone came into the room—young and slender, but with the curved hips and breasts of recent pregnancy. "I thought I heard you stirring," the stranger said. He switched on the bedside lamp. Gentle fingers touched Hayke's temples. "Good, your fever's broken. Are you thirsty? Would you like to eat?"

Hayke accepted a cup of water. "Where am I?"

"The splits. Orsen's basement. They thought it would be the best place to hide both of us." Even in the subdued light, Hayke caught traces of the other's beauty in the lines of cheek and crest.

Hayke rubbed his face. His fur felt dry, brittle. "Who are you? Do I know you?"

"I'm Alon. I've been taking care of you, which is all I can do for now."

"Are you one of them? The resistance?"

"I am now." A strange, intense expression flickered across Alon's great dark eyes. "What about you? They told me your name—Hayke—and that you're a farmer, caught up by the warders. Some falsified charges, hauled away to the slaughter with the others. Will you join us?"

"I am not sure of the Way I am to follow."

"You're Wayfolk? I suspected as much."

"And you?"

"Raised that way, but I don't see that it's done my family much good. Or anyone else in Miraz. We acted like a bunch of brainless grommets when the Terrans and their warder puppets started pushing us around. *Say yes, move on, become invisible.* Maybe if we'd stood up to them at the beginning, things wouldn't have gotten this far."

Alon's grief was a weight pressing on Hayke's own heart.

"I'm sorry, I've tired you." Alon's voice lost its hardness. He reached for a moist cloth from the basin on the bed stand and touched it to Hayke's forehead. "I didn't mean to, not you. Not after the news you brought about Birre."

Hayke stirred against the pillow. "Birre? The prisoner they took away?" It seemed everyone here knew of young Birre.

Alon's hands paused. "My mate. I saw the—" his voice stumbled, cracked, "—execution in the square, from the street. I thought he was killed with the others." He lifted his eyes and even in the dim-lit room, Hayke could see a light in them that moved him beyond words, a light he had not seen since he'd last looked into Rosen's eyes. His hands moved of their own accord, reaching out to grasp Alon's.

"He may not be alive," Alon said. "Or if he is in Terran hands, perhaps it might have been better if he *had* died. But you've given me a moment's hope and something to fight for, and that's helped me through these last days."

The dream pressed on Hayke, even as did young Alon's pain. The people rising up, lifting their heads to the sky... There was no way he could take that vision out of his memory or empty himself of its compelling *presence*. Like a path appearing in the dense tangled heart of a forest, the Way opened up before him.

Holding his glass of honey-colored wine, Lexis ambled through the central living area of the mayoral residence, nodding to each guest. Tubs of flowers, pink and musk-green, had been set around the landing of the staircase, bringing out the highlights of the opalescent marble.

The evening was going even better than he had anticipated; the pastry chefs had outdone themselves, the scent of wine perfumed the air, and music drifted through the room with just the right degree of languor. At dinner, Lexis had given a speech in honor of Commander Celestinbellini, written not by Lexis himself but by a first-rank professional speechwriter. The gratifying response combined with the effects of the wine to create a lingering warmth.

Several of the Chacarran guests began dancing in twos and threes, their posture and gestures discreetly suggesting other activities to follow later in the evening.

Lexis took his eyes from the dancers and strolled through the room. After her objections to the mass execution, he feared that Doctorvera might create a difficult situation. Lexis found her manner abrasive, her Chacarran pronunciation abominable, and the combination of her age and her pregnant appearance insupportable. He could barely keep his crest decently smoothed in her presence. But she'd left early, as had the censor Talense. Lexis was glad to be rid of them.

Across the room, several national administrators had drawn up their chairs together, talking in animated tones about the latest theater presentations. Celestinbellini himself stood in the center of a group of Terran officers and younger Chacarran notables. He turned his head as Lexis walked by.

Lexis's heartbeat speeded up and his belly tightened. He felt a new heat mingle with the glow of wine and success.

Celestinbellini stepped away from the group, moving slowly but directly toward Lexis. He moved with the powerful, almost strutting gait of polarization.

"Are you enjoying yourself?" Lexis asked in his smoothest voice. "Is there anything I can do for you?"

The Terran's exotically full lips curved upwards. "I have always been interested in dance. It seems to me to be an ideal form of communication, a way of bridging cultural differences."

Lexis found himself charmed by the Terran's odd, fluid accent. These aliens were so tantalizing.

Celestinbellini's eyes flickered toward the dancers. "No words, just two bodies joined by the magic of music."

"Would you like to learn our dances?" Lexis could hardly believe how easy it was. He set his wine glass on the nearest table and gestured toward the dance area.

"Like this," Lexis said, resting his hands lightly on Celestinbellini's.

The Terran was half a head taller and much broader in the shoulders. He wore scent, something unfamiliar and astringent, yet in no way repellant. A faint stubble covered his cheeks and chin. Lexis found these differences arousing in a way that closeness to a polarized Chacarran had never been. His own hands went lightly around the Terran's neck as he guided him through the steps. Beneath Lexis's fingers, the Terran's skin was smooth and warm. Hard muscles tensed and relaxed with each movement. With a powerful, unexpected pull, the Terran drew Lexis closer.

Lexis's small breasts flattened against the Terran's chest and he could feel the bulge at the alien's crotch. His thoughts raced ahead. The Terrans were different, permanently polarized. Grotesquely sexed, the rumors said, insatiable and possessing superhuman endurance to match their appetites. They spent their entire adult lives in a state of perpetual lust.

He forced himself to breathe smoothly. To appear eager would be to give away too much of the game.

"It's so nice, this way," Celestinbellini murmured, running his hands down Lexis's sides. "You dance with whomever you like."

"Miraz is the most exciting and sophisticated city in the world, don't you agree?" Lexis said breathlessly.

"I've seen far too little of it."

Lexis took one of the Terran's hands in his own. "There's a fine view from the second story balcony. On a night like this, the city lights are splendid." He did not add that the balcony was outside his bedroom.

"The evening is yet young," Celestinbellini replied with an odd lift of his shoulders. "I wouldn't want to take you away from your official duties. Perhaps later, when there are fewer demands on your time." His eyes rested on Lexis's before he turned away toward one of the other conversations.

The living area seemed hollow after the last of the guests departed. The musicians had gone an hour ago and the housekeeping staff hovered around the edges, waiting for the signal to begin their work.

Lexis spotted a half-filled wine glass and picked it up. He didn't know whose it was and didn't care. The pale liquid slid down his throat in a single gulp. It tasted bitter, like the ashes of disappointment. Celestinbellini had disappeared some time earlier.

He climbed the marble stairs and headed down the hallway. His door stood open, the room beyond it dark. He did not reach for the light panel. Blackness suited his mood.

Lexis opened the glass door and went out on to the balcony. Below him, the lights of the city spread out like gems. Night hid the dirt, the scars. With a little time, even the bullet holes and blood stains would fade into the patina of Miraz's living history.

My city.

Pure and ageless, the most perfect thing the world had ever produced, Miraz waited for him like a receptive lover, waited for his vision to give it purpose.

My city. Mine.

Soon his warders would finish the work of this afternoon, rooting out nests of insurrection. The rebellion would crumble like sand. The Terrans were a necessary annoyance, nothing more. Nothing they did could change Miraz's eternal essence.

Lexis caught a faint rustling coming from the center of the room, sheets sliding over one another. He stiffened. His dark-adapted eyes scanned the room and came to rest on the bed and the figure lying in it.

"I wondered how long it would take you," Celestinbellini said in a silky voice.

Lexis moved to the side of the bed. The Terran's bare shoulders and arms glowed in the soft light. A half-empty glass of wine sat on the bed table. The hairs along Lexis's spine, from the base of his neck to the deepest reaches between his buttocks, tingled. His breath came faster.

Lexis crawled on top of the bed until he knelt above the Terran, looking down at him. "Are you ready for me?"

Without waiting for an answer, Lexis bent closer. Instead of the usual downy fur of his own people, his cheeks met prickly stubble, and then, unexpectedly, the Terran's lips. The Terran's mouth spread wide under his. Although he'd heard of the Terran custom of kissing, Lexis had never in his life imagined the moist, electric shock of another mouth in such intimate contact with his own. His belly cramped, a jolt of pleasure so hard and sudden it bordered on pain. He tore his mouth away and gasped for breath.

As the Terran reached up, Lexis had not realized how big his hands were. Five broad, hard-knuckled fingers covered his breasts, pinching his nipples.

"Take it off," the Terran said, tugging at the layers of Lexis's clothing.

For a moment Lexis stared. He felt as if he were naked already, open and defenseless against desires he couldn't name. His blood hammered in his ears. The pulse throbbed all through him. His crotch was slick and wet and aching.

"Slowly. So I can watch."

Lexis stood up. His fingers fumbled at the fastenings of his tunic. He was aware that Celestinbellini had propped himself up on one elbow, and he could feel the Terran's eyes on him, measuring every movement. He hesitated. He had sometimes undressed his partners, had more often had them do the same to him for the powerful feeling of *being served.* There was something uncomfortably vulnerable in doing it alone, under scrutiny. He shrugged off the feeling as he discarded the last of his garments, his moment of unease evaporated.

He slid in between the covers and reached for Celestinbellini. After a brief caress, the Terran jerked the covers back and stared at Lexis's crotch. "You don't have much, do you?"

Lexis flushed, then as quickly blanched, his eyes fixed on the other's exposed genitals. The Terran's nub curved upwards, close to his body, dusky and swollen to grotesque size. A strange, overpowering smell arose from the Terran's body—sweat and scent and something else. Fascinated and repelled, Lexis reached out to touch the Terran's nub, then as quickly drew back when he saw the bead of glistening fluid on the tip.

Egg fluid? Surely not, it couldn't be possible, they weren't mated. Lexis's belly went cold and his genital nub shriveled. Could the Terran implant a fertile egg when he, Lexis, was not polarized?

Words would not come. He rolled toward the edge of the bed.

The Terran's hand shot out and clamped on Lexis's shoulder. With a sudden movement, Lexis found himself lying on his back, underneath the Terran. Celestinbellini's nub rubbed against Lexis's thigh. It felt like a wooden cudgel.

"Never had one this big before, eh?" All the silken sweetness vanished from the Terran's voice. "Don't worry, baby, I can't get you pregnant."

Pregnant?

Lexis quivered in terror. Did the Terran intend to put that *thing* inside him?

Celestinbellini pinned Lexis's hands above his head with one hand. Lexis squirmed and tried to pull away. The Terran's grip was brutally, exhilaratingly powerful. In a slow, rhythmic movement, the Terran began grinding his pelvis against Lexis's hip.

Lexis closed his eyes, the better to feel it. Something hot and wet, almost obscenely soft, writhed across his lips. Nausea surged through him and he opened his mouth, gagging. The Terran's tongue slipped inside.

Celestinbellini surrounded him, imprisoned him, filled him. When the Terran pulled back, still holding him fast, he made no sound. All he could do was look up into those alien eyes.

Celestinbellini's breath came in a hiss between his teeth. Sweat beaded his skin. He shifted his weight, still keeping hold, and flipped Lexis on to his stomach. With one knee, the Terran shoved Lexis's legs apart. He began probing Lexis's slit. Instead of the gentle stroking used by Lexis's chosen bedmates, the Terran thrust his fingers deep, pinching and kneading his genital nub.

Lexis winced and cried out, but his face was buried in the pillows. As he tried to pull his hands away, he felt a quick, feverish breath on the back of his neck, the exultant power of the Terran's iron grip. The struggle clearly excited the Terran. In a flash of sickening insight, Lexis realized it excited *both* of them.

Something hard and smooth pressed his perineum. The next moment, the pressure shifted to his anus. Gasping, he began to struggle in earnest. Pain exploded through him as the *thing*, the huge and monstrous *thing* penetrated the innermost recesses of his body. His vision went white. The muscles of his back and legs arched in spasm.

At first slowly, then with increasing speed and vigor, the Terran began pumping. Each thrust tore through Lexis's belly. He felt himself—not just his body but his very self—pierced, shredded, disintegrating under the onslaught.

Suddenly the Terran let out a bellow. His fingers gouged deep into Lexis's flesh, tearing fur, drawing blood. Lexis's head whirled and for an awful moment he could not feel his body except as one throbbing pulse beat. The pain crested higher and higher. A scream burst from his lungs, and then something grabbed his guts and twisted into white-hot climax, wave after sobbing, shuddering wave of it...

He gradually came back to his senses and found himself lying on his side. The muscles of his pelvis twitched, and his anal area throbbed. Something hot and sticky dripped down the inside of his thighs. Celestinbellini sat on the edge of the bed, pulling on his clothing. He turned and looked down at Lexis.

"I've heard some screaming climaxes, but nobody that passes out like you do." The Terran rose to his feet.

"Are you leaving?" Lexis whispered. He felt drained, a husk, as if a power had possessed and now discarded him. Bile filled his mouth and he fought down nausea.

White teeth flashed in the subdued light. "I never kiss and tell, and I never stay the night. Don't worry, I'll be back for more." Celestinbellini reached over and caressed Lexis's buttock, sliding his fingers suggestively down the crease and grinning when Lexis shuddered.

I can't—Lexis was not sure if he thought the words or said them aloud,—*go through that again.*

The Terran bent over. His broad shoulders blotted out the light. Shuddering, without any power to stop himself, Lexis reached up and put one hand around Celestinbellini's neck and pulled him down for one final, alien kiss.

"Until next time," Celestinbellini said, and was gone.

Chapter 40

Talense took advantage of the unseasonably mild evening to walk home, for a moment ignoring the security guard a few paces behind him. Beneath the newly budding trees that lined the Eastriver quays, he spotted Druse, his old friend from the news agency, coming toward him through the crowd. Druse lifted his crest to its full height, a frozen spray of coppery bristles. The fur around his neck rose in swift, hostile jerks until it stood out like a living collar.

A passerby cried out in alarm at the sight and another hustled his child away. Talense stared, too shocked to respond. Without a word, Druse whirled and plunged back into the stream of pedestrians.

I should have expected it. This is a new era, no going back to the old, and we all must change. Sometimes, on days like this, he wondered if he was too old and too brittle to change, if the Prophet had withdrawn his blessing and left Talense to flounder in the inversion of insanity.

His crest shivered as he remembered the moment of shock when the news of the executions had reached him. Not for hundreds of years, since the religious wars, had such a thing happened. He'd rushed over to the square, arriving even as the warders were clearing away the last of the spectators. He had not realized there would be so much blood, or how its smell would mingle with the residue of smoke from the rifles. Even now, it lingered in his nostrils.

Talense smoothed his crest and went on, but the freshness of the evening had grown stale. Arriving at the entrance to his quarters, he dismissed the guard for the night and then went in. After locking the door behind him, he pulled off his coat, hung it on the hook inside the door, slipped off his street shoes, and threw himself into the nearest armchair.

Think of the work you do, how necessary it is, the understanding you will create, the new world order you're helping to bring about...

The litany brought a poor, thin comfort. Repetition had eroded its persuasive power. Besides, the words had never been his own. They were from Sarahdavies.

A pain shot through his chest. She was ashes now, sitting in a little container on the ship that was a mere point of light in the night sky. He hadn't realized how much he would miss her.

He would tell himself it took time to build understanding, but then something would happen, like the announcement from the mayor's office that the Terrans had been instrumental in the capture and rehabilitation of Birre-az-Austre, and he would wonder if he knew the Terrans at all.

Sighing, Talense closed his eyes. His body ached, an unbroken knot of tension. It would be lovely to have Jeelan here to rub his shoulders. Jeelan was at a clan function, something to do with the middle youngsters and their reproductive health courses.

The next instant he became aware of something subtly different in the apartment, a shift in the air... Someone had been here. Was still here.

Talense heard a sound from the kitchen, small but distinct: the clink of a metal utensil against crockery. His tongue curled in fear and his crest flared briefly. His nose caught the scent of soothing menthe.

Why would an intruder—or an assassin—be brewing himself a cup of tea in my kitchen?

Step by cautious step, Talense drew closer to the kitchen. In the dim light, he saw the edge of the table and—

"Kallen?"

Talense flicked on the overhead light, boiling with relief and fury. The warder chief sat in Jeelan's chair, calmly stirring honey into two steaming cups.

"What kind of Faithless trick is this?" Talense demanded. His chest hurt. He rubbed it absently. "You scared me half to Blazes!"

Kallen shoved one cup towards Talense. "Sit down."

"Not until you tell me why you snuck into my quarters like some kind of—kind of—"

"Criminal?" Kallen looked up, his eyes grim. "Perhaps. How else could I talk to you without any... official record of our meeting?"

Talense lowered himself into his chair. The cup felt warm and solid between his fingers. He gulped the menthe, ignoring its scalding heat. The familiar taste, slippery on the tongue, soothed him. His initial outrage gave way to curiosity.

"We've had plenty of differences in the past," Kallen said, "but I've never doubted your integrity."

"Only the validity of my conclusions." Talense paused, sensing the questions behind Kallen's words.

Are you the same press who fought me with your interminable questions and your thirst for the truth? Did that thirst get buried under your new power as censor, as lackey of the Terrans?

They were the same kind of questions Druse would have asked... or

Jeelan. Since the night the clan had forced him to withdraw from the Fellowship League, Jeelan no longer asked questions.

"I've found out something," Kallen said with a shade of awkwardness, as if he were unused to admitting there was anything he didn't already know. "It's too important to keep to myself."

Talense leaned back in his chair, his hands open and empty on the table. His fur rippled, little twitches along his scalp, then lay smooth. "I'm listening."

"It's about the executions in the square. Believe it as you choose, but I had no prior knowledge of them. I never gave any orders for my people to participate in such a thing or to release prisoners to those who would."

"Are you asking me to believe you're innocent?"

"I've been a lot of things in my years, but *innocent* isn't one of them. I've done things I'd prefer to forget, but to order my warders to fire on unarmed prisoners who were offering no resistance—on *our own people*—" In those three words, a hint of emotion tinged his voice. Quietly he went on, "—the same people we've sworn to protect. *I've* sworn to protect. I would sooner cut my uniform from my own body, strip by bloody strip, than give such an order."

"Somebody in your department gave it," Talense said coolly, "and found officers willing to carry it out. Positions of power have always attracted those with the predilection for abusing it." And, he thought, a competent chief should have known what his subordinates were doing.

"We all have that potential within us. In easy times, by the grace of Oni, we are never forced to confront it."

Talense blinked. Kallen had never before made reference to the Aspect of his clan. "What's your point?"

"My point is that none of us is entirely *innocent*—to use your own word—but that doesn't automatically make us guilty. I would have refused to issue the order, I would have protested, I don't know what I would have done. I never had the chance to find out. By the time I was informed, it was over. All I could do was ask by whose orders. And ask myself how I could have been so wrong about my own officers."

Talense gestured noncommittally. "Why come to me with this? It's an internal investigation."

"That's what I thought at first. Oh, I discovered some instances of abuse, the most notable being the assignment of the least experienced investigators to Terran assaults on Chacarrans. The deeper I dug, the less sense the executions made. Contrary to the announcement at the time, these people were not terrorists. I wondered if I were dealing with a case of blackmail gone wrong. It seemed that *none* of my own people, except the jail guards themselves, were involved."

Talense laughed, a dry humorless bark. "You aren't proposing that the prisoners executed themselves? Or that Terrans somehow managed to paste crests on their heads and masquerade as Chacarrans?"

Kallen leaned forward across the table and his eyes shone with a deadly light. "I'm not *proposing* anything. I'm *telling* you that I have discovered proof the so-called warders involved in the massacre were in fact specially-trained Erlind soldiers. The Terrans brought them in their ships from Erlonn."

Every hair in Tallen's crest felt as it if were on fire. On fury-fire, on horror-fire, on terror-fire. Then fire plummeted into ice, as if the temperature of the air had fallen to near-arctic lows. As he struggled to regain control, a thought came to him, chillingly distant, as if it came from someone else:

The Terrans wanted revenge for the death of Sarahdavies and the others. They think they can do whatever they like in Chacarre and we cannot—or will not—stop them.

"The Terrans wouldn't talk to me," Kallen said bleakly. "Not even Doctorvera, who's been asking questions herself. But Lexis did. I went to his office this afternoon. He knew about it, even admitted it when I confronted him. Said it was the best thing to happen to Miraz in years and if I didn't like it, I could resign."

The air of the room turned even colder. "Did you?"

"I thought about it. While I was thinking about it, I received word that the mayor's office issued an order for my arrest. For sedition and treason most likely, although the charges weren't specified."

Received word? Yes, Kallen would have his own sources within the Department, sources he could trust, perhaps even fellow Oniites.

"Then what are you doing here?" Talense said.

Kallen's face went taut, like a rope twisted to the breaking point. "Making sure that *someone* knows the truth. Before they catch me or I disappear on my own."

Talense felt suddenly weary. The years pressed him like a leaden weight. "You've come to the wrong person. You cannot trust me."

Kallen's hand shot out with the speed of a striking snake and wrapped around Talense's wrist. "You're the only person—*the only one*—do you hear me, you tenacious, meddlesome weasel?—that I *can* trust with this thing."

For a long moment, Talense could only stare back at Kallen. "I don't know what I can do. I can't promise anything."

"Who's asking for a promise? It's enough that you *know*."

Talense pushed himself away from the table, went to the stove, and turned on the fire under the water kettle. "What will you do now? Where will you go?"

"Are you sure you want to know?"

The door to the apartment creaked on its hinges. Talense mouthed, "*Jeelan*." Kallen turned and slid the kitchen window open.

On impulse, Talense put his hands on Kallen's shoulders. "May the Prophet hold you safe through perilous change," he whispered.

Jeelan's voice wafted in from the main room. "Who's there with you?"

"I'm alone," Talense called back, and the next instant, it was the truth.

Jeelan stood by the kitchen door, his arms full of the children's folders. "Someone else was here. There are two cups of tea."

There was no accusation in Jeelan's voice, only quiet fact. He turned away, back to the central room. Talense heard the muffled sound of the folders dropping to the floor. It resonated through his aching bones. He felt as if he'd cut out half of his own heart.

Miraz: CLAN CHARGES COMPLICITY IN MASSACRE. Report by Lansky (Cleared by the Department of Information Services.)

In a surprise move last night, advocats for the Maasite Gerendre clan publicly accused a prominent Miraz family of breach of the Convocation of 1053, specifically "the deliberate and willful harboring of enemy troops on Chacarran territory." The charges specify that the Hoolite Austre sept negotiated with the Terrans to conceal and house Erlind soldiers suspected of participating in the Warder Square Massacre. It is public knowledge that Austre had leased a warehouse to the Terrans for scientific laboratories and adjacent living quarters. After it was destroyed by terrorist bombing, another building was provided and extensively modified for security.

Austre has filed an accusation of Territoriality, claiming harassment of family members by Gerendre patrols.

Many Mirazan citizens expressed sympathy for Austre, citing the recent ordeal by young Birre-az-Austre at the hands of the Freedom Movement terrorists.

Miraz: WARDER CHIEF KALLEN, 12 OTHERS DIE IN RAILCAR BOMBING. TERRORIST GROUP RESPONSIBLE. Report by Druse.

Chapter 41

MIRAZ FREE PRESS: ERLS IN MIRAZ! TERRANS IMPORT ENEMY SOLDIERS FOR WARDER SQUARE MASSACRE!

Last week, fifty innocent Chacarrans were slain by Erlind soldiers wearing the garb of our own warders. The Terrans, who engineered this horrendous spectacle, attempted to justify their heinous act by claiming that these citizens were condemned criminals. Such statements are patent lies, for these people had been tortured and held without evidence, many of them without being charged with anything other than speaking out against the Tyrants.

In vain they begged for a fair trial, for justice, for their very lives. But their pleas were met by stony silence. No mercy moved the hearts of the disguised Erls. Once the killing began, the valiant martyrs struggled vainly to escape. Before the horrified eyes of their neighbors and loved ones, they were callously cut down.

The Terrans, knowing that no loyal Chacarran would participate in this foul deed, imported the Erls to do their bidding. The Erls were flown by Terran aircar to a location outside the city and provided with Chacarran uniforms. After the massacre, the Erlind forces were hidden, possibly in one of the warehouses used as Terran barracks. No one knows for sure where they are, only that they are still among us, waiting for the next chance to strike!

Talense slapped the news sheet down in Jeelan's lap. His crest was clamped against his skull and his throat was so tight, his voice came out as a metallic rasp.

"What do you know about this?"

He'd first seen the article when one of his aides had brought it to him an hour ago. He hadn't asked where the aide had gotten an underground news sheet. He'd only stared at the headline.

ERLS IN MIRAZ.

He had told no one. He felt certain Kallen had told only him. Lexis was certainly not going to broadcast his knowledge of the Erls.

Jeelan? Had he paused inside the door, listening, before the creaking of the hinges betrayed his presence? How much had he heard?

Jeelan refolded the news sheet along its creases. "Some things you can't pretend didn't happen. Or they poison everything you do."

Something hot and tight shot through Talense's chest. He had been blind, so blind. He had seen only what he wanted to see. Moments crept by. He lowered himself to the sofa. The cushions gave under his weight.

"When Perrin asked you to stop your League activities, you said you would." Talense picked up the folded news sheet. His hand trembled. "You *promised* us—"

"I haven't broken any promises. I said I would not endanger the clan."

"You've kept on with your activities?"

"The League is all but dead, or should be."

Miraz was no longer the city Talense had grown up in, lived in, expected to die in. In his memory, he saw the Terran Compound rising like a fortress, saw the yellow light beams lashing out across the plaza. Space ships cut across the sky, leaving whitened trails like scars, carrying enemy soldiers into the heart of Miraz. He saw the alien surveillance units, their metal shapes stark against the softly weathered stone, the people hurrying past, eyes averted, crests jangled, sometimes swerving across the street to avoid his warder escort. When had all that happened? Why had he never noticed it before?

Jeelan held out his arms. Talense buried his face in the curve of Jeelan's neck. He felt the softness of Jeelan's fur against his lips and inhaled the intoxicating, familiar smell of him. Jeelan gave off a gentle, persuasive warmth. Talense drew in a deep breath. His own body felt as fragile as glass.

With a shiver, Talense drew away and captured Jeelan's hands in his. "Once I thought I would never lie to you, would never hide anything. Now I look at you and see the half of myself that has become a stranger."

Jeelan reached up to stroke the fur along Talense's jaw, an old gesture of intimacy. "Tell me, then."

"I used to think I was acting for the best of Chacarre. I believed the Terrans when they said we must be free to decide issues for ourselves, and the only way we could do that was to have all the information available to us. I believed that these 'elections' would help us cast off the quarreling and suspicion between the Clans."

"I think this is a good thing," Jeelan said, "that people know it was the Erls and not our own warders, that they understand it was the Terrans who brought them here."

"'If striving for a better, more peaceful world is hopeless, then let us embrace that folly together.'"

"Quoting Carrel-az-Ondre at me, are you?" Jeelan managed a small smile. "We could use someone with his vision. There is so much hatred out there, so much ignorance."

Talense could almost hear Jeelan saying, *And if I cannot cure the hatred, I will do what I can to mend the ignorance.*

"Hatred and ignorance," Talense heard his own voice repeat. "The tokens of our days."

"Yes," Jeelan said. "Yet it takes only a few voices of reason, like torches in the darkness, to be heard."

Something turned over in Talense's mind, like a piece of disused and rusty machinery. An idea took shape. "The Prophet said that we are granted gifts so that we may use them."

"We're a couple of dreamers, you and I," Jeelan said. "We cannot lead a troop of soldiers or run with the weasels in the underground. Yet if there were a way to conjure courage .."

Jeelan went to the cabinet at the back of the bedroom and got out the old typer machine and a packet of paper. He set the machine on the kitchen table and smoothed a piece of paper over the rectangular platen.

"Use the Prophet's gift," Jeelan said. "Use it as only you can. Write."

MIRAZ FREE PRESS: HISTORY WILL JUDGE!

My fellow Seekers,

How is a person to conduct his life in honesty and dignity, during these perilous times? Is it ethical to place oneself—and possibly one's family—at risk for the sake of signing a petition or helping a fellow Chacarran? How much easier it is to turn away, to salve one's conscience with the thought that "someone else will do it"?

Better to ask—If everyone turns away, who will be left to resist the Terran oppressors and their Erlind allies?

Who will stand up to them? Me? You?

Collaborators

I can see you now, my friend, turning away from the words on this page. They are too painful for you to bear. Believe me, I think no less of you for it. The risks are too great, the spy huts everywhere, the consequences of being caught too unthinkable. Perhaps you have already lost friends or family, taken away to either the swelling jails or, far worse, to the Terran interrogation chambers, where those who come out alive are envious of those who do not. Perhaps you only know someone who has seen these things.

I understand. I will not judge you for turning away.

You will judge yourself.

Your memory will judge you—your memory of a Chacarre where you were free to walk the streets, to meet with friends as you would, to speak your mind freely. A Chacarre where no Terrans swaggered through the streets in twos and threes. A Chacarre where pregnant people were safe from unspeakable alien assault. A Chacarre where your children can grow up, loved and free.

Your memory will judge what you do today. History will judge what you do tomorrow.

—"The Seeker"

Chapter 42

To all appearances, Padme's restaurant was closed, the front doors locked, the windows barred and lightless. Yet all afternoon and through the dinner hours, people had been coming in through the delivery entrance by twos and threes. Alon would never have believed the place could hold so many people in such quietness. The whispered conversations barely rose above the sound of their breathing. Some were advocat students that Alon knew slightly through Birre. Until now, he wouldn't have thought they could stop ranting at each other for more than a few minutes at a time.

Alon also knew Timas and his friends, especially Orsen. He knew they carried pellet guns beneath their coats. He didn't know where they got them; weapons were illegal in the city.

The farmer Hayke waited on one side of the room, still not fully recovered from his wound infection. He leaned against the wall, exchanging hushed comments with the other Wayfolk who'd come in response to Alon's own urging.

"We will not participate in violence," they'd warned him.

He'd answered, "Just come, and lend your voices," all the while thinking, *Do you think you will have any choice, any more than I had? Do you think all will be well by your merely wishing it? Or that the Terrans will leave if you ask them nicely?*

All in all, the meeting included a dozen different groups, many of which had minimal previous contact with each other. Watching them, Alon felt the first stirring of hope. They'd been working, scattered and separated, in ignorance of one another. Some, like Birre's student friends, had been active from the very beginning, the day of the plaza riot. Others had only now begun to take action. Some saw the enemy as the Terrans, others the Erls, still more the mayor and his warders. By some miracle, Padme and his network had convinced them to come together. It remained to be seen if they would take the next step and put aside their differences to work together.

"The Terrans may possess formidable weapons—the light rays, the spy mushrooms, more we don't know about." Lorne's voice, clear and quiet, pierced the silence, echoing Alon's private thoughts. "But we aren't helpless.

We have our own resources—and our knowledge of Miraz. We know her secret ways, how to disappear."

"That won't work," one of the students said. "The warders know Miraz as well as we do."

"But not the Erls!" someone else answered.

"The Erls are not the problem," Timas said. "They are only doing what they've always done, taking advantage of the situation, as is their nature. We may hate them, we may fight them, but in the final word, we understand them. The Terrans who are behind the Governing Council, the Terrans who ordered the massacre—they are not even people. They have no conscience, no honor. The only thing they understand is brute force, and that is how we must respond. There is only one way to stop the Terrans. For every Chacarran death, a Terran must suffer the same. Only when we make them pay in blood will they withdraw."

As Alon listened, a faint, atavistic shiver ran through the fur along his spine, raising it as if in readiness for action.

"What if violent resistance only provokes more violent retaliation?" Hayke had risen to his feet on the other side of the room. All heads turned now to face him. "The warders said the execution was in response to the bombing of the Terran buildings. Suppose we strike back, kill more of them, what then? Where will it end? Is that the kind of world we want to create for our children, suffering and death to be answered by more of the same?"

"We have no choice!" Alon cried. "Timas is right, they will listen to nothing else!" He gestured to Hayke. "You tell me what difference your fine pacifist words would have made! You tell me how all your prayers for harmony can bring my baby back to life!"

Words, like the boiling core of his rage turned into sound, burst from him. "No answer? Well, I have one for you! The only thing that would have stopped those vermin was killing them first! How many more of our people must die before we understand that simple truth?"

Caught in the heat of the moment, Alon raced on. "For every Chacarran death, the Terrans must pay! For every loss, for every humiliation, for every instant of pain and grief, the Terrans must pay!"

He had them now, as surely as he held them in the palm of his hand. Silence fell over the room, more eloquent than words. He saw himself leading daredevil bands along the hidden network of traverson and catacomb, striking where they would and then disappearing, turning in ambush on any Terrans who dared to follow. He saw more bombings, perhaps even the compound itself. He saw formless things that filled him with a sick, dark exhilaration. He opened himself to it, tasted burnt sulfur in the back of his throat.

They were his to command, these people standing before him, their faces rapt and eager. He had only to reach out, to infect them with his passion, to mold them into the fighting force he needed.

"From this day onward, no Terran will walk the streets of Miraz in safety. We will kill, we will strike terror. Our success will go out to all Chacarre like a shining beacon, a call to take up the struggle—until there is not a single place on the entire planet where the Terrans dare set foot. We will—"

Alon broke off suddenly. His senses, enhanced by the rising *tal'deh*, had caught the faint sounds at the front of the restaurant. An instant later, pounding shivered the side door.

"Warders!" a voice shouted from outside. "Open up in there!"

"Coming! Just a minute!" Padme called. "Quickly!" he hissed, gesturing toward the door that led upstairs to his living quarters. "Some of you, that way! The passage through the kitchen leads out on the alley."

Even as the meeting fractured, Padme jerked aside a rug in the center of the floor and pulled open a trap door. Stone slabs gleamed wetly: the pit led to the catacombs.

As Timas hurried by, Alon grabbed his rifle. "I'll hold them as long as I can," Alon said. Timas scrambled down the ladder and into the waiting blackness.

Alon took his place beside a handful of others, all of them armed. The warders weren't waiting for Padme to open the door. Someone fired a gun at the recalcitrant lock.

Alon raised the rifle. He silently thanked Birre for having taught him to shoot when they were teenagers. Meddi and Tellem had been furious.

"Are you crazy?" Hayke grabbed Alon's arm and spun him around. "Do you want to get killed?"

"Get out of here!" Alon snapped.

The weakened lock held, but the end of a baton thrust through the splintered center of the door. A gap appeared, large enough to reveal an expanse of night cut by hand lights. Something heavy collided with the door and the lock gave way. Alon spotted a dark uniform topped by the pale blur of a face, and fired. The noise of the discharge shrieked in his ears. The rifle barrel, recoiling, rammed into his shoulder.

"You're under arrest!" a voice bellowed from outside.

Alon lowered the rifle a fraction and glanced around the almost-empty room. Padme stood beside the trap door, gesturing. Hayke and three others also remained.

"Padme, go!" Alon said. He jerked his chin toward Hayke and the others. "Then you. Now! I'll cover you."

Without a word, Padme and one of the others disappeared down the catacomb entrance. Hayke reached again for Alon's arm. Furious, Alon shoved the rifle butt into Hayke's chest and pushed him toward the trap door.

From outside came muffled words, "Let me talk to him. He won't hurt me."

Alon's blood turned to ice. He couldn't move, couldn't breathe.

A familiar shape, silhouetted against the lanterns, appeared in the doorway. Alon waited, caught like a grommet in the glare of a hunter's lantern. For a horrifying instant, a stray beam of light fell across the eyes of the figure in the doorway.

Hayke yanked the rifle from Alon's inert hands and fired once at the top of the door frame. Wood chips flew from the bullet's impact. The figure ducked out of sight.

The sound of the rifle unlocked Alon's muscles. He scrambled down the ladder into the dank, frigid hole as fast as he could. A light shone palely from a distance below and then blinked out. Hayke followed an instant later, pausing only to jerk the trap door shut and bolt it from the underside.

"Quickly!" came a voice from below. Padme's, Alon thought. "They'll be through in a few minutes!"

Darkness swallowed him up. The metal rungs of the ladder, roughened with rust, cut into his hands. He forced himself to think only of the next movement—the next step, the next handhold. Hayke was only a few rungs above him.

The bottom came suddenly; Alon stepped down, expecting another rung, and met unyielding stone. Padme picked up a hand light and thrust it at him.

Alon started down the tunnel, moments before Hayke reached the landing and hurried after him. Hayke's hands were empty.

"Where's the rifle?"

Hayke shook his head. His lungs wheezed and he moved as if the wound in his side still pained him. Alon bit back further words. Hayke wasn't strong enough for this; by all rights, he should still be in bed.

They ran on with only the noise of their footsteps and their panted breaths to break the silence. Alon found himself listening for sounds of pursuit, but heard none. After a short distance, they came to a branching, several blocked-off passageways, and another way down, this time narrow circular stairs. Here they needed both hands to steady themselves. They went down and down until Alon's muscles ached in protest. The pit of his belly congealed. The temperature dropped even further. Finally they reached the bottom.

"It's safe to stop here," said Padme.

The walls, like those of the tunnels and wells, bore the marks of chiseling. A group clustered together, a dozen of them from the meeting.

Shadows cast by the hand lights gave their faces a bleak, hardened expression.

Timas, who'd been one of the first down the trap door, stepped forward. "The others—they got away?"

"Listen to me," Alon said. "They know who we are."

"But how—"

"Birre led them to us." Alon hardly recognized his own voice, so bitter. "Anything he ever knew about us, they know now."

"No," said Timas, his crest wavering. "I can't believe that. Not Birre."

"He was there," Hayke said gently. "The morning of the executions, he was taken away from the prison, perhaps given to the Terrans. Who knows what happened to him?"

"Birre would never—" Timas tried again, but this time his voice was less certain.

"Birre is no longer one of us," Alon said.

Padme sculpted the shadows with his hands. "We will mourn the comrade he used to be. He will be sorely missed." His gaze met Alon's. "What next?"

Alon thought a moment. "Anything Birre knew about—any contact, any hiding place, any method of communication—we must consider compromised. Some of the other groups might be all right if they didn't have anything to do with the advocat students' alliance. Nevertheless, we should make sure they're warned. At the very least, we ourselves will need new identity papers and new safe houses."

"Blazing damnation," said someone, rumpling his head fur. "That'll be hard. Not the papers, but the places. We can't hide down *here* forever."

"I don't intend that we do!" Alon said sharply.

"I stayed at a Wayfolk inn my first night in Miraz," said Hayke. "There may be more resources there than you realize."

"Indeed," said Padme. "I always laughed when my parents said how important it was to preserve the underground paths. I thought we'd never need them again, not in modern times. I thought hiding and secrets belonged to the past."

Hayke laid his hand on Padme's shoulder. "There is strength as well as sorrow in the old ways."

Alon smoothed his crest with one hand. "We may hide like grommets by day, but we will strike like wolves in the night."

Hayke woke in the darkness to the sound of keening. For a moment, he thought it was his own voice that had roused him, or the memory of all those nights he had sobbed himself to sleep, when the agony of Rosen's loss rose up in waves of grief too great to be contained.

He blinked, taking in the shadowy contours of the room, the outline of the door, the battered wooden chest. Alon lay huddled on a pallet along the opposite wall, his arms and legs drawn close to his body. For a moment, there was silence and then another faint sound, half-smothered against the pillow.

Hayke swung his feet to the floor, then hesitated. He remembered the *tal'deh*-fueled madness in young Alon's voice, the fire in his eyes, hot and wild enough to incinerate them all. His hands moved of their own, crossing his chest. His heartbeat slowed, the fever lifted. The teachings he had lived by all his life stirred deep in his bones.

Tal'spirë, surrender, the Way beyond madness. The state of grace.

Beneath Alon's fury, Hayke felt the other's unbearable pain. It echoed even now in his own heart.

Hayke knelt beside Alon's pallet and gently touched his shoulder. Alon's crest flared. He pushed Hayke away. "Go back to bed. I don't want your comfort."

"Don't you?" Hayke said mildly. "In your situation, I would."

"What could you possibly know about *my situation*?"

"I know that you have, after a bitter struggle and through no fault of your own, lost the love of your life. It takes a long time to come to peace with that kind of loss. Even then, some wounds don't ever heal."

Hayke put one arm around Alon's shoulders. Beneath his fingers, muscles tensed into ropes of steel. Alon's bones felt as sharp as carved shells.

Alon pulled away from the touch. Hayke let him go.

"It would have been better," Alon whispered, rocking himself gently, "far better if he had died."

Chapter 43

MIRAZ: MIRAZ YOUTH SURVIVES CAPTURE BY TERRORISTS. TERRAN SCIENCE AIDS IN REHABILITATION. Report by Ambrom. (Cleared by the Department of Information Services)

In a story that rivals the pages of fictional thrillers, the young member of a prominent Hoolite sept endured physical hardship and mental torture at the hands of Chacarran Freedom Movement terrorists, then miraculously escaped and has been restored to health, thanks to the skill of Terran mind-healers.

Birre-az-Austre, a native Mirazan, athlete, and outstanding student advocat, fell prey to the insidious propaganda of the Freedom Movement, which played upon the prevailing social unrest and the natural ebullience of his youth. All efforts by his parents, Enellon-az-Austre and Saunde-az-Vendreth, failed to deter him from this dangerous course. He disappeared into the murky underworld of dissident groups and was lured to Nantaz for the aborted insurgency.

The details of Birre's rescue remain guarded to protect the privacy of the family, but Mirazan warders, working together with Terrans and using the resources of their advanced technology, were at last able to effect his release. During his captivity, he had been mentally abused to the point of sympathizing with his captors. Terrans assisted Mirazan authorities to disentangle this young person's mind from the perfidious influence of the Freedom Movement propaganda and restore him to his proper senses.

At a brief, private ceremony, Mayor Lexis praised the young hero. "Birre symbolizes the hope of Chacarrans everywhere," the mayor said. "He is living proof that there is no peril we cannot survive and no challenge we cannot conquer."

United once more with his loving family, Birre has vowed to devote himself to liberating Miraz from the violent and subversive influence of his former enslavers.

Hayke sat alone in his room at the Wayfolk inn. Spread over a towel on the narrow bed were the disassembled parts of a pellet rifle, one of a half-dozen smuggled in from the country. It was much the sort of weapon Rosen used on weasels in the chicken coops. Rosen had taught him how to take it apart and clean it, even as he was doing now. As much as he tried to focus on the mechanics of dirt removal and oiling, he could not forget that these actions had but one goal—the killing of a fellow living person.

Can this be the Way I must follow? he wondered for the twentieth time that morning.

Hayke looked up from his work as Alon entered, his skin flushed beneath his rumpled sorrel fur. The soft curves of his body had almost disappeared. Since the raid, he bore little resemblance to the heart-breakingly beautiful youth Hayke had first met.

Alon threw his backpack on the second cot and sat down, exhaling in a gust.

"Problems?" Hayke asked.

"No, I got the papers through all right." Alon reached into the bag and took out a loaf of bread and a few bruised apples. He broke the bread into pieces, wrapped some in a scrap of rag, and put them in the bottom of the dresser. He never said where he had gotten the food and Hayke never asked. They had only a little money, given to them by sympathizers who were themselves struggling to survive, and what they did have often went for ammunition and printing supplies.

Hayke put down his cleaning rag and waited.

Alon looked up, a quick jerk that moved his face into the single beam of sunlight. "My parents came back. The warders arrested them. For questioning, Padme said." His hands curled into fists. "They should have stayed in Avallaz. I can't protect them here. What were they thinking?"

Hayke looked down at his grease-smeared hands, thinking of Torrey and Felde. "Perhaps," he said slowly, "your parents were thinking that *they* could help *you*."

Alon, having finished his bread, went to the window. Hayke watched in silence. There was nothing he could say.

His hurt runs too deep. He will not listen. There is no one he can trust. He wants to hit, to smash, to destroy.

Such fire burned in Alon that others followed where he went. His passion carried them all.

Hayke wiped his hands on a clean corner of the rag and picked up a piece of bread. "I will go by the bookstore and see what I can find out."

"We should have done something when the trouble first started." Alon turned to face Hayke. Hayke thought he had never seen such a desolate expression. "If only we had stood up to them, if only we'd struck back, made the price too high for even them to pay."

"We would have become like them, then."

"You can't fight fire with straw."

"Sometimes I wonder," Hayke said slowly, "if you are so angry that you would rather punish the Terrans than defeat them. If you would keep them here, rather than let them go back to their own place, so that you could go on hurting them."

"No, of course not," Alon replied, looking startled.

"If there were another way to have them gone, a way without violence, would you take it?"

"Even you, Hayke, must realize we don't have that choice. Maybe once, when they first came. Maybe then we could have said *no* and they would have listened. I doubt it, though. We just didn't see what they were until it was too late."

"You weren't responsible," Hayke said. He remembered Alon's expression when Birre had come through the door in Padme's restaurant. Something had gone wrong inside Alon then, something that might never be mended.

In the street outside, the sun filled the air with gentle warmth. The gauzy twist of clouds had thinned and disappeared. Hayke lifted his face to the light, but took no comfort from it. He felt as if he were moving toward an abyss, a pit of darkness. He could see no escape, no way out.

Hayke had thought many times of finding a Gathering to attend, but had always decided against it, thinking his presence might endanger the others. Now he saw what a mistake that had been. He had, in fear, cut himself off from his very roots.

In the Old Quarter, sunscreens glistened blue and white and daffy-pink in the new sun. Rock-doves cooed and pecked for crumbs in the cobbles underneath the tables outside the restaurants. The aroma of fresh bread and citron-rolls wafted from the open door of a bakery. A handful of people clustered around a wall where news sheets were posted.

The bookstore was locked, its curtains drawn. Hayke asked the neighboring shopkeepers, but learned little he did not already know, beyond the arrest and the calm demeanor of the old Wayfolk couple as they were led away.

Why, he wondered, did they come back? Out of concern for Alon or out of a deeper, intuitive sense? Had their Way led them to Miraz, even as his had?

Across the street, Padme was closing the restaurant door. After the raid, he'd been questioned by the warders and then released with a warning to stay out of trouble. The next day, a spy mushroom had been set up on the corner opposite his restaurant. Padme saw Hayke and gestured a greeting.

"Young Alon's parents have returned and been arrested. Have you heard anything more?"

"Yes," said Padme. "Word is that the Terran himself says it was an accident. It's a good thing he didn't die. Alon won't be charged with murder. The warders were ready to release Meddi and Tellem, but the Terrans wanted to interrogate them. They've taken them to the compound." Padme turned and began walking toward Westriver Bridge, Hayke at his side.

Interrogate? The way they did Birre? Hayke's fur rippled. He wondered how Padme had found this out.

Padme gestured, a graceful fanning of the fingers, the abbreviation for *tal'spirë*. Surrender, but with the inflection Padme had given it, an invitation to a silent witnessing.

"Some things are more important than safety," Padme said. "For so much of our history, we followed the yielding Way. Retreating, disappearing, and presenting no resistance, no target."

"Now the Way has led us all here," said Hayke. "For what purpose?" The mind needed reasons to explain the actions of the heart.

Images rose up in his mind, as vivid as the night he'd first dreamed them, so that instead of remembering, he saw them anew. He looked down at the plaza, even as he had on the day of the riot, and saw the people lying there, covering the pavement with their motionless bodies. His heart overflowed with emotions he could not name. The next moment, he became one of them. Cold, gritty stone pressed into his back. He felt the warmth of the sun on his face, smelled the perfume of the flower sellers' stands. He opened his eyes and stared at the sky, dazzled for an instant by the piercing blue, and stood up.

"It is a true vision," Padme said, after Hayke told him what he'd seen. "A token of the Way that has brought you here, and so many of the other Folk. May I have your blessing to take word of it to the Gatherings?"

Hayke felt a knot loosen in his chest. "I will tell them myself."

Gun in hand, Alon waited with Timas and Orsen in the night shadows. In different locations around the city, others were doing the same, ten targets in all. Alon had planned it all out, choosing this particular mission for his own.

For some nights now, they'd watched the Terran's movements, the times he came and went. He might arrive before dinner, sometimes later, but he always left around the same time, and never with more than one guard, also Terran. Occasionally, he went alone.

The street lay quiet, only a few pedestrians at this hour. Down the broad avenue, a pair of lovers stopped beside a flowering tree, sheltered from the lamp. One of the surveillance mushrooms stood on the corner outside the Mansion. It would record their actions, but Alon wanted the Terrans to know who had done this thing.

The Terran strode along, ignoring his escort, drawing closer with every footstep. He made a whistling sound between his teeth and his hips swaggered, broadcasting arrogance in the careless power of his walk.

Come on, come on. Closer, closer...

Alon curled his fingers around his gun. A faint tremor passed through his crest and down the length of his spine. He forced himself to breathe slowly, silently. Up until now, the waiting had been easy. But it would be all over in just a few moments.

Move, you Flameless garbage! What's taking you so long?

On the very edge of the area Alon had marked out in his mind, the Terran halted and turned back toward his guard.

"Hey, Harry!"

Alon flinched at the sound of the Terran's deep-pitched voice. For a wild moment, Alon considered rushing him where he stood.

Wait until it's exactly right, Alon told himself. He shook with the effort it took to restrain himself, to hold fast. *Don't give the Bird-dropping any advantage. Strike on your own timing, not his. Don't let him muddle you.*

The Terran asked the guard something, and the guard shook his head. The Terran turned, stepped into the target zone.

Alon whispered to the others, *"Go!"* He leaped into full view and landed in a crouch with the gun aimed at the Terran's chest.

"Hold it!" Alon shouted.

Timas darted from the side street and fired at the guard. Orsen, as planned, hung back, ready to help if something went wrong.

From behind him, Alon heard Timas's shots, then shouting and heavy footsteps. His attention wavered the merest fraction. The next instant, the Terran spun around, one booted foot whizzing toward the barrel of Alon's gun. Alon's fingers caught in the trigger.

The recoil of the gun sent Alon's arm snapping upward. The Terran's heel collided with the side of Alon's head and both of them slammed into the pavement.

Collaborators

Cursing, Alon grabbed for the gun, but his hands swept empty air. His legs tangled with the Terran's. He touched hair, so strange, alien and familiar at the same time. He curled his fingers in it and yanked as hard as he could.

The Terran yelled something in his own language and twisted around. A fist caught Alon squarely in the belly. Air burst from his lungs and his hands went numb. He lashed out with his feet, heard an answering cry. From somewhere to the side, Timas was shouting.

Alon scrambled, gasping, to his feet. The world went cold and gray for a moment, while figures darted through the periphery of his sight. People were screaming, running.

Out of here, fast!

Alon aimed a kick at the Terran's head. He tripped, grappled with him. More shots zinged past his ears. Suddenly, the Terran went limp.

Cursing, Alon wrestled with the Terran's weight, trying to drag him away. The next moment, Timas grabbed one of the Terran's arms. Together they dragged the Terran down the side street.

Orsen raced ahead, down the cobbled side street, to where they'd left their car. He scrambled behind the steering bar and pumped the engine to life.

Alon shoved the Terran's body into the back seat. Timas helped swing the legs inside. Alon slid in beside Orsen and shouted to Timas, "Go!" Timas sprinted down the street, heading for the nearest traverson entrance. The next moment, the car sped down the street, angling for the route that would bring them to the river.

Go, go, go!

Alon took Orsen's gun and glanced back at their passenger. The Terran's head lolled on his shoulders. Bright red blood stained the breast of his white uniform, filling the car with a metallic, alien tang.

Alon caught glimpses of startled pedestrians, another car skidding to a sidewise halt, trees, and shadows. The car's tires squealed over the weathered stone of an intersection. He could almost smell the river now.

Go, go, go!

Orsen skidded the car down the ramp. The pavement stank of algae. Circles of rust marked the iron rings for tying up boats. At one end of the landing, a slanted launching ramp disappeared into the water. At the other, a storm drain, large enough for a person to walk along if he didn't mind stooping, debouched into the river. Just inside the entrance, a weathered grille hid the opening of a tunnel leading down into the catacombs.

Orsen pulled up beside the drainage pipe. Wordlessly he helped Alon pull the Terran from the back seat. The body fell heavily to the ground. The Terran moaned. One arm twitched.

With a nod, Orsen went back to the car and released the brake. A hard shove sent the vehicle rolling down the launching ramp and into the swirling water.

Alon knelt beside the Terran. He touched the dark stain on the Terran's chest and quickly brought his hand away, rubbing the sticky blood between his fingers.

"Is he hurt badly?" Orsen said.

"How the Blazes should I know?"

"If he's going to die, anyway, we might as well put him in the river. Get it over right now, so we don't have a corpse to deal with later."

"No," Alon said quickly. "He isn't going to die. He can't die." *He has to stay alive to suffer.* With a shudder, he remembered what Hayke had said, *"Sometimes I wonder if you are so angry that you would rather punish the Terrans than defeat them."*

If there were another way, would I take it? Take it and let ashes like this live to walk away? Alon's stomach turned icy.

Nothing but foolish Wayfolk thinking. There is no other way.

Alon nodded toward the catacomb entrance. "Come on, let's get him put away. We can let the farmer look after him."

Chapter 44

Clutching his bag of supplies, Hayke followed Alon along the passageways of the catacombs. He took extra care to memorize the route, counting the branches and noting the number of paces between each turn. With practice, the intimate geometry of the city's subterrane was slowly becoming familiar.

The cell in which the Terran was held had once been an alcove for stonecutters to rest and eat their midday meal, hundreds of years ago when the catacombs were actively mined for their limestone. Six other Terrans, taken captive last night, were being held in similar, widely scattered underground cells. No one except Alon knew the location of them all.

"We've caught a big one," Alon told Hayke as they went along. "Celestinbellini. He's on the Governing Council. Also very close with the mayor." His voice took on a tinge of revulsion, although he did not elaborate further.

After unlocking the door, they bent low to enter the cell. A single lantern, set in the center, cast elongated shadows. The Terran lay unconscious on a folded blanket. A chain ran through the wall staple from one manacled wrist to the opposite ankle.

One of the Freedom Movement fighters, a student named Zumar, stood guard just inside the cell. He held his gun at ready, flinching whenever the Terran took a breath. Hayke thought he was waiting for an excuse to shoot.

"Any change?" Alon asked as he set down the food bag.

"Not a hair quivering," said Zumar.

Hayke knelt beside the Terran. Bristly stubble covered the Terran's cheeks. Hayke wondered if that was a physiological reaction to shock, like the unconscious movement of his own crest. When he placed one hand on the Terran's chest, over where he guessed the heart should be, he felt a faint, irregular vibration. "You didn't tell me he was this badly off."

"He's still alive," Alon said carelessly.

"And you don't care how long he will continue to stay that way?"

"Not if he holds on long enough for the Terrans to meet our demands."

Hayke fumbled at the neck fastenings of the Terran's uniform. The fabric was stiff with clotted blood. With Zumar's help, he opened the top part of the uniform to reveal an undershirt of silky woven material. Hayke lifted it away, trying not to open the wound underneath.

Hayke had to turn the Terran on his side to see the full extent of his injuries, and then he was relieved, for they could have been much worse. Aside from bruises and scratches, the most significant wound was from a single bullet that had passed completely through the upper chest, apparently missing the heart and great vessels. Hayke, pressing his ear against the Terran's chest, guessed the bullet might have collapsed the lung, for he could hear no movement of air on that side. The exit hole, on the front of the chest, puckered and gaped with each breath. As he pressed it with his fingers, he felt the grating of bone fragments.

Hayke smeared the edges of the wound with antiseptic paste and bandaged them as well as he could. It seemed to him that the Terran's skin was too warm, although he didn't know what was normal for these creatures.

Could it be an infection? In general, people and animals did not share the same diseases, but Hayke had no idea if the same microbes that had caused his own wound fever would also affect the Terran.

"He needs proper care from those who know his kind," Hayke protested to Alon. "I'm not a medical, just a farmer who's had to tend his own sick animals."

"We can't trust anyone else. It's you or nothing." Alon turned away. "Zumar, someone will come to relieve you at the end of the day. Until then, be strong and resolute. Victory will be ours."

"Victory will be ours."

Alon headed for the entrance. "Soon, with any luck, this one will no longer be our responsibility."

MIRAZ FREE PRESS: WHICH SIDE ARE YOU ON?

Each new dawn brings us another day of struggle, a day of a nation divided and a people at war with themselves, a day in which it is easier to point the finger of blame than to build something better.

But with whom are we truly at war? Who is to blame?

Some say our enemy is the same one who has menaced us for centuries—the Erls. Some would say they have only waited for the slightest sign of Chacarran weakness to take by subterfuge what they have never been able to gain by force of arms. Some would point to the Erlind soldiers who spilled Chacarran blood in the Warder Square Massacre.

And they would be right.

Others say the Erls are merely the tools of an even greater menace, one that threatens the very soul of Chacarre. They point to the mushrooms that spy on every honest citizen, to the compound that desecrates our ancient plaza. They point to the white uniforms, the death rays, the Governing Council that has usurped our Helm and ordered the public execution of untried Chacarran prisoners. They would say the Terrans lie with every breath when they promise us friendship and justice.

And they too would be right.

These are not simple times, when simple answers can put one's conscience to rest. These are times that call for difficult questions as well as courageous responses.

Ask yourself, in the depths of your heart:

WHOSE SIDE AM I ON? WHO IS MY ENEMY? WHAT AM I GOING TO DO ABOUT IT?

—The Seeker

Hayke climbed back to the street level and carefully oriented himself in the city. He might never achieve Alon's ease of familiarity, but he could find his way well enough. Padme was able to give him the name of a Wayfolk pharmacist, as well as a little money, more than he felt comfortable accepting but enough to pay for what he needed.

The pharmacy was small, its walls covered with shelves bearing jars of dried roots and leaves, stoppered flasks of black and green glass, many of them partly filled with elixirs, tinctures and sirops, books on medicine, and antique weighing platforms and measuring spoons. Hayke, studying the displays, recognized a few of the herbs he used on his farm animals, although he had not realized there were so many varieties. Behind the marble-topped counter, the more potent medications were stored behind glass-doored cabinets, each range of boxes neatly labeled. The place smelled of chiroseth and disinfectant moss.

Hayke greeted the owner as one Wayfolk to another. He was a little surprised by the warmth of the response.

"No matter how scattered we are," the pharmacist said, "we follow the same Way. What do you need?"

It seemed to Hayke that there was a world within a world and in this inner circle he, following the Way, could never be a stranger, friendless. "Something to treat wound fever," he said, searching for the properly unincriminating phrase. He remembered what Padme had said, *"What we do not know, we cannot be forced to tell."*

The pharmacist peered at him, eyes narrowing, then nodded and disappeared for a moment into the back of the store. He emerged a few minutes later with a plain white packet. Hayke recognized the medicine as potent against a variety of infections. It could be dissolved in water or sprinkled on food. He slipped the packet into his inner pocket.

"There's enough there for a full course," the pharmacist said. "If there's no improvement in two days—"

Hayke made a gesture of negation. "In that case, I won't be needing any more."

Celestinbellini woke with a start when Hayke entered the cell. The Terran's skin felt dry, like parchment, and the coarse hair on his face had turned lifeless. His eyes seemed to have too much white in them, even for Terran eyes. His gaze darted from the shadowy rock ceiling to the lantern, finally resting on Hayke's face. His breath came quick and light; he pawed at his upper chest. If he had been human, Hayke would have thought he was terrified.

Hayke lifted the water bottle to the Terran's lips and held it as he gulped. When the Terran lay back, gasping and coughing, Hayke laid one hand on his chest, not to feel for the movement of the ribs or the vibration of the heart, but to give him comfort, as he would any other suffering creature.

After a short while, Hayke mixed the first dose of antibiotic in a cup of water. He lifted the cup to the Terran's lips. "Here, drink this."

"What... ?"

"Medicine for the wound fever. I know it doesn't taste good, but you must drink all of it."

"No *fucking* way am I drinking that putrid stuff!"

Hayke didn't understand the Terran words, but the meaning was clear enough. "If I must, I will pour it down your throat. Believe me, I've had plenty of practice."

The Terran shook his head. The movement set off a paroxysm of coughing. In a lightning move, Hayke straddled the Terran's chest, pinning the alien's arms against his sides and immobilizing him very much as he would a recalcitrant woolie. With one hand he tilted the Terran's head back and grasped both nostrils between thumb and forefinger. With the other he shoved the rim of the cup between the Terran's teeth.

Celestinbellini struggled, trying to free his arms. Hayke dropped his weight hard on the Terran's chest and saw the quick expulsion of air. Then he poured the medicated water into the Terran's open mouth. For an instant, the Terran froze. His eyes bulged. The rim of the cup clanged against his clenched teeth. Then he swallowed.

Hayke loosened his grip on the Terran's nose. "More?"

"Let up! I'll take it!"

"It's a good sign, you know," Hayke said, swinging his knee over to one side and handing the cup to the Terran, "that there's so much fight left in you."

Celestinbellini drained the cup, tilted it to show its emptiness, and then lay back. "You must... done this before. Hope... immune treatments... hold."

"I've been a farmer all my life, and that means animals to nurse and worm and force-feed. Woolies, milker calves, puppies. Children, too. And my mate." The last words popped out of Hayke's mouth before he realized he was going to say them. But it was not surprising, really. Rosen had been so much on his mind lately.

"Someone you lost... because of us?"

Hayke made a gesture of negation. "Years before your people came. I still miss him. It's always seemed to me that life is difficult enough without having to deliberately hurt one another."

The Terran jerked upright, twisted to one side, and retched violently. Frothy, pungent liquid spewed from his mouth. Hayke scuttled aside to avoid being splashed as it hit the stone floor. A few moments later, another gush arced out, and then another. The Terran moaned and wiped his mouth with the back of one hand. Sweat beaded the bare skin of his face. Hayke handed him the moistened cloth.

Celestinbellini took it and ran it across his lips. "Gawd, that stuff tastes even worse coming back up than it did going down. Guess I'll have to take my chances with your wound fever."

Then his face turned paler and the whites of his eyes showed as slender, glistening rings around circles of black. With a hoarse cry, he buckled over, gasping and clutching his belly. A spasm racked his entire body and he vomited again, dark fluid stinking of coppery acid.

Hayke laid one hand against the Terran's back, felt him convulse again, his muscles like heated steel. The Terran brought up less each time, until there were only dry heaves.

"Help... me.." The Terran's voice came as a rasping whisper, and then he collapsed, face down.

Hayke grabbed the Terran's shoulders and rolled him over on his back. The body was unexpectedly heavy and clumsy, all long limbs and lolling head. The skin around the mouth was stained bright red with blood, the rest the color of bleached parchment.

"What's wrong with him?" Zumar approached, gun drawn. "Are you sure he isn't faking it?"

"There's no way to *fake* vomiting blood!"

"Don't know about these Terrans," the guard said. "They're not real people, you know. Not like us."

"I need more blankets, water, and towels," Hayke said, using the same tone as he would to a disobedient child. "Right now!"

The guard scrambled away without protest, leaving Hayke and the Terran alone in the tiny alcove.

Hayke laid one hand on the Terran's. The flesh yielded under his touch like damp clay. Was this the Terran version of shock? Was he even alive?

Hayke pressed one ear to the midline of the Terran's chest. He heard a quick, light beat, like a woolie cub skittering over dry ground, and then the wheezing, bubbling passage of air through the lungs. There was nothing he could do, except hope that the Terran's body had been able to expel the medicine and that, kept warm and quiet, he would have the innate strength to survive.

Hayke held the Terran's hand between his own as if he could wring answers out of the unconscious flesh. The guard's words echoed in his ears. *"They're not real people, you know. Not like us."*

No, Hayke thought, the Terrans weren't like his own people, but they were fully human in their own eyes. He looked down at the prisoner, gray and clammy, and wondered if they could each learn to listen to each other. Wondered if they could do it in time.

As the hours crept on, with still no news from Alon, Hayke kept watch over the unconscious Terran. It seemed to him that the Terran's breathing grew more regular. He hoped it wasn't just his imagination. After a time, Zumar's replacement entered the alcove, a silent older person, a craft worker, Hayke guessed.

When the Terran stirred and opened his eyes, Hayke moved quickly to his side.

"What the hell happened to me?" the Terran moaned. "I feel like shit."

"Don't tell him a Flaming thing," the guard said from across the room.

He raised his gun, half-aimed.

Hayke's crest flared. It was a miracle the Terran was still alive. "You've been shot in the chest," he said, trying to sound kindly. "I think your lung's collapsed. I gave you medicine. You reacted badly to it."

"You a doctor?"

"No." Hayke's crest slicked back. "I don't know anything about treating your kind. I had been hoping the general principles were the same as for us."

The Terran lifted his head, eyes glittering. His gaze was steady, although his muscles trembled. "Where am I?"

"You're a prisoner of the Chacarran Freedom Movement, a hostage until your people agree to our demands."

"Hostage? Christ. I thought the fuckbrain was trying to *kill* me."

"Quiet!" the guard called.

"Why don't you just finish the job and be done with it?" The Terran burst into a spate of coughing, bringing up more blood, then collapsed, gasping.

"Lie still," said Hayke. As he wiped away the red-streaked sputum, he wished he could say that he had no part in the kidnapping, but he could not bring himself to speak the lie. He had cleaned and oiled Alon's gun, he had carried messages and forged papers, and now he was treating a victim of the very violence he had made possible. How could he say he was innocent?

"We're trying to help you people," the Terran said when he was able to speak again.

"Are you?" Hayke bent over the Terran. A strange, fey mood seized him, a compound of outrage and guilt. "Are you? Were you helping my neighbor when you followed the Erlind soldiers across the border, blasted his farm into ashes, and left him homeless? Were you helping young Alon when your people assaulted him in the most unspeakable manner, when you murdered his unborn child and turned his life mate against him? Were you helping me when you brought in the Erls to massacre the prisoners in Warder Square—me among them? Shall I show you the scars from that *helping*?"

The Terran closed his eyes and lay back. His breath wheezed through his lungs. The lantern gouged shadows along the sides of his mouth and turned his eye sockets into lightless pits.

Hayke thought he had never seen a more desolate face. For some reason, the thought filled him with sadness.

Chapter 45

As the door to the Command Deck conference room whispered closed behind him, Hammadi thought how much the room had changed—how much and how little. It still held an edge of emergency scramble, a tinge of adrenaline that not even the now-functional air filters could remove.

As usual, Rhomi Calhoun was working planetary communications. Mae Brown from Nuclear Physics, along with a couple of engineering techs, sat at the additional work stations. A light panel displaying a three-dimensional projection of the central city occupied the better part of the table. Adriana Gomes looked up from her station, her skin pale. The lines of her brow and cheek stood out like crags, bone jutting through flesh. She'd shaved her head to a charcoal fuzz. As Hammadi entered the room, she started to rise and salute, but he waved her back.

"Update!" He lowered himself into the chair at the head of the table.

"We've set up a schedule of low flights over the city, visual recorders on max detail," Gomes said. "Lieutenant Adamson has teams patrolling on foot in the district where Commander Bellini was last seen."

Hammadi nodded, a short, dipping jab of his chin. She went on. "The mayor sent Adamson his personal condolences. He's promised every cooperation and ordered the new police chief, Ambyntet, to coordinate with us." She rattled off the details of map grids.

"Sir?" Calhoun said. "Sergei Bartov at the compound has uplinked a record of Commander Bellini's capture. There's a visual of one of the kidnappers. The resolution isn't too good, but we can enhance it."

"Do that," he said. "What's the situation at the labs?"

Lights on the monitor panel blinked and shifted. Hammadi leaned forward, tracking the emerging pattern.

"Reports coming in from Adamson," Rhomi said. His fingers skipped across the touchpad.

Jon Adamson's voice sounded ragged. The distortion covered any emotion in his voice. "We're at the lab facility, sir. The place is battened down tighter than a snake's ass. Apparently the Erls infiltrated the site last night, timed between watch shifts. By our calcs, they're holding two locals hostage, along with our own people."

A list of lab personnel appeared on Hammadi's monitor. Dr. Vera's name topped the list.

The muscles in Hammadi's jaws clenched. He must go on, he told himself, as if she were alive. He must not think of what it might mean to their chances of getting *Prometheus* spaceworthy again if she were not.

"We've established perimeter control and scheduled a shuttle overflight," Adamson went on. "The Mirazan police have arrived and are attempting to establish communication with the Erls."

Hammadi ran one hand over his jaw. He himself had approved the reinforcing of what was left of the lab complex, moving what they could not repair into the adjacent warehouse. Whoever fortified a place knew its weaknesses. There was no fortress that could not be taken, once those were known. He hoped it wouldn't come to an armed assault.

It was still early in the game. He didn't yet know the situation inside the labs, what the Erls wanted, or the resources of the local police. Given their past performance, he didn't think they stood a chance against an elite force in a well-defended place, but the mayor might be touchy about his local jurisdiction.

"Can we get ground-level visuals?" he asked.

"Adamson's setting up a portable," Gomes said. "It should be working in ten minutes."

"I'll try again to send a connect signal to the links inside the lab," Calhoun said. The large screen in front of him flickered grainy-white, accompanied by an ear-splitting burst of static. Hammadi couldn't see anything in the signal noise. There were three work stations with links capable of reaching *Prometheus*; Calhoun tried them all in sequence.

"Come on," Calhoun muttered under his breath. "Pick up." He flicked off the blare. "If the system's shut down on the other side, there's not much I can do."

As if on cue, Dr. Vera's face flashed across Rhomi's monitor. Her cheeks were flushed, but she didn't look hurt. Hammadi straightened in his chair, his spine rigid. Adriana bit off an exclamation of surprise.

Behind her, Hammadi glimpsed a lab table covered with the old-style glassware supplied by native companies, flasks and pipettes and distillation apparatus held upright on their stands like a crystal forest.

A voice rumbled in native dialect just out of camera range. Vera turned her head to look at the speaker. She answered back in the same language, then disappeared from view, jerkily, as if she were yanked out of the way.

"Doctor? Are you all right?" Hammadi said.

A native face appeared, round honey-gold eyes set in a mass of tightly curling blond fur. He wore something dark, cut full across the shoulders and high on the neck like a warder's uniform. Two leather straps crossed his chest, although Hammadi couldn't see what hung from them.

The native bent close to the camera, then recoiled visibly. Something crashed to the floor. His fur stood on end and his hands moved in quick, jerky gestures. Hammadi would have bet anything they were ward-off signs.

Vera's voice came across the speaker. "Just informing the local hooyas I'm in the midst of praying to my personal Aspect of the one god and anyone who disturbs me is liable to get brain-fried. Divine retribution for the sin of *communicatus interruptus*."

In light of the native's reaction, Hammadi could well believe it.

Think I look fearsome, do you? He scowled, drawing his brows tightly together. The native scrambled backward. From outside of camera range came a high, ululating cry.

Vera's face reappeared. Her eyes snapped black fire.

"Now that's taken care of," her voice crackled across the link, "I'd like to know what the hell is going on? I no sooner get the lanthanide separation apparatus set up and the circuits for the focusing lasers redesigned, than these—these pea-brained, ham-handed baboons appear out of nowhere. They've barricaded the doors with the empty ore bins, blocked the vent hoods, made an unholy mess of the heat-venting system for the furnace, terrorized the natives and my own staff, and all they can offer by way of explanation is that *you* lied to them!"

Hammadi suppressed a smile, remembering the time he had demanded what *she'd* done to *his* ship. "Stay calm. We're doing everything we can to get you out of there."

She threw up her hands. "I don't want to get out of here, I want *them* to leave so I can go back to work!"

"That's exactly what we're trying to do. Now, listen carefully. I want you to turn on the other cameras in the lab and—"

Before he could finish, she'd disappeared. A second monitor flickered to life, showing another section of lab, then another. Two natives holding primitive projectile rifles walked across the visual field. Several others pushed a metal container, presumably the ore bin she'd mentioned. The thing was waist-high and must easily hold a thousand kilos of ore. Its wheels screeched and whined.

Vera came back onscreen. "What else?"

"Can you work out a reprogramming sequence for the visual sensors in the observation modules?"

One eyebrow arched. Hammadi could almost feel the stirring of her interest. "There should be a copy of it here. What do you want to reprogram it for?"

Briefly, Hammadi outlined his plan for using the observation modules to locate and track the terrorists, based on the image Adamson had obtained. After all, whoever captured Bellini might well have set the fire bomb that killed Davies.

At the memory of the young woman, he felt a pang. He remembered how she'd gotten the conference door open in the early hours after the disaster that had stranded his ship around this forsaken planet.

"I worked my way through college as a Machinist Two," she'd explained.

"Oh? Where?"

"Mars."

And now she was gone, all that bright promise.

Hammadi wrenched his thoughts back to the present problem. His military training had taught him to make decisions based on the best way to accomplish his objective, keeping his own emotions out of the picture. Could he trust Vera to do the same?

The next moment, Vera let out her breath in a whistle. "So *that's* what set the Erls off."

"I don't follow you." Her reaction confused him. "Do you have intelligence regarding their motives?"

"It hardly takes *intelligence* to figure it out! First you promise these people they'll be serving their country's best interest and contributing to peace, then you order them into that cold-blooded massacre under the pretense of a legal execution. They're not stupid. They've got to realize from the public outcry they've been set up. Now Bellini's gone missing, presumably taken by the same people they helped butcher. You think that makes them feel *safe?* If it were me, I'd figure if you couldn't even protect your own, you sure can't do a thing to protect *me* and I'd hole up in the most secure place I could find. Wouldn't *you?*"

Hammadi didn't smile. If he were in the place of the Erlind commander, he'd bargain for safe passage home in exchange for the Terran scientists and their equipment. If Dr. Vera could convince the Erls to give her free access to a link, maybe she could negotiate her own release.

"How would you like to discuss the matter with them?" Hammadi asked.

"You'd be better off shuttling in Chris Lao. He's the one with in-depth background with the Erlind culture. Everything I know is derivative." There was a hint of dark humor in her tone. "I'll do what I can. Now—" she went on, a quicksilver shift in mood, "—here's how you reprogram the modules."

Rhomi's monitor went blank as Dr. Vera switched the link from visual to data transmission. Programming code scrolled across the screen as she entered it at her own touchpad. Hammadi recognized that she was setting the internal mechanism to identify a person from memory. The next step he'd planned would be a silent alarm, so that whenever the kidnappers stuck their noses out, their movements could be tracked and a task force dispatched.

After Dr. Vera finished, she switched to visual mode and rattled off a string of directions for modifying the electronic circuitry of the module itself. Each unit had been equipped with a protective electrostatic field capable of vaporizing hundreds of kilos of space junk. It sounded to him that she was resetting them for stun-and-capture, using a sophisticated shaped-field technique to target the positive identification.

My god, he thought. *If she can do it, it would be like being hit by lightning...* Something had gotten her very, very angry.

Listening to her now, as she calmly described how to fry the nervous systems of the terrorists, he was glad she was on his side.

MIRAZ NEWS SERVICE: SIX TERRANS SEIZED IN TERRORIST KIDNAPPING! RANSOM DEMANDS INCLUDE WITHDRAWAL OF ERLIND SOLDIERS, AMNESTY FOR KRESTE. Report by Ambrom. (Cleared by the Department of Information Services.)

Last night, Resistance terrorists launched their most audacious raid to date. In a coordinated operation, they attacked and seized six Terran officials as prisoners. Each was taken from a different location at a time when he was alone or protected by only minimal security. One guard, a Terran, was killed, and two warders wounded in the assaults. The names of the victims and the exact locations at which the Terrans were taken prisoner are being temporarily withheld, pending further investigations and ransom negotiations.

Within a few hours, a communication was delivered to the Terran Compound. Copies were also received by the Mayor's Office and were posted at various locations around the city. In exchange for the safe release of the hostages, the Chacarran Freedom Movement presented the following demands:

(1) The immediate withdrawal of all Erlind military personnel;

(2) Amnesty for Kreste-az-Ondre and all political exiles, with the restoration of Kreste as Helm;

(3) The immediate release of all Chacarran citizens being detained by the Terran Peacekeeping Force and their agents, for whatever reason.

Mayor Lexis announced that the legitimate provisional government of Chacarre would under no circumstances consider terrorist demands. "To do so," he said, reading from prepared text, "would be to encourage their criminal activities."

When asked for comment, a representative of the United Terran Peacekeeping Force said only that the matter is under investigation. A statement is expected later today.

Chapter 46

E RLONN: ERLKING DEAD! Report by Wrel. (Cleared by the Department of Information Services)

House Ar, which holds the Erl throne, confirmed this morning that Erl-tha-Estenthal Erlking, has died. The Ar speaker refused to comment on the exact cause of death. The local Terran delegation has offered assistance in the investigation.

In a separate briefing, Erl-tha-Mergetten, oldest child of Estenthal, has declared himself heir to the throne. Several claimants from rival Houses promptly invoked the centuries-old Manusillian Protocols, denied his right, and put forth their own candidates.

Hammadi took the news from Erlonn seriously. He knew from his own history that there was no better way to unify rival factions than a popular war. The last thing he needed was Erlind provoking open hostilities with Chacarre. Adamson had reported a few instances of private celebration, but the general mood in Miraz was anxious, watching to see which new House would emerge.

Dr. Vera had wasted no time negotiating with the Erls holding the lab. Within a few hours after her first conversation with Hammadi, the Erls had agreed to accept a protective escort back to Erlonn. In return, they would release the Terran hostages.

As soon as the compound notified *Prometheus* that Dr. Vera had arrived safely, Hammadi ordered a four-way link with the command deck conference room. The monitor showed Adamson in Bellini's compound office and Lao from their headquarters in Erlonn. Dr. Vera appeared in the third section. Her mouth turned down at the corners and her eyes looked tight. She was displeased about how little work she'd been able to get done before she was forced to leave the lab. Hammadi thought it a minor miracle that she hadn't refused to go at the last minute.

Collaborators

Adamson's freckles stood out against the paleness of his skin as if he'd been spattered with blood. "The Erls have apparently changed their minds and now they refuse to leave. They have enough food and water to hold out for several weeks. They're armed and can certainly withstand any attack by the locals." He outlined the situation. "They must have heard the news casts from Erlonn."

The Mirazan mayor had been peppering the compound with communications, demanding a speedy removal of the Erls, claiming a menace to the city. Which meant, in all probability, that his own office was under increasing public pressure.

"I won't authorize escalating the level of confrontation in the city at this time," Hammadi said. "But neither do I like the idea of those soldiers sitting there like a time bomb."

"Chris and I have been comparing theories on the Erls' motivation in seizing the lab complex," Dr. Vera said. Hammadi noticed the rising color in her cheeks, the heightened alertness of her gaze.

She's on to something, he thought. *She's interested.*

Lao picked up her cue. "I agree with Dr. Vee that when they felt threatened, they formed a makeshift enclose in the most defensible place they knew."

"I've noted instances of a similar reaction to social disorder in Chacarran history," Dr. Vera said, her brow pleating. "It's a reflex to run for the home compound and sit tight until the crisis blows over."

"But they were under our command," said Adamson. "If they thought themselves at risk, they should have looked to us as their superior officers. They were supposed to be highly disciplined troops."

"More importantly, how do we get them out of there?" Gomes said.

"I very much doubt the Erls will give up their stronghold simply because *we* tell them to," Lao said, "no matter what guarantees of safety we offer. For them to withdraw on our orders would mean a crippling loss of dignity—face, we'd call it."

Hammadi nodded, recalling instances from the mess in Peru where a tin general's *machismo* ended up with half his people fried. Even in this alien setting, Lao's argument made sense.

"That's the impression I have of them, too," Dr. Vera went on, speaking now to Lao as if they were having a private brainstorming. "They're alone in a hostile country, cut off from support from home. They may not want to stay any more than we want them here, but they may not see any alternative."

"The subclans that tithed these soldiers have been loyal to House Ar for generations," Lao said. "If another House prevails, they may face summary execution if they return."

Dr. Vera nodded, her expression thoughtful. "Yes, that's right. *Frightened* is how I saw them. Not only that, we're outclan, about as welcome during a crisis as a splinter in the buttocks. Whatever the reason, they seemed relieved as we left."

She must have driven them nuts, Hammadi thought. He'd seen the way she bullied his staff as well as her own. Heaven help anyone who got in her way. If she could talk the Erls into free link access of an occupied stronghold, what else had she badgered them into or out of? Thank all the powers, she was on his side.

"What do you suggest we do now, sit back and do nothing?" Gomes asked. Hammadi heard the strain in her voice, bordering on snappishness. She'd been pushed too hard too long.

"That's exactly what I recommend," Dr. Vera said. Her voice was clear and even, without any trace of offense taken. "In my opinion, the best thing to do for the moment is to wait and let the situation defuse. See how things play out in Erlonn. The Erls aren't going anywhere, not unless we ourselves provoke a confrontation."

"I thought you wanted to get your lab back," Gomes said.

"I want it back intact."

Hammadi frowned. He didn't like the idea of doing nothing. It ran counter to all his training and the dozen or more times in the field, in Peru and Indonesia, when a moment's indecision would have cost the mission. In the last few days, however, he'd recognized Vera's competence in handling the natives. He wasn't about to throw such an asset away.

"There's another thing," Lao said. "Our informants in Erlonn made it clear the Erlking's death wasn't natural. This was a political assassination. It's possible that what happened here—Erl soldiers participating in a public execution—was the precipitating event.

"And of course the major Houses were already in an uproar over our intervention after the Demmerle encroachment," Lao went on. "They'd reason that if Chacarre uses the Erl soldiers taking part in the executions—armed intervention in Chacarran domestic affairs—as a pretext to declare war, we'll come in on the side of Chacarre."

"Chacarre isn't in any position to declare war on anyone," Adamson said. "They've got their hands full with their own terrorists."

Lao's expression darkened. "From the Erlind point of view, Erl unity behind a single House is all that's kept them secure this last century."

Hammadi nodded. A thought took shape in his mind, chilling. "We have an old saying, 'Divide and conquer.' Those anti-war demos we broke up last year, could the Erls have had anything to do with them?"

Adamson's skin went a shade paler.

"Well?" Hammadi's brows drew together. "*Could* they?"

"In terms of how the Erls think," Lao said, his black eyes level and unreadable, "I'd say it's certain."

Hammadi didn't care who ran either country. They could all fry, Kreste and his terrorists and the damned Erls, along with anyone else who stood in his way. "Thank you for your input. I'll take it under advisement. On to the problem of Les Bellini and the others taken by the terrorists. Adamson, any news from the locals?"

"No, sir."

To hell with them, too. "How are the probe modifications coming?"

"Sergei Bartov's working on them now," Dr. Vera said. "We've set up a schedule, using the data from the Miraz warders to target likely neighborhoods. The highest priority are already done. The rest should be finished in three days."

"What about the demands from the resistance?" Lao said.

"We don't negotiate with terrorists," Hammadi said flatly.

Dr. Vera raised one eyebrow and gave him a scathing look as if to say, *Mutineers, but not terrorists?*

"What if these people have legitimate grievances?" Lao looked uncomfortable. "If they are desperate, maybe it's because they have no other way of making themselves heard. The withdrawal of a traditionally hostile military force and the freeing of political prisoners are hardly outrageous demands."

"We aren't holding any political prisoners!" Gomes snapped. "As for their demands, we can't allow this Kreste fellow to return. There would be an immediate outpouring of popular support and widespread civil unrest. It would destroy any hope of free elections."

Hammadi raised one hand and she broke off. "We're here for exactly one reason," he said, "and that's to get those repairs done and *Prometheus* space-worthy. Not to bring Terran enlightenment to Bandar or ensure democracy for the natives. We may have made a mistake in bringing in the Erls as backup police. We underestimated the depth of the regional hostilities. We got off lightly this time—" *Don't think about the dead,* "—and it looks like Dr. Vera can salvage the technical stuff. Next time, we might not be so lucky.

"What we need now is maneuvering room," he continued. "We can put off letting Kreste back in the country for a while. What about these prisoners? Who are we holding in the compound?"

"A group of natives sent to us by the warders for observation and questioning." Adamson looked startled. "We're trying to establish parameters for a lie detector test." He leaned over, tapping a comm-panel. A moment later, a list of names appeared on Hammadi's monitor.

"Sir?" Gomes looked over his shoulder with a return of her usual brassy confidence. "We've identified the partial visual from Commander Bellini's capture as Alon-az-Thirien." She pointed to the screen. "Could they be related?"

Tellem-az-Thirien.

Hammadi straightened in his chair. "His father?"

"Parent," Dr. Vera corrected.

"The warders think this Alon person is one of the leaders of the resistance," Adamson said. "He was wanted in connection with an assault on one of our people down here."

"A serious assault?" Hammadi asked.

"No, sir, just a bump on the head. But that incident was apparently what sent Alon underground. Next, his name showed up when his wife—husband—I don't know what to call them—"

"Mate," said Dr. Vera.

"Anyway, his mate became our first successful deprogramming subject."

Hammadi nodded, remembering. Birre-something-or-other. The family would have given full consent to a prefrontal lobotomy, they'd been so anxious to get him back, but that hadn't been necessary.

"Let Tellem go," Hammadi said. "Pick out a few others and release them, too. The terrorists want to talk? We'll beat them to the table. Get that censorship chief to make sure everyone knows we've made the first step. We want high visibility here."

Gomes drew her dark eyebrows together in a not-quite frown. "Preemptive action, sir?"

"Camouflage. We want them at the negotiation table thinking they owe us. Meanwhile, I want Tellem watched and followed, every step he takes."

In addition to modifying the observation probes, Vera began assembling a profile of the target, Alon-az-Thirien. Even if she couldn't leave the compound without an armed bodyguard, it was a relief to throw herself into the project. With the Erls still occupying the lab complex, there wasn't anything more she could do there. At times she felt herself pacing, bristling with energy. Under it all ran the unspoken thought, *I want to find the people responsible for Sarah's death. I want to make them pay for what they did.*

A picture emerged gradually, stepwise, like the simplification of an equation after the proper coordinate transformation. The complex terms would cancel out, one by one, revealing the answer. Working backwards from the initial notes supplied by Adriana Gomes, she dug through the files on Birre-az-Austre, Alon's mate, his family, his travel to Nantaz, his probable—no, *certain*—role in the arson bombings.

Why? What reason drove him to such a thing?

Collaborators

Working her way through alien psychology was a bit like learning quantum mechanics. At first, everything ran counter-intuitive. With time and hard work, she began to develop a feel for the physics of the situation. She remembered the moments when her hunches had started to pay off.

She recognized that same feeling now.

There, in the records of the local police, she found the key. A handful of notes, a report never followed up on, probably intended to be permanently forgotten. She read it in the original Chacarran, not translation. It was the sort of minor report no one would think to translate. She sat there in the warder's office, staring at the words on the paper and shaking inside.

In that moment, all the pain and rage she'd felt at Sarah's death seemed to fall away and she saw it not in isolation, but as part of a relentless escalation. Here, before her blurring eyes, was the origin, the beginning that made everything that came afterward inevitable.

Vera got up, thanked the officer on duty, and wandered into the street. She passed open-air tables where people sat drinking spiced milk and reading news sheets, a handful of children laughing as they ran and tossed a winged ball, shops displaying fine cloth, books, and tinwork. She sat down on a bench to watch. Young adults walked by with their arms around each other. Two older children helped a pregnant person with a heavy basket. A group of four or five people in brilliant yellow shirts greeted each other as if they were lovers. One carried an infant, which was inundated by kisses and caresses.

These people know nothing like rape. Not only that, pregnancy is sacrosanct. It's hardwired into their genes. With their low birth rate, every child must be precious.

It wouldn't matter to Birre that the Terrans who assaulted his pregnant mate and murdered his unborn child were drunk, half out of their minds, that they'd never ordinarily do such a thing. He would not have thought at all. He would have *felt*. And acted.

He with his fire bombs, me with my stun device. She'd designed the static charges to capture young Alon without any idea of who he was or what drove him. She hadn't cared if the electrical charge stunned him, as it was meant to do, or killed him, or left him a vegetable.

One outrage led to the next, as surely as dawn followed night. None of it would bring Sarah back, not even for an instant, or diminish her loss. Vera could see the pattern now, each round bloodier than the last. For the death of one child, the death of another and all those who'd perished in the bombing, and for that, the massacre in the police square. And for that, the kidnapping of Les Bellini and the others. And for that—when would it end?

She'd have to go carefully, and she wasn't used to either caution or diplomacy. For most of her career, she'd presented her scientific conclusions without any regard to the emotional reactions of others. Truth was truth, and she knew how good she was. She knew when she was right. Personalities didn't enter into her equations.

But now, emotion and personality might well be everything. It wasn't enough that she'd had a transformative understanding, or that she could articulate it clearly.

Somehow, she had to sell it to Hammadi.

Chapter 47

Hayke, on his way to the noon Gathering in the basement of Padme's restaurant, went by the bookstore owned by Alon's parents. The front steps had been recently scrubbed, and the stones were still wet. Inside, the lights shone and the door stood partly open. Hayke paused, blinking in surprise. He'd seen the headlines in the morning's news sheets, something about a good-will gesture, the release of suspects who'd been cleared of charges. It hadn't occurred to him that might include Alon's parents.

The door swung easily to the sound of chiming bells. Although Hayke had never been there before, he felt comfortable the moment he walked in. Books crowded the shelves. The light that streamed in through the high windows had a peculiar honey-like quality, thick and rich.

A heavy-set older person wearing an apron stood on a ladder, running a feather mop over the shelves and throwing up billows of dust. Hayke recognized him from Alon's description.

"Good day to you, friend," said Hayke.

"May the Way open before you," came the response.

"You must be Meddi."

"Indeed," said Meddi, climbing down from the ladder and extending his hands, Wayfolk style, to Hayke. Hayke had experienced the same calm in Rosen, the inner power that came from a life following the true Way.

"My name is Hayke and I've come from Alon," he said. "He's concerned about your safety."

Meddi called out in direction of the store room, "Tellem! A guest!"

Tellem was tall and restless, more so than Alon had described. Meddi said, his voice breaking at the edges, "Hayke here has seen Alon."

"Oh!" The word burst from Tellem like a cry of pain.

They love him very much, even as I love my own children.

"Please," said Tellem, struggling visibly to control his crest, "sit down, have tea. Tell us more."

Meddi silenced him with a gesture. "It isn't safe to talk freely. Not in these times, not even here in our own store. It is enough for the moment to know that Alon is alive—"

"—and well," Hayke, moved, added.

"—and that his welfare lies in his remaining hidden. What we do not know, we cannot be forced to tell."

Tellem's crest jerked upright and for a moment Hayke was afraid he'd sparked a fight. Tellem's hands moved tentatively. "Tell him—we will send no word to him. We know how great the risk is to all of us."

"Why did you come back?" Hayke asked.

For a moment, neither answered. Then Meddi said in a strange, soft voice, "We felt... moved to come, as if we were needed here in Miraz."

"For what purpose?" Tellem's crest flared again. "To fight, to kill? To negate everything we believe in?"

Meddi turned to Hayke. "The last time we talked with Alon, he had grown so hard, so desperate, he was almost a stranger to us. He would not listen."

"I never had Meddi's gift for sensing the opening Way," said Tellem. "I kept telling myself we were coming back for Alon's sake."

Of course, Hayke thought, a parent would frame things in terms of his children, a lover his beloved. The mind needed reasons to explain the actions of the heart. He himself was no different.

Suddenly, everything came clear, why he himself had been led to Miraz, the meaning of his dream, the reason he had helped the resistance, against all his doubts and reservations. What he must do now.

"Sit down, please," said Hayke. "There is something I must tell you. I know why the Way led you back to Miraz."

Tellem's fur ruffled in surprise, but they both sat down. After a moment of silence to gather his thoughts, Hayke began.

In simple words, he told them of his vision, how he saw the people lying as if dead across the plaza, how he raced through the crowd, how each one he touched lifted his eyes to the sun and rose up.

As he talked, Hayke saw the light on Meddi's face and then Tellem's, as if by the very act of speaking his dream, he had touched them. Their eyes gleamed. When he was done, they reached out wordlessly to take his hands.

The Terran Compound seemed brighter and cleaner in the sun. Even the burn marks on the pavement from the coming and going of the shuttle faded in the light. Just beyond the cordoned perimeter, Hayke took a stance beside Meddi and Tellem, Padme a little behind them. Neither the Terran guards nor the warders on the nearby street took any notice.

Hayke, like the others, stood with his feet apart, knees soft, low back relaxed, hands crossed over chest. The position was surprisingly comfortable.

He could hold it for hours if need be, as rigorous and peaceful as any seated meditation pose. He closed his eyes as the serenity and balance evoked by the posture of *tal'spirë* flowed through him.

A few minutes later two more people came to stand with them, Wayfolk by their expressions. They wished each other a fair day and then settled into waiting. Now that there were six together, the Terrans stared. Hayke could not understand their gestures, but he sensed their confusion.

A warder strode over. Glancing over his shoulder at the Terrans, he stammered, "Wha-what's going on? What are you doing?"

"Just standing," Meddi said mildly. "Would you care to join us?"

The warder smoothed his ruffled crest with a jerky movement. "Sorry, I'm on duty. But you'll have to—to stand somewhere else."

The six of them ambled off in different directions and as soon as the warder returned to his post, reformed in another location, still facing the compound.

"Excuse me?" A well-dressed merchant, yellow Sotirite token hanging from a golden chain, approached them. Like the warders, he startled as he saw their posture. "What was all that about?"

"The Terrans don't like us standing here," said Padme.

The merchant's gaze flickered to the warders, back to the compound. He lifted the chain and its clan identification from around his neck, slipped it into a pocket inside his brocade tunic, then crossed his arms over his ample breasts.

"I think I'll just... *stand here*... with you."

Free! The word echoed in Alon's mind, jittering through the bones of his skull. Ever since Hayke had brought him the news, he had been able to think of little else. His parents were free... but they intended to stay in Miraz.

Idiots! Head-blind Flaming idiots!

He slipped along a traverson, following a hidden route through the poorest section of Northhill. Occasionally he passed a door that led to a cook shop or a bakery, the delectable aromas of roasted beans or citron tarts tinging the air. Once he paused beside a corridor that opened to the bottom of a stairwell, caught by the sound of children's laughter.

The sound brought a lance of pain behind his breastbone. He tried to shake off the grief. He was no longer the same person who'd carried that child. He had to save his parents if he could. He had lost so much already.

Timas or Orsen with their constant suspicions would rage at him if they knew he was on his way to the bookstore. The risk, they'd say, how can you risk yourself?

Collaborators

The greater risk, Alon thought, was that Meddi and Tellem would stay in Miraz, visible. Vulnerable. He had to make sure they went back to Avallaz.

They will not go, Hayke had said. *Then I'll* make *them,* Alon had replied.

And it was not so much of a risk, Alon told himself. It was night, and he kept away from the brightest streets. Not even the Terran spy mushrooms could recognize him in the shadows. But if one did, what then? They must already know he was the one who took their Celestinbellini. Let them spy on him walking the streets, going everywhere he pleased. Let them look to their own backs. Let them wonder who would be next.

He could go only so far by alley and traverson. To cross Westriver, he'd have to go deep into the catacombs, a long and exhausting climb through the maze below the river, or else take the open route by bridge or underground railcar. Not railcar, too easy to be trapped. Middlebridge would be far safer. If he followed side streets, he'd be in the open, hidden in foot traffic, for only a short distance.

The quays were deserted, except for a few strolling couples and workers sweeping the debris from the day's markets. The farmers' stands and flower shops seemed to turn inward on themselves, shut up for the night. Beyond the full-leafed trees, the sky flowed in a wash of indigo, broken by a few points of brilliance low on the horizon.

The row of quay-side trees ended and Middlebridge came into view, rising in a graceful arch. Alon stepped from the shadow of the trees. There, at the intersection, sat a Terran spy mushroom, squat and rounded, with a raised ring forming its cap. Its metal housing had been covered with a substance resembling weathered stone.

Alon eased into the straggling crowd. No one took notice of him, not the cluster of Fardites with their glittering onyx clan tokens, not the heavy-set Bavarite priest wheezing behind him, not the thin, gray-clad grandparent, clutching a child by each hand. He kept pace with them into the intersection.

He glared at the piece of alien metal, not caring if the Terrans made a recording of him. He wanted them to know how he hated the mushroom, hated everything they stood for, and most especially how they had become part of the city. He thought in that moment that even if the Bird of Heaven were to come down and carry them all away, Terrans and Compound and spy mushrooms alike, he would still feel them there, in his mind.

The encircling ring popped up and out. He might have missed it if he had not been glaring at the mushroom. Such a small motion it was, not enough to make him break his stride. He caught a flash of red. Something hot and white and electric flashed over his body. His muscles locked in spasm. His arms and legs felt as if they were being wrenched from their sockets. He caught a whiff of ozone, dimly felt himself hurling through the air.

He felt nothing more.

PART IV

Chapter 48

He was not in a hospital. The walls were gray, not pale green, a swathe of unbroken blankness. Above the beating of his heart, he heard a constant, far-off susurration of air. His arms and legs would not work right. His right foot hurt. He slept and woke again, this time with more clarity. He could sit up, although not walk. The Terran who tended to him explained that the muscles in his leg had contracted so strongly, the tendon in his heel had pulled free from its bony attachment. It had been repaired by a means Alon could not understand, but still it ached with a cold, boring pain.

The weakness would pass with time, the Terran said. It was caused by the electrical charge that had been *shaped* at him by the spy mushroom. He had been unconscious for several hours. He tried not to think of what else the Terrans might have done to him then. He wondered if, even now, their machines were trained upon him. Listening to the pattern of his breathing. Watching his slightest movement. Recording the unconscious movements of his fur.

Much of the time, Alon was left alone. He hobbled around the room, searching for anything he could use as a weapon. He could not lift the bed, and the bowl that served as a sanitary facility was attached seamlessly to the floor. There were not even sheets that could be twisted into a rope. After a circuit or two, he felt too shaky to do more. He lay down and slept.

Time went by, marked only by the cycle of meals eaten without tasting and by the dimming of the lights. The Terrans made no attempt to torture him, or even interrogate him beyond polite inquiries into his name and function in the Freedom Movement. When Alon refused to answer, they left him alone.

At intervals, the door slid open. One Terran kept a light beam weapon aimed at him while the other set down a packet of food, bread and fruit, no utensils, covered in paper that shredded into powder even as he unwrapped it. Nine times they'd come now—or was it ten?

Alon found himself wishing they would do something overtly cruel, for that would give focus to his anger. He imagined Birre lying on this very same cot, pacing the margins of this room. At the thought, a riot of emotions surged up in him, a confusion of love and anger, bitter as alkali ash. It was the Terrans who had turned Birre against everything he believed in.

Birre had been so strong. He had been a leader, one of the first to take action against the Terrans. What could they have brought to bear against him? What if... what if it had not been a hideous torture but this very silence? What if it were not innocent silence, but something in the light or the air, a horrible mind-breaking weapon?

Had Birre known he was under attack? Had his thoughts jumbled as Alon's did now? Had he struggled, had he fought, had he shouted aloud in rage and frustration, and in the end, lost?

Or had he simply not realized what was happening to him until it was too late?

Alon measured the passage of time by the cyclical return of his hunger and thirst. Eventually, the terror of what might happen to him if he fell asleep wore thin. He curled up on the bed and closed his eyes.

Something jerked him awake and he scrambled to his feet, staggering on his injured ankle. He had not meant to sleep so long or so deeply. His eyes focused on the Terrans in front of him. There were two as usual, in their white uniforms, one aiming a light beam weapon at his chest. The other, Alon recognized as the one who'd first questioned him. He stood, legs braced wide, hands behind his back, weight rocked slightly back on his heels, reeking of polarization.

Alon forced himself to sit back down on the bed. His eyes moved in little jerks, as if on their own they were searching for a way out. He did not know what he would do if the Terrans started closing in.

"Your comrades have agreed to an exchange of prisoners, you for Commander Bellini," the Terran said. "The arrangements are being made right now. We will use the Octagon Temple as neutral ground."

Alon blinked in astonishment. What trick was this?

Somehow he managed to hold still as the guards bound his wrists and ankles. The soft plastic restraints forced him to hunch over as he hobbled along. They led him through a maze of corridors to another room. It too was windowless, but furnished with a desk and two padded chairs. An unfamiliar Terran bent over a low table, arranging a teapot and cups on a tray. Instead of a snug-fitting uniform, he wore loose pants and a smock of softly napped material that flowed like a gray-green river with his movements. The thick-knuckled fingers were surprisingly quick and graceful as they handled the fragile-looking cups. As Alon was brought in, he straightened up.

Alon caught a glimpse of silvery mane, naked skin covered with a spiderweb of fine lines... and full breasts rounding the gathered fabric of the smock. Alon's breath caught like a sob in his throat.

"What do you think you're doing, treating this person like an animal?" the silver-maned Terran demanded of the guards. "Take off those cuffs!"

"This is a highly dangerous prisoner," said one of the guards. "It's for your own safety—"

"I think not."

Alon heard the quiet authority in the Terran's voice. The two guards exchanged glances and then removed the restraints. Once they were alone, the Terran gestured Alon toward the chairs.

Alon sat down, rubbing his wrists. "How do you know I won't attack you?"

The Terran extended a cup of tea. "I hope you would listen to what I have to say first."

Alon's fingers closed around the cup. Flower petals floated on the steaming golden liquid.

"My name is Vera," the Terran said, sitting back in the other chair with his own cup. At first his eyes looked narrowed, tilted slightly upward at the outer corners as if he were squinting, but then Alon realized this was their natural shape. "I represent the Peacekeeping Command for the exchange today. Maybe between us, we can thrash some sense out of this mess."

Alon said, "You don't talk like the other Terrans."

Vera made a soft noise deep in his throat. "I'm no diplomat, true. I'm just a scientist with a knack for languages. You may have noticed I don't wear a uniform. And I am not pregnant."

Alon startled, a shivering along his crest that he could not control. Somehow he knew this Terran Vera could read it.

"I am not pregnant," the Terran repeated in a soft voice, perhaps meant to be soothing, "although when I was younger I could have become so. I am female.." Vera's lips stretched over her teeth, "... and more than a bit too old for such things. In my youth, I had priorities other than having children. My work, my dream of traveling to observe the birth of distant suns. I used to think of myself as a midwife to stars—a little poetry to balance all the fancy mathematics." She swirled her tea meditatively and took a sip. "Do you find that strange? My own family did."

Alon found himself unexpectedly comforted by the Terran's voice, the lilting, almost musical rhythm and strangely intriguing accent. He couldn't think what the Terran wanted from him. For the moment, apparently, she simply intended to tell her story. Alon sipped the flower tea and warmth spread through his belly. A faint taste of honey lingered on his tongue.

Vera put her cup down and leaned forward. "I have read the reports of what happened to you. The trauma. The loss of a child. I am sorry for it. I

315

wish there were a way what you suffered could be undone. The irreversibility of the time vector makes that unlikely."

"Why are you telling me this? Do you expect me to believe you're different from the others?" Alon said. Had Birre listened to these same gentle words, had he felt this same urge to believe them? Is that what broke through his defenses?

"You have no reason whatsoever to trust me," Vera replied. "I did not ask you to trust, only to listen. And to suggest that we at least try to find a way through our difficulties."

Difficulties... Prickles ran up Alon's spine, ruffling his fur. "We do only what you force us to do! We have no choice!"

"Yesterday, perhaps. But what about today? What about tomorrow?"

Alon dug his fingers into his legs to keep them still. He trembled inside, his thoughts roiling. In the back of his mind, he heard again the sickening slap of his skull against the cold street, felt the hands on his breasts, the sudden agony ripping through his body.

"There are things that cannot be so easily mended," he said, hoping his voice was not shaking as badly as his muscles. "Wrongs that can never be made right. You can't do what has been done to us and then try to wish it away."

"Some wounds can never be healed," Vera agreed. "Therefore, we have all the more reason to stop now, before any greater harm is done. Before we lose anyone else we love."

Alon's crest rippled, standing fully upright. How dared this Terran talk about *loss* and *love* as if she knew what they meant?

"I have lost a child and a mate!" Alon cried. "I will never be free of what your people did to me! What have you suffered? Who have you lost? Tell me, who?"

For a moment, Vera sat silent, eyes lowered, empty cup cradled between her hands. Not a hair moved, yet Alon was struck by the sense of powerful, inexpressible emotion. Sadness, perhaps. No, nothing so recognizably human, but piercing nonetheless.

"I had found a child of my own. Not of my body, but of my thoughts, my lifelong studies. She was in the laboratory barracks, the one that was fire-bombed." Vera's voice sounded rough. "I think of that night sometimes, I wonder if she died right away, if she even knew what was happening. What she might have become, had she lived."

Alon met the Terran's gaze. *She means it. I'm not sure how I know, but she really means it.*

His belly twisted, but not with fear, with a feeling far more terrible, and yet tinged with wonder. Listening to that quiet voice, watching that expressionless alien face, he felt the echoes of his own grief. But it was a grief

changed, mirrored.
Shared.

They finished their tea in silence. When it was time to leave, Vera would not let the Terran guards bind Alon again. No one challenged her authority.

As they went down one of the lift shafts, Alon felt closed in and suddenly dropping through space. He clenched his teeth and told himself that the Terrans couldn't read the ripples in his fur. Vera apparently could, for she laid one hand on Alon's arm, a light, noninvasive touch.

They came out in an enclosed garage and entered a car, ordinary-looking except for the nonreflective windows. Following Vera, Alon slid into the back seat beside one of the guards.

The driver started the engine. The wall of the garage lifted in folding sections and daylight streamed in. Alon caught a glimpse of the plaza outside, cordons and warders, a scattering of heavily armed Terrans. And beyond them—

There must be a hundred people out there.

They weren't the usual demonstrators—no shouting, no voices raised in anger.

Slowly the car rolled into the open plaza, parting the crowd. The warders moved the cordons and the people drew back to let them pass. Their hands were empty—no signs, no banners, no weapons—and crossed over their chests in the instinctive gesture of surrender.

"What's going on?" Even as he said it, a tendril of memory stirred, of Meddi's bedtime stories of Wayfolk history and traditions. In past centuries, Wayfolk had gathered in this manner to stand vigil when one of them was unjustly accused.

Beads of sweat stood out on the naked skin of Vera's forehead. "Just as you see—" she gestured, taking in the sweep of bodies, "—standing, watching. They've been like that since dawn. One leaves and two more take his place. When the warders tell them to move, they go. But they keep coming back, each time in greater numbers."

As they crossed the broad, arching bridge over Westriver, the crowd thinned and was replaced by ordinary traffic. The towers of Octagon came into view. The car halted outside, and Vera and Alon crossed to the main doors. The Terran guards stayed in the car. That was, Vera explained, one of the conditions under which the Terrans were allowed to use Octagon Temple.

Alon stopped in front of the carvings. He remembered the last time he'd been here, with Birre. Remembered all the misgivings he'd had, all the stories of Wayfolk killed on these very steps. He wondered if the exchange might not be an ambush with himself as bait.

Vera pushed open the outer doors. They paused for a moment, then went through the inner pair and into the center of the Temple. Alon blinked in the rainbow-hued light. As they came forward, a dense quiet surrounded him, emanating from the stones of the ancient building. Octagon might be a monument to a Faith not his, but it was also Chacarran. He had never expected to feel such a sense of welcome here.

At the end of the central aisle, in front of the altar, stood an elderly priest. His eyes looked very bright, his fur smoothed back. Ignoring the Terran, he said to Alon, "You are unharmed, my child?"

Alon nodded.

"And you agree to this exchange of your own free will?"

Alon thought the question foolish, for who would not agree to be freed? By the priest's standards, however, the question was a valid one. It gave him the opportunity to abort the exchange with a single word.

In the brief time Alon had known Vera, he and this Terran had built something between them, still fragile, hardly able to withstand the slightest misunderstanding, composed of a moment of half-imagined compassion and a few beads of sweat. The hostage exchange would be the first step toward building something more.

Gravely Alon gestured assent. The priest studied him for a moment. "Remain here, both of you. I will stand there," he pointed to a statue of Fard the Prophet. "Your counterparts will come down the aisle, and the two prisoners will meet in front of me and then proceed to their respective parties." He fixed Vera with a severe look. "Do not attempt to interfere in any way."

"Understood," Vera said, inclining her head.

The priest took his position and a few moments later two figures emerged through the little door behind the altar. They stepped into a pool of colored light. The Terran Celestinbellini leaned heavily on Hayke's shoulder.

At the priest's signal, Alon started down the aisle. The Terran did the same, occasionally grasping the wooden pews. Slowly they came together in front of the priest.

The priest held them there with the fierceness of his stare. First he turned to the Terran. "Our sacred texts do not admit the possibility of intelligent nonhuman life. Thus they have little to say about whether your people possess a spiritual unity with any of the Divine Aspects. If one were to judge by your actions here in Miraz, one might very well conclude you do not. However, each Aspect in its own way teaches infinite mercy and I am servant to them all."

Without waiting for the Terran to answer, the priest switched his focus to Alon. "And you—the death and pain of your own people lies upon you. You cannot offer the excuse that you are not of the Faith, for your own traditions are as adamant as ours."

Although Alon resented being lectured as if he were a child, he saw the opportunity implicit in the priest's harsh words. The Octagon had maintained its political noninvolvement through the centuries, and what each side needed now was here, a neutral ground.

Hayke slipped one arm through Alon's elbow, drawing him forward. Alon glanced back over his shoulder for an instant. The Terran had not yet reached the doors. In the shadows and colored light, Alon could not see Vera's face.

"What's happened?" Alon said. "Why—"

"Escape now, explain later," said Hayke. He urged Alon through the priest's door and a wood-paneled corridor.

Les Bellini staggered, as if his legs had given out suddenly, and fell heavily against Vera. She hooked her shoulder under his armpit and lifted, using her legs. He was surprisingly heavy. Not only that, he reeked of dried vomitus, blood, and mildew. Vera inhaled through her mouth and tightened her grip. He drew in his breath sharply. Under the opened front of his uniform, his chest had been neatly bandaged. He'd received medical care, then.

"Uhhh.." Under the unidentifiable grime, Bellini's face looked ashen. A spasm of coughing shook him.

"Hang on," she said. "We're almost there."

"I'm gonna be sick." His cough changed to retching.

Vera pulled him forward, wishing she'd spent more time in *Prometheus's* rehab gym. She didn't think she could lift him if he fell. The guards who'd come with the car couldn't help her. They had to wait outside. She and Bellini had to make it out on their own.

She kept her eyes on the front entrance, closer now. Ten meters... eight... Her breath hissed between her teeth. The muscles in her legs burned.

Bellini's body got heavier with each step. He started to slip from her grasp. She scrambled to hold on to him.

I'm too damned old for this. I'll have to use my brains instead.

"Get back on your feet, you nano-brained baboon! What kind of soldier are you, who needs an old woman to carry you?"

Bellini's weight suddenly lifted from her. He swayed, his mouth twisted back from his teeth in something like a snarl. "Don't need—"

"Good!" She pushed him toward the entrance. "Then march!"

Somehow she kept Bellini going past the double set of doors. The two guards rushed forward and caught him just as he collapsed again.

"He doesn't smell too good," one of them commented under his breath as they lifted him into the back seat of the car.

"Neither would you, if you'd been through what he has." Vera slid in beside him. As they started off, Bellini fell against her with a mumbled, "Sorry." She found herself patting his shoulder in a rather grandmotherly way and replying, "That's all right. You've been through a hard time. We'll get you back to the ship in no time."

One hand pawed at the bandages on his chest. His words were slurred, as if he were half drunk. "S'my own damned fault. They were waiting for us."

"Bellini." She sharpened her voice, so that he met her eyes, his own gaze hovering on the ragged edge of focus. "It doesn't matter now."

Back at the compound, the shuttle was waiting to take Bellini up to *Prometheus*, where he'd be debriefed and his injuries treated. The crowd was still there. It was an eerie experience to see all those people just standing. They reminded her of long-legged wading birds, like the ones at the lake in Kenya where she'd spent her childhood summers with her grandparents, asleep on one foot, so vulnerable it would be a crime to kill them.

A wrong deed harms the attacker as well as the victim.

Maybe more, for then she would have to live with the memory of what had been done.

Enough! She'd been reading too much philosophy. Perhaps in order to negotiate with these people, one needed to be a philosopher—or a poet. There was something in the way they moved in groups, like birds shifting direction in flight. No wonder the plaza riot was so terrible.

She remembered her grandfather's favorite saying from *I Ching*: "Perseverance furthers."

She would persevere. Treading a tightrope between one round of retribution and the next, between Alon's rage and Hammadi's determination, she would persevere.

Chapter 49

The walls of the corridor were paneled in dark wood, its finish so badly cracked that it resembled the hide of an ancient reptile. The floor had once been covered with a strip of green carpet, now worn into the color of old moss.

Lorne waited inside the priest's door. "I didn't believe they'd do it. Are you hurt? What did they do to you?"

"I'm all right," Alon said. "Keep going!"

At the base of the spiral staircase, they were joined by Timas, a gun in one hand and a lantern in the other. The four of them hurried down the staircase.

With the same talent that led him so unerringly through the traversons, Alon sensed a catacomb entrance nearby. During the turbulent centuries of Mirazan history, the priests of Octagon must have prepared their escape route.

Alon strode down the tunnel, single file between Timas and Hayke, with Lorne following at the rear. "We've got to work fast. This negotiator might turn out to be no different, but for now he's talking compromise to get his people back."

"That sounds hopeful," said Lorne.

"It's a start," Alon said. The tunnels folded around him, enclosing him. He could have made his way in the dark, yet the chill quiet disturbed him. It was just the aftereffects of his imprisonment, he told himself.

"You brought us together when everyone thought it was impossible," Timas said. Light from his lantern danced over the rough-cut walls, making them look wet. "But if you start talking about making deals with the Terrans, there will be questions. People will ask if you haven't gone rotten... like Birre did."

Alon's crest jerked upright and the fur around his neck rippled. He whirled to face Timas. "I planned the hostage raids. I led them. I say who we bargain with and on what terms."

"You'd make peace with the Terrans?"

"If it comes to that." Alon's voice echoed down the tunnel, as hard and sharp as flint.

Timas made a conciliatory gesture. "I'll do what I can." He disappeared down one of the tunnel branches.

Lorne watched him go. "He has a position to maintain. Critic, skeptic, spur. He's not an easy person, but he has a good heart. In the end, he'll listen."

"Go with him, then," said Hayke, "so he won't be alone."

Alon said nothing as Lorne's footsteps died away. He felt drained, enervated, repelled by his own harshness.

They reached a vertical shaft and climbed the rusted metal ladder set in one side. Alon recognized where he was, underneath Padme's restaurant. They came out into the cellar, retracing the same route they'd used to escape after the raid. The room seemed uncomfortably warm and bright after the catacomb tunnel. Crates and boxes lined the walls, bundles of worn tablecloths, chairs stacked and waiting for repair.

Hayke took Alon's arm. "Your parents are waiting for you."

"My parents? No, they must be left out of this."

"Do you think they came back to Miraz to be *left out?*"

Alon's chest gave a peculiar leap, as if something turned itself inside out. He felt odd, disjointed, almost dizzy. *Bird of Heaven, they probably organized the plaza demonstration!*

Back on the ground level, they made their way into a broader street, filled with people. A breeze carried the smells of garlic and herbs, then of bread as they passed a bakery, and finally the pungent smell of fresh-cut daffies. Yellow and white pennons advertised the row of shops.

Tables had been set out in front of the restaurants, many of them filled with patrons. Alon's belly tightened at the sight of two Terrans leaning back in their chairs and sipping hot spiced milk as if they had a right to be there.

Alon stumbled along, stunned by the strangeness of what he saw. He'd walked this street a hundred times before, he knew every building, every shop along it, and yet now none of them fit with his memories. Even the bookstore, as familiar as his own hand, took on a new, dangerous aspect.

Hayke pushed open the bookstore door and Alon heard the clang of the bells. Meddi stood just inside, a feather mop in one hand, Tellem behind the desk, now jumping to his feet. The two of them enveloped Alon in a smothering embrace.

"Stop this!" Alon tried to say, his mouth muffled against Meddi's well-padded shoulder. "I'm not a baby!"

"You're quite right," Tellem said briskly, drawing away. "But parents are permitted an occasional moment of weakness."

Meddi was slower to let Alon go. Alon, seeing his parent's face, wished his words had been gentler. His knees felt powdery. Meddi steered him into the big chair.

Hayke brought tea from the back of the store with a casualness that suggested he'd done it before. Alon cradled the mug of tea and tried to pull his thoughts together.

"There have been changes in the resistance movement since I was taken prisoner," Alon said. "The demonstration in the plaza, for one thing. I know that somehow you two are involved."

"To begin with," Meddi admitted after a pause in which the two parents exchanged glances. "You were so dreadfully upset with us and we weren't sure if we'd be endangering you by even talking to you. It was a very confusing time."

"That is, until we met Hayke and he told us about his dream," Tellem added. "Then everything came clear."

"Dream?" Alon glanced up at Hayke. "You came back to Miraz, putting both your lives at risk, because of Hayke's *dream*?"

"No, that's the wrong order," Tellem said, as if he were explaining something to a child. "We knew we had to come back. We didn't know why."

"History seemed to repeating itself in ways we thought were gone forever," Meddi said. "When we heard about the dream, we knew it was time to leave our safe places, to stand as witnesses so that evil would not go unremembered."

Why hadn't he seen it before? There was a network of Wayfolk stretching from Chacarre and into Erlind, Joosten, even Valada. A network honed into invisibility by centuries of secrecy, a network he could use for the Movement—

He cut the thought off. Wayfolk were the most stubborn, independent, intractable clan in all the world. They would do what they felt moved to do, and nothing else. He ought to know. He was one of them.

"I'm just a farmer with a crazy dream," Hayke said in response to Alon's unasked question. "But I can no longer take part in the bombings and the kidnappings. Timas and Orsen already know this. I came today because I'd been the one to nurse the Terran. There are some things we cannot do alone—"

"There are some things," Meddi interrupted, "we cannot do at all at the present." He put his hands on his ample hips in a gesture that Alon found endearing.

"You're right, of course," said Tellem mildly. Then, to Alon: "We'd hoped you'd spend some time with us before you go back to doing... whatever it was you were doing."

Alon shook his head. "Too dangerous for you."

Meddi drew up to his full height. He no longer looked frail and aged, but fired with an inner strength. His voice was firm under its soft expression.

"The time for hiding is over."

Alon felt so tired when they got home that the first thing he did was curl up in his old bed. It felt smaller than he'd remembered it. His body ached. Even his joints seemed worn out.

Blazes! he thought, and woke up in a darkened room. Someone shouted in anger or in pain. The echoes still hung in the air. The door swung open and Hayke came in. With a start, Alon realized that his own cries had jarred him from sleep.

Hayke sat on the bed beside Alon's knees. "When my children were small, they sometimes had nightmares, too. I used to sing them back to sleep. Their favorite was the grommet who loved the stars. Shall I sing it to you now?"

"I'm too old for that."

Pause. "Yes, I see that you are. Or perhaps too young."

Alon sighed and sat up. "What time is it?"

"You have enough time to do all the things you need to do," Hayke said soothingly. "Are you hungry?"

Alon shook his head. "I can get something later, if I need it." He intended to stand up, but his legs gave way beneath him. He fell back on the bed. He tried to speak, but nothing came from his throat, only a wheezing, gasping breath. A trembling began deep inside his body. It spread to the muscles of his arms and legs.

Without a word, Hayke wrapped Alon in his arms. Alon buried his face against Hayke's shoulder. His breath caught in his throat. He felt as if he were choking. He kept telling himself to snap out of it, to get control, even as his chest heaved in one sobbing breath after another.

I can't break down like this. There's too much depending on me.

"It's all right," Hayke murmured, running his fingers lightly over Alon's hair. "It's all right now. You're safe."

"It's not—" Alon began. It wasn't all right. Not inside.

For what seemed like a long time, Alon could do no more than burrow his head into Hayke's shoulder and take one shuddering breath after another. Hayke murmured and stroked his head. A part deep inside Alon, like a small child, opened to the rhythmic touch.

Gradually the sobs eased and Alon's breath came in gasps, high and light in his chest. For the moment, he didn't have to be brave and competent, always on guard. He could just sit here, in this old familiar room, with Hayke's body a bulwark against the world.

He said with a diffidence that surprised him, "In all the years you and

324

your Rosen were together, did you ever wonder what it would be like... if you'd paired with someone else? Or if—whether you could pair again?"

"You're thinking of Birre? Problems like those, they're not easy. They take a lot of healing, a lot of time. Time and understanding."

"There's nothing to understand," Alon said tightly, swinging his feet over the side of the bed. He went to the carved chest and began rummaging around for any clean clothing he'd left there when he moved out. "The Terrans changed him somehow. That's the end of it."

"If that were true, if you had truly given him up in your heart, then you would have no questions about pairing with anyone else."

Birre was probably back with his parents, living in that big house, safe from whatever went on in the street. *Wherever he is, whatever he's doing, it has nothing to do with me anymore.*

"I'm—I'm all right now." Alon wished his voice were steadier. He didn't sound very certain to his own ears.

"These things take time," Hayke said again. Plain words, but spoken in a way that made them seem anything but simple.

The inn host had left a carafe of tea and a tray of bread and cold boiled root vegetables. Alon ate most of it without stopping.

Hayke sat cross-legged on his own cot. He said so little that finally Alon asked him what was the matter.

"I've been thinking about my children and how much I miss them," Hayke said quietly. "I remember the night the Terrans landed. It was late summer, and we were lying out on a hill, beyond the fields. The hay had just been mown and the smell was sweet, so sweet. Stars filled the sky, not like here in the city. Torrey was teasing Felde about what he'd do if he ever met a real alien. And Felde said he'd play his music for them."

Alon pressed one hand to his belly. His child would never make music for the Terrans or anyone else. Pain flared, but this time it seemed a wave, not a piercing stab. More sorrow than fury, it rose and gently subsided. He thought of the Terran Vera and their shared grief. It had changed him somehow, even as Hayke had. It surprised him that such tender feelings should have such power.

All this time he'd been acting out of pain and anger, wanting nothing more than to smash every Terran he saw.

The harder I smashed, the harder they smashed back.

325

Shortly, the others began arriving—Timas, Orsen, Lorne, Padme. Their eagerness resonated in the little room, filling the air with a close, familiar tang. Alon sat on his cot, while the rest crowded together with Hayke or on the floor.

"We've got five hostages left," Alon said. "In return, we'll demand amnesty for Kreste and anyone who's helped him, and an end to the spy mushrooms."

"You think this negotiator will agree?" Orsen said, his crest ruffling in skepticism.

"Perhaps not," Alon said. "We'll see how serious she is."

"There will be problems about those Faithless mushrooms," Lorne said from his place at the foot of Hayke's cot. "The warders like them, say they cut down on crime."

"The warders are half the problem!" Timas said with a snort. "They weren't so bad under Kallen, but this new chief—"

"Who, Ambyntet?" said Alon.

"We've heard rumors he's set up a secret force," Padme said, "one responsible for assassinations made to look like ordinary accidents. We've heard that Kallen's death was arranged under orders from Lexis."

"Do we have proof of that?" Alon said.

"Not yet," Timas said, with a gesture that looked murderous.

Alon pressed his crest against his skull, remembering when he'd pleaded with Lexis for Birre's freedom. "If that's true," he said, "we must get Lexis out of power. If we go after Ambyntet, Lexis will appoint someone just like him."

Around the circle, the others gestured agreement.

"You could become mayor yourself, if the Terrans hold elections," said Hayke. "They're supposed to be open to anyone."

Alon masked his surprise. Wayfolk rarely sought the visibility of a political career or had the clan connections for it. But if Lexis, who'd been no more than a third-rate poetry teacher, could rule a city, why not him?

He shook the thought away. "We've got to keep pressure on the Terrans. The watchers in the plaza—that's a good start. There must be no more attacks, no more bombings, no kidnappings."

"If we back off, the Terrans will think they've won," Orsen growled. "We'll lose everything we've gained."

"Not backing off," Hayke spoke up. "Shifting tactics."

"Tactics!" Timas spat out the word.

Alon held up one hand. "Let Hayke speak. The plaza vigil *does* have an effect on the Terrans, even if we don't understand what it is. I saw that for myself."

"Changing times call for changing means," Lorne said. Padme gestured agreement.

"We should kill them all," Orsen said, but less vehemently.

"We should surround them with mirrors," Hayke said quietly. "Never alone, never unwatched. Isn't that what their spy mushrooms have done to us?"

"Any time a Terran leaves the compound, our own people go with him," said Alon, catching the spirit. "Twos and threes, but we don't approach them. We don't interfere. All we do is follow and watch. If they threaten us, we retreat, just like in the plaza. Others take our place. Every Terran will know that his actions are witnessed and remembered."

Timas laughed. "They'll just hide in their compound!"

"I hope so," Lorne said dryly. He turned back to Alon. "It's a good idea while we're negotiating."

"What about you?" Alon asked Orsen and Timas. "Will you join us, or at least agree to keep the peace?"

The two of them gestured agreement, Timas first and Orsen more grudgingly. The bond that held them was uncertain and flimsy. How much strain would it stand? What would break it? What would hold? What unforeseen event would fracture this alliance, sending each of them off on their own?

Alon glanced from one face to the next, wondering that they had come together at all. Neither clan ties nor shared vision joined them, not even Hayke, who followed his own stubborn Way. With an odd shiver, Alon remembered his own moment of trust with the Terran Vera. The thought came to him that he might have more in common with her than with Orsen or Timas.

We come together to use each other, whether or not we understand each other. Each of us for our own purposes. But purposes could change.

Had *his*? Had he become something other than what he'd been, touched by Hayke's dream and Vera's compassion and the first slow steps of his own healing? Or perhaps by his sudden, unwanted insight that Chacarre and the Terrans had become inextricably linked, each needing the other, each unwilling to admit it?

He didn't know. He would have to go back to the compound to find out.

Chapter 50

Returning to the Terran compound was the hardest thing Alon had done in his life. What, he demanded of himself, did he think might happen to him? He had safe-passage, authorized by the official negotiator. If the worst came to pass and he were once more taken prisoner, he would risk no one else by his decision.

Around him, the city hummed with activity, the streets with their tiny shops and flower stands, the open-air markets lining the quays, the arching Westriver bridge. The breeze from the river touched his face with its faint, wild tang.

As Alon approached the plaza, the compound came into view, towering above the age-softened stone of the surrounding buildings. Seeing it, his thighs began to shake. His crest jittered. Each step became a hurdle in itself.

A cluster of people ringed the compound entrance, standing with their arms crossed over their chests. There were fewer than yesterday, the day of his release. He blinked—had it been only yesterday? They stood quietly, faces composed, eyes alert. He envied their serenity.

As Alon neared the watchers, they parted to let him pass. For the briefest moment, he felt himself surrounded by them, enclosed by their stillness. It was enough that the watchers would be there, marking his entrance and waiting for him to come out again. He took a deep breath and mounted the steps.

"Hey! You!" One of the Terran guards blocked his path.

Alon, clinging to his tenuous courage, felt the eyes of the crowd on his back. *Whatever happens here, they will see and remember.*

The Terran must have thought it, too. "Please state your name and business. Sir."

"I am Alon-az-Thirien, here to meet with the negotiator Vera. I was given free passage."

The Terran bobbed his head in that peculiar gesture of theirs. "I'll have to check you for weapons."

Alon sensed the heightening in the crowd's alertness. "Then do it here. Outside."

While the second guard kept his weapon trained on Alon, the first searched him, using both his hands and a flat box, some kind of instrument. Then Alon was free to enter the compound foyer. Just before the doors swung shut behind him, he turned and glanced back at the watchers.

The image of them standing there, so still and calm, brought a surge of strength. He supposed it was a foolhardy thing to go into his enemy's stronghold alone, unarmed, and yet at that moment his very vulnerability became a source of courage.

To go unarmed among his enemies... Unarmed, but not unremembered.

It struck him that memory was the most potent weapon of all.

The Terran guard led Alon through the foyer and into the bowels of the compound, along passages as gray as tarnished metal. The air held the same staleness, like the exhalations of Terran machines. He himself had changed.

Inside him, in a place no Terran science could reach, the sweet Chacarran sun filled him with its warmth. He felt it every step, even in the confines of the elevator tube and the office in which Vera waited for him.

Two seats of molded plastic had been drawn up around a table. A carafe and two empty glasses stood on it, along with two writing tablets. Alon lowered himself to the seat opposite Vera.

Vera's nostrils flared. "The guard said you'd come alone. Have you been courteously treated?"

"How can we talk about hope and trust and new beginnings in a place like this?" Alon gestured with one hand, taking in the featureless walls. The movement stirred the air, set up little breezes of metallic-stinking air. "It's no different from the cell you put me in."

"Where, then?"

Alon took his time answering. "We are talking about the future of Miraz, of all Chacarre. So let's go out there—stroll along the river or through a park, buy some fruit at the farmers' booths, sip tea outside a bar. Stand under the open sky, walk down a street with a thousand years of history in its stones. Find something in the life of the city as a starting point."

One corner of Vera's mouth twitched. She lifted her shoulders, sending a gentle movement through her breasts. "We could compose poetry."

Alon laughed aloud. "Very bad poetry, I'm afraid."

The Terran's hands moved restlessly on the table. She clasped them together as if to hold them still. "We'd both be vulnerable to anyone who wanted to sabotage the negotiations. And then there's the issue of privacy."

Alon moved toward the door. "Are you coming?"

"I have no choice."

More watchers had gathered in the plaza. Some of them detached themselves from the main crowd and followed Alon and Vera. They crossed the plaza, heading south, and skirted the busy mercantile district.

Before him and behind him, Alon sensed a hundred small moments of life, an elder holding the hand of a child, mates strolling arm in arm, someone opening a door for a pregnant, a merchant greeting an old friend. He caught glimpses of his image in the shop windows, distorted by the imperfections in the glass and backed by ghostly images of fabrics and garments, piles of bread loaves or cheeses dipped in colorful waxes, toys or books or furniture. The city wrapped him in a pattern of richness.

I am walking with a Terran through my own city, he thought. *She is an alien, a scientist she said, and I am nothing but a Wayfolk book seller.* No words could mar the moment, walking down a sunlit city street.

"Look! Ah, there!" Vera tilted her head back, face to the sky, and pointed as a covey of rock-doves burst over the tops of the buildings.

Alon stopped to buy a bottle of wine and cheese buns, then guided Vera to the strip of park that ran along the bankers' street. Their silent escort followed, watching from a distance. They sat on a bench under a tree in the cool, earthy-smelling shade. Alon sipped the wine. It was tart on the tongue, with a pleasant woody aftertaste. He handed the bottle to Vera. She held it under her nose and then returned it, untasted.

"Thank you, but no. Your wine is not for me."

Alon leaned back, watching the Terran, acutely aware of the silent watchers. They were too far away to overhear any conversation, and yet their presence changed everything. He still couldn't read the expression on the Terran's hairless face, but it seemed to him that Vera was also feeling those eyes on her. Perhaps she also was struggling to find a Way.

Vera, as if aware that Alon was staring at her, shifted on the bench. "How shall we begin? Are you prepared to discuss the return of the hostages?"

"Are you prepared to give us what we asked for?" Alon countered.

"Not everything and not right away, no."

Alon sighed.

"There must be no more violence," said Vera. "Whatever else you and I may fail to resolve, we must find a way to stop the cycle of escalating retaliations."

Alon made a gesture of agreement. "Can you make Hammadi understand that? Can you control Lexis and his warders?"

"You're asking me my limitations while we're just beginning negotiations?" Vera said.

"I'm asking you not to offer what you haven't got."

Vera said nothing.

"We must have our country back," Alon said after a pause.

"I know."

"And the only way to accomplish that is for both of us to feel as if we've won."

"I know."

"And you Terrans, of course, are not to be trusted."

Vera's mouth twitched in what might have been a smile. "I know," she said softly.

For a long moment they sat in silence. A breeze, warmed by the sun, ruffled the leaves above their head. Two young children scampered down the gravel path, rolling a brightly patterned ball, with a laughing parent close behind.

"Then," Vera said, "we are in complete agreement."

The negotiations went better than Alon expected. Together he and Vera were able to devise a sequence of exchanges that made it appear that each side was standing firm for its own demands. Hammadi, the Terran chief, would not budge on the subject of the return of the Helm. The Provisional Governing Council would surrender control only to a government that represented the will of the people, he said. It didn't matter that 150 years ago, Carrel-az-Ondre had become the first Helm out of universal desperation. What was only a beginning to the end of centuries of clan feuding and rivalry was to Hammadi ancient history. In the end, Alon and his allies agreed.

The heavy doors of the Octagon swung closed behind Alon. He blinked, surrounded by the now familiar darkness, before stepping into the spectrum of light cast by the high windows. The priest came forward and made a gesture of greeting. Alon responded politely. The Temple no longer felt a strange, intimidating place. Alon and Vera had arranged to meet in the little office behind the altar. The site was a good compromise, offering both a neutral location and privacy.

Today Vera was late. After she arrived, as they exchanged pleasantries, she seemed distracted. Alon thought it must be because of the watchers who had continued to grow in numbers and pressure. He remembered how she'd reacted to them on the day of his release.

"The Terrans can't even find a place to piss without five of us watching," a minor city official had bragged. His words had been quoted in some variation in every bar and inn, so much so that a few days later, the phrase *five of us watching* had become a joke in itself.

"Is there some new problem?" Alon asked, careful to keep any mischievous twitch from his crest.

Vera was usually direct to the point of bluntness. It was one of the reasons Alon found himself enjoying working with her. Now she seemed indecisive. She talked about the latest incident at the warehouse complex that the Erlind soldiers had taken over.

"You have only to wait the Erls out," Alon said. "Sooner or later they'll run out of food or whatever House prevails in Erlonn will order them home. What's the rush?"

Alon could read Vera's gestures well enough to recognize how disturbed she was. "We can't wait until *sooner or later*," she said. "We need access to that lab now."

Lab? Alon remembered there was a scientific facility in the complex. He gestured a question, then repeated it aloud for her understanding. "Why?"

"The work I was doing there was vital to repairing our space ship. Without it, we cannot leave orbit. We're stranded here." She leaned back in her chair and blew out a deep, gusty breath. "Hammadi would have a seizure if he knew I'd told you. But I don't see any detriment to your knowing why we stay on. It's not because we enjoy oppressing less-developed civilizations. It's because we have no choice."

"You will leave when your space ship is repaired?"

"That was our intention. We only started meddling in your affairs to ensure the political stability we needed for the manufacture of our replacement parts. It's a good thing your technological level is as advanced as it is, or we'd be here for decades."

By then, how much would Chacarre have changed? Alon felt as if Vera had thrown a bucket of icy water in his face. "Then we must get the Erls out as soon as possible."

Vera shook her head in that peculiar Terran gesture. It made Alon dizzy just to watch her. "We've tried everything. We've offered them safe conduct back to Erlonn, we've ordered and reasoned. Maybe they'd leave if their own superiors commanded it, but there's no government yet in Erlonn. So we've been waiting, and meanwhile, their presence has become a sore spot with the Mirazans."

The more widespread the protest, the greater the chance that Hammadi would revert to a harder stance.

"Erls don't retreat, gracefully or otherwise," Alon said. "In all the centuries we've been enemies, we have learned that."

Vera raised both hands in an enigmatic but eloquent gesture. "What, then? What would *you* propose in my place?"

"You'll have to force the issue," Alon said, "or they'll sit there until they starve. So offer them the chance to remain in Chacarre with full citizenship. Put a tight deadline on it. That way, anyone who stays will be *presumed* to have turned traitor. Any Erl with a shred of loyalty will be scrambling to show he's not at heart a Chacarran."

"That's certainly something we haven't tried. Do you think they would accept Chacarran citizenship?"

"They might find it difficult to go back, after being exposed to Chacarran culture." In Chacarre, any defectors might well be seen as political refugees and met with some degree of sympathy.

Vera chewed on her upper lip and drew her brows together in an expression that made Alon want to laugh, it looked so much like a child's comic toy. "What about clan loyalties? Is it possible these Erls would cut themselves off from their own families, like—like singletons?"

Alon winced at her misuse of the term. "They're Fardites, and you know what that means." Maybe she didn't know what that meant. Patiently he explained that there were procedures for any of the Prophet's followers to apply to the local Eighth Aspect priest, or to Octagon itself, for that matter, for support services—food, medical care, housing in a Fardite enclose instead of the splits. They'd soon be absorbed into a larger clan, through pairing or adoption.

They spent the next several hours working out the details for the release of the remaining Terran hostages. Vera left the small office, exiting through the main body of the Temple. A handful of watchers undoubtedly waited to trail her back to the compound.

Alon heard a soft tapping on the door. It must be one of the priests, checking to see if the office were empty now.

Birre stepped into the room. Even shadowed in the doorway, he shimmered in Alon's vision. "I've been trying to see you for days. I've left messages at the bookstore, with your parents, everywhere.."

Birre had lost weight, his slender grace now whittled into gauntness. His burnt-color fur had dulled, his eyes grown too large.

Alon's body wouldn't move. "I never got any messages."

"There's no explaining what I did. I know that. I can't justify it, not even to myself. I never intended—that much you've got to believe." Birre stumbled over his words, his hands moving in half-intelligible gestures, maimed and ineffectual.

The room felt suddenly too small.

I loved him once. We loved each other.

Alon felt a pain, an aching so deep it went beyond the physical and he had no words for it.

"Sit down," he said as gently as he could. "Tell me what happened."

Birre perched on the edge of the chair. He clasped his hands together as if to stop them from shaking. "I don't remember much after the raid. I didn't go back to the compound—I didn't—I—The hospital released me about a month ago, I think, and then it took a while for the drugs to wear off. My parents kept me at home."

A prisoner. As if they were ashamed of him.

"I left as soon as I c-could," Birre went on, stumbling over the word. "I'm working again now, on the Eastriver docks. Manual labor. My parents don't know where I am, or if they do, they've left me alone."

Alon looked away. "What about advocat school?"

The moment stretched on. Alon looked back and saw Birre's eyes wide and staring.

Without thinking what he was doing, Alon got up and went to Birre. He took one of Birre's hands in his, felt the work-roughened fingers. Birre quivered, a twig about to snap.

"I was a prisoner of the Terrans, too," Alon said. "I don't know what would have happened to me if I hadn't been exchanged so soon. I thought about you the whole time. How much stronger you were than me. What they could have done to you."

Birre seemed to crumple in on himself, falling forward. Alon scrambled to his feet and caught Birre in his arms.

Come back to me.

"I can't," Birre said. The whispered syllables touched Alon's hair with the merest stirring of air.

Alon felt the thin shoulders with their muscles like twisted wire. He touched his lips to Birre's hair. Tenderness flooded him, half pleasure, half melting pain.

"Stop!" Birre raised his head and pushed away, standing shakily. "Please stop. You don't know what you're doing. How can I bear it, seeing what I can't ever have again?"

"You can. *We* can—"

"No!" Birre raised one hand. "Just let me say this and then let me leave. There aren't any happy endings to this story, Alon. Maybe someday, when what's broken inside me—I don't know. But I do know that what you're doing now is too important. I can't change what I did, no matter why I did it, no matter if I wasn't responsible. The only thing I can do now is to stay away from you. It was selfish of me to come."

"No! Don't say that!"

Birre had turned toward the door and now paused, his shoulders hunching. He flinched, trembling visibly now. He looked as if he expected a physical blow.

"What I mean is," Alon said, taking a deep breath, "when all of this is over, we will find a way of loving each other again. Only that."

Slowly Birre nodded. A light passed over his eyes, a hint of their old fire. "You keep on with the Terrans, you hear? You keep pounding them and pushing them until you've won and they're gone. You do it for both of us." Then he jerked open the door and slipped through.

Alon didn't bother to get up. It was fitting to be alone in a room where Birre had not completely closed the door.

Chapter 51

Every one?" Hammadi repeated. He'd taken the link from Dr. Vera in his own quarters, and it was a good thing, for none of his staff could see the expression on his face.

"Every damned one." The gleam in her eyes was brilliant enough to etch the phosphors of his monitor.

After Dr. Vera started negotiating with the terrorists, there had been no more kidnapping attempts. Even the attacks on the observation probes had fallen off to almost nothing. Hammadi grudgingly conceded that her approach had merit. The Erls' continuing intransigence had been the one remaining impasse. She'd managed, by an unbelievable combination of soft-hearted civilian reasonableness and outright bullying, to solve that, too. She'd even asked his permission before broaching the idea of offering Chacarran citizenship to the Erls. He'd given the okay, thinking it was a lunatic idea if he'd ever heard one, but he had nothing to lose. He'd thought at best a few of them might accept. But *every damned one?*

"Of course," Dr. Vera went on, "you don't want to hear about the unbelievable mess they left. They weren't deliberately destructive, they just had no idea what they were shoving out of the way in so cavalier a fashion. Sergei's supervising the clean-up team even as we speak."

She signed off cheerily, leaving Hammadi sitting in silence. Sighing, he ran one hand over his jaw. With the Erls out of the lab, Dr. Vera and her staff could get back to work. If nothing else went wrong, if there were no more terrorist attacks, if she could pull off one of her technical miracles.

They might actually get out of here. Back into space. Back home.

Suddenly, he thought of his garden, the rocks arranged on the raked sand, the pond with its water lilies. The butterflies. The sunshine drifting through the wisteria arbor, dappling the book on his lap. The laughter of his adopted daughter. The image shook him more than he expected.

If there was one thing Hammadi had learned in his months orbiting this gawdforsaken planet, it was to take nothing having to do with the natives for granted. What were they doing these last weeks, shadowing his men everywhere? Chacarrans didn't react like any civilians he'd dealt with before.

But if he couldn't rely on his own judgment and experience, what could he trust?

MIRAZ: TERRANS ORDER FREE ELECTIONS; LEXIS DECLARES CANDIDACY. Report by Ambrom. (Approved without changes by the Department of Information Services.)

In a press conference late this morning, the assistant Terran commander, Jonadamson, announced the intention of the Provisional Government to hold "free and democratic elections" in accordance with previous agreements. In order to avoid social chaos, he said, elections would proceed in a step-wise fashion, with only some officials being chosen each time.

The first and most important office to be restored is that of Helm. Despite calls for the immediate reinstitution of Kreste's administration, Jonadamson insisted that this post be open to all candidates. "If the people want Kreste back, they are free to vote for him," he said.

Immediately following the press conference, Miraz Mayor Lexis declared himself a candidate. The response from the audience was mixed. Long regarded as a popular hero of the Miraz Plaza Riots, Lexis took over his current position after the previous mayor, Chellen, was assassinated. Lexis has frequently been a subject of attack in the unauthorized press for his luxurious lifestyle and the severity with which he has dealt with civil disturbances. He has been accused of having a role in the Warder Square Massacre, although these charges have never been substantiated.

It was Lexis's intention that the people would decide they didn't want Kreste back. Kreste represented the direst threat to Miraz and to all of Chacarre. By a single action, by fleeing at a time when Miraz needed him most, he had betrayed everything the office of Helm represented. He had violated the ancient covenant of the trust by placing his own personal welfare above his clan, his city, his nation. Carrel-az-Ondre, first Helm of Chacarre, would never have done such a cowardly, self-serving thing.

How, by all Eight Aspects and the Tears of the Flaming Bird, could Kreste ever be trusted again?

And who could take his place, if not Lexis himself?

To this end, Lexis hired Chellen's publicist to plan his campaign and advise how he might put his position as mayor to best advantage. He would have preferred to enlist Kreste's old staff, but most of them had disappeared and those who still remained in Miraz flatly refused the job, clinging to protestations of retirement or ill health.

"You understand," said the publicist, "that I have never taken on a task quite like this." Small and wiry, he never stopped waving his hands, as if by constant churning he could generate success. Within a few minutes, his effervescence made the roots of Lexis's fur itch.

"*No one* in Miraz—in all Chacarre—has ever done such a thing. The goal of publicity has always been the communication of material private to the clan. We've always been able to assume a common background and interest. Announcements having to do with the city governance were handled by the Bureau of Internal Affairs. Their writing, as you must surely realize, is about as inspiring as boiled callet."

The publicist paused, drawing breath. Lexis kept his eyes on the pale peach walls and wished he didn't need such an odious, unsettling person.

"It's too bad we can't hire someone like Talense to write your press statements," the publicist rattled on. "His work is brilliant, and he's accustomed to addressing all the different clans. Or this Seeker, from the underground press."

"My name must never be associated with any illegal activities," Lexis said.

"Of course, what he writes is seditious trash. Nonsense, really. It's that he says it in such an eloquent manner. No matter how strenuously you disagree with his arguments, you must admire his way of presenting them."

If Lexis couldn't get this Flameless Bird-dropping out of his office, he would surely throttle him. "Are those the announcements for me to look over?" he asked, picking up a sheaf of papers. "Then let's meet again, but not until I've had a chance to study them. My clerk will let you know."

"Of course," the publicist said, gathering up his materials with satisfying haste. "Perhaps Commander Celestinbellini, who has been so helpful to you in the past, will also be available. I have heard that he returned to Miraz yesterday."

After the publicist left, Lexis stood at the window for a long time. He thought of summoning one of the young aides he'd gathered around him since he'd become mayor. He had not taken another bed mate since the kidnapping. He had not been able to even consider it. Perhaps that would distract him now. He would lie on the cushioned bed, the air perfumed with rosellia and fragrant night-white, while eager fingers stroked his body.

He would remember the nights, the whispered heat, the taste of the alien mouth on his, the grotesquely swollen nub filling him, searing him, ripping his flesh—

Enough!

His slit had gone wet, remembering. His knees felt like glass. His hands trembled.

Lexis went back to the desk and sat down. He smoothed his crest and stroked the silk of his tunic across his belly. He adjusted the small picture-speaker that Terrans had installed in the office. It was set to communicate with Celestinbellini's office in the compound.

A moment's flicker, and a Terran figure came into view, facing at an angle to the screen. Looking away from him, talking to someone Lexis could not see.

Lexis's stomach turned inside out. "Bel—" he began, the private name the Terran commander had given him to use.

Celestinbellini looked up with those gloriously melting eyes. Lexis's stomach went hot.

"Mayor Lexis." Celestinbellini's eyes did not change as he spoke. "Is there anything I can do for you?"

"Are you alone? Can we talk?"

"Just a moment." The Terran turned and spoke a few sentences in his own language.

Lexis said, "I'm glad to see you're well. I was worried about you. I'm sick thinking what you must have suffered at the hands of those criminals! There is no atrocity they will not stoop to. As you know, I have been opposed to dealing with them from the very start. But it was worth it to have you back safe. You look very well now."

"Thank you for your concern."

"Perhaps I could express it in a more... personal way. When can you come to me?"

"I—" Celestinbellini made a noise low in his throat. "I don't think that will be possible."

"Indeed. Why not?" Lexis smiled inwardly. This new shyness was most intriguing. Charming, really. It would be interesting to see what difference it made in bed.

"There's been a change in policy. To put it bluntly, no fraternizing with the natives is permitted."

Lexis flared his crest in a way he knew Celestinbellini admired, the hairs jutting upwards and then falling to either side like a living fountain. "But surely—"

"Let's not make this any harder than we have to," Celestinbellini said with the first trace of feeling yet. "I don't have any choice in the matter. I'm an officer in the United Terran Peacekeeping Command. I gave an oath to put my duty above personal considerations, no matter how pleasant they might be."

"Have it your own way, then!" *Let him think he's won.* "But if you want to live and work in Chacarre, you'll have no choice but to deal with me!"

With a dismissive gesture, Lexis cut the link. He got up and began pacing. The movement sent blood flowing through his arms and legs. The pounding of his heart and the tingling along his spinal hairs felt wonderful.

Once I'm Helm, he'll have no choice. Then he'll come crawling back...

Chapter 52

Ferro wandered along the rocky shoreline east of Haven, his hands thrust deep in his coat pockets. Gusts of frost-edged air ruffled his fur. Even in summer, the winds from the Ice Sea cut to the bone. He paused to gaze southward, to watch the light sheeting off the water. He had gotten into the habit of these walks, solitary except for the two guards that Na-chee-nal insisted accompany him everywhere. They were both young, one a farmer from the northern coastal region who'd handled guns all his life, the other an intense, serious student from Cenza. Both accepted him as Kreste without question, which still brought mingled feelings of sadness and resolve.

Overhead, sea birds shrieked out curses in their secret language as Ferro headed back toward Haven, along the path through the rocky beach. There might be news from Chacarre, hand-carried for privacy. The two guards lengthened their strides to keep up with him.

As he approached the wharves, he noticed a group gathered around a new arrival, a fishing vessel, he guessed, and Chacarran by its build and markings. Curious, he moved through the crowd, thinking that perhaps there was news from the mainland.

The ship's captain climbed out from the hold and onto the dock. His coat and coveralls were splotched with engine oil, his face lined and weather-reddened. He smelled of fish and salt air. When he saw Ferro, he paused, wiping his hands on the ends of his heavy knitted scarf. "You're Kreste?" he said in the lilting Chacarran of the northwest coast.

Ferro smiled and extended his hands. The captain bobbed his head, took them for a moment.

"What's the news from home?" Ferro said.

"Like I was telling them," the captain said, nodding at the onlookers, "the sheets are full of this election talk. Nobody knows what to believe. There's a few announced they'll run, but most are waiting to see what happens. If you come back—" he broke off, glancing around, and ran one hand over his salt water-streaked fur.

"Come on up to headquarters," Ferro said. "You can tell me all about it." *In private*, he meant.

The captain looked relieved. "I've got some packages for you down in the cabin."

Ferro gave orders for the boxes of supplies to be brought up. The packet he carried himself. When they reached the headquarters building, he took a few moments alone in his office to put aside the money and examine the letters. None looked as if they'd been opened in transit; several had been sealed in outer envelopes. He opened these and scanned their contents. One crisp white envelope, the address printed in formal block characters, was hardly the sort of thing one of the resistance fighters would send.

The letter inside was on official stationery of the United Terran Peacekeeping Force. Not the Liaison Committee, not the Provisional Government. Ferro had been standing, but as he read the letter, he sank into a chair. He read it twice to make sure he'd understood. It was a guarantee of safety and diplomatic privileges, as well as confirmation of the offer of amnesty, signed by the captain of the Terran space ship, Hammadi himself.

It was for Kreste, of course. As Kreste he could go back. And his charade would last only so long as he didn't meet anyone who'd known Kreste. It had been a miracle and a tribute to the Islanders' isolation that he hadn't been recognized before now. Most of the Chacarrans he met were fishers or an occasional runaway farmer. There had been a double handful of exiles from Miraz and Avallaz, some of whom had known Kreste. A few had guessed his secret, and others he'd been able to convince he was still Kreste's assistant.

He snapped alert as Na-chee-nal came in.

"Who's that waiting out front?" the Valad asked. "Another boat courier?"

"He brought some supplies," Ferro said. "A little money. Letters."

Na-chee-nal narrowed his eyes, scrutinizing Ferro. "Something bad in there?"

Ferro folded the letter and tucked it into his pocket. "We'll discuss it later. I don't want to keep the captain waiting."

Na-chee-nal made a gesture of impatience. "He's just a common fisher. No one would entrust anything important to him."

"He's Chacarran."

"And I'm not, is that what you're saying? I who gave up my own country and my own career, to fight at your side? I who—"

"Are you *jealous?*"

"Of *him?*" Na-chee-nal made a snorting noise.

Ferro called the captain in. One of his guards brought in tea for the three of them. After grunting a greeting, Na-chee-nal sat sipping his in silence.

Ferro put the fisher at his ease within a few minutes, asking him about

344

his ship and the sailing weather, then about conditions at home, what people were saying, what they might be thinking but didn't say.

"Lexis, he's the mayor of Miraz, he's running for Helm," said the fisher. He leaned forward as he talked, his attention focused on Ferro, except for occasional glances in Na-chee-nal's direction. "Out my way, people don't like him much on account of how he never was elected to anything in the first place. He only got in because of Mayor Chelle being killed. Seems a person shouldn't profit so much from another person's misfortune. There's a lot of stories. Rumors. We're working folk, what do we know? Some would choose him if they didn't have any other choice."

"And if they did have a choice?"

The fisher paused and studied Ferro with eyes gone pale, as if from too much staring at the sea. "Pardon my speaking frankly, but some are saying you won't come back. They say if you meant to, you would have spoken out by now. They say you're scared of the Terrans, you've lost touch with what's happening at home, you don't have what it takes to lead anymore. All sorts of things. I guess people need to believe there's someone out there who hasn't given up, someone who's kept fighting, no matter what. Here's a chance, but they don't see you taking it. Maybe I've spoken out of turn, but you asked me what I think."

"And if I came back?"

"Oh, that's easy! No choice there!"

Ferro heard the flare of hope in the fisher's voice. Kreste had become a hero as much because people needed one as because of anything he'd done. He felt the heat of Na-chee-nal's warning glare: *Don't commit yourself.*

"It's not a simple choice, you know," Ferro said. "I have to decide what's best for Chacarre, as well as what's the popular thing to do."

"Oh yes, well, we understand that. I'll tell them back home, then, that you're thinking of it?"

Ferro got to his feet and the fisher did likewise. "Tell them.." He led the way to the door, then paused with one hand on the latch. "Tell them I have not forgotten them."

The fisher made a gesture of satisfaction. Na-chee-nal escorted him from the building. After they left, Ferro sat down, staring out the window. In all the time he'd traveled on errands for Kreste, all the time he'd spent in that incredibly dreary hole in Erlonn, Ferro had never felt such an acute longing for his own country.

After a few minutes, Na-chee-nal came back into the office. The room seemed instantly warmer and more dangerous.

"So. What was useful in that?"

Ferro's crest rippled briefly. "Actually, something we should have realized ourselves. As long as there was no chance of a restoration of a

Chacarran government, we were the embodiment of resistance, defiance, hope. With this Terran proposal, whether it's legitimate or not, well, if we don't go back, people will see it as outright abdication. That all we ever meant to do was hide out in the Isles and play at being outlaws."

Na-chee-nal scowled. "I don't care what this fisher says. It sounds like a Terran trap."

Ferro managed not to smile, Na-chee-nal's response was so predictable. "You're right, of course, and it's entirely possible the Terrans themselves planted that story to do just that. But this," he took out the letter and held it out to Na-chee-nal, "this changes everything."

Na-chee-nal read it quickly, his fur rippling. "I don't see why. It's just another ruse, no more credible than any other."

"He did not have to send the letter, signed with his own name."

Na-chee-nal's muscles bunched, rigid. "You going back? Or thinking of it?"

"I must. Unless I really do intend to be no more than a footnote in history."

For a long moment, the only sound in the room was that of Na-chee-nal's breath through his clenched teeth. The Valad's fur had risen, giving him the appearance of even more imposing bulk. Ferro sensed the mixture of anger and fear, like an acrid scent.

"You cannot go back," Na-chee-nal said at last.

Ferro faced him, resolute. The challenge had been building between them for months now, delayed only because they had a common cause. "Why? Because *you* think it's too dangerous? Because *you* presume to judge what chances I may take and what I may not?"

"Anything worth doing carries risk," Na-chee-nal admitted. "The greater the danger, the greater the glory. But that is not why you must not go."

"Then why not?"

"Because you are not Kreste. The people will be furious at how you tricked them. They'll be screaming for your blood."

Ferro waved aside the Valad's last comment. There was a chance the people would choose him anyway, because he was the one who'd carried on in the leader's name, the one who'd kept hope alive in Chacarran hearts. Would they care who he'd been before?

Na-chee-nal would fight him every step of the way. It would be no different from anything that had gone before, since the day the Valad had appeared in Haven. Na-chee-nal had his own vision, his own purposes, which were not necessarily Ferro's. They had been useful to each other so far.

"I've made my decision," Ferro said. He was amazed at how calm he sounded, how resolute. The time for debate had passed. "I'm going back to Chacarre. I'll say I'm Kreste's representative until I get to Miraz. Then I'll tell the truth and run under my own name. The only question left to discuss," he added, "is whether you will come with me."

MIRAZ: (MIRAZ NEWS SERVICE: SPECIAL EDITION): KRESTE ACCEPTS AMNESTY, ANNOUNCES CANDIDACY! PLANS TO RETURN TO CHACARRE TO CAMPAIGN FOR HELM. Story by Druse. (Story printed on rush notice without submission to the Department of Information Services.)

Breaking his exile, Kreste sent a formal communication to the Terran Provisional Government, announcing his acceptance of the amnesty offered him and declaring himself a candidate for Helm of Chacarre. The Terran representative and negotiator, Doctorvera, held a news conference in which he read aloud Kreste's letter. For complete text, see page three.

The trip across the Channel, this time in an Islander boat, was sunny and smooth, in sharp contrast to the flight north. Sea birds wheeled and screeched overhead, mindless cries that at times sounded both joyous and tormented. Silvery fish followed in the wake of the boat, sometimes leaping above the water. Their dorsal fins caught the light like rainbow sails. In the distance, great beasts from the depths, migrating to colder waters, sent up spumes that hung in the air like cloudy pillars.

Ferro had no better sea balance than before, but he remained on deck for most of the trip. He wanted to see the first gray outlines of the Chacarran mainland emerge from the misty horizon.

Already he was beginning to find the presence of Na-chee-nal's hand-picked guards oppressive; even here on the boat, one or another of them watched his every movement. But he would gain nothing by trying to dismiss them. The journey might hold many dangers, for Kreste had enemies. The plaza news conference had all the makings of a disaster—the Terrans with their light beam weapons poised on top of the compound, the warders, armed resistance fighters, a large crowd, tense and perhaps angry, frustrated certainly, antagonistic speakers whose political careers hung in the balance. But he would have Na-chee-nal by his side. The Valad might argue every decision, but he would defend Ferro with skill and ferocity against all dangers.

The wind hummed in Ferro's ears and blew his fur about wildly. He felt himself driven by forces he could sense but not control. He could only pray to Maas, Sixth Aspect of the god, whose attribute was charisma and demonic inversion, apathy, that it was mere nervousness about the task ahead and not premonition of what could go wrong.

Ferro arrived in Miraz two days before the news conference. He came at night by railcar from Ellien, a small town on the northern outskirts, with Na-chee-nal sitting beside him the whole way, one hand clutching a knife underneath his vest, and his elite guard scattered about the car.

They arrived just after dinner time and found a hotel near the rail station. The room was dreary and cramped, in need of a good scrubbing and a fresh coat of paint. He stood at the window, opened to let out the summer day's heat, and saw only the grime-coated wall of the opposite building. Rock-doves screeched out of sight. The twilight seemed dingy.

He sighed and threw himself down on the bed. Na-chee-nal, sitting in the single chair that he'd placed by the door, grunted in sympathy.

"It is difficult for me, also, to be penned like a hamstrung plains runner," the Valad said. "I should be reconnoitering. Planning for contingencies."

Ferro's crest rippled. Reconnoitering was not exactly what he'd had in mind. "I'm not worried about getting there safely. I trust you to do that."

He ran his fingers through his crest. It felt greasy, as if it had taken on a coating of grime from the room. "The tricky part will be to hide Kreste's absence from the Terrans. They will want everything and everyone in place before the conference starts. I can meet with the negotiators and make the arrangements while posing as Kreste's aide. But eventually they will ask where he is... and I will have to tell them."

Na-chee-nal sat on the bed beside Ferro. "You will win them over. This much I know, as surely as I know the strength in my own two hands. You may not bear Kreste's name, but you are worthy of his office. I have not stayed for all these long months because I knew you to be a weakling."

Ferro, stung by the undertones in Na-chee-nal's voice, looked at him with newly awakened eyes. *He doesn't serve Chacarre, he serves me. But the part of me that might have loved him back died along with Kreste.*

Before Ferro could think of what to say, Na-chee-nal got up and returned to his own chair. He sat there, wrapped in a stiff dignity, as if he knew he had given away too much of what was in his heart.

Chapter 53

Hayke awoke on the day of the candidates' speeches with a sense of unease, an aching of the roots of his crest. It reminded him of the sudden change of season when summer had gone on too long and the first storms of autumn burst across the heavens, laden with blustery rain.

On the other side of the inn room, Alon lay curled like a child, sheets wound around his legs, one arm folded under his head and the other hanging off the side of the bed. The sun's first pale rays gilded the hair on his bare shoulder. He had grown tougher in the last few weeks and lost much of his ethereal beauty.

Hayke wondered how much Felde and Torrey had changed, all the things they'd said and done that he would never be a part of. Things that were gone forever, even as Rosen was.

Let it go, he told himself. *The Way will bring all things right again.*

Sighing, he straightened up and went to wash. When he returned, Alon was sitting up, rubbing his eyes.

"I got a message from Vera last night," Alon said, rising and stretching. "She asked me to meet with her and Celestinbellini before the speeches today. Then we'll all go sit on the stage as sponsoring dignitaries."

Hayke ruffled his crest as if to say, *You, a dignitary?*

"A bit of drama, I admit," Alon said with a sheepish gesture, "but I like Vera's idea of presenting a united endorsement of the elections. It's taken us a while to get used to the idea. Even Orsen, with all his doubts, has come around to it as the best compromise."

Hayke gestured agreement. If the people saw Alon, a hero of the resistance, standing beside the Terrans, that would answer the charges that the elections were a sham. Although he could not have said why, the idea of Alon standing on a platform in the plaza troubled him.

"I will go with you," he found himself saying.

Alon glanced at Hayke with a startled expression, then continued dressing. "All right, since you offer. You've as much right to be there as any of us."

Collaborators

The sun burned off the night's river-mist as Alon and Hayke stepped into the street and headed south. The morning's bustle had the texture of barely restrained excitement. Instead of rushing to work, people stood and talked in groups, making animated gestures. Aproned merchants swept the area in front of their shops, while flower sellers set out their wares. Over and over again, Alon heard the name, "Kreste."

The farmer's market filled the Westriver quays. Alon and Hayke passed stands laden with fruit, greens, and sugared barley, potted herbs, jars of jellies as clear and brilliant as gemstones, honeycomb, speckled eggs, dried apples, and jugs of golden brew. A fruit seller, recognizing Alon, smiled and offered him a fist-sized melon called lover's-knot, bursting with sweet juice. Alon cut it open and shared it with Hayke, as they stood at the riverside, apart from the bustle of the crowd.

Across the river, the clutter of buildings in the blocky, square-fronted style of two centuries ago, glowed softly in the morning sun. Octagon, with its towers of weathered stone, shimmered in the light, foretelling the day's heat to come.

"It's as if," Alon said aloud, "as if everything we've worked for is coming together this morning."

"I wish I could be sure," said Hayke. "I've wondered if the vision of my dream might not be something real—something that will happen today. I thought the people were dead and they were only stunned. Could it mean something even more terrible? I just don't know."

Alon glanced over at him, but Hayke's eyes were fixed ahead. Hayke said, after a pause, "I fear what it might mean."

"Sometimes, everything frightens me," Alon said quietly. He paused, then went on in a rusty voice, as if the words were too long unused and his throat had forgotten how to pronounce them. "Things that change, things that stay the same. Life itself is terrifying. The best we can manage is to try to make a little sense of it."

And to give comfort to one another, as you have given to me.

"'Why should we fear the changes that lie ahead?'" Hayke quoted the old Wayfolk proverb. "'Change has brought us everything we value'." He paused, his eyes clouding over.

"And taken it away again," Alon murmured, knowing that Hayke was thinking of his Rosen.

And he can never touch his hand, or see his face, or hope that Rosen might find a measure of happiness somewhere else.

We are not lovers. We are companions, each with our own separate loss, easing each other's loneliness.

350

Just as he and the Terran Vera were.
The thought shook him to his roots.

Chapter 54

Ferro strolled through the narrow streets of Miraz's Westbank district, savoring each moment. The ancient buildings had never seemed as graceful as now, when the morning sun cast delicate shadows from the lintel carvings. He passed intersections where the original alignment of the stones forming the corners had not been absolutely true vertical, and over the centuries the walls had settled, leaning perceptibly toward each other as if greeting their neighbors with a dignified nod. Already the restaurants had unfurled their multicolored awnings, casting puddles of tinted shade over the cobblestones.

Na-chee-nal stalked at Ferro's side and the two young guards trailed behind, snatching glimpses of the shop windows whenever they dared, exchanging secretive, gestured comments about the jewel-hued Shardian silks, translucent porcelain and glass from the Drowned Lands, the brass and silver serving-ware with intricately rendered clan emblems.

Na-chee-nal wasn't happy about Ferro's circuitous route, the length of time and exposure; he'd much rather have Ferro under roof and behind walls, and he'd said so several times already.

This is my city, the heart of my country, and that's true whether I am its leader or only one singleton citizen. Ferro did nothing as frivolous as stop to buy a sugar-dusted pastry or a citron ice. Na-chee-nal's value lay in his watchfulness, and it would be prudent not to provoke him too much. Not today.

Ferro touched the pocket where he carried the text for his speech. Once the masquerade was over, he might not be able to walk so freely in the city.

They crossed the arching bridge over Westriver, and the Terran compound came into view above the surrounding buildings. Ferro was struck by how it had changed. The last time he'd been in Miraz—when Kreste was still alive, he remembered with a shock—the compound had seemed like an excrescence, a scabby, deformed wart on the smooth paving of the plaza. Ferro had envisioned an accommodating Aspect taking a medical's scalpel and scraping it off. The image had brought him a sort of delusional comfort on more than one dreary Island night.

The growth had now taken hold, penetrated deep into the substance of the host body, elaborated with outbuildings and security barricades. As Ferro stared at it, a shiver crept along his spine, sending the fur along his crest rippling, so closely did the transformation resemble the process by which a Chacarran enclose might expand with the generations.

Or the way a cancer might infiltrate healthy tissue, until no surgeon's skill could remove it without killing the patient.

The main compound itself had been extended, like an out-thrust tongue surrounded by barricades where the warders walked patrol. This part of the compound looked new. The glossy white panels and sheets of green-tinted glass showed no trace of the weathering of the older structure. Coming closer, Ferro saw that it functioned as a transport corridor leading from the main part of the compound to a platform area. The platform extended into the open space, where an audience could surround it on three sides. The speakers would be able to travel between the platform and the security of the compound without any exposure.

And I thought Na-chee-nal was overprotective.

Safety was bought at the risk of imprisonment. Once inside, there would be no escape if things went wrong, if the Terrans changed their minds, if the offer of amnesty turned out to be a ruse.

Ferro got his first look at the watchers he had heard about. They stood in silent clusters, eyes alert, crests serene, arms crossed in the gesture of surrender. They parted to let him approach. In their presence, Ferro felt an eerie sort of calm. Even Na-chee-nal responded to it, his fur lying smoother against his skull, his posture less blatantly aggressive.

Ferro halted at the barricade and introduced himself as Kreste's representative. The Terran on duty invited him to enter, the only stipulation being a weapons search. Predictably, Na-chee-nal objected, but he capitulated when Ferro offered him the option of staying outside.

The Terran held out his hands, clearly meaning for Na-chee-nal to surrender his weapons. Hissing audibly, the Valad handed over his gun and the big knife in his belt sheath. The Terran took these and placed them in a silvery wrapping, then took a short metal stick from a loop on his belt. When he pointed it at Na-chee-nal, the Valad's crest jerked half-upright, a wedge of dark stiff hair running like a razor along his crown. The bulbous handle of the rod turned red.

"*All* your weapons, please," said the Terran guard.

"Are you accusing me of cheating?" Na-chee-nal used the Valad word for doing less than one's utmost. His crest raised to its full height, the individual hairs fanning out. He reached into his boot, drew out another knife, and then a third from inside his sleeve. Ferro, watching, felt sure Na-chee-nal had not relinquished everything. Even if he did, he would still be a formidable opponent.

The Terran placed the knives with the rest. Then, with an expressionless face, he asked Na-chee-nal to spread his arms and legs so that he could be further searched.

Na-chee-nal drew his lips back, showing his teeth. The fur on the sides of his neck ruffed out.

"Just a routine precaution," the Terran said. "For everyone's protection."

The Terran reached out one hand. Na-chee-nal hissed again, looking as if he'd like to bite it off. The Terran hesitated. Na-chee-nal's fur quivered. The air vibrated with a faint hum. One of Ferro's young guards trembled visibly, and the other looked about to faint.

Ferro didn't know whether to laugh or run. He'd never seen the Valad in outright challenge mode before. A confrontation of legendary merit was taking place right before the eyes of the Terrans. And the Terrans were missing it.

Go carefully here. Treat nothing as it seems. Remember these Terrans are not human, no matter what their outward appearance.

The watchers moved closer, still in that calm, submissive posture, without the least hint of aggression.

We see what happens here, they seemed to be saying. *We will remember.*

Ferro took a deep breath. Spectacle was one thing, but being remembered as a Nameless egotistical fool who couldn't even control his own bodyguards was quite another.

"Na-chee-nal, my friend," he said quietly. "Would you prefer that this Terran person do less than his very best for all who will attend today? How would it serve me if you impair his ability to do his duty for the sake of your pride?" He inflected the word to mean *personal indulgence* rather than *the welfare of the clan.*

After a heartbeat, the Valad gestured assent. He stood like a lump of bronze while the Terran patted the folds of his garments.

"You two," Na-chee-nal growled at the two aides, "stay out here." Fur slicked against their skulls, they gestured their obedience. The story would be all over Miraz as soon as two young guards could bring themselves to talk at all, how Na-chee-nal faced the Terrans, how Kreste the Helm found a way through the showdown. They would someday tell their grandchildren about it.

Lexis arrived at the compound in a formal mayoral convoy surrounded by warder vehicles. His own private car was followed by two others, holding a half-dozen of Ambyntet's specially selected officers. As they passed the long side of the plaza, Lexis noticed that the usual scattered groups had grown and would soon merge into a crowd. Those damnable watchers seemed to be everywhere. Their heads swiveled to follow Lexis's entourage.

A year ago, before that first riot, he would have been terrified to address even this small an audience. Now he brought up the vision of the crowd, silent and rapt, waiting for him.

"Together, we will move our city forward. Not back to the past, clinging to tradition for its own sake, but into a new and glorious future, partners to the stars, preserving what is good and obliterating what is not."

It was not, perhaps, the most eloquent of speeches. He hadn't written it and wasn't sure which of his advisors was responsible, possibly Chellen's publicist, although Lexis thought the prose rhythm too good to be his work.

No matter how well the speech might succeed, Lexis had given thought to other preparations. Early on, Ambyntet had hinted of the possibility of an "accident" that might befall Kreste. Certain poisons produced the symptoms of a heart seizure and yet left no residue. Ambyntet was skillful enough to find a way of administering them undetected, a needle ring or palm dart. Lexis hadn't asked the details.

The idea was appealing, for even if Kreste wasn't killed outright, a public display of weakness, combined with his cowardice in abandoning Chacarre, might well prove deadly to his political chances. The drawback was that should something go wrong, should someone witness the administration of the drug, should Ambyntet be suspected and accuse Lexis of complicity... no, in the end, Lexis decided the risk was too great.

Lexis had settled on another option, one that could not so easily be traced back to his offices. It would be easy enough to arrange, given the large number of people expected in the plaza and how excited they would be, some anxious, others jubilant. It would take very little to push such a crowd into outright panic. The Terrans would intervene with their light beam weapons, as they had before. In the ensuing chaos, Lexis and his warders would emerge as guardians of order.

The cars halted behind the primary structure and the guards got out first, rifles ready. A detachment of warders scanned the streets for any hint of trouble. Lexis climbed out of the car and stood for a moment, back straight and face lifted to the sun. Had it really been so long since he'd enjoyed the freedom of the open air? The brightness pained his eyes.

Ambyntet's people motioned Lexis inside, while others remained on guard at the entrance. The interior of the compound had been rearranged again. No traces remained of the old foyer and museum. Instead, Lexis and his guards entered a holding pen, caught between two sets of locked gates. A bank of lenses ran along the top of one wall. The doors appeared to be glass, but Lexis didn't doubt the material would stop pellets, even at close range.

After the brief moment of sunshine, the indoor air seemed thin and old, its life half used-up.

On the other side of the second door, Jonadamson waited. The young officer wore strips of colored fabric and bits of metal across one side of his chest, probably clan tokens.

They proceeded down the short corridor. "Is Kreste here?"

"I don't believe so." Jonadamson halted and placed his palm on a wall panel. The door slid open. The room was, Lexis noted, windowless and secure, and utterly dreary. An attempt had been made to brighten it. The chairs were upholstered Chacarran-style in fabrics of red-orange and sienna. The central table bore trays of Mirazan pastries and a vase of flowers, arranged in a style that was unusual yet pleasing, subtly suggestive of movement. Lexis studied the design, puzzled. He knew all the best florists in Miraz and this was none of their work.

A moment later, the door at the far end whispered open and three people entered. Lexis's belly twisted at the sight of Celestinbellini, talking in animated tones with two Chacarrans as he escorted them in.

Lexis blinked, recognizing the notorious head of the resistance movement. When Lexis had seen him last, Alon's skin shone beneath his fur with a pearly radiance. Now the glow had faded and his beauty had hardened, the once-sensual curves of breast and hip no longer visible through his clothing.

Alon met Lexis's gaze, but not a hair quivered. His eyes seemed unnaturally steady, like those watchers outside. The Chacarran beside him, the one with the unusual colorless fur, seemed possessed of the same infuriating stillness.

Celestinbellini inclined his body forward from the waist, his movement as graceful as the opening in a courting dance. "Welcome, Mayor Lexis. Do you know everyone?"

Bell! Lexis kept his crest smooth and his voice even. "We've met."

"Under somewhat different circumstances," Alon said.

Watching the two resistance leaders, Lexis could have sworn there was something between them. Something abnormal. They couldn't be lovers, not with Alon already paired.

Lexis felt Celestinbellini glance in his direction. He could not read the expression in those dark eyes. It could mean anything—passion, loathing, indifference, a plea for forgiveness, implacable hatred. Heart pounding through his skull, Lexis took the farthest seat. Ambyntet, silent as a shadow, slid on to the chair on the other side, while the rest of his escort stood against the wall at alert.

Just then, a Terran officer entered the room and whispered in Celestinbellini's ear.

"If you'll excuse me, gentlemen, there's a matter I must attend to," Celestinbellini said, rising to his feet. "Please make yourselves comfortable, help yourselves to refreshments, and if there's anything else you need, all you have to do is ask."

Before the first dignitaries arrived at the compound, Vera had gone back to her quarters, intending to be there for only a few minutes. While standing in the elevator tube on her way to Les Bellini's office, she had a sudden flash of insight into the efficiency limitation of the sensitizer-activator system for the focusing lasers. She'd been wrestling with it for a week now, unable to solve the non-uniform gain distribution problem. Since she was wearing formal clothing, a tailored jacket over loose-cut pants of Mirazan silk, she had no wrist link and no materials for jotting down equations. Rather than risk forgetting a crucial detail, she rerouted the tube, rushed to her room, shoved aside the piles of rumpled smocks, read-onlies, and Chacarran technical manuals, and started entering notes on her bedside terminal.

One idea quickly burgeoned into another. A heady exhilaration thrilled along her nerves as she realized that she'd solved the problems induced by uni-axial stress during crystal growth as well. Her fingers flew over the touchpad. She lost all sense of the passage of time, only the passage of ideas.

The internal link to her quarters sounded, as irritating a sound as humankind could devise.

"Damn it, later," she muttered.

Buzzzz.

Vera swore in Mandarin, a deviously nasty curse Chris Lao had taught her, and touched the link. She recognized the voice of one of the security guards posted at the compound entrance. It took her a few moments to realize what he was so upset about. Bellini had given strict orders that only the authorized speakers and their attendants were to be admitted.

The person who'd shown up in Kreste's place was not Kreste. Not only that, he was accompanied by a very large, very belligerent Valad bodyguard.

The boy at the gate was smarter than he looked, Vera thought, to call her and not Bellini, who was now—*god, look at the time!*—entertaining the other dignitaries.

"Just hold him there," she said. "I'm on my way."

It took Vera only a few minutes to reach the front doors. In a quick glance, she assessed the emissary, using every scrap of Chacarran psychology she'd figured out. He was small and neat, conservatively dressed in clan-neutral colors, and considerably more composed than his companion, whose neck ruff flared out, the individual hairs twitching slightly. A faint odor clung to the Valad, an undertone to the rancid-fat smell of his ornate vest. A sulfur compound, she thought.

The emissary proffered a letter of introduction signed by Kreste, together with the official invitation and safe passage. Not a hair in his crest quivered as she read the letter.

It took her a few minutes to go through the letter, reading carefully to make sure she understood each word. She finished and looked up. He'd been watching her. He said, "You can read Chacarran."

"Yes." *And you don't miss much.*

She motioned to the security guard and said in Terran, "Ask Commander Bellini to join us." She chose a room that had been partitioned off from the museum area, on the ground floor and convenient, yet distinct from the official reception area. It had once been a bay for spectrometers and cryogenic detectors, and Vera tended to see it still in those terms, the ghosts of the equipment that had once carried her dreams. The only seating was a couple of storage lockers. No one sat down.

Bellini walked in and glared at Na-chee-nal as if they were born enemies. Vera noted the Valad's barely contained aggression. His natural inclination would undoubtedly be to draw the largest knife he carried and lunge at Bellini, screaming in rage and delight. She wondered if the security people out front had taken all his weapons. She didn't think so.

"Did I misunderstand your message, Doctor?" Bellini said. "I thought there was a problem with Kreste's presence."

"There is," Vera said. She glanced pointedly at Ferro.

Ferro maintained his calm demeanor. "A minor matter. Kreste will not be speaking today. I will be standing for him."

"My question is whether to allow a substitution at this late date," Vera said.

"You have seen my authorization, signed by Kreste," Ferro said. "Do you challenge its authenticity?"

"For one thing," Vera said, "the invitation and amnesty offer were extended to Kreste personally. We understood that he himself would participate."

"We Chacarrans don't use such elaborate procedures. It's not unusual for one clan member to stand for another or for business contracts to be made between families, not individuals. If Kreste could have come himself at this time, he would have done so. I have complete authorization to act on his behalf."

"They've been expecting Kreste," Bellini said. "Another riot, even one we're prepared for—"

"You would make this judgment, without even knowing what my speech contains?" Ferro's voice ripped through the air.

He had, Vera realized belatedly, spoken not as himself, a mere emissary, but as someone with considerably more authority, someone accustomed to making decisions and issuing orders.

"I am responsible for maintaining order in this city." Bellini didn't seem to have picked up the shift in Ferro's diction. "We must consider the consequences of the substitution."

"Kreste has fully considered the implications," Ferro said, as if that were all that mattered.

"There's also the effect it might have on Kreste's campaign," Bellini said. "Lexis will be speaking in person, the Hoolite candidate as well. People could decide that Kreste didn't care enough to do the same. We could cancel the conference and reschedule at a time when Kreste could appear."

"No," Ferro said.

"We must remain neutral in these elections," Bellini said.

Can't the man think of something more creative to say? What's he using for brains, boiled cheese? "These people are new to the process," Vera said. "They may not realize all the factors that go into public opinion."

"*Your* factors may not be valid for *us*," Ferro said. Vera heard the heat in his voice.

"Very well, we will go ahead as scheduled," Bellini said, "with the following change. Kreste will speak last. That way, even if there is a disturbance, the rest of the program will already have been completed."

Vera sighed and nodded. It was as good a decision as could be hoped for under the circumstances.

Chapter 55

A Terran guard ushered Talense to a room within the compound, where the other dignitaries waited. He quickly assessed the group, marking the absence of those he expected to be there and the presence of those he hadn't met before. The Hoolite representative, who was to give the introductory remarks, looked as if he'd rather not be sharing the same platform with the others. He wore his elaborate enameled clan badge like a shield.

Talense gestured a greeting to Lexis and took an empty seat. He recognized the young resistance leader, Alon, and his adjutant. Hayke, that was the name. Beside Lexis sat the new warder chief, Ambyntet. Talense had met him on a dozen occasions and thought him competent if taciturn.

Celestinbellini and Doctorvera entered the room, along with a Chacarran dressed in subdued, ordinary clothes. The Chacarran looked familiar, but Talense could not place his name. Close on their heels came a Valad in traditional vest, its stitched designs blurred by years of accumulated grime.

Immediately, Talense sensed a secretive tension between Lexis and the Terran Celestinbellini. Rumor, brought to Talense's ears through Jeelan's resistance contacts, had it that they'd been lovers before Celestinbellini had been taken hostage. At the time, Talense had put it down to malicious gossip, but now he was not so sure. Not that it mattered one hair's-weight who Lexis brought to his bed. There were far more important things to worry about, like where Kreste was.

"It's time to begin." Celestinbellini motioned everyone to the door.

"Where's Kreste?" Alon said, rising.

"We cannot begin without him," said the Hoolite.

"There will be a slight change in the order of the program," Celestinbellini said. "Mayor Lexis, you'll be speaking first, after the introductory remarks." The others began filing out the door, following Jonadamson.

"I suppose he's waiting separately," Lexis said in a voice like a petulant child's. "Using what's left of his prestige for a dramatic entrance. He undoubtedly thinks he'll gain an advantage that way." He gave the Hoolite a sharp glance. "But I'm ready for him."

Talense, shivering inwardly, thought, *In more ways than one?* Notions like that seemed to pop into his mind these days, as if his thoughts no longer belonged to him. He watched Lexis lean over and murmur something to Ambyntet.

"We have made every effort to ensure that the entire election process, including today's conference, is conducted in a fair and impartial manner." Celestinbellini drew his brows together in a bushy chevron in the center of his brow.

They left the main body of the compound and proceeded down the sheltered corridor.

Celestinbellini, along with a handful of city notables and delegates from the eight clans, mounted the platform. Talense spotted several small, lensed boxes, placed high and pointed at the platform area. No doubt, Hammadi had ordered them installed to watch and record the entire proceedings.

The Terran guards ushered everyone to their seats. Those who were not to speak sat on the back row, Talense among them. He found himself behind Lexis and beside Hayke, one place over from Ambyntet. To his other side sat the big Valad. In the front row, beside Lexis, were Celestinbellini, young Alon, the negotiator, Doctorvera, and the Chacarran who was presumably Kreste's adjutant. What was his name? Ferro, that was it, a functionary from the embassy in Erlonn. The seat reserved for Kreste remained empty.

Talense felt like a harp string taut almost to breaking. The noise and the eye-blinding glare from the plaza jumbled with his questions about Kreste, the historic importance of the event, the memories of the plaza riots. Down below, warders and white-suited Terrans moved along the edge of the barricades. All of them appeared armed. He wondered if, high above him, other soldiers were tending the same light beam weapons that had so successfully put a stop to the riots.

The noise of the crowd shifted as Celestinbellini stepped to the front of the platform. The Terrans had installed a sound amplification system, which had been explained to them earlier. They had only to stand within a marked circle. Anything they said, whether shouted or whispered, would reach the entire plaza.

Talense pretended to take notes on the Terran's welcoming remarks, while keeping his eye on Lexis.

It is not the Way, Hayke told himself again with all the firmness he could muster, *to shrink from what we fear may happen.* He was here because the dream had come to him. He could feel it, like the massed heartbeats of the Wayfolk scattered in the crowd before him, like a primeval imperative. He dared not allow himself to imagine beyond the moment. The seeds of the dream had taken on their own life.

The Terran commander took his position in the speaker's circle, crisply dark against the brightness of the day-lit pavement and the mosaic of the crowd. The speech itself meant little to Hayke, empty phrases extolling the virtues of democracy and cooperation. The silence of the crowd moved him far more deeply. Like them, Hayke found himself not only listening but waiting. Waiting for Kreste, he thought, and perhaps for something more. It disturbed him that Kreste's chair on the platform remained unfilled, although he supposed that was for security reasons and that Kreste would make his appearance at the last minute.

The Terran was mercifully brief in his remarks. After a neutral introduction, Alon stepped forward into the indicated circle. He had not intended to speak formally. "It's my presence that makes a difference," he'd told Hayke earlier, "not any wisdom I might happen to utter."

But Alon did not stand there like a person who intended to say only a few meaningless phrases. He always moved gracefully, but now he held himself with such quiet dignity that Hayke could not have looked away, even if he had wished to. It was not a personal glamour, but the mysterious and inexorable unfolding of the Way.

Alon moved past the speaker's circle to the very edge of the platform. He lifted his arms as if he were going to fly out over the crowd. No one on the platform moved to stop him.

Alon began to speak. His voice, unamplified, could not have carried over the vast open space of the plaza, but the exact words didn't matter, only the unspoken bond between the people below and this single person on the platform. A sigh rippled through the listening crowd, sweet as a twilight breeze over a field of ripened grain.

Hayke blinked, looking now with more than his physical eyes. He saw the plaza like a vast field, ready for the reaping, felt the heavy-headed stalks bending in a gentle wind, yielding.

But it too rises up again.

The moment passed. Alon lowered his arms. Hayke looked out on a plaza that superficially resembled the scene a few minutes earlier, the same patchwork of colors and faces. But this time, there was a subtle difference.

Waiting...

Chapter 56

Ferro felt as if he had suddenly developed a new sensory modality and his usual perceptions had been superseded by something more powerful, encompassing. The platform embodied the world he knew—circumscribed, layered with nuance and undercurrent. In the plaza, he sensed something else, as if a wordless elemental force moved the people standing there.

Once, the raw wildness of that force would have terrified him. Now he felt exultation bordering on awe. Here on the platform were the familiar elements, the subtle shifts of alliance indicated by the distance between Lexis and the warder chief, the glances that passed between the resistance leader and the Terran negotiator, the changes in posture as the censorship chief took his seat, the flickering movement of the Hoolite's eyes, the unconscious rippling of fur. Here it mattered whether he spoke as Kreste or as himself.

But out there, in the open air, in the uncompromising light, bracketed between the glowing facades of the ancient buildings, Miraz itself took on form and intelligence. It cared nothing for his name, his clan, his alliances. Only who he was. Only what he could bring to this moment.

Bring what?

After the Hoolite delivered a short introductory speech, Lexis rose. Standing precisely in the center of the marked circle, he drew out his written speech and gestured dramatically before beginning to read. Amplified by the Terran machinery, his words thundered out over the plaza. He spoke of the pride of Chacarre, its illustrious history, its honor, and of the importance of preserving that heritage.

It was a good speech, a stirring speech. Once it might have carried them all in its wake. But the temper of the day had shifted. Surely Lexis must feel it, too. Heritage was no longer something to be preserved, but to be created, invented, realized, and not singly, clan by clan, family by family, but from the heart and very core of the nation.

Lexis wants to hold on to the way things are, out of fear that change will make them worse. Chacarre is not such a fragile thing that it must remain forever frozen in time.

Things have happened here that can't be so simply undone, all harm canceled, all blame absolved, all sins forgiven.

Out in the plaza, the crowd remained quiet, attentive. Beneath the stillness, Ferro sensed their vitality. The mood shifted from waiting into imminence.

The Terran commander spoke Ferro's name. There was a burst of protest from the other dignitaries on the platform. A few people in the forefront of the plaza cried out and surged forward, gesturing. They demanded, "Where's Kreste?"

A thrill shivered along Ferro's spine. Let them rise up against him as impostor and betrayer of Chacarran hope. But let them listen first. He would let their judgment stand—but only after the pretense was ended.

Let me be judged by what I have done, what I myself have created.

There was nothing more, Ferro reflected, that anyone could ask.

Ferro stepped to the edge of the marked circle. He felt eyes on him, not just from the crowd, but from the people behind him. Some he imagined sympathetic—Na-chee-nal, the resistance leader, Alon, and his friend. Some neutral—the censor chief, Talense, Doctorvera, and the other Terrans. Hope and suspicion from the clan delegates. A knot of coiled tension from Mayor Lexis, doubtless wondering how much of a threat Kreste really was if he must send a substitute.

Ferro gathered his thoughts, recalling the speech he'd planned. He'd never addressed so many people at once, not even in his dreams. Before Haven, he hadn't even spoken formally to smaller groups, not since he'd been in school. In the Isles, he'd avoided direct exposure, at first because he was still afraid someone would recognize him as not being Kreste, then later simply because it was the style of leadership he'd become accustomed to. Now his crest tingled, every single hair straining at its roots. His vision sharpened, as everything he saw gained new, crystal-hard edges. The immensity of the crowd, and his body's response to it, surprised him.

Ferro started slowly, as if he were beginning a conversation, gesturing with his hands, earnest but friendly. He touched the chords of tradition, of pride in a system that had not only survived but triumphed over so many crises in the past. Kreste had been part of that tradition, he said. He reminded them it was not only Kreste's personal leadership but his ability to adapt, to find new roles in changing situations, that had made him great.

"Kreste knew the arrival of the Terrans would lead to irreversible changes in the balance of international power. Even when he was caught up in events no one could have foreseen, he fought for the welfare of Chacarre. Then, when he no longer had a choice, when he could no longer act effectively here, he chose exile so that his family—all our families—would still have hope. So that the fire of Chacarre might burn somewhere, no matter how dark things might seem here at home.

"Who can truly know what that exile meant to him? Isolation? Despair?

Defiance? Who can understand the courage it took to leave not only his clan and his city, but his entire nation? To go to a far-off land, like an uprooted tree cut off from the source?

"I cannot tell you what Kreste had to give up in order to retreat to the Isles. But this much I can tell you, that in that moment of decision, that moment of sacrifice, he became more than a single individual. He became the soul of our entire race."

The people who'd cried out for Kreste were silent now. A reservoir of grief waited. A word from him would free it.

"You do not know me," he said quietly. The Terran voice amplifiers carried the harmonics of a sob in his voice. "But Kreste knew me. I was with him, by his own choosing, on the flight from Miraz. I was with him on the fisher's boat crossing the Ice Sea Channel. And I tell you that nothing— *nothing*—must stand in the way of what he gave so much to accomplish. The dream we shared—of Chacarre once more free."

The crowd's silence deepened. For this moment, they were his.

Ferro crossed his hands over his chest, as if surrendering himself to the justice of the crowd. "I am not the Kreste who left these shores. This is true. He died shortly after we arrived in the Isles. But I am the Kreste who, for all these months, has urged you to hold fast to hope. I am the Kreste who returns to you now as a choice for a free Chacarre.

"In his place, I suffered the Isles exile. In his place, I kept his dream alive.

"I come back to you now with this simple truth. I have served you in Kreste's stead, but I am not Kreste."

A stunned silence followed his words. Then someone near the front of the crowd scrambled to his feet and raised one hand, shouting, "Kreste! Kreste!"

Within instants, more people pushed their way forward. Cries of "Kreste!" intermixed with "Ferro! Ferro!" so that the two names blended into a single sound.

Ferro took a step toward the edge of the platform, toward the crowd. The time for Terran barriers had passed. He was a singleton no longer. For life or death, he belonged to them now.

When Celestinbellini announced that the final speaker would not be Kreste himself, a ripple of surprise passed through the other speakers and dignitaries on the platform. Talense felt it through the tendrils of pain that crept upwards from his breastbone along his neck and jaw. His right arm trembled, fingers curling into claws.

Collaborators

The pain will pass. It's physical tension, that's all. Just a few minutes more, and it will be over. The words in his mind carried Jeelan's intonation, his soothing rhythm.

Talense forced himself to concentrate on the events unfolding before him. He'd suspected from the beginning that Kreste might refuse to come. Kreste had no reason to trust the Terrans, and the personal risk was enormous.

A few moments later, the pain ebbed, leaving a taste like mildewed copper in Talense's mouth. His right arm felt as brittle as glass.

As Ferro began to speak, Lexis turned in his seat and gestured for Ambyntet to lean closer. The movement startled Talense.

Ambyntet must have been the one to arrange the railcar accident. He killed Kallen. This time, the voice was Jeelan's, clear and strong. It overrode the distant words of Kreste's emissary. Talense could feel his mate's presence, a hint of scent, a whisper of warmth on his facial fur. He blinked and glanced around, knowing it was impossible.

He killed Kallen. But Lexis gave the orders.

Lexis said something to the warder chief. Talense could not make out the words above Jeelan's insistent voice.

Now Lexis plots to kill Kreste. Or, failing that, his emissary. Talense! You must stop him this time!

Talense's good hand shot out, moving of its own accord, and gripped Lexis's shoulder. Underneath the expensive fabric, the flesh was soft, pulpy. Ambyntet tensed, one hand moving toward his pocket.

"I'm watching you," Talense said, pitching his voice so that only Lexis could hear him. He shifted his gaze pointedly to Ambyntet. "And I'm watching *him*."

For a moment, Lexis stared back, pupils dilating. A faint smell of overheated sulfur clung to his fur, stinging Talense's nostrils.

"I don't know what you're talking about."

Without warning, Talense felt as if he'd just slammed into a wall of silvery ice. Something hard and cold, a vise of frozen iron, crushed his chest. The pain stole his breath. The edges of his vision went cloudy. Nerveless, his fingers fell open. Lexis jerked away.

"What's this?" came a gentle voice at Talense's side. It was the white-haired farmer who'd saved him on the day of the riots, now young Alon's aide. "Are you ill, my friend?"

Talense swayed in his seat, gulping air. His heart fluttered against the cage of his ribs like a bird straining to be free. "It... will pass."

The crowd's protest subsided, listening now as the emissary continued his speech. Lexis, with a parting glare, turned his back to Talense.

Talense slumped in his seat. He swayed, caught himself with his good hand on the arm of the chair. Somewhere, pain rose and fell in waves. It seemed to belong to someone else. He took a breath and then another. There was nothing more he could do.

The moment Kreste's proxy stepped forward, Lexis's fur prickled. Something had gone wrong with his careful plans. This Ferro did not carry himself like an underling. He took the speaker's circle like a person accustomed to command. His opening comments rang through the plaza.

As Lexis listened, his crest quivered. He jumped when Ferro announced that Kreste was dead—*Dead! Kreste dead!*—and that Ferro had taken his place. *Kreste is dead.*

Jubilation surged through Lexis, tinged with an unexpected sense of relief. He had been right to wait. There was no need to resort to poison or subterfuge. He could win the election fairly, and the triumph would be all the sweeter.

During the brief, shocked pause that followed, Lexis twisted in his seat, leaning toward Ambyntet. Before he could say anything, a hand grabbed his shoulder. Talense's eyes glittered and his crest raised slightly. The edges of his teeth looked very sharp. His fur had a rank, acrid smell.

Stay calm, Lexis told himself. *There's nothing he can do here, in so public a place.*

"I'm watching you."

"I don't know what you're talking about." Lexis jerked free from Talense's grasp. He had to think, to get back into control. Lexis's heartbeat took on a feverish quality.

Then he realized the censor chief looked ill—perhaps he was ill—perhaps the stress of his position had taken its toll. Then Lexis could stall for time, let the disease take its course. If not, if he were wrong about Talense being in poor health, then a touch of Ambyntet's needle dart would be enough to silence him. Every course of action carried its own risk. Lexis couldn't decide what to do. Time, he needed time to think, to plan.

The noise from the crowd changed as people shouted out different names—Kreste, and Ferro. Some milled around, gesturing to their neighbors, pushing toward the platform. The warders at the barricades moved to meet them. The dignitaries on the platform shifted uneasily on their seats. Lexis caught a chopped-off phrase from Doctorvera, something about letting Ferro speak.

The brewing chaos rumbled through Lexis's bones. The slightest action, he thought, would ignite the crowd. It would be the plaza riot all over again. The warders were armed and ready, their emotions primed by the events of the past year. This time, however, he would not be down in the midst of it, vulnerable. Up here, he was safe. The Terrans would protect him.

On ground level, white-uniformed Terrans darted forward, their light beam weapons in hand. Above, more Terrans would be preparing the larger beam, which could sweep the entire plaza. The Terrans would have no choice but to defend the compound and everyone in it. Lexis himself could not have planned the confrontation more perfectly.

From behind Lexis came a crashing sound, sharp and sudden like splintering wood or the report of a gun.

Lexis scrambled to his feet. His chair toppled over behind him. Someone rammed into him. He shoved the person away, an instant later realizing it was the Hoolite elder. The Hoolite sprawled across Lexis's feet, almost knocking him down. Lexis spotted Talense lying on the floor, his skin like blue-gray chalk.

"Medic!" Doctorvera's voice rose above the clamor.

Ambyntet drew his gun with one hand, grabbed Lexis's arm with the other, and pulled him to the side of the platform.

With a savage roar, the Valad in the second row rushed forward, so fast his body seemed to blur. Lexis hadn't realized a person could move that quickly. The next moment, the Valad crashed into Ambyntet and carried him to the floor. His huge hand clamped over Ambyntet's gun. The warder chief twisted like a whipsnake in the Valad's hold. His legs lashed out, churning the air. His heels pounded the platform. The Valad, on top of him, bellowed in rage.

Somehow, Ambyntet got one knee up, shoved the Valad's hips aside, and wrenched the hand with the gun free.

A few of the dignitaries pushed forward, but most stood as if paralyzed. Their faces, glimpsed in a blur, looked distorted, barely human. Lexis flinched at the bright, percussive sound of a pellet gun firing.

People seemed to be rushing in all directions at once, toward the two still struggling on the floor, or else backwards for their own safety. Doctorvera crouched on the floor by Talense, her back to Lexis. He couldn't see what she was doing. Lexis caught a glimpse of Hayke, standing with young Alon. To the side, the Hoolite elder shouted for calm.

Celestinbellini rushed forward, shouting orders. He hooked one arm around the Valad's neck and hauled backwards. Lexis's heart leapt in his throat as the raw, molten power of the fight swept over him.

His eyes locked on Celestinbellini, struggling with the Valad, the bulge of his muscles through his uniform, the way his lips drew back from his teeth, the glint in his eyes. The musk of Terran sweat filled Lexis's lungs. He remembered the bruising grip of those hands, the hardness of that body, like blood-warm marble. If he died in this moment, he thought, it would be with those images imprinted forever on his mind.

The Valad managed to twist the gun out of Ambyntet's grasp. It clattered and slid across the floor. People rushed toward the two fighters. One of the Terran aides and a warder grabbed the Valad's arms. Someone started yelling in Terran.

"Murder!" someone in the crowd screamed. The cry was quickly taken up by others. "Murder! Assassin!"

The howls of the plaza crowd and the shouting on the platform blended to a roar. Lexis paid it no heed. He thought, with a sudden, fatalistic clarity, as if some other power were putting the words in his mind: *It is too late. They will never believe I'm innocent now.*

At the same time, *Everyone saw Ambyntet with the gun. Everyone heard it fire. That's what they'll remember. Now, when no one is watching...*

Lexis picked up the gun. The metal felt warm and solid against his palm. His fingers slipped into position on the firing lever. He straightened up, facing the center of the platform and beyond it, the crowd. From above, in the upper stories of the compound, yellow light beams shot out across the crowd. The scene reminded Lexis of a lightning storm—the flashes of brilliance, the rumbling thunder, but most of all, the electric sizzle in the air.

Memory surged through Lexis. He remembered the burnt-sulfur smell, blended now like an exotic perfume with the salty tang of Terran bodies and the memories of nights writhing under Bellini's hands. He swayed, dizzy. An unnamable emotion, dark and lubricious, filled his belly.

Ferro stood at the very edge of the platform, silhouetted against the brightness of the plaza. His arms stretched out as if he were poised for flight.

For a moment, watching him, Lexis almost believed it. On a day like this, anything was possible. Anything.

Without thinking, he raised the gun and fired. Ferro dropped off the platform like a hamstrung woolie.

In his mind, Lexis saw the body slamming into the pavement, and the crowd, like savage beasts, closing in on it, rending it with their teeth. He thought of hot blood, of pain and sweat, the reek of alien musk, fingers digging into his flesh, pulling him open, his own body convulsing in pleasure.

Lexis forced himself away from the sight of the plaza. He must act quickly, decisively. He must hide the gun where it would be found later, perhaps behind the seating risers. When he turned around, the first thing he saw was Celestinbellini, with his light beam weapon aimed directly at Lexis.

"Drop it."

Something sweet and poisonous spurted through Lexis, shaking him to his core. He couldn't untangle the riot of words and sensations. His body rocked with the pounding of his heart.

"I found this," someone else said with his voice. "It's evidence."

Collaborators

As he reached out to take the gun, Celestinbellini's eyes glittered, hard and opaque. Until that moment, Lexis had not realized how very alien he was.

Chapter 57

Sirens blasted the air, sending jolts of pain through Alon's skull. Beams of yellow light lashed out. He rushed past the struggling fighters to the edge of the platform. The crowd had burst through the barricades and now engulfed the warders who stood in their way.

It no longer mattered whose name the crowd shouted—*Ferro* or *Kreste* or *Alon*. These were the syllables of the moment. Something else spoke through their blended voices, a beast awakened from an ancient sleep.

Ferro stood on the edge of the platform, spreading his arms as if to take flight. At that instant, the gun on the platform fired again. But Ferro was already in motion, jumping off the edge, and the shot missed him.

Alon whirled around to see Lexis standing there. Lexis's fur stood out in indecipherable patterns, so jumbled it lost all meaning. In one hand, he held a gun and he pointed it straight at Alon.

Alon stared at Lexis and then at the gun. He felt like a grommet caught in the path of a hunter, unable to move, to even breathe. The next moment, Lexis turned away. His eyes looked blank, as if he hadn't even seen Alon.

As if he no longer saw anything at all.

From the edge of the platform, Alon looked down. He glimpsed Ferro, caught and buoyed by a dozen eager hands, before the crowd swallowed him up.

Bodies lay, tumbled and graceless, wherever the light beams had struck. In between the rows and piles, people stood bunched together. Many held on to one another. Those nearest the platform drew back, peppering the air with their shouting. A few, braver or angrier than the rest, pushed forward again.

Timas and Lorne had made their way to the front of the crowd. Timas put one hand inside his vest, gesturing angrily with the other. He shouted, over and over, "Murder! Murder!"

The Terran guards stood watching, their hands ready on their own weapons. Alon scented the temper of the crowd-beast. *Tal'deh*, rage, shimmered in the air.

Images surged behind his eyes—fallen bodies glossy with blood, the caustic burnt-sulfur reek of madness kindling everyone it touched, raging through the city...

... Octagon bathed in fire, bright blood splashing down its steps, Westbridge crashing into the river...

... a sea of people surging through the central district and then to Northhill, roaring, mindless as a whirlwind, devouring not only Terrans but everything in their path...

Someone touched him. The vision shattered. He turned to see Vera. She gestured toward the passageway leading to the compound and safety. In the faint smell of her sweat, he tasted her fear and knew it was not for herself. In that moment, he could read her as easily as the back of his own hand.

The warning siren sounded and the people in the front ranks of the crowd halted. A few of them gestured and cried out. Vera shouted something in Terran. It sounded to Alon more like a curse than a command.

People waited, but no more light beams came. The racket from the crowd died down; Alon could not understand why, but he sensed the welling calm like a physical pressure, a held breath. The plaza stretched before him like a storm-battered field. Only a scattering were still on their feet. Huge swathes marked where people lay as if dead.

The rest of the crowd crouched down, huddled like bed mice. The tang of *tal'mur*, overwhelming fear, rose up from them like an effluvium.

From the plaza, Alon heard sobs of terror. His body responded instinctively. His heart raced, and his eyes searched for a route of escape.

No! The word tore from the depths of his being. *I will not give myself over to either the madness of anger or the madness of fear. Instead, I will find the Way beyond them.*

Tal'spirë. *The state of grace.*

Without thinking, Alon brought his arms up to cross his chest. His heartbeat slowed, strong as a river. A pulse of warmth suffused his body. His fingers brushed soft curves, a lingering reminder of his pregnancy. This time, no answering grief pulsed through him, only the comfort of knowing he would carry the memory of that lost joy to the end of his life, engraved in the shape and texture of his body.

Alon's vision cleared. He caught the sullen glow that was Lexis, and Vera's sharp-edged, crystalline light. The crowd he saw as a bed of embers, ready to flare up like an inferno or die away into ashes, glowing bits of fear and loyalty, compassion and bitterness, a dozen other passions jumbled with dreams, and all of them blanketed by the demanding, reflexive response.

Tal'deh! Tal'deh!

Hayke was no longer on the platform. He had already reached the plaza; he knelt beside the nearest fallen, a student perhaps. With his new clarity of vision, Alon could see the faintest shiver of Hayke's crest.

Hayke rose slowly, brought his hands up, mirroring Alon's, and crossed them over his breasts. An instant later, other people followed him in the gesture. Somewhere in the crowd, Alon knew, Meddi and Tellem were doing the same, along with Padme and the rest of the Gathering. Birre, too, was there, his breath catching in his throat. Alon felt them all. One and then another, they raised watchful eyes to the platform.

Alon dropped his hands to his sides. A dozen thoughts passed through his mind, impulses to go down with Hayke, to confront the Terran commander, to call out to Timas and the others. Each one passed through him like the rattling of dry leaves as he waited for the Way to open.

In the pause that followed the last sweep of the plaza, Celestinbellini gave a rapid series of commands, halting the firing of the light beams and arranging for the removal of Talense's body. Within moments, Terran guards ushered Lexis and the two brawlers into the depths of the compound. Alon spared a flicker of pity for them, for he knew what would happen to them there, not from any act of cruelty on the part of the Terrans, but from their very alienness.

Silence spread across the plaza like ripples over a pond.

"... spooky.." one of the Terrans murmured to another and gestured at the crowd.

The other said, "I bet not even old Hammadi has seen anything like that!"

No, Alon thought, *you haven't. Nor have we. The old ways, the traces of our animal instincts, still linger in us, the call of* tal'mur *and* tal'deh. *But we are more than our heritage. Whatever direction we find for ourselves, it will not be yours.*

Celestinbellini, having restored immediate order, walked up to Vera and Alon. His face furrowed as he studied the plaza. "What the devil is going on out there? I could have sworn they were going to rush us."

"These people have no devil," Vera said. "And they *did* rush us."

"Something stopped them. Damned if I know what it was."

The silence in the plaza deepened as more and more people rose up, arms crossed in the posture of surrender. A wave passed through them like the sea smoothing over towers of sand. A little way into the crowd, a space opened up. Ferro stood there.

"Terrans!" His voice rang out.

With the waiting, listening part of his mind, Alon heard the rose-cream buildings along the boulevards pick up Ferro's cry and sing it back to the bronze statue of Carrel-az-Ondre, the first Helm. The rivers echoed it, the markets along the quays, and the towers of Octagon and Old Hospital.

"Terrans!" The word hung in the air, defining all of them, aliens and humans alike.

"Terrans, listen! There will be no elections! We will have no more of your alien ways! I am Helm of Chacarre, chosen as was the first Helm, over a century ago."

"I warned you," Vera said to Celestinbellini in a low voice.

Ferro raised one hand in a gesture that even the Terrans must understand. "We take our country back! We take it back now!"

For a long moment, a heartbeat, there was no answer. No one moved on the platform. Then Celestinbellini took another step forward, standing close enough to Alon to touch him.

"Come up to the compound," Celestinbellini called out, using the voice amplifier machines, "and we will continue this discussion."

Timas, standing near the front, yelled, "How do we know you mean it?" and someone else cried, "We can't trust him!"

Others shouted, "Terran slime!" or "Bird droppings!"

Alon sensed the guns out there, even if he couldn't see them. These people weren't all Wayfolk. They were followers, moved by the current of the moment. A current that could shift in an eye blink.

The crowd rumbled. Echoes of anger resonated through Alon. Any one of them could move—a shot, a volley of fists. The waiting silence would shatter. The beast within the crowd would surge to life.

Tal'deh! tal'deh! rang the ancient cry for blood. The thought made Alon dizzy.

"Come down to the city," Ferro replied, gesturing so that everyone in the plaza could understand him, "and I will talk with you."

Celestinbellini did not reply. Alon saw the close-cut hairs on the Terran's scalp as a sort of crest, primitive and mute. He smelled the salty alien tang, heard the quick, indrawn breath. A few of the others muttered words Alon could not catch but whose meaning was plain enough.

Jonadamson moved to the commander's side. Reddish blotches covered his pale skin. He stank of fear. "Sir, I can't allow—"

Celestinbellini gestured his aide away. Alon could feel his scorn of caution, his need to act before the moment passed, to match the grandeur of Ferro's leap.

The Terran commander walked to the edge of the platform and looked down, as if contemplating the drop. Down in the plaza, the beast of madness waited, bound by no more than a gossamer web.

"Anything can happen out there," Adamson said. "It's a mob situation, plain and clear. You won't solve anything if you get killed in the process."

If he dies, someone else will take his place, someone even worse. And getting rid of him will not return what I... or any of us... have lost.

"He's right," Alon said. "Anything can set these people off. The reflexes of fear and rage are too strong. It won't matter if you go armed and surrounded by your own guards or naked and alone, you will have no defense. Your light ray weapons will not help you."

Celestinbellini's eyes narrowed, alien and unreadable. Perhaps he was thinking of his time as Alon's hostage. Perhaps he was thinking that Alon, too, had been a prisoner. "If you have a better idea, let's hear it."

"You can't go down there," Vera said suddenly. Her chin lifted and her eyes blazed. "But I can."

You can die, too. Alon didn't care if Celestinbellini got torn apart or trampled into bloody bits. But he did care what happened to this one pregnant-looking, wrinkle-faced Terran.

From deep inside him, something spoke and he recognized what it was. "No," he said. "You can't go down there. But *we* can."

Together Alon and Vera made their way through the crowd. A handful of people sitting on the ground glared at Vera with sullen, ruffled crests and refused to move. Alon led her around and through the congested knots. Always, a path opened up before them.

Like water, ever to the sea... Alon thought with an inward smile.

As they moved through the crowd, there came a point where they were beyond any possible help from the compound. It was like setting to sea in a paper boat.

They halted in front of Ferro. Ferro gestured a formal greeting to Vera. She stood very still, except for the rise and fall of her breasts with her breathing, the ripple of the silky Chacarran fabric of her garment. Her mouth narrowed, as did her eyes, deepening the creases.

"Captain Hammadi believes the only way to be certain it is truly the will of the people is to hold an election," she said.

Ferro's crest stayed smooth, but his eyes glinted. "Tell your Hammadi not to waste idle breath lecturing us about Terran principles. He pretends to be concerned that we rule ourselves and then tries to impose this alien election process on us."

"The will of the people—"

"Has no meaning whatsoever here! Not even the most demented inversion of the Eighth Aspect would support such a thing! We will take our own country back, in our own way."

Restive, the crowd shifted. Few of them could hear the conversation, nor were there sufficient visible gestures for them to follow.

"We will not surrender to your Terran ways," Ferro said, "not so long as the Bird of Heaven spreads its shining wings across the sky. We are

Chacarran, even though you cannot possibly understand what that means."

You are Chacarran, Alon said silently. *You are the Helm who sent us encouragement and orders all those heartsick months. But I... I am something else.*

"For the moment, then, let us set aside the question of a Helm election," Vera said mildly.

"Why? What will be gained by postponing the elections, only to hold them later?" Ferro said with a scornful lift of his crest.

"Would it be acceptable to hold elections for other offices?" Vera asked.

Alon's fur rippled. He remembered the conversations they'd had during the negotiations for the hostage exchanges. If the Terrans could not back down, neither could Ferro. He was Helm by the consensus of the Clans; every Chacarran in the plaza had felt it and knew the irrevocability of that fact.

Alon said, "The post of mayor of Miraz will be open."

"Whose side are you on?" Ferro's crest snapped up, then subsided.

"How have the mayors of Miraz been.." Vera hesitated delicately, "*traditionally* selected?"

"Sometimes the office passes dynastically within a clan," Ferro answered. "Other times it changes. There's no single fixed procedure."

"So there's nothing in Chacarran law or custom to *exclude* elections?"

"It's an unusual method, true." Ferro looked unhappy. Alon watched him weighing whether to press the issue or save his breath for more important arguments.

"If the Terrans are willing to back down on the issue of the Helm, why not give them this?" Alon said. "The office is vacant. There will have to be an investigation. We all saw Lexis with a gun in his hand."

"I'm willing to discuss it," Ferro said. "That is, if your Captain Hammadi would agree to cease his interference and acknowledge our own Helm."

Vera's shoulders hunched. "Let it stand as a proposal, the first of many I will take up with the captain."

That seemed to satisfy Ferro, at least enough to agree to a time and place to meet. Vera extended her hand, Terran-style. Ferro ignored it, but he gestured formal agreement.

All around them, people scrambled to their feet, embracing their neighbors. Their voices sounded happy and excited. Some pushed their way toward Ferro, shouting. Others burst out singing. They cared nothing for specifics; all they knew was that their Helm had met the Terran on his own Chacarran terms. Chacarre had won.

Chapter 58

MIRAZ: CITY MOURNS DEAD. Report by Druse.

Leave-taking rituals were held in Miraz Plaza today for the Chacarrans killed during the riot that followed the news conference earlier this week. In a special ceremony featuring both Chacarran and Terran eulogies, thousands came to honor the six who died. All but one of the deaths, according to medical workers, were directly attributable to the effects of the Terran light ray weapons. Among the dead was Talense-az-Mestre, of the Interclan News Agency. The cause of his death is under warder investigation.

Terran commander Celestinbellini, who yesterday formally surrendered his title to the new administration headed by Ferro-az-Kerith, offered a public apology on behalf of his race.

"The stun setting was designed to be harmless," Celestinbellini said, "and it was applied with the intention of preventing a greater loss of life. In our best judgment at that time, any alternative course of action, including that of simply doing nothing, would have resulted in even more casualties. However, we accept full responsibility for the consequences of its use and deeply regret this tragedy. On behalf of myself and the United Terran Peacekeeping Force, I offer my most sincere condolences to the families of the deceased."

MIRAZ: ALON ELECTED MAYOR. MIRAZ WARDERS PETITION FOR RETENTION OF TERRAN SPY UNITS. Details at 10.

MIRAZ: LEXIS FACES MURDER CHARGES. Report by Lansky. Former Mayor Lexis, already in custody under investigation of the death of

Department of Information Services Director Talense, now faces charges stemming from the death of former Warder Chief Kallen. Mayor Alon's special investigative unit yesterday received documents implicating both Lexis and Warder Chief Ambyntet in the supposed 'accident' that resulted in Kallen's death six months ago.

MIRAZ: TERRANS TO DISMANTLE COMPOUND!!! Report by Druse. Terran spaceship captain Hammadi announced today that his forces will withdraw from Chacarre, beginning next month. Central to this action is the complete dismantling of the compound in the plaza. The United Terran Peacekeeping Force has agreed to repave and repair as much as is needed to restore the plaza to its original condition.

As part of the terms, the nation of Chacarre and the city of Miraz granted the Terrans permission to establish a small ongoing presence. In a separate treaty with the nations of Erlind and Valada, the Terrans have agreed that no alien weaponry of any kind will be permitted.

The Terran embassy will be housed in a suitable structure, equivalent to that of any other official embassy representation. Security will be provided by Miraz warders. Each of the Terrans nominated for the embassy must be interviewed and approved by a council of clan representatives.

Negotiations concerning the disposition of the Terran surveillance units, popularly called "spy mushrooms," are still underway. The warders have petitioned Ferro's office to be allowed to maintain the units for crime deterrence.

It is believed that hundreds of small arms, imported into Miraz by resistance fighters, are still at large. The newly-formed Terran Friendship League has publicly called for an armed Terran force to protect Chacarre in the event of another Erlind invasion.

MIRAZ: AMBYNTET INDICTED, MURDER CHARGES DROPPED AGAINST LEXIS FOR INSUFFICIENT EVIDENCE.

On a bright Mirazan midday, the sun cast softly dappled shadows through newly leafed branches. A couple walked with their arms around each other's shoulders, absorbed in each other, their voices like the cooing of water-doves. A child carried a balloon in the shape of a Terran space ship. Two Terrans stood guard outside the house where Kreste had once been held, their eyes alert and weapons ready. People sauntered by, wearing light spring colors. Some stared curiously at the Terrans, for these were the last aliens they might ever see. Within a few days, they would all be gone, for how long no one knew.

Lexis walked up to the entrance and paused. Except for the watchful stare of the Terran guards, no one took any particular notice of him. He wore an ordinary, slightly drab tunic and leggings. He'd sold or given away his costly robes. His clothes hung on him, accentuating his thinness. He lived simply, from one day to the next.

After the charges against him were dropped, he'd moved back into his parents' apartment. At first, he did whatever work was needed. Recently, the baker had asked him to help in the shop, so now Lexis spent his days surrounded by the aromas of nut butter, caramel, and whipped honey. Yet the flavors eluded him. Everything tasted like dried straw.

As Lexis stood there, a breeze sprang up. It carried a subtle mix of fragrances, early blooming skyflowers, pungent daffies, sweet cooking spices, cloves, and chiroseth.

Through all the long winter, there had been not a word from Celestinbellini. Then, as the ice broke and thawed, the Terrans announced their plans to leave. Forever, presumably, or for long enough it made no difference.

A few had chosen to stay behind.

When Lexis had read the news story, he felt a surge of something hot and urgent, the closest thing to arousal since Bellini had last held him.

Surely he will come to me again.

Now the compound was gone, the pavement smoothed over by Terran machines, leaving only a faint, rough discoloration that a few winters would erase. Almost all the aliens had shuttled up to their space ship. Celestinbellini arrived in Miraz that morning, spent it in the mayor's offices with Alon-az-Thirien, and then came here, to this house that had been given over for the use of Doctorvera.

Lexis waited, bony shoulders hunched against the balmy day. He ran one hand over his skull, but his crest would not lie smooth. His skin felt hot, as if he burned inside.

The door opened and the Terran guards came to attention. Celestinbellini appeared on the threshold, talking to someone who stood in the shadows. Doctorvera, presumably. Lexis remembered hating her once, resenting her. Now he felt nothing.

Collaborators

The Terran commander's uniform shimmered in the spring light. Watching him, Lexis thought, was like seeing a poem, each syllable a movement, captured for the instant and then forever gone.

Celestinbellini started down the street. Lexis stepped forward, to be blocked by the guards.

"Please, I must speak with you."

Celestinbellini motioned the guards back. His nearness pierced Lexis in a flash of heart-breaking beauty. Lexis's knees melted.

"Let's go inside," Celestinbellini said. "There's a private room we can use."

Hope flaring, Lexis followed him into the house. It was cool, the entrance area lit only by the slanting light from windows in the stairwell. He expected to find the house filled with Terran oddities, machines, and alien intrusions, but there were none. The place was utterly ordinary by Chacarran standards. The room off the entrance area was small, its furnishings worn but comfortable. He lowered himself to a padded bench.

Celestinbellini sat on the edge of a chair with frayed tapestry covers. He leaned forward, elbows resting on his knees, hands moving in fretful circles. "I wanted—I intended to say goodbye to you. There were always too many things to do. You know how it is."

Lexis found his voice. "You're leaving."

"I'm going home," Celestinbellini said, with that peculiar bobbing of the head. Lexis no longer found it strange; only this morning, he would have given anything to see it again. "I'll miss this place."

"And me?"

"We had a good time together. I won't deny that. I'd have liked there to be more of it. But things... things happened."

Lexis waited a heartbeat, then another. To steady himself, he held on to the bench frame so hard that his finger joints cracked with the strain. His throat felt swollen with all the things he dared not let out. But there was no more time, no other chance. He might never see Bel again after this moment. There were too many things unsaid in his life.

"To me, it was more than a good time."

Celestinbellini stared at him, oval eyes opaque. His eyes flickered to Lexis's belly. Lexis thought he was wondering if he might be pregnant. For the first time, the idea didn't repulse him. Instead, he felt a flicker of sadness that it had never been possible.

"No, not that," he said. "But I am bound to you in ways I can't describe. I *belong* with you. I want to go with you."

"I'm sorry, that's out of the question."

"I will die if you leave me," Lexis said. "Can't you see I'm dying already?"

"You feel shitty now, but you'll get over it. Take my word for it, nobody ever died from unrequited love."

Trembling, Lexis reached into his tunic pocket and drew out a folded paper. Celestinbellini opened it and read it slowly, mouthing the Chacarran words silently.

"It's a poem, isn't it? And you wrote it?"

Lexis nodded, using the Terran gesture.

"I'm no expert on these things, even in my own language." Celestinbellini let his breath out. "It's... it's beautiful."

"Please," Lexis struggled to keep the begging out of his voice, "take me with you."

Celestinbellini slapped his thighs and got to his feet. He took a stride towards the door, then paused and looked back. "It's not up to me, you understand. You've been a subject in a criminal investigation. People—my superiors—will claim you used our relationship to get out of a bad situation here."

"I can't undo what's been done," Lexis said. "Any of it, even this. The bond was forced on me. I never chose it. It happened before I realized it."

Celestinbellini came to stand next to Lexis. He put his hand on Lexis's head, ran his fingers over the jutting crest. "Poor soul. Just like that farmer who poured medicine down my throat, thinking it would help. Stuff damned near killed me. I'm not sure it's good for any of us to have so much to do with each other."

Lexis laid his face against Celestinbellini's leg. The fabric of the uniform was cool and slick, the muscles underneath hard. The rhythmic touch on his hair reached into his core. Something loosened inside him. His breath came in a sob.

"I'll ask the captain if you can travel with us as a representative of Chacarre, maybe a native poet. I owe you that much. Of course, you may change your mind and curse me when we arrive on Terra and you're the object of fanatical public interest. Don't say I didn't warn you." He moved away. Lexis swayed as if he would faint.

"There can be no personal relationship between us, you understand? That's over and done with. I never promised you anything." Celestinbellini held out the paper. "Impressive as this may be, it changes nothing."

"I understand." *I understand more than you know.*

Lexis closed his eyes, knowing what would come next. Hammadi would say no. Lexis had spoken with him enough times over the Terran linkage devices to be sure of it. Celestinbellini would let the matter go without protest, secretly glad it was out of his control. Lexis himself would watch the night sky, searching for the dot of brilliance that was no longer there.

He would not die. He would want to, yearn to, but he would not. He

383

thought of the other poems, left back at the enclose, the way the words flowed from the pit of his soul and on to paper in intricate, perfectly balanced designs. There would be more over the years, whole cycles of them stemming from the hurt that would never heal. They were good, far better than he ever dreamed he could produce.

No, they were great. They would outlive him. He would have everything he thought he wanted—fame, immortality, respect—except for the one thing most desired.

Hammadi stood at the window and looked out over the city. He wished he could somehow pass through the window and experience the city, touch it, feel it, smell more than the tantalizing whiff he'd caught between the shuttle and the embassy. From here he could see the expanse of the plaza, sunlight on the bronze statues, the rows of trees with strange names, the rose-cream buildings, the twin rivers stretching like silvered ribbons, the arching bridges, the sky that unearthly shade of blue. Across Westriver, Octagon Temple rose above the quayside trees, its towers like bleached marble.

This was his first and last chance to see Miraz. He'd waited until the repairs on *Prometheus* were complete, every detail double-checked, every pre-flight test run. Even now, his visit had been accompanied by the greatest secrecy and security.

He turned his head. Vera stood just inside the door, hands behind her back. She was wearing a two-piece outfit of soft, nubby material, dull gold trimmed with geometric patterns embroidered in black and orange. It was a native design, curiously flattering. Or maybe she'd lost weight and gained muscle tone from her months planetside.

"It's a beautiful city," he said. "We must have had places like this a few centuries ago. Will you be sorry to leave?"

"I'd like to stay here."

"I thought your passion was studying the birth of stars," he said. "You can hardly do your spectroscopy here."

"My passion, as you put it, has always been science." As she spoke, she lifted her hands and gestured with them, complicated patterns woven in the air like sign language.

"Science isn't about measuring things. It's about asking questions, about asking what the answers mean, about getting inside the heart of the universe. About being alive and human. Physics was just a key to worlds beyond my wildest imagining. The mathematics turned my head inside out, like learning to think in a dozen new languages at once. I'd work and work and nothing would make sense, and then something would click and I'd never see things the same way again."

Hammadi heard the excitement behind her words. He'd seen that fever in her eyes before. He knew better than to try to talk her out of staying. He hadn't realized until that moment how much he'd miss her.

"Chacarre is like that," she went on. "Since I've been here, I've had to question every assumption, every habit of thought and procedure. I've have to look into myself as well as outside. I'm greedy. I want to make the most of what's left of my life."

The city, rose and ivory and yellow-green, silver and blue, blurred in Hammadi's sight. Vera had never talked to him this way before. He suspected she'd never talked to anyone quite like this. It was as if she'd taken him inside her private world, not the sophisticated scientist, but the woman.

"It will be years before another ship arrives," he said. *Think what you're doing. This isn't a field trip. It's a life sentence.*

Vera's face wrinkled into a grin that started at her eyes and kept going. He'd seen her smile so rarely, he hardly recognized her. Gone were the hard edges, the electric crackle.

"Oh, yes," she said. "I have no doubt I won't live to see it. But my ideas will. Like children who've grown up and left home, they'll mutate over the years, becoming mine no longer. Isn't that the goal of intellectual inquiry? To connect ourselves with each other, with the world, with the universe? To become, as the poet says, a stream in the river of time?"

All the way back to *Prometheus*, Hammadi found himself envying the captain who would return to see what Vera's legacy had become.

Epilog

Twilight softened the Miraz skyline and lights marked clusters of houses, jewel-strung lines of streets blurred by softly falling snow. Alon stood at his bedroom window, watching the transformation from light to darkness to light again. Behind him, the mayor's mansion lay quiet except for the muted bustle of the house staff, clearing away the dinner party debris.

Another sound focused his attention, footsteps he knew as intimately as the beating of his own heart.

"You're still here." He turned to face Birre, who hesitated at the doorway.

"Should I go?"

"Go where?"

Birre stepped into Alon's arms. He still felt fragile, with an inner core of tension. Alon recognized the same wariness in himself, no matter how relaxed he might be outwardly. He wondered if either of them would ever be free of it.

Birre laid his head on Alon's shoulder. He wanted to stay the night, Alon knew, but he couldn't ask. They hadn't talked about it since spring, when the Terrans had shipped the last of their forces up to their orbiting ship. The pressure of dealing with Birre's anxieties had been more than he could bear. That argument had ended with Alon demanding they keep separate quarters, himself here in the mayor's mansion, Birre in his family's enclose. At the time, Alon believed it was for Birre's sake, that Birre wasn't yet ready to leave his family.

He remembered the first time they'd made love since their reconciliation, the way Birre clung to him and whispered, "Please.." and then, "I'm sorry, I'm sorry."

We keep trying to make things the way they were, even as we make sure that will never happen. There is not one of us who has not—by our actions or by our silent acquiescence—collaborated to bring this new world about.

Birre's fingers tensed on Alon's arms. Alon felt his silent pleading as a ripple of physical pain. Gently Alon kissed the curve of Birre's neck. He would not send Birre away, not again, not when so much else had been taken from him. He had no choice; they were mated for life. Just as he had no choice to be Chacarran and Wayfolk, to be who he was, to raise his voice for a new vision of what might come from the ashes of the past. The Faith had the right image for it—the Bird of Heaven, ever Burning, ever renewed.

Like water, ever to the sea.

Fire and water. Hope and death. Terra and Chacarre. They would survive.

Hayke and his children met Vera at the railcar station in the village. Although she'd enjoyed the journey from Miraz, her body was sore and aching, claiming its age. During the trip, she'd made notes in her journal, enjoying the sensual pleasure of writing with ink on real paper. The journal was from a stationer's in Miraz. She had dared not keep even a handheld computer, although the technological evolution on this planet had been thoroughly disrupted already. She wrote in Chacarran sometimes, at others in her own language.

Demmerle was a lovely region, hills that reminded her of southern France with their sprawling orchards and fields rippling in shades of palomino gold and brown. The villagers themselves had been polite but curious, pulled one way by their fears and another by their reflexive, protective response to her pregnant appearance. This no longer bothered her; she could imagine a time when its absence would seem strange.

After dinner, eaten on the porch as the sun dipped behind the hills and the earth exhaled waves of heat, they carried blankets into the fields. Hayke had been harvesting hay, and the stubble gave off a sweet, musty smell.

Vera lay back on her blanket, watching the last milky light fade from the horizon. The constellations looked almost familiar, even their names: the Archer, the Water-Dove, and the Serpent, which Wayfolk called the Grommet.

Torrey, as restless as any student she'd ever known, excused himself after a short while. Hayke explained he was courting with the neighbor's oldest, Adso. "Still playing at it, not knowing what they're getting into."

"Do any of us, when we first love?" Vera said.

Hayke laughed. "It will be a good match. They've known each other since they could walk."

He paused, looking east, and Vera imagined he might be remembering the invasion from Erlind, the fear and the running, the destruction of Verne's house and barn. Alon had told her a little of that story, enough for her to feel its echoes in her own people's history.

"And little Felde?" she said. She felt the rustle of straw as the child sat up, listening.

"He's no farmer," Hayke said. "He wants to study music in Miraz. Alon's offered to sponsor him."

Silence deepened. The smell of the earth turned cooler and richer. From a nearby hedgerow, a bird began singing, a lilting three-tone melody. Another answered, a variation of the song, as if it had been imperfectly learned and then passed on. For some reason, it made Vera think of Sarah. She still kept the stuffed animal with her few personal possessions. A tear slipped down her face. She reached up to brush it away and then realized that even if Hayke saw it, he would not understand.

These people do not cry.

Never since she had decided to stay in Chacarre had she felt so very much alone.

As if in answer, Felde lifted his reed flute and began to play. The notes flowed from one to the other, filling the night air. Sometimes Vera thought she heard a fragment of a familiar lullaby, then a Greek *hasapiko*, then a free-tone poem. Each phrase built to the next, connected and whole. It was the most beautiful thing she'd ever heard. She would gladly have died in that moment, with that joyous sound in her ears.

I will end my life here, on this planet, and perhaps someday some other crazy old Terran-born woman will sit on this very field and listen to music like this. Perhaps we will even make music together.

The thought filled her with a peace beyond words.

The End

Appendix I: The Faith

Aspect	Name	Tone	Color	Attribute	Inversion
1	Sotir	ur	yellow	loyalty	blindness
2	Kesh	chee	orange	endurance	cancer
3	J'	san	red	joy	infection
4	Hool	rai	purple	fertility	starvation
5	Bavar	dol	blue	hope	natural disasters
6	Maas	ma	green	charisma	apathy
7	Oni*	soo	white	Old: vitality New: victory	sterility
8	Fard (The Prophet)**	heh	black	change	insanity

    * Oni was once thought to be the final Aspect of the god, hence the old usage, "Seventh Name", meaning "Ultimate".

    ** Fard was a historical figure who was incorporated as the embodiment of the Eighth Aspect. A few Fardites believe this to be an incorrect interpretation of the Prophet's teaching, the need to unify the seven sects into one monotheistic faith.

Bonus: World-building in *Collaborators*

"Once Upon a Time, in a City Far, Far Away . . ."

Every story has a beginning, not just in the text itself but in the mind of the writer. Sometimes we begin with an image or a phrase that's so evocative, so mysterious and compelling we just have to find out what it means. At other times, a character will pop up and demand that her story be told. Or we'll look at something quite ordinary and wonder, "What if?" What if this were different or that happened at another time? What if the rules of physics worked in ways at odds with accepted reality? What if magic-or vampires, or angels, or superheroes-shaped the world?

In this case, my story began with a place. A city. Not any city, one specific city. My family and I had an opportunity to live in France for about nine months.

We arrived in Lyon in January 1991, shortly after the beginning of the first Gulf War, and none of us knew quite what to expect. We were nervous, being Americans abroad at such a tense time. It was (by California standards) bitterly cold, the streets covered with ice and slush. I had a little high school French, very rusty, and I'd injured my back before we left, but I went out every day, getting the kids enrolled in school, finding out where to buy bread (the corner *boulangerie*, of course) and when Rhône Accueil, a sort of international welcome gathering, met. We had some pretty dreadful days when everyone was sick and not adapted to the cold or to the French way of doing things. But with patience and open minds, we settled in. My older daughter attended a private bilingual school, where she was something of an exotic celebrity, coming from California, and the younger one soon made herself at home at the *école maternelle* (and came home chattering in French). I wrote every day, working on the revision of *Northlight*.

The snow melted, the sun warmed earth and air, the little garden of our house blossomed with spring flowers, and the city, which had seemed cold and distant, opened its arms to us. I suspect the hospitality had always been there, but it took us a while to come to a place of mutual appreciation. I also suspect that the improvement in my French, coupled with my willingness to "adapt myself" to French customs, opened many doors for me. The Lyonnais were intensely proud of their city and eager to tell me all about it.

Collaborators

And what a city it was! Situated at the confluence of the Rhône and Saône Rivers, Lyon was once called Lugdunum, the capital of Gaul. Later it became a hub of the medieval silk trade, a center of culture and commerce, and finally the heart of the French resistance to the Nazi occupation.

Our house stood on the western hill, where the Romans built their fort overlooking the peninsula where the two rivers flowed together. Everywhere in our neighborhood, I'd come across Roman ruins—from the amphitheatre still in use for summer concerts to bits of aqueducts and baths. Below us lay the *Vieux Quartier*, where people lived and worked in buildings that dated from the Renaissance. The cathedral, St.-Jean, was begun in the 1080s, took 300 years to complete, and is still in active use. In its courtyard, I found fragments of a 4th Century Christian church, and believe that the site was used for a much older pagan temple. Although I'm not Catholic, I attended Mass from time to time (in French, of course) to experience the millennium-long continuity of faith practice. As an American, I had little experience with buildings or artifacts older than a few centuries, and very few of those were still being used as they had been originally intended. And, of course, St.-Jean was *the* place to be seen, to meet people, and to make connections.

As I explored the city, either alone, with Anglophone friends from Rhône Accueil, or with my family, I was repeatedly struck by how history permeated every aspect. Some buildings showed damage from cannon balls during the French Revolution. Plaques marked places where citizens were executed by the Nazis or Jewish families were deported. Because the buildings in the older areas form solid blocks, passageways called "traboules" permit public access and many of them date back to the Renaissance, when they allowed silk merchants to transport their goods without getting wet on rainy days. "We French seek to preserve our patrimony," a Frenchman said to me, "but you Americans seek to create yours."

After visiting the tiny *Musée de la Résistance*, I became interested in how many varied ways the French responded to the German occupation. Some protested from the very beginning for religious or ethical reasons, but others went along, whether from fear or apathy or entrenched antisemitism, or simply because the war did not affect them personally. Yet others sought to exploit the situation for personal power or financial gain. Some became active only when their lives were affected.

I was so intrigued by the complexity and range of responses, the idea of stayed in my mind even when I returned home. When my older daughter and I returned to Lyon in 1994, the old *Musée de la Résistance* had been replaced by a modern museum in the building that had once been used by the Gestapo. The new exhibits gave me even more information. My daughter and I visited the village of Le-Chambon-sur-Lignon, featured in the documentary film, *Weapons of the Spirit*. The Protestants of this village, no strangers to persecution themselves, saved thousands of Jewish children by smuggling them into Switzerland and, when asked why they risked their own lives, replied simply that it was the right thing to do.

I knew then that I had to tell this story. Because I'm not a writer of history or historical fiction, but of science fiction and fantasy, I would tell it in the genre I knew. I would set my tale on an alien planet, in an alien city... but one that I loved even as I had come to love Lyon.

Bonus: Add Some Characters

The central inspiration for *Collaborators*—that individuals respond in a variety of complex and contradictory ways to a situation of occupation and resistance—immediately suggested many types of characters: the rebel, the idealist, the opportunist, the political player, the merchant willing to sell to anyone if the profit is high enough, the sadist who exploits the powerlessness of others for his own gratification, the ambitious person who doesn't care who his allies are, the negotiator, the peace-maker, and the patriot.

These are all interesting roles, offering scope for compelling confrontations, but they are not in themselves *characters*. They're slots into which characters might fit at any given time, as those characters progress along their own life story arcs. The temptation is to take such a slot, insert a character, and then have him behave in that way and only in that way throughout the story. This is the classic "spear-carrier" persona, whose only function is to come onstage, carry his spear (or throw it, or make a speech, or die in some plot-appropriate way), and then disappear. He might have a few warts or wrinkles or a bit of backstory, but only in service to his predetermined *function*.

Effective characters work in just the opposite way. They go about their lives in their idiosyncratic ways, with their own histories and families, dreams and neuroses. Interesting as these might be, they do not in themselves constitute a dramatic plot, only a series of linked episodes. Then something— whether it's an internal event like a new goal or an external one like an invasion by a space-faring race—catapults the character into a dramatic course of action. The overall problem/crisis/goal informs and shapes the character's choices, but at the same time the character—her personality, history, viewpoint, relationships—drives the action in a unique way. So I needed to find out who some of these characters were, both alien and Terran, throw them into an escalating situation, and see what they did with it.

One of the first characters to speak to me arose from an unexpected source. I never knew either of my paternal grandparents, for both had perished in the lawlessness and pogroms in Ukraine shortly after the first World War. My father told me about how his mother ran a bookstore that was the center of intellectual (and revolutionary!) thought in their village, how, when that village was destroyed, she kept her two children alive as they wandered the countryside for two years, going from one cousin's house to another but never staying very long. He spoke of her courage, her idealism, and her unfailing love. Some piece of her, or her-as-remembered, stayed with me, and I wondered if I could create a character with that strength and devotion to her children. I began to write about Hayke, who opens the book as he lies in a field with his two children, gazing up at the stars and wondering what these star-people might be like. Hayke had other ideas about what his life was like besides merely following in my grandmother's footsteps, and everything changed once it became clear to me that the alien race—the Bandari—were gender-fluid. Hayke, like my grandmother, was a widow (using the term generically to include both sexes), and one of his children was born of his own body, but the other of his dead spouse's, and he told me he felt an especial tenderness for the latter child.

The other Bandari announced themselves as the story line took shape. Alon and Birre, the young lovers, presented a wonderful way to bring the reader into the world of how Bandari form families, with the added dimension that they come from different religious traditions, so there are conflicts not only between the native race and humans, but even within the pair-bonds of the characters. As events proceeded, with the cycle of violence escalating, each became radicalized in a different way, according to my initial concept that not only do people respond in a variety of ways, but their perceptions and decisions change with experience and evolving circumstances.

Even though the ground action takes place in an area roughly the size of Western Europe and most of the characters live or come from Chacarre, I didn't want all the national territories to be the same. I wanted differences in language, dress, attitudes toward authority, etc., between Chacarre and its rival, Erlind, and also within Chacarre itself. Every once in a while, a new character would surprise me, like Na-chee-nal with his "barbarian" vigor and his smelly woolen vest, or Lexis, the dangerously repressed academic poet.

The Terrans presented a different challenge because in many ways, they were more homogeneous than the Bandari. They inhabit a single spacecraft and although there is a natural division between crew and scientific personnel, for the most part their goals are shared and their hierarchies are well-defined. Left unchecked, that's a recipe for boring, so I added some friction, a few divergent motives, a highly stressed environment... and into this walked Dr. Vera Eisenstein, genius. Most of the inspiration for her character came from the women engineers and physicists I'd gotten to know (thank you, Society of Women Engineers!) with a touch of Dr. Richard Feynmann thrown in. She doesn't play by anyone's rules, she cares far more about science than diplomacy, she's simply too good at what she does to disregard, and her mind never stays still. I had a ball cooping her up in the infirmary and watching what kind of trouble she'd get into, but I didn't realize at first that she would become a pivotal character, one capable of acting for the greatest good despite the depth of her loss. I'd been thinking about her passion in terms of science, not in terms of her capacity for love nor in terms of her ruthless commitment to understanding everything she sees around her, whether it is a problem in laser spectroscopy or alien psychology or the nature of her own grief.

Bonus: Designing a Gender-Fluid Race

As the concept for *Collaborators* took shape, I realized that one of the key issues was power: power that comes from advanced technology, power that comes from military superiority, power that comes from idealism, power that comes from love, power that comes from political advantage. But also and especially, power that relates to gender. In fact, I don't think it's possible to address the issues of power without talking about gender.

People—that is, we Terran-humans—often confuse gender, sex, and sexual orientation. Sex identification arises from biology, and most of us are either male or female genetically and phenotypically. That is, we possess either XX or XY chromosomes, and our genitals conform to the norm. These are not the only possibilities (you can have XXX or XXY, for example) and problems arise from the societal demand that every person fit into one or the other category. This has nothing to do with "masculine" and "feminine," which are cultural interpretations, or with who a given individual is sexually attracted to. The binary division of male and female, while appropriate for many people, does not work for everyone.

Gender, on the other hand, has to do with how you experience yourself, a personal sense of being a man or a woman (or both, or neither). Each of these is distinct from sexual orientation, which has to do with an enduring physical, romantic, and emotional attraction to another person. Gender has been described as "who you want to go to bed as, not who you want to go to bed with."

A few years ago, I attended a workshop at the Ben Lomond Quaker Center on "Gender, the Search for Self, and the Search for Acceptance," facilitated by Chloe Schwenke, an ethicist who is herself a transgender woman. Although much of the workshop centered on personal issues of gender and identity, it struck me that as a writer, I discover much depth and richness by asking the same questions.

In science fiction and fantasy, we have been playing around with such notions as more than two sexes/genders, none, fluid sexes/genders, and a diversity of gender role expressions. Every so often, a story that takes a new or not-new-but-splashy look at the field garners a lot of buzz, particularly in the queer and queer-friendly community. Yet much genre writing continues to perpetuate the world view of two oppositional and fixed genders, each with equally unyielding behavioral expectations. For many writers and readers, a character or society that goes too far outside the familiar becomes so uncomfortable as to fracture sympathetic identification. It strikes me, however, that even within the limitations of conventional portrayals of sex and gender, we can reach for greater depth. We can go beyond the Caveman Model of Gender Roles, the Separatist All-Men or All-Women Worlds, the Rambo-in-Drag/Supersensitive Male dichotomies and other variations already done to death.

To give you an idea what I'm talking about, here are some questions from the workshop. I've rephrased them to apply to characters, rather than personally.

- How does your character know "what" that person is? What feelings, sensibilities, and other forms of awareness (other than simple body awareness) most make that person feel male, female, or somewhere in between?
- Can you describe your character in non-gendered terms?
- Does gender influence the spirituality of your character? How?
- Has your character experienced a dissonance between what is expected and what was felt internally? How does the character deal with this tension? How does the character's sense of integrity and honesty affect the response?
- How does this character (and the surrounding culture) consider the issues of equality and fairness between the masculine, feminine and androgynous?
- How does the character's experience of gender affect the perception of the Divine, either within or outside the cultural norm?

In writing *Collaborators*, I wanted to create a resonance between the tensions arising from First Contact and those arising from differences in gender and gender expectations. It seemed to me that one of the most important things we notice about another human being is whether they are of "our" gender. What if the native race did not divide themselves into (primarily) two genders? How would that work biologically? romantically? socially? politically? How would it affect the division of labor? child-rearing? How would Terran-humans understand or misinterpret a race for whom every other age-appropriate person is a potential lover and life-mate? Not only that, but in a life-paired couple, each is equally likely to engender or gestate a child.

For the sake of linguistic simplicity, I adopted the convention of using the masculine pronoun as the generic universal for my alien race. I wrote this story in 1992-1994. Today I might make a different choice.

Bonus: More on Designing a Gender-fluid Race

We humans tend to think about gender as binary, and the concepts of fluidity (changing from one to the other, not necessarily once but perhaps many times during a lifetime) or being both male and female (or neither) are fairly recent additions into conventional public discourse. Fluidity is not the same thing as being transgendered (which is where a person's gender—their identity—and their sex—their biological/genetic category) are not the same. Both are different from sexual orientation, which has to do with attraction to another person. All too often, if a species that does not fit into the female/male division is portrayed in media, they're shown as sexless, not only androgynous but lacking in sex drive.

I take exception to this. I see no reason why sexual activity should not be as important to an alien race as it is to human beings. We have sex for lots of reasons, reproduction being only one of them. It feels good—no, it feels *great*. It creates bonds between individuals, whether as part of lifelong commitments or otherwise. It's physiologically good for health, both physical and mental. So for my alien race in *Collaborators*, I wanted sexuality to be important. I had the idea that before pair-bonding, they'd be androgynous in appearance, neither distinctively male nor female, but highly sexual (at least, post-puberty). Sex would be something they'd enjoy often and enthusiastically with their age-mate friends. However, the intimacy created by too much sex with the same person would lead to a cascade of emotional and physiological effects resulting in a permanent, lifelong pairing. The pairing, a sort of biological marriage obvious to everyone around the couple, leads to more changes—polarization into genders, with accompanying mood swings, aggression, inability to focus—preparing the bodies of the couple for reproduction. Each partner would appear more "female" or "male," which sets up many occasions for misunderstanding with Terran-humans who think in terms of those divisions (and react accordingly). The Bandari, on the other hand, would wonder how people who are permanently polarized can get any work done, and they consistently react to Terran women as if they were pregnant, and therefore to be protected at all costs.

Just as we've instituted the canonical Talk about the birds and the bees, or sex ed in schools, so the Bandari natives would have systems of preparing their young people, trying to ensure that pairing does not have disastrous political or inter-clan consequences. We know how badly that works in humans, so it's likely to be equally ineffective with Bandari teenagers, too.

About the Author

Deborah J. Ross is an award-nominated writer and editor of fantasy and science fiction, with over a dozen traditionally published novels and five dozen short stories in print. Recent releases include *A Heat Wave in the Hellers and Other Tales of Darkover; Thunderlord,* and *The Children of Kings* (with Marion Zimmer Bradley); and *The Seven-Petaled Shield* epic fantasy trilogy. Her short fiction has appeared in *F & SF, Asimov's,* and *Star Wars: Tales from Jabba's Palace,* and the Book View Café anthology, *Nevertheless She Persisted,* and has earned Honorable Mention in *Year's Best SF.* She has served as Secretary to the Science Fiction Fantasy Writers of America (SFWA), the Board of Directors of Book View Café, and the jury for the Philip K. Dick Award. When she's not writing, she knits for charity, plays classical piano, and studies yoga.

Also by Deborah J. Ross

Darkover novels (with Marion Zimmer Bradley)
Arilinn (forthcoming)
The Laran Gambit (forthcoming)
Thunderlord
The Children of Kings
Hastur Lord
The Alton Gift
A Flame in Hali
Zandru's Forge
The Fall of Neskaya

The Seven-Petaled Shield trilogy
The Heir of Khored
Shannivar
The Seven-Petaled Shield
Collaborators
Northlight
Jaydium

Collections
A Heat Wave in the Hellers and Other Tales of Darkover ®
Transfusion and Other Tales of Hope
Azkhantian Tales
Other Doorways: Early Novels
Pearls of Fire, Dreams of Steel